Andrew G. Harrison slipped the stack of photographs out of the manila envelope. Which one of these images was she? The exploited child? The loving woman? Whichever she was, it had become Andrew Harrison's task to sit in judgment on Savannah Royale Marsdon.

Savannah was twenty-eight in the fifth photograph and the zoom lens on the hidden camera had caught her smiling up at the man beside her. Andrew Harrison ignored the achingly familiar face of her companion. He picked up a magnifying glass and studied this last photograph more closely, focusing on her face. The provocative three-year-old had matured into a woman of strength and character, a woman any man would be proud to have stand beside him.

He lay the magnifying glass aside and drummed his fingers on the cool marble. Choices made by others for that three-year-old child had dictated the way the world would react to her for the rest of her days. Other hands had set her on the road that brought her to this moment. Now her life lay in his hands.

He got up slowly, feeling the weight of time pressing down on his fragile bones, and walked over to the phone. When the voice answered at the other end of the line, Andrew Harrison said, "I've decided."

ROYALE

DONA VAUGHN

Tudor Publishing Company
New York and Los Angeles

Tudor Publishing Company

For information address Tudor Publishing Company,
255 E. 49th Street, Suite 25D, New York, New Yor, 10017.

ISBN: 0-944276-04-0

Printed in the United States of America

First Tudor printing—May 1988

For Renate

PROLOGUE

Andrew G. Harrison slipped the stack of photographs out of the manila envelope and riffled through them thoughtfully. All of them had the same subject: one female face repeated over and over in infinite variation.

He shuffled the photographs with a sudden youthful flourish that belied the age spots on the backs of his skeletal hands. One by one he dealt five of them out like cards on the cool Italian marble of the tabletop. Behind him in the master suite of the main residence of his six acre Santa Barbara estate, a floor-to-ceiling glass wall framed a breathtaking three million dollar view of the Pacific coastline. Andrew Harrison ignored it. The task before him required his entire concentration. He was playing for a woman's life.

He set the rest of the photographs aside and, one by one, flipped over the five remaining.

Fate had manipulated the cards. Age three, twelve, fourteen, twenty-one, twenty-eight: the entire woman lay before him. But which one of these images was she? The exploited child? The loving woman? Whichever she was, it had become Andrew Harrison's task to sit in judgment on Savannah Royale Marsdon.

He moved the five photographs into chronological order, aligning them with an old man's finicky preciseness. He was a fair man. He would give each photograph its chance to speak for the woman.

The first was a rarity. It had been one of a set of twenty-four prints—a nude, three-year-old Savannah, preening with provocative innocence for the camera. Every other print, save the one in his hand, had been destroyed by a man who had paid five thousand dollars for the privilege. The remaining print was stunningly beautiful, as had been the others. A man might as well destroy the Mona Lisa, Harrison thought.

The second was a portrait of Savannah at twelve. Child-Woman. There was a wanton, dreamy look in the gold-flecked green of her eyes that stirred a part of him he had thought long dead. The man who took that photograph was a genius, he acknowledged grudgingly.

The third was a blowup of a news photo of Savannah at fourteen that gave no hint of where it had been taken. But Harrison knew; the entire nation had known. There was such pain on that young face that he found he could not bear to study it with the care it deserved. He went on to the next.

The fourth was a wide-angle shot of Savannah at twenty-one as she emerged from a limousine impossibly elongated by the camera, a forlorn figure in widow's black, her face heavily veiled. Harrison sighed. The expression hidden behind the black veil might have tipped the scales one way or the other.

Savannah was twenty-eight in the fifth photograph and the zoom lens on the hidden camera had caught her smiling up at the man beside her. Andrew Harrison ignored the achingly familiar face of her companion. He picked up a magnifying glass and studied this last photograph more closely, focusing on her face. He could not fault the judgment of her companion. The provocative three-year-old had matured into a woman of strength and character, a woman any man would be proud to have stand beside him.

He lay the magnifying glass aside and drummed his fingers on the cool marble. Choices made by others for that three-year-old child had dictated the way the world would react to her for the rest of her days. Other hands had set her on the road that brought her to this moment. Now her life lay in his hands.

He got up slowly, feeling the weight of time pressing down on his fragile bones, and walked over to the phone. When a voice answered at the other end of the line, Andrew Harrison said, "I've decided."

"Yes?"

"Kill her."

BOOK I

Irene

Chapter 1

Savannah checked to make sure the dressing room curtain was pulled completely closed before she stripped down to her panties. Sometimes other models laughed at her, but she hated undressing in front of anyone else. Ever since she turned twelve four months ago, and her flat chest had begun to swell into firm little breasts, it bothered her even more. She wanted to ask her mother to wait outside, but she already knew what the answer to that would be. Mama never let her out of her sight at photographers' studios. She was always telling Savannah what bad people photographers were and how she should never let herself be alone with one. Being by herself in the dressing room wasn't the same thing at all, but Savannah knew Mama would never see it that way.

She half-turned, shielding her breasts from her mother's eyes with one arm, and reached for the white blouse hanging on the dressing room wall. The pale half-moons on her fingernails shone through the thin cotton as she took the blouse from the hanger.

"Bra or not?" she said over her shoulder.

"Not," her mother said.

Savannah tossed her mane of golden brown curls out of the way and slipped on the blouse. She turned to stare at herself in the mirror as she buttoned it. Not just her nipples, but the warm brown circles of her aerolas were clearly visible through the fabric. "Mama!"

"Not," Irene Royale said firmly. She extinguished one cigarette with a sizzle in the half-inch of coffee remaining in her Styrofoam cup and lit another, studying her own reflection in the mirror, unblinking as a lizard.

Savannah knew better than to argue when Mama got that closed look on her face. Mama had looked like that for the past six months, ever since the subject of moving to Los Angeles had first come up, and now that they were here, it wasn't getting any better. Savannah had lived in New York since she was three months old, and no matter how many times Mama told her that Los Angeles was her home and that she was really a California girl at heart, she knew it just wasn't true. She hated everything about Los Angeles, from the people to the cars. Especially the cars, she thought with a little shudder. Mama was a terrible driver. Maybe she was just out of practice because they had lived in New York so long, or maybe it was something else, the Bad Thing that Savannah didn't want to think about. Whichever it was, they didn't have to have a car when they lived in New York, so that was one more reason to hate Los Angeles.

Irene exhaled impatiently, sending cigarette smoke eddying around Savannah and making her cough. Hurriedly, Savannah reached for the jeans and struggled into them. They were so tight she had to jump up and down to get them over her rear. For a while she thought she was going to have to lie down on the dressing room floor to be able to zip them, but finally, with Mama's help, she managed to pull them together across her flat stomach and edge the zipper up slowly, so that the metal teeth wouldn't bite into the tender, untanned skin above her panties.

Savannah started to pull the blouse out of the waistband a little, so that her nipples didn't strain so obviously against the fabric, but Mama brushed her hands away. "Let it alone," Irene ordered in a stern voice. "You've fooled around long enough." She crushed the cigarette out on the floor of the dressing room and shoved Savannah through the curtain.

Kit Nelson couldn't figure out what was wrong. At twenty-five, he was still a boy-wonder and women loved him, all women, from teenagers to grandmothers—but especially the models. They loved his bronzed surfer's body and his snakeskin cowboy boots. They loved his sun-streaked squeaky-clean hair and the frenetic energy with which he made love to them, as though they might vanish at any moment. They didn't know that was exactly what he was afraid of. He had been a lanky six-footer, awkward, thin to the point of emaciation, when he first arrived in Los Angeles with his camera equipment, his virginity still intact after nineteen solitary years in a tiny town that

had never heard of different drummers. Half the high
school football team had taken turns trying to beat
the weirdness out of him: the other half had tried to
rape him. If it hadn't been for a doting grandmother
sending his photographs in to every contest she could
find, he often thought he would have been dead or
queer by now. With her help he finally amassed
enough prize money to get to California, and once
there, a very strange thing happened. There must
have been something in the thick, smoggy air that
agreed with him better than the thin, sun-parched
stuff he'd been accustomed to breathing in West
Texas. Kit was transformed. His skin tanned without
burning for the first time in his life. He began to
work out, and his muscles grew along with his body.
For a while he had to buy a new set of clothes every
couple of months, until he leveled off at a perfectly
proportioned six foot three. That was when Kit discovered that, along with a talent for photography, he
had a talent for women as well. For all his frenzied
efforts the past five years, he still hadn't made up for
the long dry season that had gone before, but he was
working on it and enjoying every minute. He was on
top of the world, all right. So how come he couldn't
coax a decent smile out of this frozen little New York
bitch.

"That's it, darlin'," he called to the girl on the
platform. "Point your buns at the door and smile."

Obediently, Savannah struck the pose. The jeans
stretched across her rear and thighs, and the thin
cotton shirt clung lovingly to the promising mounds
of her breasts. "Now break my heart with your

smile,'' Kit told her. With another model he might have murmured, ''Think about my cock, babe, and all the fun we're gonna have. That should do it.'' More than once he had stopped a session to take a model into his office and ball a look of ecstatic delight onto her face and then brought her back and shot it before it faded. But this chick's *mother* was standing right behind him, for Crissake.

Kit shrugged and tried to forget the silent woman as he studied the girl on the platform. Eighteen going on eternal woman, he thought. He had never seen such perfection in his life. Even the heavy-handed makeup job couldn't mute it: creamy ivory skin with golden undertones, clear green eyes with golden flecks, golden brown hair tumbling past her shoulders. She was a symphony in gold and just to look at her made his balls tighten.

But the photos were going to be dead. Kit had a sixth sense about that. He could tell without even developing the film that this session wasn't going to make it. He shoved his sun-streaked hair away from his face. Somehow he was going to have to unfreeze the little bitch.

''Come on, baby,'' he urged, with the laughing lilt of promise in his voice that made most models peel out of their teddies and beg him for it. ''Turn it loose. Shake your butt. Muss your hair.''

Savannah leaned over, letting all that golden brown hair fall forward and hit the floor, and then straightened into another pose. But the magic rapport that had to be there, *had to,* between the model and the camera, wasn't. ''Come on, honey,'' Kit begged, desperate now. "Think about all the one-handed readers." The clear green eyes looked at him with innocent wonder. "The guys who are going to get it off by looking at your boobs through that shirt, for Crissake!"

And that was even worse. If she was ice before, she was a glacier now. "Shit," he muttered at the camera.

"Mr. Nelson?"

He had forgotten Savannah's mother. For one stark moment he felt the same terror he had the day the football coach caught him pissing in the team's Gatorade, but then it faded. He wasn't that skinny oddball kid anymore. "Yes, ma'am?"

"If I could talk to you privately for a moment. . . ."

He barely suppressed the sigh. "Right now isn't the best—"

"Please, Mr. Nelson. There are a few things we need to discuss before you continue," Irene Royale said, her voice colorless and cold.

The woman reminded him of a little brown hen, clucking about her one chick. She was probably going to drag him into the hall and complain about his language. "Okay, Mrs. Royale." The sigh escaped before he could stop it, but the woman didn't seem to notice. "Savannah honey? Take five." Kit followed the woman into the hall.

Outside the studio she hesitated and glanced down the hallway at the blonde receptionist. "If we could talk somewhere a little more private . . ."

Kit resisted the urge to glance at his watch. He was good with women—all women, not just the ones he bedded—because he didn't rush them. He gave them plenty of time. He'd give Mrs. Royale her chance, even if it cost him half an hour of shooting time. It might just give him a hint on how to warm up that block of ice in the studio.

"This way, Mrs. Royale." He led her to his crowded little office and avoided looking at the couch in the corner where he might be balling the look he wanted onto Savannah's lovely little face this very minute if her mother hadn't tagged along this morning. When they were both seated, he said, "Now, Mrs. Royale—"

"Irene."

Kit straightened in his chair, like a bird dog that had just caught an almost imperceptible scent. He looked her over, really looked at her, for the first time since she had walked into the studio with her daughter in tow.

Irene Royale wasn't so old, Kit realized, maybe thirty-seven or thirty-eight. The girl must have picked up her height from somewhere else, because Irene was only five foot five or six, and Savannah was at least three inches taller. Aside from that, Irene was Savannah all over again, but older and without the golden undertones that lit her daughter's skin and eyes. The green of Irene's eyes was grayed, muted, but there was a look there that he recognized, a look that said she chewed men up and spat them out when she was through with them. Kit fairly quivered with anticipation. He *loved* a man-eater.

"I'm sure you've noticed that Savannah is very nervous, Mr. Nelson."

"Just Kit, honey."

"Kit." The sultry note in her voice hadn't been present in the studio in front of her daughter. Kit leaned forward. "She's worried about moving to Los Angeles. She had a lot of friends in New York. Photographers she worked with regularly, whom she trusted." Irene shrugged. Mesmerized, Kit watched the way her breasts moved behind the brown silk of her dress. "But none of them saw her . . . potential. They wanted to keep her a little girl. But she's not a little girl anymore. You can see that."

Kit jerked his mind back to the conversation. "Well, sure, but—"

"I told her California was the promised land, but she doesn't believe me yet. I picked you on purpose, Kit. I've seen your work. You're the one who can show Savannah as she really is. Your photographs can make people, the right people, realize her potential."

"She's got the potential, all right. If she'd just relax with the camera. . . ."

Irene was toying with the first button on her dress. Kit watched in total fascination as her fingers caressed the tiny ivory button, carved into the shape of a rose. Irene leaned forward and the button strained against the pressure, threatening to pull free. "She never had a father, Kit. It makes a girl insecure. If she thought there was a man here in Los Angeles who was interested in her . . . who cared what happened to her . . . who would help her with her career . . . then she would relax."

A picture popped into Kit's mind of the three of

them, him and Savannah and Irene, on his king-sized
bed, bare-ass naked on the white fur throw. He shifted
in his chair to ease the sudden tightness of his pants.

Irene's fingers continued to play with the tiny
ivory button. "If she thought you would take us to
some parties, introduce her to some film people, that
sort of thing. . . . She would be marvelous on the
screen, Kit. Can't you see her up there, all honey and
gold? . . ." Irene leaned back, her eyes half-closed.
Her face took on a dreamy look that made him want
to scramble across the desk and grab her. "If she's
got this much at twelve, can't you just see her in a
couple of years when—"

"Jesus Christ!"

Irene's eyes flew open. "What is it?"

"Jesus H. Christ!" Kit was on his feet. His frantic
glance bounced from Irene to the couch and back to
Irene. "The kid is twelve years old?"

Irene Royale nodded, and Kit blushed right through
all that lovely California tan.

At first Savannah sat on the edge of the platform,
legs crossed primly, waiting for Mr. Nelson and her
mother to return. A faint sheen of perspiration glis-
tened on her skin. She mopped it away and worried
about how the blouse was beginning to cling to her
damp skin. If only she had a wristwatch. There was
no clock in the studio, but she was sure Mama and
Mr. Nelson had been gone more than thirty minutes.

After a while the blonde receptionist stuck her
head in the door and said, "Where's Kit?"

"He's talking to my mother," Savannah told her.

She looked expectantly at the receptionist, hoping the woman would offer her a Coke, or at least a glass of water.

The blonde had a funny expression on her face. She ignored Savannah completely as she walked around turning off the floodlights and muttering to herself. She slammed the studio door as she left.

It was cooler with the floodlights off. Savannah leaned straight back until she lay looking up at the ceiling, letting her blue-jeaned legs dangle off the edge of the platform. It was quiet in the studio, so quiet she could hear the sound of the receptionist's typing. After a while it stopped and then she could hear the click of heels down the hall, past the studio door, and in a few minutes, the rushing gurgle of a toilet being flushed. Then the heels clicked back down the hall and the typewriter began to tap again.

Savannah kept staring up at the ceiling until gradually her eyes drooped closed, and she let herself think about the Prince.

She thought about the Prince a lot. He was like no one she had ever met in real life. Sometimes she thought he might be her father, but since Mama had no pictures of her father and refused to answer even one single question about him, she couldn't be sure. She wasn't even sure what the Prince actually looked like. She knew that he was tall, taller than Savannah's own mortifying five foot nine. She guessed she was glad of her height in a way, because without it she wouldn't have a chance as a model, and Mama had explained to her in great detail what their lives would be like without the modeling money coming in. They would be Poor.

Savannah knew what Poor was. Once, when she was six, they were shooting a commercial for children's dresses on a Bronx street and a bag lady had lunged through the crowd of spectators and grabbed Savannah. She hugged the terrified little girl to her bosom, murmuring something over and over. The other children told Savannah later that the bag lady had said, "My little girl. I've found you at last." They teased Savannah about it until she cried. They said she was the bag lady's daughter and some night the bag lady was going to come and get her and put her in a bag and never let her out again.

For weeks afterward Savannah would wake up yelling and covered with sweat from a nightmare of being stuffed in the old woman's bag. She could still remember, as clear as anything, the way the cloth of the old woman's dress had scratched against her cheek when the bag lady hugged her against the suffocating softness of her huge bosom, and the horrible stench that invaded her nostrils as the old woman clutched her so tightly with her rough, gnarled hands that she couldn't even turn her head.

She would never forget that smell. An adult would have known it was a combination of cheap wine, sweat, and years of dirt. Savannah couldn't identify the individual components, but she knew what that smell was. It was the odor of Poor. That was what was going to happen to her if she didn't do everything her mother told her to do. She would be Poor, and that smell, that horrible, terrible smell, would be all around her forever, for the rest of her life. So Savannah worked very hard to do exactly what her mother wanted.

Still, it wasn't enough. There were things outside Savannah's control that threatened them, that wanted to make them Poor. There were arguments that Mama had with the Agency, and the ad people, and the photographers. No one yelled, but Savannah could tell they were arguments just the same. Once when a photographer went stomping by Savannah without even ruffling her hair or saying hello, she heard him mutter something about "stage mothers," but she had no idea what he meant. Last year the arguments had grown more frequent, and the Bad Thing had gotten worse and worse. Sometimes Mama had slept past noon, and sometimes she smelled almost as bad as the bag lady. The phone stopped ringing and Mama finally canceled the answering service. No one had any jobs for Savannah in New York anymore, and she knew it had something to do with Stage Mothers and the Bad Thing.

That was when she first began to realize that what they needed was the Prince. She wasn't stupid enough to think he would come riding up on a white horse. She was a child of the city. She knew he would be in a taxicab or a limousine.

She daydreamed about the Prince constantly. She could never be certain what his face looked like. Every time she tried to focus on him in her thoughts, it was the same as when she tried to read a story in her dreams. If she tried to read, the words would dissolve and fade away before she could really see what they said, and it was the same way with the Prince's face. The more she tried to focus on his eyes, his nose, his mouth, the more everything blurred and vanished. So she couldn't be sure of what he really looked like. The only thing she was sure of was that when the Prince did come, everything was going to be all right. He would take care of Mama and her, and make the terrible Poor smell go away, and fight the Bad Thing like it was a dragon. Then she and Mama and the Prince would all live happily ever after.

When Mama told her they were going to move to California, her first thought was that the Prince wasn't going to know where to find them. She had hidden notes for him all over their apartment, telling him the new address. As she lay on the platform, eyes closed, waiting for Mama and Mr. Nelson to return, she crossed her fingers for the hundredth time and hoped that the Prince would find the notes and come for them soon.

The blonde receptionist came back twice to see if Mr. Nelson and Mama were through talking yet. She still didn't offer Savannah anything to drink, and the second time she left, she slammed the studio door so hard Savannah was afraid it would come off its hinges.

The first thing Savannah noticed when Mama and Mr. Nelson finally did return was that Mama's hair was different. Mr. Nelson and Mama were talking about something, but Savannah wasn't really listening. She was busy trying to figure out exactly what it was that was different about Mama's hair. Then she realized Mama had spoken directly to her. "What, Mama?"

"I said Kit is going to take us under his wing and show us L.A. Isn't that wonderful?"

Savannah nodded doubtfully. She knew what it was that was different about Mama's hair now. When she left to talk to Mr. Nelson it had been coiled in a neat little bun on the back of her neck. Now it was knotted loosely on top of her head, with little tendrils curling out around her face.

"Let's go and freshen your makeup," Mama said. "Kit's going to do wonderful things for you with his camera."

Mr. Nelson had been fiddling with his camera, but now he straightened up and said, "Can't you see you're going about it the wrong way, Irene? Too heavy handed. You need to scrub her face and start again. Get rid of the tight clothes. You can dress up any kid her age and make her look like a whore, but—" He caught Savannah's gold-flecked gaze on him and she was fascinated by the blush that spread up his face all the way to his hairline. "But that's not where her appeal is," he went on doggedly. "Sensual innocence. That's what the kid's got that's special. That's what you need to bring out." Another wave of crimson swept across his face. "Believe me, it'll be just as effective as T and A—better, if it's done right."

Savannah wanted to stick her fingers in her ears. Now they were going to have another one of those arguments that wasn't an argument. Afterwards she and Mama would go back to their new apartment and the unopened boxes and wait for the phone to ring. And wait. And wait

Irene walked over to where Savannah sat on the edge of the platform. She lit a cigarette and stood gazing down at her daughter's upturned face. The smoke curled out around Savannah: the terrible smell of Poor reaching out for them. She braced herself, holding her breath, waiting for the words that she knew would start the bad times all over again.

And then Mama said, "You know, you're right, Kit. You're a fuckin' genius in more ways than one."

Savannah looked up at Mr. Nelson and was rewarded by a third blush. She was astounded. She never knew anyone could blush so many times in a row.

"For Crissake, Irene. The kid—"

"The kid is going to be famous, Kit. You're going to make her a fuckin' millionaire!"

Savannah was not really paying attention to Mama's words. She was studying her mother's face. The closed look was gone. Everything was going to be all right. Soon the Prince would find the address she had left for him and come to get them. Savannah smiled.

"That's it!" Kit Nelson yelled. "Smile like that for the camera, babe, and we've got it made."

Chapter 2

Kit cleared a space on his desk with a sweep of his forearm and sat down to examine Savannah's proof sheet. His first quick glance told him that at least twelve of the shots were outstanding. A couple were even better than that. Heart racing, he forced himself to examine each one of the different pictures. He spotted the one failure in the center of the second row. The camera had caught her in mid-blink, eyelids drooping. The rest of the shots were perfect. The kid was a real pro; she could afford to reproduce the entire proof sheet as her composite if she wanted to. She had the consistency of a much older, much more experienced model . . . and the camera loved her.

Kit reached for the magnifier and leaned closer to study the facial expression on one of the full length shots, a wanton dreamy look that made him yearn to know what she had been thinking of when the camera froze it on film. He dropped the magnifier and shoved the proof sheet away. There was no question of Savannah's true age in these shots. She was definitely a twelve-year old. Irene had washed the eighteen-year-old, eyelashes spiky with mascara, down the drain and reapplied the makeup with a lighter hand. She had accepted all of Kit's suggestions without question, from clothes to eyeshadow, and the results were on the sheet in front of him. Everything he had promised Irene was right there in the contact prints. Sensual innocence. A provocative sexuality that reached right off the page and stirred his penis into painful tumescence.

Twelve years old. That merely enhanced it.

Twelve.

He grabbed the proof sheet and crumpled it into a tight ball before pitching it into the wastebasket with the beer cans and candy wrappers.

He leaned back, staring down at the crumpled ball of paper. She had to be the shiest little girl he had ever met in his life. And obedient. If her mother told her to kiss a frog, she'd only hesitate long enough to ask which one. A regular Girl Scout.

Twelve years old.

And absolutely gorgeous. She was the most beautiful thing he had ever seen in his life. Child-woman. Without his guidance Irene would bury all that under layers of makeup and dress the kid in T-shirts with her tits sticking out, when the truth was that the kid didn't even *need* tits at this stage of the game. She had something else, something better. He'd be damned if he knew the name of it, but he did know one thing for sure. Irene was right. He *was* a fuckin' genius in more ways than one. He could take that kid and let the whole world see all those golden undertones, all that innocence and all that . . . that *sensuality*. He could make every man wish he had her in his bed and every woman wish she were twelve again. The skinny teenager who had come slinking out of Texas with pimples and a suitcase full of Fruit of the Loom briefs, courtesy of his grandmother, could do that for her, while some hot shot photographer from New York City could only screw it up.

Kit fished the crumpled proof sheet out of the wastebasket and smoothed it out before he reached for the phone. It rang twice at the other end before a colorless voice answered with a chill, "Yes?"

"Irene, this is Kit. I just looked at Savannah's proof sheet." The moment dragged out until he took pity on the woman at the other end of the line. "Savannah's gonna have the best goddamned comp this town's ever seen!"

In just six months Savannah's new image made her the hottest property in the country. From printwork, fashion and advertising photography, she launched into commercials. By the end of the year she was flying back and forth between New York and Los Angeles on a regular basis. Her face appeared on the covers of *Vogue, Harper's Bazaar, Glamour*, and *Seventeen* that year. Her phenomenal success had made Kit Nelson nationally known as a photographer of nymphets, and he was besieged by mothers of girls as young as three, who hoped their daughter would be the next Savannah Royale.

At thirteen Savannah starred in her first feature film, *Streets*. It was a plotless, arty story about a baby pro, a teenage hooker who seduces an aging businessman and makes him her slave, and it was filmed in lovely, lingering detail.

Irene refused to allow Savannah to read the entire script. She cut it apart and made a special copy for her daughter with only Savannah's cues and speeches. Since it was shot out of sequence, and because Irene hustled her off the set as soon as she finished her part of each scene, Savannah had no idea what the picture was about. When the director said, "Smile," she smiled; when he said, "Cry," she cried; when he said, "Look sexy," she thought about the Prince. She didn't even know there had been any nude scenes until she read an article in *Seventeen* that explained her mother had insisted on a body double for her.

Between her schoolwork, her modeling and commercial work, and the film, Savannah had no time for any social life. She and her mother had a bigger apartment now, and a live-in housekeeper, Mrs. Browder, who was always telling Savannah how lucky she was to have a mother who loved her so much.

Savannah was beginning to wonder. Somehow her mother's obsessive interest did not seem as much like love as it had when Savannah was younger. Sometimes Savannah wondered what her mother's ultimate goal was. They had enough money now to live comfortably, but still Irene pushed for more.

When *Streets* was finished, Irene refused to let Savannah see it. Savannah began to understand that Irene was purposely trying to keep her a child by restricting her reading matter, her TV viewing, the films she saw, and the people she met—but she could not understand why. She sensed that Irene was preparing her for something, pushing her toward some predetermined destiny, but she had no idea what it might be.

The critics hated *Streets*; the public loved it. They couldn't seem to get enough of Savannah. Articles about her appeared everywhere, questioning her morals, her upbringing, what the mere fact of her existence was doing to the fiber of American society.

Savannah had no time to worry about American society. She was hard at work on her second film, *Night's Daughter,* a period piece about a Victorian miss, still in the schoolroom, who becomes the object of an elderly roué's lusty pursuit. Irene made Savannah a special script once more, but Savannah convinced her stand-in to steal her a copy of the real one. As a consequence her acting improved, but her opinion of her mother worsened.

Irene was drinking more heavily and she was seldom home at night. Mrs. Browder, their housekeeper, had become a virtual jailer. She refused to allow Savannah to go anywhere alone, even to the library. "Your mother gave strict orders," was all Savannah heard from morning till night from the housekeeper's lips. She yearned to rebel, to snatch a little freedom for herself.

Fate and the director of *Night's Daughter* stepped in to lend her a hand.

Cara Wade was Savannah's body double in *Night's Daughter* and under ordinary circumstances Savannah would never have been allowed to meet her. However, Irene came down with a bad case of the flu, and was forced to turn the job of escorting Savannah on and off the set over to Mrs. Browder. Jeffrey Hanks, the director of *Night's Daughter,* was a perfectionist, and Mrs. Browder soon grew bored with sitting through the endless retakes. The housekeeper began to spend the time, while Savannah was on the set, knitting and dozing in the young star's dressing room. For the first time in her life, Savannah was free of her mother's watchful eye. She was fourteen.

First she was able to watch the other actors finish the scenes she was in, something she had not been allowed to do before. And then Jeffrey Hanks found out from Savannah's stand-in that Irene was not in attendance. The director seized upon the opportunity to expose Savannah to other parts of the film. He had decided there was a void in Savannah's portrayal of the Victorian miss. Thyra, the young Victorian girl, had enticed the roué with a foreknowledge of where her efforts would lead—knowledge gained, according to the script writers, from watching the servants' sexual antics below stairs. It was this foreknowledge, missing from Savannah's clear green gaze as the camera focused on her gold-flecked eyes, that Jeffrey Hanks was determined to put in those innocent eyes while he had the opportunity.

He juggled the shooting schedule so that the nude scenes with Savannah's body double were next, and then he made certain that Savannah was there to see them. With studio personnel stationed unobtrusively about the set and near the dressing room to detain or deflect Mrs. Browder if the housekeeper should awake to her duty, Jeffrey Hanks shot every sensual scene in the movie, one after another, with Savannah watching wide-eyed beside him.

When Savannah caught sight of Cara Wade, her body double, for the first time, she couldn't help but think that double was entirely the wrong word. She would have given anything to look like the other girl. Cara was four years older, four inches shorter, and had real breasts that bobbled around like Jell-O under the hands of the actor who played the roué. She was also friendly as a puppy. With barely a nudge from Jeffrey Hanks, Cara took over Savannah's education. She explained to the thunderstruck girl exactly what was happening in each scene, what the movie goers would think was happening, and exactly how each physical act would feel to Thyra if it actually was happening—since Cara had a wide and varied experience with the opposite sex.

By the end of the eighth day of Irene's illness, Savannah knew almost as much about sex and the male of the species as the girl she was to portray.

The flu felled Mrs. Browder in Savannah's dressing room on the ninth day of Irene's illness. When the studio phoned to say the housekeeper was on her way home, but that Savannah was still on the set, panic gripped Irene. Someone, someone she could trust, had to be with Savannah at all times. That was essential to her plan. But who could she ask? Weak with fever, she clung to the phone and tried to think.

At first Kit Nelson didn't recognize the hysterical, sobbing voice on the other end of the phone. When he did, he broke out in an icy sweat. "Irene?" The phone threatened to slide out of his hand. "Is . . . did something happen to Savannah?"

By the time he pieced her disjointed phrases into a coherent tale, Kit's heartbeat had slowed to normal. "I'll be glad to pick her up." He soothed the distraught woman. "No problem." He winced as he thought of what Evie would say when he told her to cancel the rest of the day's shooting, but he went steadfastly on. "I can be there in less than an hour. . . . Promise. . . . Of course . . . I'll get over there right away." Kit hung up the phone and sat staring at the couch in the corner of his office. He couldn't figure out why Irene had called on him. Over the past two years they'd had sex, great sex, a dozen times, but she'd never given him a hint of what was inside that self-contained exterior. Those past few minutes on the phone she'd displayed more emotion than she ever had before in Kit's presence. In or out of bed.

Evie's reaction was predictable. He and his blonde receptionist replayed the same argument they'd had over and over ever since Irene and Savannah had walked into the studio that first day. "She's too old for you, Kit," Evie said for the hundredth time. "And I don't just mean in years. She is the most cold, conniving bitch I've ever—"

"Come on, baby," Kit said with a grin as he shrugged on his jacket. "You know I still love you the best."

"And the way she watches that kid is sick. Just positively sick. I tell you, she gives me the creeps."

Evie slammed a desk drawer so hard she broke a fingernail. "I get the feeling she's getting ready to sell the kid to a white slaver and all she cares about is keeping Savannah a virgin until the deal goes through!"

Kit felt his grin fade. "Don't be silly," he said, but his voice lacked conviction. Too many times in the past he'd had the same thought about Irene himself. For the first time since Evie had come to work for him, he walked out without giving her a playful good-bye kiss on the cheek, and left her staring open-mouthed after him.

Kit had a long time to consider Evie's suspicions as his Corvette idled in a lengthy line of traffic, threatening to overheat. It did nothing to improve his rapidly deteriorating mood when he finally located Savannah's dressing room and discovered she was still on the set. He suspected the first studio goon of giving him the wrong directions to the sound stage. When he finally reached it, a second goon kept him waiting outside for a good twenty minutes, ostensibly to check his presence with Jeffrey Hanks, but actually to allow the director time to finish shooting the scene in progress. The early warning system Hanks had set up for Mrs. Browder was working perfectly.

By the time the second goon returned to tell Kit he could be admitted to the set, Kit's anger had heated up to match the temperature of the concrete burning through the soles of his shoes. He was too mad to notice Savannah was not in costume and that the bath-robed actress she was excitedly exchanging whispered comments with was her body double. "Come on," he said, grabbing her by the arm. "Irene's having kittens."

* * *

Savannah allowed Kit to drag her off the set without a single protest. She was too busy digesting Cara Wade's last remarks. The body double had taken one look at Kit Nelson and gone into a fake swoon. "How come you never told me you had something like that on the string?" she demanded of Savannah.

Savannah turned around to stare over at Kit. She had never thought of the photographer that way before, but her cram course in sex education made her do so now. "He's a friend of my mama's," she told Cara. "He's not interested in me."

"He could be." Cara giggled. "I mean, he's breathing, isn't he?" She leaned closer. "I can tell from here, that body would make the effort worth your while."

Savannah looked at Kit consideringly. Somehow she didn't think he was the Prince. She had never thought of the Prince as having that kind of tanned surfer's build or sun-bleached hair. But still . . . Savannah had never been kissed in her life. Not really. Movie kisses didn't count. She wondered if she could get Kit to kiss her, a real kiss, the kind Cara had been describing to her. "How can I get him interested in me?" she asked the older girl desperately. "I know Mama must have told him to bring me straight home. He'll never—"

Cara's eyes sparkled with delight and mischief. "What kind of car does he drive?"

"A red Corvette."

"Okay, it's a scorcher out. After he gets through changing the flat tire, he's going to be hot and thirsty.

All you have to do is suggest he take a couple of minutes to stop for something cool to drink.''

"How do you know he has a flat?"

Cara grinned. "He doesn't yet. Just don't hustle on your way to the parking lot, okay?" She turned away as Kit approached.

As Savannah followed Kit off the set, she realized that his long-legged stride was covering ground at an alarming rate. At this pace, they'd be at the parking lot too quickly for Cara to carry out her plan. "Kit?"

"Umm?" he said, striding on, hands jammed in his coat pockets.

"Kit!"

He stopped and looked down at her with a brotherly grin. "What is it, kid?"

He still saw her as a baby. This is never going to work, she thought hopelessly. "I . . . I need to stop by my dressing room. I left some books there that I'll need tonight."

"Okay, kid. Lead the way."

She kept him waiting outside the dressing room while she re-did her makeup and then, when he banged impatiently on the door, she grabbed up the first two books she saw.

Kit didn't even look at her as he started off again, hands in his pockets once more, shoulders hunched, staring at the ground. He didn't glance up when Cara passed them on the way back from the parking lot, her bathrobe blowing open to expose a generous expanse of thigh, and he missed the long, slow conspiratorial wink she gave Savannah.

The flat tire caught his attention. "Oh, shit," he

groaned and then glanced at Savannah and blushed. He tossed his jacket into the back of the Corvette and unlocked the trunk, muttering under his breath.

Savannah was sure now that Kit wasn't the Prince as she watched him jack up the Corvette and change the tire. Even if the Prince did turn out to look like a surfer, he would never blush. The Prince would be so suave and debonair nothing would ever embarrass him. And the Prince would never, ever, in a hundred million years, have those big circles of wetness under each arm, and streaking down the back of his shirt.

By the time Kit had tossed the last of the tools and the punctured tire back into the Corvette's trunk, Savannah had almost decided to call the whole thing off. Almost. If it hadn't been for one thing. She knew that as soon as Irene recovered she was going to be a prisoner again, and she wouldn't have another chance for years to test her newfound knowledge. She was going to kiss Kit Nelson, really kiss him, before the afternoon was out.

She was thrilled when Kit agreed without any persuasion at all that they should stop someplace and have a drink. She was lost in a romantic vision of the two of them alone in a booth in a dark little bar, sipping something terribly sophisticated from long-stemmed glasses and staring deep into each others eyes, when Kit whipped the Corvette into a root beer stand.

She managed to swallow her disappointment and smile brightly as Kit ordered two large root beers. "To go," he added as an afterthought. "Your mom was expecting you home a long time ago," he told

Savannah with a chuckle. "She's gonna think I kidnapped you."

As soon as their root beers arrived, the Corvette snarled to life once more.

Kit seemed to have forgotten Savannah was in the car with him. His hands clenched the steering wheel with such force that his knuckles were white, and once he muttered aloud, "Maybe I should just come right out and ask her."

"What did you say?"

"Nothing, kid," he told her. But she could see the grin didn't quite reach his eyes. "Just something I need to talk over with your mom." She could feel his awareness of her click off as though someone had turned a switch, and she knew with a sudden desperation that she was blowing her one chance.

When he pulled into the apartment house's parking lot and cut the motor, she was almost frantic. "Kit," she pleaded. "I . . . I need to talk to you about something."

"What is it, kid?"

"Do you think of me as a little girl?" Something stirred behind his eyes, something she had never seen there before. A dull red washed across his cheekbones. He turned and rolled down the car window. A hot blast of air invaded the Corvette's interior.

"That's a crazy thing to ask me, kid," he said without turning back.

"Look at me, Kit."

He let his glance trail over the golden symphony of her face. Two years of photographing nymphets, he thought, and all their mothers want them to look like this. He traced the innocently provocative pout of her lips with a trembling finger. She leaned toward him and he was trapped like a fly in a web, in the gold-flecked green of her gaze.

Savannah remembered everything Cara and the directors had told her, and she put every last bit of it into her face at that moment. She looked at Kit just like he really was the Prince. "Could . . . Could you kiss me, Kit? Just . . . Just once."

Kit Nelson groaned and it gave Savannah the funniest thrill of pleasure in the pit of her stomach to know she could make a man sound like that, a strange mixture of disgust and desire, and then Kit pulled her to him and his lips came down on hers.

His mouth moved against hers, grinding her lips against her teeth. She was disappointed when she realized it was going to be just like the movie kisses. She was more like a spectator than a participant, not really involved. Then Kit pressed against her more urgently, forcing his tongue between her lips. She tried to pull back, but his arms were holding her so tightly that it reminded her of the bag lady. Even the smell, the hot, sweaty, male smell of him, reminded her of that terrible day.

She tried to pull free, pressing against his thighs, and one flailing hand found his erection. She gasped, jerking her hand away, and Kit forced his tongue all the way into her mouth until she thought she would gag with the horrible slimy feeling of it.

Then the Corvette rang with a tremendous deafening explosion. Kit jerked away from her and flopped a couple of times against the car door, a strange red stain spreading across the front of his shirt.

Mama was standing outside the car in her black nylon nightgown, holding a gun in her hands. Her lips were moving, but Savannah's ears were still ringing from the explosion and she couldn't hear the words.

Kit's flopping stopped with a wrenching shudder. He fell over against the steering wheel and lay still. Far, far away in the distance, Savannah could hear the sound of a car horn, and even further away than that was the sound of a woman's voice, screaming over and over, "You bastard! You tried to ruin the plan!"

The police came.

First, two uniformed men in a regular squad car; then two men in suits in an unmarked car; then another squad car, and another, until Savannah lost count.

And the others.

Reporters and TV newspeople. The neighbors, no longer content with peering out their windows. Thrill seekers, drawn by the crowd and the flashing lights.

Until at last the parking lot was as full of people as a crowded movie set. All of them talking, moving, breathing.

All except Kit.

Savannah stood beside a pale, trembling Mrs. Browder who had come staggering out of her bed and downstairs, and watched them load Kit's body into an ambulance. Except for the men who were lifting the stretcher, no one else seemed to notice he was being taken away. It was Mama who was the center of attention.

Wrapped in a sheet someone had brought her, Irene stood quietly between the two uniformed policemen while the newspeople badgered her for answers to their questions. She just kept shaking her head, saying nothing.

Savannah stared at her mother. There was something hiding behind Irene's tight smile, something that, of all the people milling around in the parking lot, only her daughter could understand. Something shining through the unblinking green of her eyes as Irene ignored the reporters and TV cameras and stared across at the ambulance.

Savannah's stomach lurched.

Triumph!

That was what lay in the green of Mama's steady gaze as she watched the men with the stretcher. Triumph.

But why?

"They should leave the poor thing alone!" Mrs. Browder sobbed as the ambulance doors slammed shut. "Someone should make them leave Mrs. Royale alone."

A policeman came over to stand beside Savannah. He looked at her curiously. "Did he do that to you?"

Savannah pulled her gaze away from her mother and looked down. For the first time she realized that Mama had ripped the front of her dress when she yanked Savannah from the Corvette. The bodice was torn almost down to her waist and the lace of her bra was showing through. She pulled the torn edges of the fabric together and stared at the policeman.

"Come along," he said, taking her arm. "You can change clothes while your mother gets dressed. You, too," he told Mrs. Browder. "Then you're both going down to the station with her." The policeman reached out to take Mrs. Browder's arm as well, but she jerked back out of his reach.

"Not me," the housekeeper gasped. "I wasn't down here. I was upstairs. I don't have anything to do with this. You take the girl, but leave me here."

"You, too, lady," the policeman said. This time when he grabbed Mrs. Browder's arm, he held on.

He escorted both of them upstairs and turned Savannah over to a policewoman. The woman went with Savannah into her bedroom. She was young, with short, bouncy blonde curls ringing her face, but her eyes were gray flint. "Hurry up, kid," she said when Savannah hesitated. "Put on something else."

"I . . . I'd like to be by myself," Savannah told her.

The policewoman's lips smiled but her eyes didn't. "No chance, kid."

Savannah snatched another dress out of the closet. She kept the closet door between her and the policewoman as she wriggled out of one dress and into another, letting the torn garment slip to the floor at her feet.

The policewoman walked over and picked up the dress, held it up to examine the ripped fabric, and then stuffed it into a plastic bag.

"What are you doing with my dress?" Savannah

asked her when the woman started out of the room with it.

"It's evidence," the policewoman said.

When Savannah followed her into the living room, she found that Mama and Mrs. Browder had changed, too. Mrs. Browder and Savannah rode down to the station house in one car while Mama rode in another. Except for the policeman in the parking lot, no one had asked Savannah anything. She wondered if she should explain to someone that it was Mama who ripped her dress and not Kit. But the two policemen in the front of the squad car were staring straight ahead, their faces stern and unfriendly, and Mrs. Browder was muttering to herself about the indignity of being hauled off to the police station. Savannah laid her forehead against the window and closed her eyes.

At the station house, Mama disappeared through a door with three men in suits. The two policemen who had driven them took Savannah and Mrs. Browder into another room. There was a long table with a scarred top and five battered straight-backed chairs around it. One of the policemen left.

The other one sat down in the chair at the head of the table and lit a cigarette. He took off his cap and tossed it onto the table in front of him. "Might as well relax," he told Savannah and Mrs. Browder. "She's making a statement. It'll be a while."

Savannah had no idea what that meant, but Mrs. Browder sighed and sat down, so she did too.

After a long time, a tall, distinguished-looking man in a navy three-piece suit came into the room.

Savannah watched him, curious. He didn't look like the other policemen.

The man nodded at her without smiling. "I'd like to talk to Savannah alone now," he told the policeman.

"Sure, Counselor." The policeman retrieved his cap and left.

"You, too," the man told Mrs. Browder when she made no move to follow.

Mrs. Browder leaned back in her chair. "Just who are you to be ordering me around?" she asked belligerently.

"I'm Carl Franklin, Mrs. Royale's lawyer. Are you Mrs. Browder?"

"I am," Mrs. Browder said with an emphatic nod. "Are you going to be my lawyer, too?"

The lawyer chuckled. "You're not going to be charged with anything, Mrs. Browder." He pulled out one of the battered chairs and sat down beside Savannah. "Now if you'll just step out in the hall for a few minutes, I'd like to speak to Savannah alone."

Mrs. Browder crossed her arms and glared at him. "I'm not to leave her alone with anyone. Mrs. Royale's orders."

"Irene knows I need to question her alone," Carl Franklin said reassuringly.

"Well . . ."

"It will only be for a few minutes," the lawyer told her. "I have most of the facts from Mrs. Royale already."

"I guess if she said it was all right . . ."

He remained prudently silent and Mrs. Browder heaved herself up with a sigh. When the door had closed behind the woman, he moved his chair closer to Savannah's. "I don't want you to worry about anything, Savannah. I've had a long talk with your mother and I don't think we're going to have any major difficulties. It's a clear case of justifiable homicide. Trust me, Savannah. Everything is going to be fine."

Far down inside herself, like the beginnings of an earthquake deep within the earth, Savannah could feel herself beginning to tremble. There were words she needed to say out loud. Words she needed to taste on her lips. "Kit is dead."

It came out shaky and strangled. Carl Franklin leaned over and patted her hand. His hand was dry and cool against hers. "That's right, dear. There's nothing for you to worry about. He won't bother you ever again." His long fingers curled around her hand and caressed her palm.

Savannah snatched her hand back. "But he's *dead*!" she cried. It was beginning to sink in now. No one was going to yell, "Cut," or "It's a take." Kit wasn't going to get up, brush himself off, and give her one of his big sunny smiles. "He's really dead!"

"Now don't let yourself get—"

"She shot him! Mama *shot* Kit!"

"It's all right, Savannah," the lawyer insisted. "Everyone will know she did it to protect you."

She blinked, trying to clear away the bloody vision of Kit that was threatening to block out the lawyer's face. "What?"

"How far did he get?" Franklin leaned closer. She turned her head away, but she could feel his breath on her cheek as she stared straight ahead at a blotchy patch of paint on the far wall. "When he ripped your dress, did he put his hand in your bra?" The lawyer's voice was low and husky. "Did he fondle your breasts?"

Savannah shook her head. There were words on the wall beneath the paint. Someone had tried to cover them up, but they were bleeding through.

"I'm sorry to have to ask you these things, Savannah, but your mother needs your help." His voice dropped to a persuasive whisper. "She helped you."

Cops are cunts, the words on the wall said. *Fuck 'em.*

"He was a rapist, Savannah. Lord knows how many other young girls he took advantage of. You were lucky. If it weren't for your mother . . ."

She twisted around to face the lawyer. "Mama *shot* him!"

He nodded. "And you should be proud of her. She's a brave woman. She did what she did for you, Savannah." He put his hands on her shoulders so that she couldn't turn away from him. There was something in his face that reminded her of Kit. Of the way Kit had acted in the car when she asked him to kiss her. "Did he put his hand on your thigh?" Carl Franklin asked her. "Did he touch you inside your panties?"

She tried to twist away, but he held on. "Let me go," she pleaded.

"Do you want your mother to go to jail, Savannah?"

The cold promise in his voice froze her where she was. She stopped fighting him. "Jail?"

"Do you want her to go to prison? Just because she tried to protect her daughter?"

She stared at him, terrified. What if they found out the truth? What if they found out that she was the one? That it wasn't Mama's fault, but hers? What if they found out that she had asked Kit to kiss her? The lawyer said something else, but there was a roar building up inside her ears, drowning out the sound of his voice. If they found out, they would put *her* in prison instead of Mama, and that would be worse than Poor. Worse than anything.

The lawyer gave her a shake. She could see his lips moving, but she couldn't hear anything. The roar in her head was drowning out everything else. "I want Mama!" she shrieked. "I want my mama!"

The policeman rushed back into the room, followed by Mrs. Browder. The lawyer talked to the policeman, waving his hands helplessly as Mrs. Browder tried to quiet Savannah. Savannah stopped shrieking and began to cry instead, with great tearing sobs that ripped at her throat. She couldn't stop sobbing until they bathed her face with cold water. But even after the sobs stopped, silent tears continued to trickle down her cheeks.

The lawyer and Mrs. Browder bundled Savannah out of the police station, through the crowd of newspeople outside and into a long maroon Lincoln. The lawyer drove. There was another crowd of reporters waiting outside the apartment house. Kit's Corvette was still in the parking lot. When Savannah saw it, the sobs began again.

The lawyer and Mrs. Browder half-dragged, half-carried her up the steps while the cameras followed. By the time they shoved her through the door into the apartment, she was shrieking again. She never even saw the waiting doctor or his needle.

Irene was home the next day. She spent the rest of the week trapped inside the apartment by newspeople and crowds of the curious outside.

Mostly Savannah stayed in her room. When she came out, she drifted like a ghost through the apartment. She never spoke to Mama and Mama never spoke to her. The doctor came by and took Savannah's temperature every day. He looked down her throat and thumped her on the back, and listened to her chest with his stethoscope, but he never said anything about Kit or what had happened. He never gave her any other medicine after that first day.

Still, the effects of the sedative seemed to linger on. There was a cottony cloud around her, insulating her from the real world, from what was happening, and Savannah was glad. She knew that if she looked too closely, she would start crying again. And if she started crying again, she knew she would never be able to stop.

The inquest was on a Tuesday. There were five men and five women on the coroner's jury. Irene Royale testified for less than half an hour. The jury took only fifteen minutes to deliver a verdict of justifiable homicide.

As soon as she heard the verdict, Evie slipped out of the courtroom and raced down the hall, out into the sunlight. She dodged through the traffic as horns blared, desperate to reach her car before Irene Royale could leave the courthouse.

Her hands trembling, Evie unlocked the trunk of her car and grabbed the shopping bag. The shifting liquid feel of it as she lifted it out of the trunk made her queasy. *For Kit,* she reminded herself. She slammed the trunk and hurried back the way she had come. The shopping bag with its sloshing liquid contents beat against her legs as she ran.

Savannah recognized the blonde woman pushing her way through the crowd outside the courtroom before Irene did, and she stopped, ignoring the lawyer's impatient mutter. Savannah knew Kit's receptionist had never liked her, but now there was something really frightening on Evie's face as she shoved closer to Irene.

Evic elbowed her way the last few steps and reached down into the shopping bag. She pulled out a plastic container.

"Mama?"

Savannah's whisper of alarm was lost in the noise as the reporters pressed closer, but Irene had realized her daughter was no longer beside her. She reached back and grabbed Savannah's arm, yanking her forward just as Evie ripped off the container's cover and heaved its contents at Irene.

The shower of thick red liquid caught Savannah full in the face and cascaded down her body, drenching her hair, her dress.

"I know what you did!" Evie screamed at Irene as

the first policeman reached her. "I know why you did it!"

The blood was everywhere, inside Savannah's bra, between her fingers, dripping from her hair, even in her shoes. Mama and Mrs. Browder took her back into the courthouse, to the women's rest room. A policeman stood guard outside the door while Mama and Mrs. Browder sponged the worst of it off with paper towels. But they could do nothing about the smell. It clung to her hair, her dress, making her gag.

Irene shoved her against the wash basin. "Throw up in here. Not in Carl's car."

Two policemen escorted them back outside and through the crowd to Carl Franklin's Lincoln. Savannah caught the grimace on the fastidious lawyer's face as she climbed into the back seat with Mrs. Browder. She sat with her knees together, terrified that the blood still covered her, that it might leak through her thighs like a period and seep out onto the maroon velvet seat. Her teeth began to chatter.

"For Christ's sake, roll down the windows," Irene told the lawyer as he slipped behind the wheel. "It smells like a fuckin' slaughterhouse in here."

The studio shot around Savannah for two more days and then called and demanded she return to work. Irene drove her daughter down herself.

The dressing room had a closed musty smell about it as though Savannah had been away for years instead of less than two weeks. She wandered around the room, trailing her fingers through the dust on the tabletops, while Irene made some phone calls. No one had even come in to water her plants and half of them were dead.

Her own face leaped up at her from the ivory satin of the daybed. Someone had left a copy of the *National Enquirer* lying there. Savannah picked it up.

The whole front page was given over to her and Kit. There was a selection of the most provocative of Kit's photographs of her, none of which she had ever seen before, and a photograph of her standing in blood-drenched shock on the courthouse steps. And in the center of the page, a grainy shot of Kit's face, slack-jawed in death, pressed against the steering wheel of the Corvette.

Irene snatched the paper out of Savannah's hands before she could read the story, but the image of Kit's face was already burned into her brain.

When Savannah walked back on the set of *Night's Daughter*, the look Jeffrey Hanks had wanted was finally in her eyes.

Chapter 3

By the time Paul Marsdon arrived, the ground floor of Jeffrey Hanks' Beverly Hills villa was already jammed with humanity. From the oak-paneled entry hall to the aquamarine waters of the heart-shaped pool, glowing like a jewel in the early evening dusk, the party goers filled every available square inch of space. As he slowly forced his way through the wall-to-wall revelers, Paul realized he knew nearly everyone there. Hell of a place for a man my age to make a fool of himself, he thought and detoured to the bar for a double Scotch.

He wasn't sure he trusted the impulse that had drawn him here tonight, and that was unusual for him. He was a man who lived by his hunches. They had made him both rich and powerful. But this impulse . . . this one scared him. He was fifty-eight years old. He kept himself in shape; his body didn't look it, but the years were there, nevertheless. He had avoided a lot of traps in his life, but now he was about to leap into one with his eyes wide open. One that he never thought would be a problem for him. Despite three wives, seven children—the youngest of whom was twenty-two—and a mistress, Paul Marsdon had never been in love. Well, he was in love now, heaven help him, and with a seventeen-year-old girl he had never met.

He finished that Scotch and fortified himself with another double before he set off again in search of his host. It was slow going, through the sea of people, all of whom required a word, a pat, a handshake, a smile. Jeffrey was always ahead of him in the crowd. "He was *just* here," he heard half-a-dozen times, but the director was not to be seen.

Paul wearied of it finally and turned aside into the less-crowded living room to enjoy the impressive city view while he sipped his second Scotch, the last he would permit himself that evening.

Night turned the window into a mirror as he stood there, and he observed his own reflection in the glass with increasing moodiness. She probably wouldn't be able to guess his true age unless he told her, he thought, but what would a young girl think of that profile? He had been handsome as a boy and he knew without conceit that he was handsome still. His warm brown hair had not grayed and there wasn't an ounce of slack flesh on his lean frame. But his eyes had seen too much, old man's eyes in a still-youthful face, and there was a certain arrogance in the hook of his nose, the thrust of his chin, that a girl her age might find disturbing.

He should leave right now, he thought. Now, while Savannah was still a luminously golden screen image. Before she became flesh and blood with thoughts and feelings. Except that it was already too late for that.

He knew more about her than anyone else, except perhaps her mother. Thanks to the very efficient and extremely expensive private detective he had employed, he even knew a few things about her that her mother did not. There was an inch-thick file of clippings, photographs, and reports in the safe at his Malibu house, the one to which he alone had the combination. Some people never generated that much information about themselves in a lifetime, he thought. If Irene Royale persisted in her efforts what would Savannah's file look like when she was thirty?

There was an accompanying file on Irene herself. He had known for the past three and a half years what the woman planned, ever since the death of that photographer. She had begun to send out definite signals last year, but her asking price was far too high for the people to whom she had made overtures. Fortunately, the woman had very little imagination. There were certain oil-rich Arabs who would have . . . but she either had not thought of that or had not known how to approach them. Although, as her intent became plain, it would only be a matter of time before someone like that sought her out. He would have preferred to wait one more year, but he knew he didn't dare.

Paul turned slightly, gauging the effect of his nose in the dark window, and shook his head at the glass. He had no doubts of his power over women. His looks and his money had combined to bring him anything he desired in the past.

But a seventeen-year-old girl? That was a different matter.

"Paul!" The reflection of Jeffrey Hanks' sharp-edged, serious face joined his own in the dark window glass. "So this is where you've been hiding. I was starting to think you hadn't made it."

"I was late. As usual." They shook hands. He and Jeffrey were of an age, Paul thought suddenly, but Jeffrey, with his thinning hair, stooped back, and fussy old man's manner, looked it, while he, thank God, did not. Forgive me, Jeff, he thought. It's not that I think less of you, old friend, but I need all the help I can get right now.

"Well? What did you think?"

"What?" Paul jerked his thoughts back to the present. "Think about what, Jeff?"

"The film, man! What else?" He was fairly dancing with impatience. "What did you think of the film?"

Two and a half hours this afternoon spent in dreamy wonderment as he watched her captured in flickering light on the screen by a master director. "It was your best work ever, Jeff. And hers." It was not just an empty social lie. He meant it, and Jeffrey could hear the truth of it in Paul's normally restrained voice. "Thanks for arranging the screening for me."

"The kid is a dream to work with." A note of regret colored Jeffrey's words.

"But?"

"The mother."

"You've worked with stage mothers before. You've worked with *her* mother before."

Jeffrey shrugged his thin shoulders. "I'm getting too old for that sort of hassle."

"Nonsense," Paul said, a shade too heartily. "Genius like yours never grows old. To make a film like I saw this afternoon . . . You can handle a mere mother."

Jeffrey gave his old friend an amused look. "Want to meet her and judge for yourself? If you've got something she wants, she'll have you out of those pants before you know what hit you. And I understand the broad is *good*."

"But you haven't . . . ah . . ."

Jeffrey's slow, gentle smile transformed his face. "Even if I *liked* women, she wouldn't be my type. As it is . . . Come on, Paul. I want you to see for yourself that the rumors are not exaggerated. I think Irene is out by the pool."

"And Savannah?" He was proud to note there was no betraying tremble of anticipation in his voice.

"Is not more than five feet away, I can guarantee you. When Irene starts to prowl, she'll send the kid home, well-guarded. You know, I feel sorry for Savannah. The only place she gets to live is on the screen. It's a hell of a life for her."

Paul thought about the screening that afternoon. Rough cut and all, Jeffrey Hanks' newest film was an obvious masterpiece. "But you take advantage of that, don't you, Jeff?"

"You betcha'. The kid's got a lot of fire in her. It's got to come out someplace. Since Irene won't let her have any other outlet, it boils out on film. I'd be a fool not to use that. Want another drink before we beard the lion?''

"I've had my limit for tonight.''

Jeffrey lifted an eyebrow. "Don't count on it. There's something about the girl that makes you need a good stiff drink afterwards. Even a man of the world like yourself. You'll see.''

Paul caught sight of Savannah first. Stretched out on a lounge by the heart-shaped pool, she was wearing a flowing mocha caftan in airy cotton gauze that clung lovingly at her breasts and hips to the still-wet coffee brown maillot beneath it. Her damp hair trailed over the edge of the lounge and hung nearly to the ground. She would be even more stunning when her body matured, he thought. A real beauty. That long-legged coltish figure with the small high breasts and prominent nipples was only a hint of what was to come. In four or five years time . . . Paul realized his palms were sweaty as a teenager's as Jeffrey led him over to meet the young actress's mother.

Irene Royale occupied her own lounger, next to her daughter's, her back to the two men. She wore a backless tank top and an ankle-length skirt in somber gray cotton jersey, her only adornment a gold brace-let on her left wrist. She was forty-three according to the reports Paul had received, fourteen years younger than himself, but when she swung around suddenly, as though somehow sensing his presence, Paul felt young, bashful, awkward.

She was a plain-looking, self-contained little woman,

shorter than Savannah, fuller at the hips and breasts, and her skin was aging badly. Liquor, cigarettes, and who knows what else, he thought. Its texture reminded him of a lizard skin purse he'd bought his last wife for their wedding anniversary just before they'd decided to see their separate lawyers. She had the same green eyes as her daughter, but the spark, the golden fire that lit up Savannah's face, was missing from Irene's unblinking gaze.

And yet . . . there was something. An undefinable aura that promised she *would* be good in bed. Paul knew instinctively that despite her age, bad skin and all, she could snap her fingers and any man at the party would be hers with the exception of Jeffrey Hanks, whose sexual nature leaned in another direction.

And himself. He had been fourteen when his father took him to the select house in San Francisco for his sexual initiation. Even after all these years, he could still remember the smell of the bed sheets the next morning. Now, looking at Irene Royale, he was reminded of that same smell.

Jeffrey introduced him to Irene with a flourish. "I just can't believe you two have never met," he added chattily to cover her stony silence. "Paul is simply one of my best friends."

Paul noted with grim inner amusement that both Jeffrey's wrist action and affected patterns of speech had become more pronounced in Irene Royale's presence. It was almost like watching a terrified prospective victim trying to ward off a vampire with a cross. "I've seen your daughter many times on the screen," he said smoothly. The woman's assessing gaze swept

over him. Paul kept his face as carefully expression-
less as a poker player's. He was gambling for the
highest stakes of his life. "She's an excellent actress."

He glanced over at Savannah herself. Dreamy and
preoccupied, she was staring into the glowing aquamarine waters of the pool, apparently unaware of his
presence. Some of the articles written about her
had implied that she was a little stupid, but Paul had
watched the girl carefully on the screen and he knew
it wasn't so. She was simply a very private person in
a very public occupation.

And, oh my God, was she beautiful in person! The
screen image had only hinted at the loveliness before
him now.

"Savannah!" Irene prodded. "Say hello to Mr.
Marsdon."

The girl looked up blankly. She had obviously
been a million miles away. She nodded at Paul disin-
terestedly, not really seeing him, and returned to
watching the water.

When he glanced back at Irene, Paul knew immediately that his mask had slipped; his face had given
something away. The avaricious gleam in her gray-
green eyes confirmed it.

Paul excused himself as quickly as he politely
could and followed Jeffrey back to the bar to order
the uncustomary third drink of the evening that his
old friend had predicted he would need. He downed
most of it in two gulps, ignoring Jeffrey's delighted
laugh. Savannah hadn't glimpsed the naked yearning
that had flickered across his face for a brief moment
when he stared at her, but her mother had. Paul

grinned to himself, a small, tight grin directed at the bottom of his glass. He had meant for Irene to see it.

Paul threw himself into a new physical fitness program with a vengeance. He had always taken reasonably good care of himself, but now he worked out every day.

Judging by what he had seen of Irene, he expected a call sooner, but it was two full weeks to the day before he heard the chill, colorless voice on the phone. The woman was a formidable angler. She knew how to play her fish once it was hooked. One look at Paul's face the night of Jeffrey's party had convinced her the hook was set.

She invited him for lunch the following day. Her excuse was that Savannah had expressed a desire to get to know him better, but when he arrived at the chic, contemporary house, set on a private knoll above Beverly Hills, he could see that it simply wasn't so. Savannah appeared to be at a loss as to where she had met him and was just as bewildered at being included in the formal luncheon.

Even the pure joy of gazing at Savannah as she sat, demure and virginal in a high-necked, long-sleeved lacy white dress, a mere arm's-length away, faded under Irene's unblinking gaze. It was a stiff silent meal and Paul was nearly as happy as Savannah when it was over. She escaped to her room with a murmured apology as soon as Irene dismissed her.

With Savannah's distracting presence removed, Paul found he could focus on his surroundings. The house itself was a contemporary jewel, with high ceilings and entire walls of glass and mirrors, the furnishings an elegant counterpoint to the architectural design. He gazed at Irene Royale with new respect as he followed her into the living room.

"Savannah needs male guidance," she said when she was seated beside him on the spectacular over-stuffed white sofa that faced a window-wall with a city-to-ocean view. She had shed the jacket of her severe black suit when Savannah left them. As she leaned toward him, Paul could see her nipples through the thin fabric of the deceptively simple, extremely expensive little blouse that had been hidden beneath it. "Someone she could lean on. Someone she could trust." Irene moved so close he could feel her breath hot on his cheek, the pressure of her breasts against his arm. "You could be that man, Paul. She trusts you a little already."

It took every ounce of his self control not to jerk away from her hand as she brushed his hair back from his face. He cleared his throat. "I . . . I would like to be that man, Irene. With your permission, I'd like to call again."

They stared into each other's eyes then, almost like lovers, searching each other's souls. After a moment, both of them felt satisfied; they had each found what they were seeking in the other.

"Savannah will be so pleased," Irene said at last, her lips thinned into a humorless smile. Paul knew she could feel his revulsion at her touch, but he knew, also, that she would make no issue of it. The game was too nearly won. The prize too dear and close at hand.

*   *   *

Paul began his formal courtship of Savannah immediately. Following that first lunch, he appeared at their hilltop residence regularly for lunches and dinners, like a kindly, non-threatening uncle, always supervised by Irene's watchful eyes. He took Savannah to the zoo, to the ballet, to gallery openings, always with Irene in tow like a duenna. His attempts to draw Savannah into any conversation lasting more than two sentences were dismal failures; she was reticent in Irene's constant shadow. For the first time in forty years, he had a problem with nearly constant erections. Irene Royale's knowing grin mocked him constantly.

Six weeks after his courtship of Savannah and her mother began, Irene met Paul at his office on a Wednesday morning at his invitation. He had planned to wait six months before making the offer, but he found he could not. He had helped Savannah celebrate her eighteenth birthday the night before, and having accepted him as a friend of her mother's, she had hugged him and kissed him soundly after she opened her present.

He had masturbated three times, like a teenager, that night before he had finally been able to get to sleep. The strain of it still showed in his face for Irene to read when his secretary showed her into his office. Irene's body was all but concealed by her loose-fitting, cowl-collared, charcoal silk jumpsuit, its fullness nipped in at the waist by a black cinch belt and then released to flow down her hips into wide pyjama legs that swirled around her surprisingly slim ankles as she walked. Her hair was brushed straight back from her forehead and she wore enormous black sunglasses that hid, not only her eyes, but half her face as well. Except for the leather case she carried, she might have been an aging actress, coquettishly drawing attention to herself by attempting to disguise her identity. Yet, as always with Irene Royale, there was something more. Some hint of raw sexuality that Paul found disturbing.

He waited until his secretary had discreetly closed the door behind her as she exited before he said, "Take off those damn goggles and let me see your eyes."

After Irene slipped off the sunglasses with irritating slowness, Paul almost wished she'd left them on. The triumphant sparkle that lit her gray-green eyes was unnerving, a parody of Savannah's gold-flecked gaze.

Irene closed the sunglasses with a snap and dropped them in her purse. "She's a virgin," she said bluntly.

"How do I know that's the truth?"

"I have a doctor's report." Irene unsnapped the briefcase and took out a paper.

Paul took it from her without letting his fingers touch hers and perused it quickly. "This could be faked," he mused.

"You've been with her. Been around her. You know it's the truth."

"I'll want to keep this."

She shrugged. "If you meet the price."

"And the price is?"

"One million dollars. Five hundred thousand now. Five hundred thousand when I deliver her to you."

"And what do you require from me?"

"Don't mark her up."

"You plan to resell her?"

Irene nodded. "Not that it's any business of yours. I've been waiting a long time for this. I plan to make the most of it."

"Why didn't you start sooner?" It was a question that had tormented him for a long time.

"I had the opportunity, but no one would meet the price."

"Until now?"

"Until now," she agreed.

"I want it in writing," he told her.

"Why?" She was genuinely curious.

"The commodity you are selling me is extremely perishable. I want to be able to reassure myself that the transaction actually happened."

Irene shook her head. "You must think I'm nuts. I'd be a fool to put something like that in writing."

Paul opened the top drawer of his desk. He began to lay out crisp piles of new bills. "I have fifty thousand here. I'll have the remainder of the first five hundred thousand delivered to your home this afternoon."

Irene licked her lips. "You don't really think I'd be crazy enough to . . ."

Paul slid one of the piles back into the desk drawer. "Of course, if you'd rather not go through with it. . . ."

"Wait." Irene caught his hand. It was all he could do not to recoil from her touch. "I didn't say that."

"Then let's get started," he said briskly. He pointed to a typewriter in the corner of the office. "I hope you can type. I'd rather not have my secretary involved in this. She still has a modicum of respect for me."

"I'll bet she does." Irene grinned nastily. "She's almost young enough to be interesting, right?" She seated herself at the typewriter and waited, fingers poised. "What do you want it to say?"

"I, Irene Royale, agree to sell Paul Marsdon the sexual services of my daughter, Savannah, for . . ." He broke off. "What is the time period we're talking about, Irene?"

She grinned up at him, challengingly. "One night."

". . . of my daughter, Savannah, for one night's time, in exchange for one million dollars in cash, five hundred thousand now and five hundred thousand when she is delivered to him or his agent. I hereby swear, and attach a medical report to show, that my daughter is a virgin. I place no stipulations on Paul Marsdon's behavior with my daughter except that Savannah is to be returned to me 'unmarked' within twenty-four hours' time, so that I may resell her services."

In the middle of that last phrase, Irene's hands ceased to move on the typewriter keys.

Paul thought for a moment that he had pushed too hard, that she would surely refuse to type those last words. Then he realized it was something else that had stilled her fingers; he felt her hand stroking his thigh. There had been no erection to trouble him today, and he shriveled even more from her practiced touch.

She laughed at him. "You only like them young, don't you? I've seen you around Savannah, you old fool. You can't keep it down."

"If I weren't an old fool, I wouldn't be paying you one million dollars for her . . . services," he pointed out, trying to ignore the bile rising in his throat.

She laughed again and finished typing the last phrase he had dictated. "Anything else? A clinical description of what I expect you to do to her? Or do you like the dirty words? Is that what gets you hard, old man?"

"That's enough," he said with deceptive mildness.

She ripped the page from the typewriter and scrawled her signature carelessly across the bottom of it. She tossed the page in his direction.

Paul caught it before it could flutter to the floor. He folded it together with the medical report and stuck them both in his breast pocket. "Why are you doing this, Irene?"

"You have the nerve to ask me that?" She crossed to the desk and unsnapped her briefcase.

"I'm only offering to purchase what you had already decided to sell." He looked at her closely. "How long ago did you decide to do it? When you brought her back to California? Or before that?"

Ignoring him, she began to stuff the money into the briefcase.

"What about her father?"

She paused and looked up. "What about him?"

"Does he know where she is? What's become of the two of you?"

She scooped the last of the money into the brief-case. "You think all those little details will help you get your thing hard for her? Well, forget it. Try something else. I have some nude photographs of her that were taken when she was three. Another five thousand and they're yours."

The bile was rising, threatening to gag him. "Sure," he muttered, nodding. "OK."

"You want me to bring her to you?" She might have been arranging the delivery of flowers or furni-ture. "Or will you pick her up?"

"My driver will be at your home Friday afternoon at five." Paul sat down on the edge of his desk and forced himself to meet her eyes. "What are you going to tell her?"

"Nothing." Irene looked at him defiantly. "If you think I'm going to soften her up for you, forget it." She patted the briefcase. "I'll be expecting your delivery this afternoon. Just make sure your driver brings the rest of it on Friday afternoon or she doesn't go with him."

"Of course." Paul felt compelled to add, "I'm an honorable man."

Reaching over, Irene patted him on the genitals. She laughed when he recoiled from her touch. "Of course you are, Paul. Just as honorable as all the other bastards in the world with outside plumbing." She slipped the huge sunglasses back on her face and puckered her lips at him in an obscenely mocking kiss. "It's been swell doing business with you. I just hope all my 'customers' will be as easy to deal with.''

When she left, Paul walked over to the credenza by the window and pulled out the concealed bar. He poured himself two medicinal fingers of Scotch with trembling hands and swallowed it in two gulps. Resolutely, he shut the bottle away again and went back to his desk.

He sat down and took the papers from his pocket, unfolded them carefully and smoothed them flat on the desk in front of him. He read both of them through, from start to finish. Then he laid his head down on his desk and wept.

Chapter 4

The Friday morning after her eighteenth birthday was the last time Savannah ever dreamed about the Prince. She awoke at eight, all in a panic, thinking she was late to school. It was several moments before she remembered that high school was over for good. She had graduated two weeks ago.

Eighteen and a high school graduate! She sat up in bed and hugged herself with glee. No more lessons in her dressing room with teachers from the Los Angeles Board of Education. She was through with all that. Through with feeling like a lonely, out-of-step freak. She could do anything she wanted now. Go to college. Travel. Anything. The possibilities stretched out before her like an endless road. She wouldn't have to ask anyone's permission for anything, ever again. After eighteen years her life was finally about to begin.

The first thing she was going to do with her newfound independence, she decided, was redecorate her bedroom. Its prissy little-girl decor had been featured in both *Seventeen* and *Young Miss* in the last two years. Thousands of teenage girls had copied it right down to the pale pink wastebasket.

Savannah hated it.

She hated the pale pink dotted-swiss curtains and bedspread with their extravagant lace ruffles. She hated the pale pink walls and the pale pink shag carpet. All that pink made her feel as though she were drowning in a bowl of melted strawberry ice cream!

She didn't hate the stuffed animals and dolls people kept giving her, but they bothered her. She had never been allowed to play with them while she was still young enough to want to, and now that she no longer did, their button-eyed stares accused her.

It was a baby's room, she thought. A five-year-old would love it. Nobody seemed to notice that Savannah Royale had grown up.

Nobody except Paul Marsdon.

She fingered the necklace he had given her for her birthday at dinner on Tuesday night. A grown-up present, not some stupid teddy bear. An original design, he had said when he fastened the clasp. Made just for her and no one else. She liked that, having something that was hers alone.

She unfastened the clasp and slipped the delicate gold chain from around her neck so that she could look at the pendant. The dainty gold bird fascinated her as it poised in her palm, wings spread, ready to take flight.

She had felt like that herself, she realized, ever since her birthday. Felt as though she were poised on the edge of some awesome discovery. Did everyone feel like this when they turned eighteen?

She wondered if Mr. Marsdon would be there for lunch. Most days he was and she had come to look forward to his presence. Mama was different when he was around. Not as stern. Something about Mr. Marsdon put Mama in a very good mood, but Savannah hadn't been able to figure out what it was.

At first Savannah had been startled when Mama included her in the meals and outings with Mr. Marsdon. But when she realized that nothing had changed, that Mama still had no intention of leaving her alone with anyone, not even a kindly elderly gentleman like Mr. Marsdon, she relaxed and began to enjoy herself almost as much as Mama did. He was really nice, she thought as she plumped up her pillows. He always tried to make sure she was included in the conversation, even if Mama ignored her as usual. Savannah just wished that she knew more about the world, about life, so that she could string two sentences together without lapsing into blushing silence. If only she were not so embarrassingly, tongue-tied *stupid*! He must think she was a *baby*!

The phone rang downstairs. Savannah slipped the necklace back around her neck and waited. When the photographers from the teen magazines had come, there had been a pale pink Princess phone on the nightstand, and they had each taken half-a-dozen shots of Savannah giggling into it, just as though it were a regular fixture in her room. When they were gone, Mama had unplugged it once more and that was the last Savannah had seen of it. The downstairs phone was the only one in the house and Savannah wasn't even allowed to answer it. Either Mama or Mrs. Browder answered every call.

The phone stopped on the fourth ring.

She wasn't going to let this go on, Savannah thought. She was eighteen now. It was high time Mama stopped treating her like a baby. Like a prisoner. If only she had a friend, someone who could talk to Mama for her. Someone who could convince Mama that she needed room to grow.

Savannah touched the tiny gold bird nestling in the hollow at the base of her slender neck. Mr. Marsdon! He would be the one to do it. He would help her; she knew he would. She had taken one look at him that first morning when he came to lunch and had known immediately that she could trust him.

She smiled up at a patch of sunlight on the pale pink wall and then closed her eyes and snuggled back down into the pale pink sheets, letting herself glide back into sleep. Almost at once the dream began.

She was in the garden, in late evening, stretched out on one of the marble benches, as cool and still as the stone on which she lay. Yards and yards of some diaphanous white fabric covered her completely and trailed down to the ground on either side of the bench like huge gauzy wings. Beneath it her body was firm and golden in the dying light and the heavy scent of tea roses filled the air.

Slowly she became aware of a man standing nearby. The deep purple shadows of evening that slashed across the manicured lawn cloaked his identity, but she knew it was the Prince himself, come at last after all her years of waiting.

He came forward silently and knelt beside her. Savannah realized that he was waiting for a sign from her, some indication that his love was returned.

She tried to grasp his hand, but her fingers were numb and lifeless. Frantically, she tried to lift her arms, eager to finally embrace him, but she could not move. She had become a part of the marble beneath her and she knew that only the Prince's kiss would save her from the paralyzing cold that was creeping toward her heart.

But as she realized that, the Prince stood up, and she saw that he had blank button-eyes like the teddy bears that lined the walls of her room. A guilty blush burned all over her body. He turned and strode away, leaving her alone with the heavy scent of the roses.

Rough hands grabbed at her and shook her. As they did, the fragrance of roses changed into the suffocating smell of Poor. The bag lady was back, and this time Savannah knew she wasn't going to escape.

She tried to scream as she struck at the arms that held her, but she could force no sound through the tight, panicked muscles of her throat.

"Stop that, you brat!"

Mama's voice sheared through the fabric of her dream. Savannah stopped struggling and shrank back against the pillows, away from the smell of whisky on her mother's breath.

Irene sat down heavily on the side of the bed. "What's wrong with you, for God's sake?"

Savannah pulled her sheet up around her shoulders and stared blankly at her mother, still confused from the dream. "You . . . you scared me, Mama."

Irene laughed harshly. "You have an easy life, don't you, little princess. Sleep all day, if you want to. Lounge by the pool. When I was your age . . ." Her voice trailed off, and then she went on, bitterly. "Time to get up, little princess. Time you put that lazy little ass to work."

Savannah was awake now and fury flamed through her veins. "Don't you talk to me that way! Acting is hard work. You're the one that's lazy. You don't make any money; I do. You just try to drink it up as fast as—"

Irene's slap knocked her head back against the headboard.

Savannah stared at her mother, stupefied. She couldn't believe those words had actually come pouring out of her. She couldn't believe Mama had slapped her. Mama had never slapped her before. She had never given her a reason to before.

Irene leaned closer and the nauseating smell of whisky on her breath nearly choked Savannah. "You stupid little slut," Irene hissed. "Don't you ever talk to me like that again. If it wasn't for me, you wouldn't be anything. You'd be a stupid little nobody in some backwater town, knocked up by the first bastard that got in your pants."

Savannah looked at her calmly. It was as though that slap had erased some barrier. She could see Mama truly for the first time without the crippling fear that had always held her paralyzed before. "Is that what happened to you, Mama? Is that what made you like you are?''

Irene stood up abruptly. "You're not ready for that bedtime story. Not today. Get up and get your hair washed and set. You've got a big evening ahead of you.''

"Are we going somewhere?''

"You are.'' She left without giving Savannah a chance to question her further.

Savannah got up and put on her robe. Surely Mama hadn't meant she was going to let her go someplace alone. Mama had never done that. But then, Savannah had never been eighteen before. Her heart gave a little leap. Maybe, just maybe, things were changing.

But the red imprint of Mama's hand on her cheek argued differently. Savannah waited until it had faded before she ran downstairs, taking the steps two at a time, and raced into the kitchen.

Mrs. Browder was setting a place for one. "Mama's not eating?'' Savannah said to the housekeeper.

"She had a bad night. Her insomnia was acting up. She decided to go back to bed for a little while.''

"You mean she stayed up all night drinking again,'' Savannah said cynically as she took her seat.

"Don't you talk like that about your mother, young lady! It's not respectful.'' Mrs. Browder snatched back the plate she had been about to set before Savannah. "Maybe you just won't get any breakfast.''

Something had definitely changed within her, Savannah thought. She was not the same person this morning. "You know,'' she told the housekeeper slowly. "I'm the one who earns the money that keeps this place going. If it weren't for that, you wouldn't have a job here. Maybe I ought to fire you.''

"Your mama controls the money, Miss Hoity-Toity and you and I both have to do what she says." Mrs. Browder dropped the plate on the table with a thump. "Now eat your breakfast."

Savannah pushed back from the table. "Maybe I still have to do what Mama says, but I don't have to do what you say. Not anymore."

"You sit right there and eat your breakfast."

Savannah left the kitchen, slamming the door behind her.

Mrs. Browder yanked it open. "Your mother will have something to say about this."

Savannah whirled around. "I'm sure she will when she gets through sleeping off her liquor. But in the meantime you can just leave me alone."

The housekeeper gasped and took a step backwards. "What . . . what about your breakfast?"

"Eat it yourself." The look on Mrs. Browder's face was a reward in itself. Savannah escaped back to her room and threw herself on the bed in a fit of giggles. Things were going to be different, all right. She was an adult and it was time everyone started treating her that way.

Starting today.

Irene slept until after four. When she awoke, she was in a foul temper that two quick drinks did nothing to assuage. Savannah's hair was the first thing to incite her rage.

"I told you to wash it and set it," she yelled, after

walking into Savannah's bedroom without knocking, "not pile it up on top of your head like that."

Savannah met her glance in the mirror and went on pinning her hair up. "I did wash it, Mama. I just wanted to try a new style. I'm tired of looking like a baby."

Irene stubbed out her cigarette on the edge of the dresser. Before Savannah could move away, her mother reached out and began yanking the hairpins out with both hands, letting the golden brown tresses tumble back down around her daughter's shoulders.

Savannah twisted away, tears springing to her eyes. "Don't, Mama!" she cried, all her newfound confidence vanishing in a second. "That hurts! You don't have to—"

"You fix it like you always wear it." Irene shoved her trembling hands into the pockets of her robe. "You don't change anything without my permission. Especially not today."

"I don't understand you!" Savannah cried. "Why won't you let me—"

"You just do what I say." Irene smiled down at her without warmth. "Mama knows best."

Mrs. Browder knocked gently on the open door. "Mrs. Royale? I just wanted to let you know that—"

"Why are you still here?" Irene's rage foamed up again. "I told you I didn't want you here this afternoon."

"I just had a few more things to—"

"Get out," Irene said flatly. "If you can't follow a simple instruction, then you can be replaced."

Mrs. Browder shot a startled glance at Savannah.

"I don't know what that little brat has been telling
you, but I was only doing what you—"

"Get out!" Irene snatched a bottle of perfume off
Savannah's dresser and flung it at the housekeeper.
Mrs. Browder jumped back, and the bottle struck the
door and bounced off without breaking. The housekeeper scuttled away without another word.

Irene turned on Savannah, who was staring at her
with wide frightened eyes. "You. You fix your hair
the way I told you and get yourself downstairs in
fifteen minutes."

"Yes, Mama." Her voice was barely above a
whisper as she tried to control the trembling of her
chin. Something was terribly, terribly wrong. Had
Mama gone crazy? With her robe gaping open and
her hair tangled and matted, she looked like an old
woman. Like the bag lady. She smelled like the bag
lady, too. Like sweat and whisky. Savannah shrank
back as Irene took a step toward her.

"Don't look at me like that, you little bitch! You're
not going to cheat me out of what's coming to me. Nobody's going to cheat me out of what's coming to me."

The dresser was pressing against Savannah's back-
bone. "I . . . I don't know what you're talking
about, Mama. I'm not—"

"You be downstairs in fifteen minutes." The grim
promise in her mother's voice made Savannah shiver.
"Or I'll drag you down by the hair of your head."

Mama was at the bar when Savannah came downstairs. "I see I managed to get through to you," she
said, her words already beginning to slur together.

How could Mama get *so* drunk *so* quickly, Savannah wondered as she dropped down on the sofa and propped her long legs on the coffee table. Mama had said nothing about changing clothes, so she had kept on the soft blue T-shirt and brief white shorts she had put on that morning. Irene herself was still in her robe. Although she had taken time to comb the tangles out of her hair, she hadn't put on any makeup yet and her face looked hard and old. Like the bag lady, Savannah thought with a shudder as the doorbell sounded.

"Get that," Irene told her.

"Me?" Her voice came out in a surprised squeak.

"You. You can do something as simple as open a door, can't you?"

Savannah felt an angry flush wash over her cheekbones, but she managed to bite back a reply. She wasn't about to provoke Mama again. She stomped down the hall and threw the door open without even bothering to look through the peephole.

A huge black man in a chauffeur's uniform stood there, holding a suitcase. His eyes seemed to stare right through Savannah without really seeing her. "Is Mrs. Royale home?"

"Bring him in here," Irene shouted.

The man stepped into the hall and closed the door behind him.

"Wait!" Savannah said frantically. Surely Mama had forgotten how she was dressed. "Wait here just a moment. Please?"

The man's face remained impassive. He nodded.

Savannah left him there and hurried back to the

living room. Irene's eyes narrowed as Savannah entered alone. "Where is he?"

"Mama! You're not dressed! You can't let that man—"

"Bring him in here. Now."

She knew there was no arguing with Mama when she had *that* tone in her voice. Not when the level in the whisky bottle had dipped so low. Savannah marched back down the hall, her shoulders stiff and straight, her embarrassment burning on her face for the stranger to see. "My mama will see you now," she told him. "This way." She led the way down the hall to where Irene Royale waited.

"Mrs. Royale?" the man said when he entered the room. "Mr. Marsdon sent me."

Irene set her drink down so hard it sloshed all over the bar. "It's about time you got here."

He glanced down at his watch. "Five o'clock, ma'am. As agreed."

"Don't you contradict me, you stupid black bastard!"

Savannah cringed. She could see a muscle jump in the man's massive jaw, but he said nothing.

"Did you bring it?" Irene demanded.

He held out the suitcase.

She grabbed the handle with both hands, almost staggering under the weight of it. "You stay right there," she told Savannah. "Don't you go anywhere until I say you can leave."

Savannah stared at her in amazement. "I don't understand, Mama," she said plaintively.

Irene ignored her, hurrying from the living room

and up the stairs. When she heard her mother's bedroom door slam shut, Savannah turned to the stranger.

The chauffeur was still standing in the center of
the room. She thought he must be the biggest thing
she had ever seen in her life. He was almost seven
feet tall and she saw with a fascinated glance that
under his cap he was completely bald. Should she
offer him a drink? she wondered. That was what
Mama usually did when men came.

She tried to catch his eye, but he was staring
straight ahead at some nonexistent point in space.
She could have been a piece of furniture for all the
attention he was paying her. "Ah, excuse me, sir?"
she began tentatively. "Would . . . would you like
something to drink?"

"No, miss," he said gravely. There was no friendliness in the brief glance he turned on her, no anger,
no emotion at all. He might as well have been a
robot.

"You can sit down if you want," Savannah told
him. "I'm sure my mother will be back soon."

"Thank you, miss, but I prefer to stand." His
glance returned to that same nonexistent point in
space. Savannah sat down on the sofa, knees primly
together, and waited for Mama to return.

It was at least ten minutes before she came back
downstairs, a smile on her face. "Okay," she told
Savannah. "You can go with him now."

The black man started toward the hall. Savannah
stood up, but she made no move to follow him. "Go
where?"

"He's going to take you to Marsdon."

Savannah was confused. Her mother had never allowed her to go anywhere alone before in her whole life and here she was practically pushing her out the door with this stranger. "I don't understand, Mama."

"I'm sure Mr. Marsdon will explain everything when you get there," Irene said with a smirk. She sat down on a barstool and lit a cigarette, clearly enjoying herself.

Savannah could feel the pulse pounding in her neck. "But . . . should I change clothes?"

Irene's glance swept over her from head to toe. The brief shorts exposed the whole length of Savannah's slim, tan legs and her golden brown hair was tumbled around her face in glorious disarray. "Go like that," she muttered. "It may help the old man."

The chauffeur shifted impatiently. "Ready, miss?"

Savannah was close to tears. A nameless panic had gripped her. Something was about to change and she was afraid. "Mama, please! I don't understand what's happening!"

Irene turned back to the bar and poured herself a fresh drink. "Get along with you," she said cheerfully. "Don't keep the man waiting."

Savannah hung back. A chance at freedom, however slight, however brief, was not to be turned down lightly. But she could sense there was more to it than that.

"Go on, I told you," Irene said roughly.

"Miss?" The chauffeur bowed slightly. "If you'll follow me."

Savannah did. At the door she paused and glanced back. Mama didn't look up. She was smiling down at the glass in her hand.

The chauffeur led Savannah out to a huge black limousine that was blocking half the drive. He helped her into the back of the limo with the same care and attention as if she had been all dressed up for a party. There wasn't a hint of a smile on his face as he closed the door, but Savannah just knew he was laughing at her. She felt ridiculous perched on the buttery-soft leather upholstery in her T-shirt and shorts. Surely this wasn't how Mr. Marsdon expected her to arrive or he would have sent a jeep instead of a limousine. Why hadn't Mama warned her?

They drove in silence for almost five minutes before Savannah finally got the nerve to ask, "Where are we going?"

The chauffeur glanced at her in the rearview mirror. "Mr. Marsdon will meet us at his Malibu residence, miss."

"Oh." His Malibu residence, with the emphasis on Malibu. So Mr. Marsdon must have other residences in other places.

For the first time, Savannah realized that she knew absolutely nothing about Paul Marsdon, what he did, or where he lived. Nothing except that Mama had allowed him to come to their house and take them places. Now Mama was sending her alone to meet him.

What was going to happen next?

She scooted forward and tapped the driver on the shoulder. "What's your name?"

"Carter, miss." He watched her in the mirror.

"What if I asked you to take me back home, Mr. Carter?"

His hand moved so swiftly that she didn't realize what was happening until a click sounded on either side of the passenger compartment. He had locked the doors.

Savannah forced herself to draw air into her lungs. Whatever happened, she wasn't going to be a baby. "I guess that answers my question," she said with a calmness that sounded forced and hollow to her own ears.

The driver remained silent.

Marsdon's Malibu residence was a Mediterranean-style villa built around a center courtyard alive with colorful flowers, bougainvillaea, and shade trees. An enchanted place, Savannah thought when she caught sight of it. It was there that they found Paul Marsdon.

"Wait here, miss," the chauffeur told her and marched forward stiffly, cap in hand.

Mr. Marsdon rose when he saw them and started her way, but the chauffeur's hand on his arm detained him. The man leaned down and said something to Mr. Marsdon. Savannah could only catch a few words: ". . . didn't even tell her I was coming . . . frightening little girls. . . ."

That last phrase galvanized her into action. Whatever happened, she wasn't a little girl anymore. She walked forward and extended her hand. "It's nice to see you again, Mr. Marsdon." His hand was warmer than she had expected; his palm, moist. "I hope you'll excuse the way I'm dressed, but Mama didn't tell me I was supposed to be ready to go anywhere."

Carter sniffed audibly.

"Call me Paul, please." Mr. Marsdon turned to his chauffeur. "That will be all for the moment, Carter."

Savannah glanced around. "You have a lovely house," she told Mr. Marsdon as the chauffeur left them.

"Thank you," he said with extraordinary graveness. She wondered if she sounded as young and foolish to him as she did to herself. She could feel her cheeks warming under his scrutiny.

He took her by the arm and led her over to the blue-cushioned chairs on the other side of the courtyard, beside the fountain. "Sit down, Savannah. We have to talk."

She obeyed without hesitation. There was something different about Paul Marsdon tonight. Something she didn't understand. But she still trusted him. "I don't know why Mama let me come here tonight, Mr. Mars—Paul. She's never done that before." She shook the curls back from her face. "Do you know why?"

"Yes I do. That's what we're going to talk about. But first I want you to read something." He took two folded papers from his coat pocket and handed them to her.

She looked down at them. "What are these?"

"Just read them. Please. And then we'll talk."

Slowly Savannah unfolded the papers and began to read. When she had finished, she stared at him, her eyes enormous green emeralds, her face pale.

Paul Marsdon took her right hand in his two large ones and held it tightly for a moment. "Don't be afraid," he told her. Then he explained to her what they were going to do.

Downstairs the phone was ringing. Irene groaned and pulled the pillow over her head, but she couldn't shut out the persistent sound.

"Mrs. Browder! Answer that damn phone!"

The phone continued to ring.

Irene groaned again and sat up. "Mrs. Browder?" she yelled. "Are you here?"

The phone continued to ring.

Irene got up slowly and staggered down the stairs. By the time she reached the phone she was in a raging fury. "Who the hell is this?" she snarled when she picked it up.

"Mrs. Royale?" a man inquired.

"What son of a bitch wants to know?"

"I'm Vincent Tate, legal representative for Paul Marsdon. I have some urgent business to discuss with you."

"It's the middle of the goddamned night," she complained, but her fury had vanished as abruptly as if someone had flipped a switch. Something was up. She could sense it. If that old bastard had marked up Savannah, he was going to pay for any plastic surgery she needed. It's not coming out of my money, she promised herself.

"It's seven A.M., Mrs. Royale. And this business won't wait."

"Savannah's due back at five tonight." Irene grinned at the phone. She reached over and snagged a nearly empty bottle of Canadian Club from the bar. "How-

ever, if he wants to buy another day of her time . . .
for the same price, of course.'' She took a healthy
swig of the Canadian Club straight from the bottle
and wiped her mouth with the back of her hand. She
was slowly starting to feel human again.

''Mrs. Royale. . . . What I have to discuss with
you is best done in person. Not over the phone.'' He
paused. ''I can be there in half an hour.''

Irene took another healthy swig. ''Come ahead.''

''Right,'' he said and hung up.

Irene replaced the receiver and stared at the bottle
in her hand thoughtfully. The weasel was probably
trying to get his money back. Too late for that. It was
safely stashed. All those years she had spent waiting
for this opportunity had made her smart. Some creep
like Marsdon was going to have to get up pretty early
in the morning to take it away from her. She finished
up the bottle before she staggered upstairs to shower.

What did one wear to entertain an old bastard's
lawyer, Irene asked herself when she came dripping
out of the shower. She threw half a dozen dresses out
on the bed, but the effort of trying to make up her
mind was too tiring. She put her robe back on and
went downstairs to the bar to wait.

Tate arrived in twenty-nine and a half minutes,
immaculately dressed. He wasn't bad looking, in a
prissy, old-maidish sort of way. When she sat back
down she let her robe open slightly to hint of her
nakedness beneath it. ''Want a drink, Mr. Tate?''

''No, thank you, Mrs. Royale.'' He waited with
unconcealed impatience while she poured one for
herself. ''If we could get down to business now. . . .''

"What does the old fool want? His money back?" Irene grinned. "Not a chance."

"Mr. Marsdon wanted to reach an agreement with you concerning his wife before the news media learns of the marriage. He thinks it better for all concerned if you present a united front . . . and that nothing is said about the arrangements you attempted to make with him."

"What wife?"

"Savannah Royale Marsdon."

"He can't do that!"

"He already has, Mrs. Royale. All perfectly legal, I assure you."

"She wouldn't have agreed—"

"She did agree. Quite readily, Mr. Marsdon said. Now." He became all brisk business. "I have prepared an agreement between you and Mr. Marsdon. For the sum of fifty thousand dollars a year, you agree to make no attempt to see or contact your daughter again. If you make any such attempt, the money stops. Automatically. Permanently."

Irene laughed at him. "She won't stay with him. She'll come home to me. All I have to do is snap my fingers and—"

"I think not, Mrs. Royale. Mr. Marsdon has arranged for you to talk to your daughter one final time before the agreement goes into effect." Tate picked up the phone and dialed. "They're in Las Vegas," he explained. He gave a suite number to the party on the other end of the line. After a moment he said, "Tate here," into the phone while his eyes studied

Irene's incredulous face. "I'm there now. Yes. Yes.
I told her. Yes, Mr. Marsdon."

"Give me that phone," Irene screamed at him.
She jerked the phone away, not caring that the robe
had slipped halfway open to expose her body, slack
and naked beneath it. "What the fuck are you trying
to do, you old bastard? You bring my baby home!"

Paul Marsdon's voice was calm, controlled. "She's
not your baby anymore, Irene. You have forfeited the
right to have anything to do with her."

"You ball-less wonder! You let me talk to her
or—"

"Certainly."

In a moment, Savannah's soft voice came on the
line. "Mama?"

"Savannah, honey. This can't be true. You didn't
marry him, did you?"

"Why, Mama? Would you have preferred that I
just let him screw me?"

Irene jerked the phone away from her ear and
stared down at it for a moment before she raised it
again. "How can you talk like that? What has he
been telling you?"

"He showed me the papers, Mama." Savannah's
voice grew faint. "The one you signed. The one
from the doctor."

"It's a forgery," Irene said desperately. "I never
signed anything. You come home, Savannah. You
come home right now and I'll explain—"

"There's nothing to explain. Paul just confirmed a
lot of suspicions that I've had for a long time. You

really ought to be grateful to him for the money, Mama. I asked him not to give you anything at all.''

    "Savannah—"

    "Good-bye, Mama."

BOOK II

Paul

Chapter 5

Of all the arrangements Paul Marsdon made for his wedding, it was clothing that presented the biggest problem. He knew Savannah would need an entire wardrobe, had known it from the moment he first approached Irene Royale beside Jeffrey Hanks' heart-shaped pool. The problem was how to acquire it. For a man who had clothed three wives, four daughters, and one mistress from the skin out, Paul knew remarkably little about the techniques of acquiring those clothes.

Size was no problem. Savannah's measurements were public knowledge. But beyond size was an entire range of considerations he had never addressed personally before: color, style, fabric, accessories, underclothing, and who knew what else.

And it all had to be perfect, exactly what Savannah would have chosen herself. This was a project that needed a woman's touch, but what woman could he approach?

A professional buyer was out of the question. When

the story of his marriage broke—and he had no illusions on that score—he didn't want someone coming forward to add that little tidbit to the gossip. Besides, there was always the possibility that word might leak out beforehand; he couldn't take the chance that Irene might learn what was going on before his plot was in motion. So who could he ask for assistance.

Not his current secretary! The thought of the look that would be in her eyes made him cringe. Not his wives. Not his daughters. Certainly not his daughters-in-law.

Of all the options open to him, there was only one he could afford to exercise. Only one person he could afford to trust with this most delicate of missions.

Garnet Hoffman.

Garnet had been his secretary and lover for twenty years. Seven years ago, she had retired from both positions to take up residence in a low-slung contemporary house tucked away in a wooded Malibu canyon with two Lhasa Apsos and three Persian cats. The house was in Paul's name, but he never dropped by without phoning first—even though Garnet never gave any evidence she appreciated that small courtesy on his part—and there was never any sign of another male presence in the house.

Although the sexual side of their relationship had faded, Paul visited her often. He had found it was not as easy to divorce himself from his office wife as it had been to cut the emotional ties to his three legal wives. He missed her advice, her intuition, her confirmations of his judgment. A visit to Garnet was like opening a fine bottle of wine: there were always rich nuances to her that only a connoisseur could appreciate fully.

If she had noticed his growing obsession with Savannah Royale, she had not mentioned it. The time between his visits had stretched out longer and longer. Now, he realized with a shock, it had been almost four months since the last time he had lain in the hammock in her Malibu garden watching her comb her animals' sleek coats, laying his latest business strategy before her, and chuckling over her insight.

Garnet was the answer to his dilemma, but did he have the right to involve her? She had come to work for him between wives number one and two. She had even coached him along in his pursuit of number three while warning him all the time it would not work. But now he realized, with a new awareness given him by his love for Savannah, that his marriages had hurt Garnet deeply. When she learned of his marriage to Savannah would that not be the deepest cut of all? Or would she be more deeply wounded not to have been a part of it? Because now he saw quite clearly that while he had thought their relationship had matured into a mutual friendship, Garnet loved him as deeply as he loved Savannah.

In the end he thrust aside the memories of Garnet's twenty-seven years of devotion and love; it was Savannah Royale who filled his thoughts completely in this moment. That decision was made at considerable cost to his self-esteem, and when he called Garnet to tell her he was stopping by, his voice was so brusque she did not recognize it at first. He had to identify himself for the first time in their more than quarter-century together.

*   *   *

Paul used his key to let himself into Garnet's house. A yapping chorus of welcome from the two dogs and a yawn of indifference by the one remaining member of the former feline trio greeted him. But no Garnet.

When she did not answer his hail, he went in search of her. He found her sitting in the living room staring out at the creek. An elaborate tea service was set out on the low table in front of her.

He felt as though he were in a sickroom. "Garnet?"

"Would you like some tea, Paul?" she asked, as though he had only been out of the room for a few minutes instead of four months. "Or would you prefer a drink instead?"

"Tea would be fine." When he sat down beside her, he found himself studying her familiar elegant profile as if seeing her for the first time. She was a small, fine-boned woman. Bird-boned, she had told him the first time he took her to bed. Today her hair was coiled in a precise French roll. Only for him, in their most intimate moments, had she worn it down, in a soft blonde cloud. Cool, crisp, efficient, she had been a tyrant in the office. She was dressed just as crisply now in an immaculate white blouse, a trim gray skirt, but as she poured the tea her hand shook so badly that the hot liquid splashed out onto the table top. The cup clattered in the saucer as she handed it across to him. Her eyes were huge in the small oval of her face.

"Garnet? Has something happened?"

"I'm not very good with money, Paul. It just

seems to . . . to drift away. I have less than two hundred dollars in my checking account until your check comes at the first of the month.'' She stood abruptly, wringing her hands, and walked over to the window-wall to stare out at the creek once more.

The strange note in her voice had roused the dogs. The Lhasa Apsos came trotting in from the hall, tails waving, and settled themselves on either side of her feet, casting reproving glances at Paul.

''I'm afraid I don't understand what—''

''It's just that I may require a little loan, Paul,'' she said without turning around. ''To get myself settled somewhere else, you understand.''

He was mesmerized by the emotions playing across her face. She had been twenty when she came to work for him. Somehow, over the years, it had been that fresh-faced girl he had continued to see; even when the girl had been long replaced by the elegant office tyrant. Now he saw what he had not seen for the last seven years: the faint patterning of lines across that well-kept face, the crinkles at the corners of the eyes. Age creeping up as steadily on her as it was on him. Now he knew what the emotion was in that face.

Terror.

He crossed the room and enfolded her in his arms. ''Did you think I was kicking you out? We've been together too long for that.'' Outside in the garden, the hammock was swaying gently in the breeze, as though he had just gotten up from it a moment ago.

Garnet's voice was muffled against his chest. ''It's been so long since you were here. And your voice on the phone . . . You sounded like a stranger, Paul.'' She choked on his name and the dogs whined at their feet.

He held her out from him and looked into her face. ''I would never do that. You're too much a part of my life. It's just that the matter I've come to discuss with you is very . . . delicate. I wouldn't even mention it to you if there were anyone else I could turn to.''

''Nonsense,'' she said briskly, her shoulders straightening. She looked like a tiny, trim drill sergeant. ''You know there's nothing you can't discuss with me, Paul. Not after all these years.''

''I wouldn't want to hurt you, Garnet. I would never want to hurt you.'' He hesitated. But the impulse that had brought him here in the first place would not let him stop now. ''I'm getting married again.''

The joy that lit her face was genuine. ''Paul! I'm so happy for you!'' The dogs, recognizing that the crisis was past, yapped cheerfully. ''This calls for champagne, not tea!''

''You may not think so after you've heard the details,'' Paul told her ruefully. ''I'm marrying an eighteen-year-old girl.''

Her expression wavered and then firmed. ''Why that's just fine. I'm sure you will be very happy. And I hope that our . . . friendship will continue, Paul, just as always.''

''Of course it will, Garnet. Nothing could change that.''

Now she was genuinely curious. ''But what on earth did you want to talk to me about today?''

Paul sighed explosively. "Clothes!"

"Clothes? For you?"

"For her. Not only am I marrying a girl younger than any of my children, I'm stealing her away from her mother without a stitch of clothing."

"Why, Paul! How romantic."

"Not for her." The memory of gold-flecked eyes reproached him. "She'll be confused, afraid. And she'll have nothing to wear."

"And you want me to . . ."

"To buy her things. Everything." He pulled a notebook out of his pocket and handed it to her. "These are her measurements. She'll need everything from the inside out. Clothes, underwear, handbags, shoes. Get it for me, Garnet. Please." He was begging, and he was a man most unused to begging. "Charge it to your accounts. I don't want her to feel uncomfortable or out of place during our first few days together."

"You want me to go alone? To shop for her?"

Paul nodded.

Garnet glanced down at the notebook and then back at him, amused. "But this isn't enough, Paul. It won't do at all."

"All her measurements are there," he protested.

"But not her coloring. How will I know what colors to select? And where will you be staying? What kind of weather am I shopping for?"

"We'll be married in Las Vegas. And then we'll honeymoon on the Island." He hated even mentioning the plans out loud. Especially the Island. He and Garnet had been young lovers there once. He had the oddest feeling that he was being unfaithful to Savannah in some way.

"And the coloring . . ." Garnet snatched a pencil from the table and began making swift notes in the efficient way he remembered from their years in business together. "She'll need makeup and— You won't be giving her a chance to pack a thing?"

Paul shook his head. "I'm afraid not."

"Are you abducting her?" The question was playful, but when he didn't answer right away, the notebook slipped from her fingers. Her hand darted to her mouth. "Oh, Paul! You wouldn't!"

"I'm buying her!" All the self-loathing he felt in that moment was in his voice for her to read.

Garnet swayed, and for a moment he thought she might faint. Then her iron control reasserted itself. She knelt gracefully to recover the notebook. When she rose, the glance she turned his way was clear, untroubled. "And the coloring, Paul? I'll need to know that."

"Don't you want to know why I'm buying another human being like a slave, Garnet?"

"I know you, Paul. I've known you for twenty-seven years. That's all I need to know. Except for the girl's coloring."

He stared at her for a moment and then turned and strode back across the room. For a moment she thought he was leaving, but then he returned with the magazine that had been lying on her coffee table and shoved it at her. "There," he said roughly. "That's her coloring."

Garnet glanced down at the magazine. The girl on

the cover was the young actress/model whose face seemed to be everywhere these days. "She has the same coloring as Savannah Royale? What a lucky young woman she is."

"She *is* Savannah Royale."

After Paul left, Garnet sank down on the sofa, the notebook forgotten beside her. She clutched the magazine with trembling hands, studying the beautiful young face on the glossy cover. Her own youth had never seemed as far away as it did at that moment.

Today had been a false alarm. But it was a warning, too, of how quickly she could go from pampered to destitute. Whatever had been between Paul Marsdon and herself—whether it was love or simply friendship—was ending. There was nothing in her name to show for the years they had been together, not even this house. Only Paul's whim and the few dollars that remained in her checking account stood between herself and poverty.

It was time Garnet Hoffman started looking out for herself. First, the charge accounts. Garnet knew instinctively that Paul would not question a single figure on the shopping spree for his bride-to-be. With the help of a few salesclerks, Garnet knew she could milk a tidy little sum from the charge accounts Paul had set up for her. And after that . . . there would be other opportunities. She was sure of it.

Until the spots of moisture began to dot the glossy magazine cover, Garnet didn't realize she was crying.

To Paul's intense relief, Savannah didn't ask where

her elaborate wardrobe had come from when Carter delivered her to the Malibu house. She simply accepted the fact that when he sent her upstairs to change there were clothes waiting there for her: a dress, underclothes, shoes. She gave them no more thought than she would the clothes for a fashion shoot, except that this time she didn't have her own bag with her, and makeup was provided as well.

A line of expensive leather suitcases sat in the foyer when she came back downstairs, and a few minutes later, the chauffeur placed the small leather makeup-bag she had used with the rest of the luggage.

They took Paul's jet to Las Vegas. A high-rollers' penthouse suite at the MGM Grand was ready for them when they arrived. A maid unpacked Savannah's bags and took the billowing white wedding dress, which had occupied one huge case all by itself, off to be pressed, while Carter drove Paul and Savannah to the county courthouse to get the marriage license. There was no blood test or waiting period. All that was required was her proof of age, and Paul had that with him.

When they returned to the Grand, two maids brought the wedding dress back to the suite and waited in patient silence in Savannah's bedroom while she combed her hair and applied her makeup. When she was ready, they stood on tiptoe to slip the yards and yards of ivory peau de soie and chantilly lace over her head, and to drape the long lace veil over her hair mantilla fashion, letting it fall gracefully around her shoulders and flow down the length of the train. She added the face veil of tulle and stepped into the peau de soie shoes, which had been packed with the dress. The maids oohed and ahhed over her. They drew her over to the mirror so she could see herself. "You look like a princess," one of them said with a sigh.

Savannah stared at herself, overcome by the vision in the glass. Her face, behind the tulle, was radiant. She did look like a princess.

An image of the Prince wavered in her mind, and then shattered when one of the maids exclaimed, "The garter! Your 'something blue.' It was packed with the dress," she explained as she handed it over to Savannah. "Do you have the rest?"

They were horrified to find she did not, and the other maid loaned her a handkerchief. "That can be your 'borrowed.' The dress will be your 'new,' but what about your 'old.' "

There was no "old." Savannah realized for the first time that she was leaving all her possessions with Mama, but suddenly that didn't matter. Her hand darted to the tiny gold bird that hung from the thin chain around her neck—Paul's birthday gift to her—and she knew she had brought her most important possession with her. "This is all I need," she told them.

The wedding ceremony was performed in the five-thousand-square-foot suite, which had been transformed while she dressed into a floral fantasy by extravagant arrangements of white roses and orange blossoms. White satin ribbons supported by flower-covered stanchions formed the aisle. The minister waited between two graceful candelabras wound with ivy and roses, as Carter, who had traded his chauffeur's uniform for a black morning coat and dark gray striped trousers, escorted her to Paul's side. Members of the Grand staff served as witnesses.

Savannah clutched the bouquet of large white orchids with trembling fingers and darted one quick glance at Paul, stern and handsome in his black morning coat, before she said, "I do." When the minister pronounced them man and wife, Paul kissed her solemnly on the lips.

The minister and the hotel staff stayed for the wedding breakfast buffet and the vintage champagne. Savannah, with Paul's assistance, cut the elaborately-iced seven-tiered cake. The onlookers applauded appreciatively as Paul fed her the first bite and she fed him the second, and Savannah blushed.

Shortly afterwards, everyone discreetly departed. Paul waited until he and Savannah were alone in the suite and then phoned his lawyer to tell him that the ceremony was over and he could notify Irene Royale that Savannah was now legally his wife. Then he opened another bottle of champagne and poured each of them a glass while they waited for the phone to ring.

Savannah handed the phone over to Paul. The stream of abuse that poured out of the receiver in a tinny little faraway voice seemed as unreal as everything else that had happened to her in the past few hours. Savannah stared down at the ring Paul had slipped on her finger during the ceremony, watching the way the gold caught the light.

"Good-bye, Irene," Paul said abruptly and re-placed the receiver with a definite click. Without looking at Savannah, he removed his boutonniere and dropped it in an ashtray. "It's finished," he said.

Savannah waited, unsure what to do. There was a strangeness in the room now that had not been present before. Everything had seemed so clear cut a few seconds ago. Paul Marsdon had rescued her, had brought her to Las Vegas, had married her. Now she was Savannah Royale Marsdon. Until this moment, she hadn't begun to realize what that meant.

Paul rose and poured himself another glass of champagne. He crunched the bottle back down into the ice without offering Savannah a refill. Staring out the window at the neon Nevada dawn, he said, "You might want to nap for a while before we leave for the Island." Then he disappeared into one of the bed-rooms, not the one that held Savannah's new ward-robe, and closed the door firmly behind him.

Savannah realized that he was shutting her out; what she couldn't understand was why. She rose with a rustling of fabric and went into her own bedroom to change out of her wedding dress.

Paul was shaking so badly when the door closed behind him that he felt like an old man with the palsy.

Scruples.

It was a hell of a time to develop scruples. But there they were all the same.

The enormity of what he had done hadn't really sunk in until he hung up the phone. Something twisted within his chest as he remembered the trusting way she had looked up at him with those clear green eyes. He had done it, exactly what he had set out to do.

Savannah Royale was his, body and soul.

Especially soul.

He knew better than anyone else just how tight Irene's leash had been. It wasn't just that he was the only man in Savannah's life, for Christ's sake. He was virtually the only other person the girl knew, thanks to her mother's watchfulness.

Savannah would love him; he had no doubt on that score. She had no other choice. Like a duckling that imprints on the first thing that it sees when it comes out of the shell, she would imprint on him. Because he was the first and only significant person in her life after Irene, Savannah had no more choice than that just-hatched duckling. So all his babble to himself about how he was saving her from Irene was just so much crap. He had freed her from one cage to put her in another, more gilded one.

Savannah was so isolated, so protected, that she wouldn't even recognize the bars around her for what they were.

But he would.

Paul showered and changed. When he came out, Savannah was sitting in the exact spot she had occupied when he left the room. Only she, too, had changed, and Paul saw that Garnet had chosen well. The soft beige linen suit made Savannah look older, and more sophisticated—the pampered wife of one of the wealthiest men in the country. Who would guess looking at that gorgeous creature that she was a criminally naive eighteen-year-old virgin?

He was so filled with disgust, for himself, for Irene, that he didn't trust himself to speak.

She watched in silence as he phoned the airport to alert his pilot.

When he hung up, she said, "There isn't anything . . . anything wrong, is there?" Her eyes were wide, confused.

"No, no," he said quickly. He reached for the champagne, anything to avoid meeting her glance again. He was afraid she could see right through to his soul. "We'll be leaving for the Island in a few minutes. I'll have the maids come up and help you pack."

"All right," she said obediently. He risked a look as she uncurled those long legs and stood up, and then wished he hadn't.

When the door had closed behind her, he called the desk, and then he paced around the room, coming finally to a halt in front of the remains of the wedding cake.

What in the hell was he going to do?

They were halfway to the airport before Paul realized he had never explained where they were going. The Island, he had said, with arrogant assurance that she knew as much about him as he knew about her. That she had read the countless feature articles that had appeared on him and knew about his different residences, where they were, what they were called.

Now, as he remembered how quickly she had acquiesced when he told her to get ready, he realized that would have been impossible. It had not been part of Irene Royale's schemes to let Savannah know that much about him, about anyone. Savannah was following blindly, trustingly, like the duckling, imprinted on the wrong "mother," trustingly followed the human researcher.

He had slipped so easily into Irene's role that it was terrifying. To have the kind of power he had at this moment over another human being was unlike anything he had ever felt before. He had never owned someone body and soul and he found he did not like the little thrill of excitement it gave him every time he thought about it. Was that feeling the reason why Irene had done what she had? he wondered.

This morning his dream was fulfilled in every part. He had prepared so carefully, down to the tiny little healed incision on his balls that insured there would be no children for the two of them. At the time he had told himself the vasectomy was so that later she would be free to start a new life, to have children with someone nearer her own age. But now, as Carter steered the car through the early morning traffic, Paul realized that was a lie. He had not had Savannah in mind when he let that son of a bitch take a knife to his balls; he had been thinking only of himself. Children would have diverted Savannah's attention from him. He was a greedy selfish bastard who wanted everything about her to be his. Body and soul.

He had always been a hard man in a business deal. That was how he had made his millions. But always, *always,* he had believed he had a conscience, that there were some lines he would not cross. Now he knew that was not true and the thought sickened him.

As the car slowed, he realized he was like a man who had bought a fabulous stolen art treasure. What could he do with it now, except admire it in private. Surely a masterpiece deserved to be seen by the world, but if the world saw his treasure it would be taken from him.

No matter how wrong he felt he had been, he couldn't just let Savannah walk away, not only for his sake, but for her own. She would be easy prey for the first person that wandered up. Perhaps even Irene.

His hands had curled into unconscious fists. He couldn't do that. He couldn't set her free. God forgive him, he was afraid to touch her because of what it would do to his immortal soul, but he was equally afraid to let her go.

So what was he going to do? Keep her locked in a vault forever? Paul hunched down in his seat, miserable at the thought.

Chapter 6

Paul's jet landed at Coolidge Airport on Antigua. Savannah had time for no more than a quick glimpse of the passing landscape out the windows of the limousine as Carter whisked her and her new husband to English Harbour and a waiting yacht. A ten-minute boat ride brought them to the Island.

The Island.

How could two small words sum up the magic Savannah found waiting for her on this small dot of land in the clear blue waters of the Caribbean? As soon as she stepped up on the dock, she knew that something wonderful was going to happen to her here. The gentle trade winds tugging at her hair and the sun, bathing her skin with a warmth that made her want to shiver with sheer pleasure, were telling her so. Somewhere deep inside of her there was a hard-shelled protected *something* that was feeling the first faint stirrings of life. Inside that hard little center was the *real* Savannah and she knew that the quivery, breathless feeling that had taken possession of her in the last few seconds was the way a rose must feel when it realizes it's going to bloom. Or how a caterpillar might feel when it realizes that all along there has been a butterfly hidden inside its ugly squirmy little body.

Afterwards she had no recollection of coming up from the dock across the smooth carpet of lawn, or of what Paul had said or done as he conducted a brief tour of the airy, sprawling house. She was only aware of the seconds ticking away as she waited for him to stop talking and let her escape to her own room, aware that each moment he kept her here, shut away inside these walls, was time stolen from her life-to-be, from the awakening that was to come.

When at last he released her, she raced upstairs with the exuberance of a child on the last day of school and shooed away the maid who had been unpacking her clothes. She tore into the luggage, one piece after another, tossing clothing haphazardly around the room, searching frantically for what she knew had to be there. The unknown someone who had arranged for all of this wonderful and perfectly appropriate clothing, who had known to the last ounce and fraction of an inch, her height, weight, and measurements, and even the kind of sanitary protection she preferred, had provided everything *else*, so she knew it had to be there. It simply *had* to be.

Finally her fingers closed upon two wisps of chrome yellow Lycra: the briefest, barest bikini that could have existed. There were other swimsuits, too, of course. The unknown someone would have seen to that: maillots, tanks, bikinis, a whole wardrobe of swimwear. But nothing so brief and bare as the yellow Lycra bikini. Only her own skin could have been more revealing.

But it was not revealing her body that she had in mind; that was the furthest thing from her thoughts. She wanted only to expose herself more fully to the tingling magic she had felt when she stepped out on the dock, to let the Island and the sea breeze and the sand, fine and white as sugar in a china bowl, and above all the water, the bright, unbelievably blue water, possess her.

Savannah spent the rest of that first long, lazy afternoon lying on the sand, rising occasionally for a cooling dip in the clear blue Caribbean waters.

How strange it was to remember that she had spent her life on one coast or another, in New York or Los Angeles, and how close she had been to the ocean in those two cities. All she remembered now was the shuttling back and forth across the great middle of the country between them, imprisoned in the belly of an airplane. It was as if she had never seen an ocean before—for that matter, never seen *anything* before. For always, *always,* there had been Mama between herself and the rest of the world—at worst, a barrier; at best, a filter.

Now she was finally free and as self-absorbed as an infant making its first contact with the world. Everything fascinated her, from the fine white sand clinging to the taut skin of her thighs, to the sound of breaking surf from a distant reef, to the antics of the seabirds further down the beach.

When a servant came to tell her dinner would be

ready soon, Savannah left the beach like a sleep-
walker. She showered in the bath hut near the beach
and, wrapped in a huge towel, let herself be led
across the breezeway that connected the hut with the
house. In her room, she slipped on the underclothing
and dress already laid out on the bed for her. She
wore her still-damp hair knotted at the back of her
neck, and only the faintest hint of makeup to hide the
flush of sun on her skin.

Paul talked to her at dinner and she nodded and
smiled occasionally, but the words were from somewhere far away and made no sense. All she could
think of was that the beach would be waiting for her
again tomorrow, eternal and timeless.

At last Paul fell silent and simply feasted his eyes
on her beauty. Savannah was so caught up in her
own thoughts that she never noticed his words had
ceased.

After dinner they went to their separate bedrooms.
Savannah woke once during the night and lay awake
listening to the wonderful sounds of the surf and the
wind from the water.

She spent a week simply lying on the sand and
bathing in the water. A lounging chair and an umbrella were set up on the second day and refresh-
ments appeared periodically with a thoughtfulness
she never noticed, arriving seconds before she became aware that she was thirsty or hungry. She had
only to stretch out her hand and whatever she wanted
was already there, waiting. An assortment of oils for
her skin was replaced daily on the low table beside
her lounging chair. With them she found a brush, to

comb the sea-breeze tangles from her hair, and pins and combs to contain it—but those she never used. She was not aware of the hands that placed the food and drink and other things beside her. She had no idea Paul watched her like a voyeur from the sprawling house half-hidden in the flowering bushes behind her, sending the parade of servants with anything she might desire before even the hint of want could rise within her.

Paul spent every moment that Savannah was on the beach gazing at her from the balcony of his room, the room that was to have been theirs. The thought of what might have been made his palms slick with sweat, and he almost dropped his binoculars into the hibiscus below. He had never undergone such torment as he did now, watching that long-legged coltish figure with its small high breasts, basting in the Caribbean sun, knowing that legally she was his to fondle and possess, to kiss and caress, but that morally he could not.

His balls ached constantly. He could not sleep and the coldest of showers did not diminish him as he thought of her lying in the immense antique four-poster bed in the room just beyond his. In the midnight quietness he thought he could hear her tossing and turning, the soft sound of her breathing, the thudding of her heart, and then he realized it was his own ragged breathing and his own heart's painful thudding that he heard. He cursed himself for a fool and a coward as he lay awake, staring up at the moonlight-washed ceiling. Surely there would be no hell for him in the afterlife; he was suffering unbearably for his sins in this one.

On the morning of the seventh day, Savannah became aware that some vital part of her, which had been missing all her life, but which she had never known existed before now, had become hers. Something within her had become whole. For the first time since she had set foot on the Island seven days earlier, she was aware of more than the sand and the sun and the sea. She was no longer self-absorbed, but hungry for the world. A flood of sensations had deluged her, and spongelike she had absorbed them all. But now they had done their job and she was no longer the same person who had stepped off the deck of Paul Marsdon's yacht a week ago. She was a brand new person, born here on the beach, on the clean white sand, and a whole new world of possibilities stretched before her.

To the watcher on the balcony, nothing had changed. The gleaming body lay on the beach like a golden statue in the sun.

Woman.

Eternal.

Timeless.

There was no external clue that the binoculars could capture; but the change was there.

The first sign came when Savannah left the beach in mid-afternoon instead of waiting for the long graceful shadows of the palms to stretch across it like slender purple fingers of evening. Paul gripped his binoculars so tightly that his fingers ached as he followed her progress up the beach.

Although Savannah had not summoned her, a thin black woman was waiting for her at the door of the bath hut with a fluffy white bath towel in her hands. Just as she had waited every day for the past seven days, Savannah realized with a small shock of awareness; as though waiting there, statue-still, towel in hand, until impulse or whim might drive Savannah off the beach, was her only function in life.

Savannah took the towel and sent the woman away so that she could shower in privacy, but now, like a latter-day Robinson Crusoe, she was suddenly aware of *others* on her island. For the first time since she had landed on the Island, she was curious about the airy sprawling house Paul had brought her to and the people within it.

She finished her shower and, swaddled in the huge bath towel, padded across the breezeway to the house. She was faintly conscious of her nakedness beneath the towel, of the way her nipples quickened at the touch of the terrycloth, but her curiosity left no room for modesty or embarrassment. She wandered through the downstairs rooms throwing open the louvered shutters so that the Caribbean sun could come flooding into the bright white rooms through the jumble of greenery that surrounded the house: frangipani bushes with alabaster flowers, lush hibiscus, coconut palms, and sea grape trees. Inside was an equal jumble of furnishings. Though the rooms were large and spacious, they were crammed with furniture in a variety of styles and periods. The servants waited silently, watching her with dark attentive eyes until they were sure she required nothing from them, and then went on with their tasks. Though they had served her efficiently for seven days, Savannah knew none of their names and did not recognize their faces. Nor, she realized as she retreated up the wide mahogany staircase to her room, did she know where Paul's room was.

Savannah closed the door of her bedroom behind her and then let the towel slip to the floor. The ceiling fan hummed above her head as she studied herself in the mirror, the same curiosity she had turned on the house she now directed at herself. Seven days of the Caribbean sun had turned her skin to burnished bronze everywhere except for the two narrow strips of white that betrayed her modesty. Two white strips, Savannah realized as an uncomfortable blush warmed her face, that made her look not nude, but naked.

What would Paul think if he saw her like this? she wondered

I'm a married woman, Savannah told herself. *Married but . . .*

But what?

Unconsummated was what the dictionary would say.

Unfucked was what Cara Wade would have said.

Why hadn't Paul made love to her? Was there something wrong with her? Something about the body in the mirror that he did not like? Something about *her* that he did not like?

Savannah knew what should be happening between a man and his wife. Cara had explained it all to her on the set of *Night's Daughter*.

A vivid picture of Kit slumped against the steering wheel of the Corvette flashed into her mind and her stomach twisted with the pain of remembering.

Savannah turned away from the mirror, and one by one she threw open all the louvered shutters that made up one entire wall of her room. A rush of sea wind caressed her skin and knotted fresh tangles in her hair as she stepped out onto the balcony. From this height she could see over the lush greenery and down the carpet of lawn to the white sand of the beach where the empty lounge chair waited in the shade of the umbrella.

What would Mama do if she could see her now, standing naked in the sun?

Savannah had already stepped back into her room before she realized that she didn't have to think about Mama anymore. She didn't have to think about Kit either. Kit, Mama, and everything that had happened before were in another life. When Paul Marsdon married her, he closed the door between that life and this one. It would never open again.

Savannah pulled on a fresh swimsuit, a crystal blue maillot, and went back down to the beach.

He had retreated into his room when she left the beach, closing the shutters behind him, and he waited, suspended in time, as she wandered through the house. He followed her progress through the ground floor rooms by the banging of shutters, wondering what she was doing but too timid to go downstairs and see for himself. Then he heard the door of her room, right next to his, open, and after a long silence, those shutters, too, were thrown open to the sun. Then she was gone again, and the house was silent once more except for the soft movements of the servants going about their tasks.

For the rest of the afternoon, even though he knew she had returned to the beach, Paul sat in his dark, shuttered room, refusing to allow himself the agonizing pleasure of watching her from the balcony. There were urgent messages piling up in the downstairs study, business matters that needed his immediate attention. Before long, the tone of the communiques' would grow strident. He had hoped to stay on the Island until some relationship had grown up between them, some semblance of a real marriage. For the first time since he had put his plot into motion, he was forced to realize what a vain hope that had been.

The vain hope of an equally vain old man.

At first she didn't notice that her glass, once emptied, was not promptly refilled; that the dainty remains of the tiny, crustless sandwiches lay drying on the plate. When she realized that the parade of servants had stopped, she had only a moment to wonder idly at the reason before the joyful thought came to her that she could linger on the beach as long as she wished if no one came to call her in.

She lay staring at the vast expanse of blue before her, a warm buzzing in her blood. A dreamy eroticism had taken possession of her as she lay glistening with oil and she was content to enjoy it alone for now. She lingered on the white strip of sand until dusk, until the frogs and crickets had begun their chorus, before she finally rose reluctantly and made her way to the bathhouse.

The thin black woman was waiting for her at the door of the bath hut, the eternal fluffy white towel in her hands.

"What's your name?" Savannah asked her as she took the towel.

No surprise registered on the ebony face. "Elizabeth, miss," the woman said. Her voice was soft as the trade winds.

"Thank you, Elizabeth," Savannah told her.

The faintest trace of a smile lightened the woman's solemn face before she left Savannah to her shower.

The rush of water drowned out the insect sounds of evening and Savannah lost track of the time as she rinsed the salt and sand from her body and her hair. Her eyes were shut tight against the soap, and it was startling, when she finally opened them, to see that it had grown dark out while she luxuriated under the warm water.

In her room she ignored the dress and underwear already laid out on the bed and wore instead a simple ankle-length tube of white cotton that clung just above her breasts, leaving her shoulders bare. Her hair hung damp and free, curling into wisps around her face as she moved around the room.

Paul was waiting in the den when Savannah descended the stairs looking like a tall young goddess, all golden tan from a week of Caribbean sun. He had seen the bill on the dress she wore: eight hundred dollars for a cotton dress as simple as a nightgown.

It was worth every penny, he thought, and then his heart leaped into his throat as she passed between him and the light from the dining room beyond—he realized she was wearing nothing beneath the dress. Absolutely nothing.

For a moment he remained frozen in time, and then he glanced around anxiously to see if any of the servants had seen the forbidden vision.

Savannah walked past him into the den, and as he followed her he found the clean fresh scent of her more tantalizing than the most expensive perfume.

She looked around the room curiously. "Who decorated this house, Paul?"

His glance followed hers, and for the first time in years he really saw the amazing hodgepodge of furniture that had collected here. Elegant rattan rested side by side with refined antiques. Whimsical wicker was scattered nonchalantly across priceless oriental rugs. The final result was not an interior decorator's studied electicism, but simply a jumble; this place might have served as the attic for all his other houses. Wives, daughters, daughters-in-law, and a mistress was the answer to her question, but he couldn't bring himself to say it. While he had told Savannah of his previous marriages, he had not realized until this moment just how much baggage he was bringing to this marriage from his former life. But as he looked around the room, it was painfully obvious. He could see so clearly the imprint of each of the women in his life: a piece of furniture here, a charming accessory there. Even Garnet was here, especially Garnet, and he didn't want to think about her right now, particularly now with Savannah standing there in a dress he had prevailed upon Garnet to choose for her. "No one really," he said at last. "It all just—accumulated."

"It's very nice," she said quickly, with a little girl's attempt at politeness that told him she didn't think it was nice at all.

"If you want to try a hand at redecorating, feel free," he offered and was startled by the dumbstruck look on Savannah's face. He suddenly realized, with a blinding flash of hatred for Irene, that Savannah had never been offered an opportunity to shape or control her own environment. When he assured her that he had indeed meant what he said and that she could call in any assistance she wanted, including a decorator from the States, it was as though a dam had broken in their relationship. She chattered gaily all through dinner, full of ideas for the house, and he found himself wondering what his other houses would look like through her young eyes.

This time she joined him in more than one glass of wine with dinner, and when they were finished, the flushed look of her face and the way her words tripped over each other with eagerness warned him that she might be feeling the effect of the alcohol. Still, he couldn't resist the impulses to seal his offer with a bottle of champagne, and she agreed immediately.

They moved out onto the terrace for their celebration. While Paul waited for Joseph, who had been butler at the Island house for a quarter of a century, to fetch the champagne, he sat in utter contentment, watching the bright sprinkling of stars over the dark sea and listening to the rushing, breathless sound of Savannah's voice.

She had never told him anything of her life with Irene and now he found she did not need to. As she discussed her plans for the house, her appalling naiveté told it all. She had no idea how sheltered she had been; she had no idea how boundless was the freedom that was now hers—or of the amount of money at her disposal. Although she had signed the prenuptial agreement his lawyer had insisted upon without a murmur or question, Paul had immediately changed his will in her favor. Her money from modeling and acting would have made her well-off for the rest of her life. Her portion of his estate would make her one of the wealthiest women in the country. Yet, he could tell from her conversation that she had no idea what any of that meant. She had absolutely no idea of what anything cost.

And now a recollection surfaced; something he had noted but had not previously comprehended. Savannah never carried a purse. Paul realized yet another extent of Irene's control over her daughter; Savannah had never been allowed to carry her own money. How might she react when she realized how completely her mother had kept her from leading a normal life? The task ahead of him was formidable. To educate her without letting her realize how terribly uneducated she had been. Otherwise her fragile self-confidence might be totally destroyed.

At the clink of ice in the champagne bucket, Paul turned and caught sight of Savannah standing between him and the light from the den. He was at once hotly aware of the body beneath that simple cotton dress.

Embarrassed as a teenager by his erection, Paul waved Joseph away brusquely and kept his back turned to Savannah as he struggled with the cork. Here he was planning to comport himself like a kindly elderly uncle and there was Savannah's innocent sexuality reminding him of his own wicked lustfulness. His hands shook as he poured the champagne and his voice was hoarse as he proposed the ridiculous toast to her future decorating efforts. All he could think of was that he needed to have some female explain to Savannah that she shouldn't parade around in front of him that way—

And how utterly absurd any female of his acquaintance would think that request, since Savannah was his wife and not his niece or daughter.

The joy had gone out of the mock celebration for him and he drained his glass with a grim purposefulness. Savannah must have picked up his mood for her chatter faltered and stopped, and although he poured them both a second glass of champagne, neither of them touched it as they sat there in silence. After a few minutes, Paul excused himself and went up to bed.

He undressed in darkness; there was enough light from the moon through the open shutters and he was unwilling to face his own reflection in the harsh glow of electric lights. He was already in bed, wearing only the trousers of his pajamas, lying on his back with his arms crossed behind his head, staring up at the ceiling and wishing fervently that he had not given up smoking twenty years ago, when the door to his room opened and closed softly.

The moonlight didn't reach that far. He couldn't see who had entered and now stood there in the darkness that pooled around the door.

He wasn't alarmed right away. His first thought was that Carter had come to tell him about some problem that required his immediate attention. The huge black chauffeur doubled as bodyguard and confidant and had for the past forty-five years. "Carter?" he said softly.

When there was no reply, Paul reached for the bedside table drawer where a loaded Smith & Wesson .38 revolver lay. The rustle of clothing stopped him.

The sound of a woman removing her clothes in the darkness.

He was instantly erect. One of the maids, he thought. I'll send her away. But the pressure of months of abstinence caused him to strain at the cloth of his pajamas. He was not meant to live like a monk. He never had; there was a string of marriages and a mistress to prove it.

Whatever crazy moral sense had gripped him the past few days was still in effect, however. Savannah was his wife, and even if he could not bring himself to touch her—to violate her was how it seemed to him now—neither could he seek release with someone else. So his throbbing penis was already beginning to subside when the woman joined him in the bed, seeking his erection with warm, knowing hands.

He had already grasped her shoulders to push her away, when Savannah's tremulous voice came out of the darkness above him. "This is how Cara said you should be."

"Who?" he asked hoarsely, although he knew she was talking about Cara Wade, her body double on *Night's Daughter*, just as he knew everything about her from the thick file in his Malibu safe—but he would have said anything, *anything* at that moment to keep Savannah's hand grasping his manhood as he swelled to life once more.

But then she moved against him with a determined innocence that could only have come from lessons heard but not practiced, and Paul found that he was, after all, the man he had always believed himself to be.

Chapter 7

The Island was their base. From there they ranged all over the surrounding islands, doing all the ordinary tourist things Savannah had never done before and Paul had not done for years. Occasionally they talked about her nebulous plans to redecorate the house, but she put off doing anything about it. The fact that Paul had offered was enough for her now. She was having too much fun to tie herself down with an interior decorator. So she pretended to look for accessories to add to the jumble, and Paul indulged her in that as he did in everything else.

Carter went with them everywhere. Gradually, Savannah became aware that he was not only their driver, but also their bodyguard—and that he was embarrassed.

Why, she did not understand. Passionate and lengthy as their lovemaking was, it was an intensely private thing, conducted in the room that had been Paul's and was now theirs—never out in public. So she could not understand what it was that embarrassed the chauffeur so.

Then, one afternoon on Antigua, a flower seller pushed an armful of blossoms at Paul and said, "Buy them for your beautiful daughter."

Before Savannah grasped what was happening, Carter inserted his huge frame between Paul and the flower seller and was ushering Savannah and Paul into the car with a minimum of fuss. Savannah might have dismissed the incident entirely if it had not been for the tips of Paul's ears glowing pink. Of Carter's embarrassment there was no outer sign, but she knew it was there. And now she knew that Carter was embarrassed not for himself, but for Paul.

On the way back to the harbor, she found herself studying Paul's profile covertly. She could remember quite clearly how she had thought him elderly in the beginning. She must have been more of a baby then than she had realized. How had he ever been able to stand her when they first met?

The handsome face beneath the warm brown hair was anything but elderly. Paul looked exactly like what he was: a rich powerful man, used to making decisions and having them obeyed. The time when she had thought otherwise seemed a million miles away. He was her husband, and she knew every inch of that lean, tightly-muscled body beside her. All the places where he liked to be touched, and kissed, and stroked. Just the thought of it sent a little thrill of desire racing through her.

That night she hugged Paul to her fiercely, and her passion awakened an answer in him that more than satisfied her. She had said nothing of that afternoon's incident, and for all she knew, he didn't realize she had seen his embarrassment. "I love you, Paul," she told him, snuggling closer to him in the wonderful afterglow of lovemaking.

"You're only grateful," he said hoarsely. "But that's enough for me, Savannah."

No matter how much she threatened and cajoled, tickled and caressed, he would not admit she could love him.

When she finally gave up and drifted off to sleep, he stayed awake, staring up at the ceiling, trying not to think at all.

Carter never looked directly at her; he always focused on a spot just over her head. At first Savannah found that amusing. The longer it continued, the more challenging she found it to try and make him focus on her. But no matter what she asked him and how appealing she made her voice, he still spoke to that nonexistent point in space just above her head.

He had developed another annoying habit, as well. Every morning at breakfast with a reproachful look he would drop a sheaf of messages beside Paul's goblet of orange juice. The first few days Paul ignored the stack of papers and went on talking with Savannah about their plans for the day. The stack continued to grow in size each morning, and by the third day, "urgent" was scribbled in red across the top of some of the messages.

On the fifth day, Carter fanned out the messages so that Savannah could see from across the table that "urgent" was written on every one. "Are you going to do anything about these?" he asked Paul.

"What are those, Carter?" Savannah asked.

As always he refused to look directly at her. "Messages from Mr. Paul's businesses. Things he should be attending to." *Instead of fooling around with you,* was the unspoken message.

"Is that right, Paul?"

He looked like a little boy discovered with his hand in the cookie jar, she thought fondly. "Maybe I should get caught up on a few things," he said slowly. "I'll do it tonight, when we get back from Antigua."

Savannah studied Carter's face. "But Carter thinks you should have caught up on those things several days ago, doesn't he?"

"Carter's not on his honeymoon. Besides, I promised I'd take you shopping today."

"Carter can do that while you catch up on your work," Savannah told him. She fought hard to resist the mischievous desire to giggle aloud when she looked up at Carter. "Can't you?"

She had finally achieved what she wanted; his gaze was focused directly on her. But now that she had his full attention, she was sorry she had done it. She didn't like the scornful look he turned on her. It reminded her of the night he had brought her to Paul's Malibu house, the night he had called her a little girl. "Certainly, Mrs. Marsdon."

That was the first time anyone had called her by her married name, and she should have been proud—instead she felt as though she had just been reprimanded.

"If you're sure," Paul said slowly, his eyes straying to the pile of papers beside him.

"I'm sure," she said. "As a matter of fact, I think I'll go and dress now. I'll be ready in about half an hour, Carter."

"Yes, Mrs. Marsdon." The steady black gaze was focused above her head once more.

When she came back downstairs to tell Paul she was leaving, he was still at the breakfast table reading through the papers and making notes in their margins. He barely acknowledged her good-bye.

They docked at English Harbour to pick up the car. She looked longingly at Nelson's Dockyard, but a cruise ship's passengers were swarming through the restoration and she had no desire to be caught up in so many tourists. Once in St. John's, she directed Carter to drive to St. Mary's Street. She had already learned during her excursions with Paul that St. Mary's was the main shopping area. She began in Kensington Court, taking her time going through the dozen or more shops, weighing with equal gravity the merits of African-printed caftans, straw placements, and bone china.

She was wandering idly through a shop full of resort clothes when all at once several thoughts struck her at once with dismay. She had no idea where they were going after they left the Island, so she had no idea what souvenirs would fit into whichever of Paul's residences they settled in. Nor did she have any friends or family to bring souvenirs home to, since she certainly wasn't planning to have any contact at all with Mama. And worse, most assuredly worse, she had no money. Not a penny of her own. Paul always paid for everything. It simply had not occurred to her that she would need any.

She glanced up quickly. Carter was hovering discreetly in the background. What was she supposed to do, she wondered, ask the chauffeur to pay for whatever she picked out? Her cheeks burned at the thought. She grabbed a madras skirt and held it up to her waist to check the length while she tried to think.

"Have you decided on something?" the salesgirl asked her.

Before she could answer, Carter was beside her, his hand already on his wallet.

"No," she said quickly. She thrust the skirt into the salesgirl's hand and strode out of the shop without waiting for Carter's reaction. On the street, she paused and looked longingly toward the Kensington House. Paul had taken her there for a drink earlier in the week, and she was thirsty now, but she had no intention of asking Carter for anything.

"Shall I get the car, Mrs. Marsdon?" he said smoothly, as though he had no idea why she had bolted from the shop.

Behind that bland exterior, he was probably laughing his head off at her stupidity, she thought angrily, but she replied, "Yes, do that," just as smoothly.

As soon as he turned away, she hurried off in the opposite direction, losing herself in the crowd, and then darted through the doorway of the nearest shop. She pretended to be browsing through the beads and inexpensive shell jewelry near the window while she watched Carter searching for her. As soon as he entered the shop next door, with Arawak pottery in the window, she rushed back outside and hurried down the street in the other direction. She ran for a block before she stopped to catch her breath, earning a stitch in her side in the process. Somewhere along the way she lost her sunglasses.

Shielding her eyes from the glare, Savannah looked back the way she had come. Carter was not in sight. She had no idea what she was going to do, but the feeling of being free made her almost giddy.

Near where Temple Street crossed St. Mary's Street, she stopped in front of a small jewelry shop with a fascinating display in the window. A few absolutely stunning sterling silver pieces were scattered with artful carelessness across a bed of loose shells and purple and green coral. Savannah was intrigued by the contrast between the natural shells and the man-made silver objects. She was so caught up in the displays she didn't realize there was anyone else within a million miles until a male voice said, "I was wondering when you were going to do that."

Savannah turned, startled. A tall dark-haired young man, not much older than herself, was standing right beside her. They were almost the same height. "Do what?"

"Shed your keeper."

"My keeper?"

"That big black dude who's been watching you like you were the crown jewels. I've been following you ever since you left English Harbour, waiting for a chance to talk to you alone."

"I didn't notice you."

"I know. It nearly broke my heart. I half killed myself wrestling a taxi away from two old lady tourists back at English Harbour and I said to myself at the time, 'She didn't even notice you.' "

"Why did you want to talk to me?"

"I wanted to tell you you're beautiful and ask you to have dinner with me."

He was smiling at her in such a warm, friendly way that she found herself smiling back. "I can't do that."

"Why not? You ditched your keeper just for me. Why can't you have dinner with me, too?"

"I didn't 'ditch' Carter because of you," she protested. "I did it because I was mad."

"Mad about what?"

"About going off without a penny to my name, that's what. I can't even buy something to drink, let alone any of this wonderful jewelry."

"And you're thirsty, aren't you? I can see the symptoms of extreme dehydration setting in."

She *was* thirsty, very thirsty, and angry with Paul for putting her into such an embarrassing situation with Carter. A tentative smile played across her lips while she considered the offer. He did seem very nice.

"That's better," he said softly. "After all, I'm a fine upstanding citizen. I know your father would approve of me."

"My father?" She frowned.

"I saw you with him yesterday."

"That's not my father." She was smiling again. "That's my husband."

Something changed in his face and she wasn't sure what. "Then I know you'll enjoy a drink," he said. The way he said it, with a scornful undertone to his voice that had not been there before, made it clear that he was now offering more than just a drink.

"I don't think so." She started to turn back to the window.

He grabbed her by the arm and yanked her around to face him. "Don't get sulky now that we're finally on the same wavelength."

She tried to pull away but his hand was like a vice on her arm. "I don't know what you're talking about."

He stroked her cheek with the backs of his fingers. "We're going to have a good time. You'll see. I'll bet you're as hungry for that as you are thirsty for a drink, aren't you?"

"Let me go," she pleaded, and all at once Carter was there like an immense avenging angel.

Before the young man quite realized what was happening, Savannah had been yanked from his grasp and he was sprawled on the sidewalk.

"Thank you, Carter," she said gratefully. "I don't know what I would have—"

"Get in the car, Mrs. Marsdon," he said coldly. "I'll take you back to the Island."

She obeyed him, cheeks burning. He left a streak of rubber on the street as he sped away. Savannah turned to look back through the rear window. The young man was still lying where Carter had left him, rubbing his jaw. Carter took a corner so fast that she was nearly thrown across the car, and she concentrated on hanging on to the armrest.

Carter drove in silence until they reached the harbor. He screeched to a halt and all but yanked her from the car, hurrying her toward the yacht as though someone were after them. Savannah could see the surprised faces of the crew.

She dug in her heels and pulled her arm away. "Stop this, Carter. What's wrong with you?"

He kept his voice low, but it was throbbing with anger. "I've worked for Mr. Paul for more years than you've been alive, Mrs. Marsdon. I won't be party to your little games!"

"I don't know what you think was going on, but you're wrong."

"Am I? Just when did you arrange to meet that boy? Yesterday? I saw him watching you and Mr. Paul."

"I didn't arrange to meet him at all. I just happened to run into him."

"And you just happened to try and lose me back there at Kensington Court so you could go running off to meet him."

"That was because of something else," she said, hating the humiliation that burned on her cheeks.

"And what was that, Mrs. Marsdon?" he said scornfully.

"You know what. You knew I didn't have any money to pay for anything. You were just trying to embarrass me, weren't you?"

"Most women carry a purse with money and credit cards in it, Mrs. Marsdon. Why don't you?"

He said it quietly; he might as well have slapped her. She would never be like everyone else; Mama had seen to that. She turned away and plunged blindly toward the yacht.

He caught up with her just before she reached it and took her arm. "Don't make a fool of yourself in front of the crew," he said quietly when she tried to pull free.

"Just in front of you." She stopped struggling and looked up at him. "You don't like me, do you, Carter?"

"It's not my place to like you, Mrs. Marsdon. You're Mr. Paul's wife and I take care of Mr. Paul."

"Well, Mr. Paul is my husband and I love him. I don't care what you tell him, but I just want you to know that I wasn't trying to meet someone else. I'm not interested in anyone else."

"I'm not going to tell him anything, Mrs. Marsdon. Either I was wrong and it won't be necessary, or I was right, and he'll find out soon enough for himself."

When they got back to the Island, Paul was still working. He stopped briefly for dinner, and then went back to his study afterward. He came to bed very late that night and fell asleep as soon as his head hit the pillow. He rose before she woke the next morning, and by the time she came downstairs, he had already eaten breakfast and was back in the study again.

Savannah hesitated outside the study door, trying to decide what to do. She wanted to talk to him about yesterday, but not about the young man and Carter's anger—Carter could bring that up if he wanted and she would deal with it then. Instead, she wanted to tell him about the jewelry store she had seen, but she knew she shouldn't interrupt him.

Carter was keeping conveniently out of sight this morning, but she sent one of the maids for him.

"Yes, Mrs. Marsdon?" he said when he joined her in the dining room.

"I want to go back to St. John's today."

What he thought was clear on his face. He gave a quick negative shake of his head.

"Don't be stupid," Savannah told him. "I want you to take me back to that jewelry shop on St. Mary's Street. I never got to see inside it. I'll be ready to leave in about half an hour."

He didn't unbend an inch, but he didn't shake his head again either.

"Oh, and Carter?"

"Yes, Mrs. Marsdon?"

She grinned at him. "Be sure and bring some money."

The faintest trace of amusement flitted across those black eyes and then vanished so quickly she couldn't be sure it had ever existed. "Of course, Mrs. Marsdon."

The jewelry shop was even more fascinating on the inside than she had believed possible. Savannah lost all track of time as she gazed at each piece, enjoying the abstract forms the artist had chosen.

The saleslady hovered for a while, but soon grew bored and drifted to the window to watch Carter pacing back and forth beside the car like a sentry on duty. "Friend of yours?" she asked Savannah.

"My chauffeur," Savannah said, and the saleslady's interest perked up once more.

"Would you be interested in having a custom piece? The artist will be here tomorrow if you'd like to talk to him."

"I'd love to," Savannah told her. "I'll be back then."

She had Carter pick them up a quick lunch, which they ate in the car, and then drive on to visit several other jewelry stores, but none of the jewelry she saw that afternoon had the same quality as that in the first shop. Savannah searched one shop after another, taking longer than she should have, trying to define that quality to herself. She gave up at last and let Carter take her back to the yacht. Tomorrow she would talk to the artist himself, she thought. Maybe he could name that elusive quality in his jewelry for her.

She had stayed on Antigua longer than she had intended, and they were late getting back. Nevertheless, Paul was still working when they arrived. Carter checked with the maids and came back to tell her that Paul hadn't stopped for dinner.

She told Carter to go ahead and have dinner served, then she went into the study. "It's time to eat, Paul."

"Savannah! Did you have a good time today? What did you do with yourself? I'm afraid I've been neglecting you."

"Carter took me to St. John's again. I had a wonderful time. I was looking at jewelry in some of the stores." She was dying to tell him about the jewelry she had seen. Maybe he could puzzle out for her the mysterious difference between the jewelry in the little shop on St. Mary's Street and the other jewelry she had seen today. But before she could even begin to describe it, she saw that she had already lost his attention.

"Things have really stacked up at home," he said, waving his hand at the papers on his desk. "I hate to do this, darling, but we're going to have to go back sooner than I had expected."

"When?"

"Tomorrow."

She thought about the artist she was to have met and then resolutely pushed that from her mind. "That's fine, Paul. Now come and eat."

As Carter turned right off Sunset Boulevard and guided the Rolls through the impressive iron gates into Bel Air, Paul took Savannah's hand, trying not to show the misgivings that suddenly possessed him. He loved this neighborhood for its peace and privacy, but how would his Old Bel Air address seem to a girl Savannah's age. Barbara, his youngest daughter, had hated Bel Air so much that she had talked her mother into giving up this house in the divorce settlement in exchange for a higher profile Beverly Hills address where she could live shoulder to shoulder with her neighbors instead of hidden from the tourists and sightseers behind thick hedges and the rolling landscape. She had wanted to go to Beverly Hills High School as soon as she was old enough, instead of the

Upper School of the Westlake School for Girls. Barbara still preferred sidewalks and conspicuous consumption, not elegance and seclusion, and she was only five years older than his new wife.

Paul was swept by a wave of total helplessness. The enormity of what he had done was staggering. Marrying a girl forty years younger than himself was bad enough, but now he had compounded his troubles by bringing her back to Los Angeles. The thought of Barbara reminded him that he couldn't put off introducing Savannah to his children forever, much as he dreaded that moment. Understanding that he had children from former marriages was one thing; seeing how much older they were than herself was something else.

When the Rolls swung into his driveway and paused before the gate, Savannah scooted forward to peer through the tinted windshield toward the densely planted landscaping beyond. Paul realized he was holding his breath as he waited for her reaction to her first glimpse of the house. He forced himself to take a deep breath as Carter drove through the gate, but he couldn't look away from her face. Nor could he interpret the expression of stunned surprise the first view of her new home, through the twisted sycamores and Chinese elms, brought to her features.

He turned to glance at the house, trying to see it through her eyes. Did it seem too pretentious, this huge old Mediterranean villa perched on five acres of the choicest landscape in Old Bel Air? Even though it had been less than a month since he last saw it, the mansion looked larger than he remembered. Too late

he found himself wondering if she would have preferred an apartment to a house.

"Paul?"

"Yes?"

"I asked you how long you've had this house."

Longer than you've been alive, my darling. "A
long time," he mumbled aloud. "It was built in
1928. I had it completely remodeled when I bought
it." He balked at divulging the details. There were
words he did not want to say to her, words like: the
divorce settlement, my second wife, my two youngest children. Her hand had turned to ice in his, and
he realized he was sweating.

He was vastly relieved when the maid met him at
the drive with a sheaf of messages in her hand. He
gave them a quick glance. "Something's come up,"
he told Savannah. "I'll have to go in to the office for
a few hours."

He escorted her up to the front door and then
hurried back to the Rolls.

"You should have carried her over the threshold,"
Carter said as he held the door for Paul.

Paul leaned back, not saying anything. The tightness in his chest didn't ease until the gates swung
shut behind him.

Savannah stood in the center of the magnificent
oak-paneled three-story entry hall. When she tilted
her head back to look up, she felt just like she was at
the bottom of a well. All of the luggage had been
stacked just inside the door, and she had a crazy

impulse to pile all the suitcases on top of each other and try to climb out.

"Welcome back to L.A., Mrs. Marsdon," the maid said. "Would you like to go upstairs and freshen up? I'll have your luggage brought up to you immediately."

Savannah nodded, not trusting her voice.

Paul was rich.

The full reality of that had struck her as soon as she glimpsed this house. Of course, she had known he had money, a lot of money, but as she followed the maid up the stairs she realized that he must have more money than she could possibly comprehend. Instead of pleasing her, the thought terrified her. It was the press of all that money which had pulled him away from her on the Island and brought them back to Los Angeles sooner than they had planned. She saw with hopeless resignation that the same thing was going to happen here.

On the Island, she had been a pampered princess out of a fairy tale. Now she was back in Los Angeles, and the Island was half-a-world away.

Paul arrived each evening with the same rushed apologetic air. "Business," he would murmur in explanation as he greeted her with a kiss. The first night, he insisted they have their before-dinner drink in the opulent living room with its spectacular cathedral ceiling, but its hugeness had been depressing shared by just the two of them. After that, they took to spending the time before dinner in front of the massive stone fireplace in the oak-paneled family room, while he shared his day with her.

She listened with such wide-eyed wonder that it made everything that had happened to him seem important and worth recounting. He had never fancied himself a storyteller, but Savannah's interest made him blossom.

Dinner was always in the formal dining room. Once or twice a week, when they went to the dinner table, Savannah would find a wrapped present beside her plate and open it with a squeal of delight. He brought her diamond necklaces, books of poetry, and lavish bottles of perfumes she had only owned before by the quarter-ounce.

They had no guests, because Paul could not bring himself to share a single moment of her time. Nor did he accept any of the invitations that poured in. There had been several questioning phone calls from one or another of his children, but he was putting off seeing them for as long as he could.

After dinner he would retire to the library to finish up whatever work he had brought home from the office. Savannah would curl up in a chair across the room from him and read until he was ready to go to bed.

Some nights they made love in the vastness of their king-sized bed, and some nights she merely snuggled against him in a curiously defenseless way that made his heart ache for her. In the mornings, they had breakfast in the sun-drenched breakfast room and then Carter took him to the office.

At first he called home every day, but since she

never answered the phone herself, he was afraid she considered his calls an intrusion. Gradually he stopped phoning, forcing himself to forgo the additional pleasure of hearing her voice. Instead, he sent his secretary out shopping for her more and more often. Almost every night found a new present beside her dinner plate, and roses were delivered to her once or twice a week.

"You're spoiling her," his secretary teased. "She must be the happiest woman in Los Angeles."

Every morning Savannah pulled the drapes aside and stood at a window in the cavernous living room, watching the Rolls disappear down the drive toward the gate and wondering how in the world she would get through the empty hours until Paul returned.

Chapter 8

"Will we be celebrating your birthday today, Mr. Paul?" Carter asked.

"What the hell kind of question is that?" Paul said, meeting Carter's glance in the rearview mirror as the chauffeur angled the Rolls to a smooth stop in front of the Marsdon Building.

"A sensible one." Nolan Carter had been Paul Marsdon's chauffeur and companion for enough years to earn him certain privileges as far as he was concerned. "Shall I remind Mrs. Marsdon that she should be picking up a birthday present for you this morning?"

"And why would you do that except to harass me?" Paul said sharply.

"A man's fifty-ninth birthday shouldn't be ignored," Carter answered placidly.

"This one is going to be."

The thought had crossed his mind as he eased out of bed that morning, his joints stiffer than usual, that today was his birthday. But Paul had no intention of bringing it to anyone's attention. Especially not Savannah's.

Carter had only been needling him and he knew it.

Carter took a minute to buff a spot off the shiny finish of the passenger door after Mr. Paul went into the building. Why in the world had he tormented the man like that? he wondered. Mr. Paul was embarrassed enough without Carter on his back, too. But he just couldn't leave it alone. He wanted to scratch at it like a mosquito bite. He wanted to scratch it so bad he listened extra hard to all the little digs and jabs people aimed Mr. Paul's way and kept count of them like they were scores in a game.

But the sorry truth was that it wasn't Mr. Paul's folly in marrying that girl that bugged him half as much as the little girl herself.

You had to watch her every minute, or that sweet nature of hers would be under your skin and you'd be dancing on the end of her string as bad as Mr. Paul was, and he wasn't about to let that happen. He took off his cap and rubbed the perspiration from his bald head with his forearm. After the run-in with that young man on Antigua left him with a set of bruised knuckles, he knew he had to watch her closely, for her own sake as much as Mr. Paul's. She just couldn't be as naive as she seemed to be—only he knew she must be. He had met Irene Royale.

He got back in the driver's seat, slamming the door with extra force. Trouble was, she reminded him too much of his own Theodora. He and Theodora's mama had been separated for twenty-seven years, ever since Theodora was five. It hadn't been his idea to break up the marriage. When Odessa left with the baby, he tried every way in the world to get her back. He would have agreed to do anything she demanded—anything except the one condition she gave him, which was to quit Mr. Paul. He'd been working for Mr. Paul's family for fourteen years when Odessa tried to get him to go into something else. He'd been eighteen when he went to work for Mr. Paul's daddy, and Mr. Paul had been a skinny little squirt of thirteen, into every kind of mischief in the world. Since Nolan Carter was the youngest and the quickest of the servants, he'd gotten the job of looking out for Mr. Paul, and he'd had it ever since. For forty-five years.

He had been thirty when he married Odessa and he'd known then he shouldn't do it. But that eighteen-year-old girl had the sparkliest black eyes and the flounciest way of walking! It had flat taken a man's breath away to see her coming down the street.

Mr. Paul's daddy had encouraged Carter to tie the knot, not that he had needed much encouragement. Lord, that woman had been hard to keep up with. She was a wild woman in bed and spunky as all get out everywhere else. Theodora had shown up a year later, with snapping dark eyes like her mama's but a decided preference for her daddy's shoulder as a place to perch.

Thinking about that made him turn the car toward the U.C.L.A. campus.

*   *   *

She was in her office, barricaded behind a stack of student papers, and she didn't look up when the door opened.

"Hello, Theodora."

She kept her eyes on the paper she was grading. "These days everybody calls me Teddy, Daddy. Mama, my students, the president of the university. You're the only one who still calls me Theodora." She flipped that paper noisily and went on to the next one.

Just gazing at the top of her head was beginning to irritate him, but he told himself that this time he wasn't going to lose his temper with her. "I thought they called you Dr. Carter."

Now she did look up, and it was Odessa's eyes he saw flashing at him. "Are you here for something special, Daddy?"

"I had a few minutes between errands. I wanted to see how you're doing."

"I'm doing fine. So's Mama," she added pointedly.

"That's good," Carter said, turning his chauffeur's cap round and round in his hands. Even though it had been Odessa who'd up and left, Theodora still held him responsible for it. Mr. Paul had been sent to Korea and Odessa had just about talked him into leaving Mr. Paul's daddy's employ and looking for some other kind of job. Carter had been willing because after looking out for Mr. Paul for so long, doing anything else for Mr. Paul's daddy just didn't seem right. But then Mr. Paul had come back from Korea with that piece of shrapnel in his leg, and going off on his own didn't seem like such a good idea to Carter anymore. Not with Mr. Paul needing more looking after than he ever had before in his life.

Carter was wondering how to exit gracefully without stirring up any more of the old animosity when she said, "And how's Mr. Paul's new young wife?"

He hated the way she emphasized Mr. Paul's name, making it sound like he was a slave owner. "Mrs. Marsdon is just fine," he said stiffly.

Theodora snorted. "I'll bet she is!"

"You're jealous of her?" Carter said in amazement. "Theodora, she's just a little· girl."

"Pretty smart little girl to marry a rich old coot like Mr. Paul."

"That's—" He stopped. What could he say that wouldn't compromise his loyalty to Mr. Paul? Or just plain make things stickier with Theodora? Talk about a no-win situation. "I'll be going now, Theodora. I have to get back to work."

She wouldn't give it up. "How long they been married. Six months? Nine? I'll bet she's already seen more of my daddy than I did all the time I was growing up."

"She never had a daddy at all."

"Now she's got mine."

The plea in her voice made them both uncomfortable "Theodora . . ."

She gestured at the papers in front of her. "I have to finish grading these by tomorrow."

"Please tell Odessa I asked after her," he said with formal stiffness.

"I'll do that, Daddy."

Her eyes were already back on the paper, as though she couldn't stand to look at him anymore. He let himself out of her office.

Walking down the long empty corridor he felt a pain in his right shoulder, the one she used to ride on when she was a baby. Must be arthritis setting in, he thought.

None of the lights were on in the front of the house when Paul got home, and it worried him. "Was Savannah supposed to go anywhere tonight?" he asked Carter.

"She never goes anywhere by herself, Mr. Paul. You know that." Carter frowned. "Even if she had, why would all the lights be off? Better let me go in first."

Paul started to object, but trying to keep Carter from doing what he thought was his duty was harder than trying to stop a tank. He just pushed past Paul and into the house.

Paul followed close behind but it was Carter who heard the whisper of noise in the living room. Once again he went first, Paul right on his heels.

The lights came on and cries of "Surprise!" "Surprise!" filled the air. It was a big party—the huge living room was full to overflowing with guests. Every friend he had ever made in Los Angeles was there, and then some.

But that wasn't the worst of it. Like ghosts of Marriages Past, his ex-wives and his children seemed to fill every corner of the room. When he smiled, Paul could feel his skull through his skin.

His vain hope that Savannah might not be there floundered immediately. She stood near the windows, slightly apart, a gentle bemused expression on her face.

Paul's first angry thought was that Carter had been behind this, but one glance at Carter's grim face told him otherwise. At least he hadn't suffered *that* betrayal. Calmer now, he looked around the room, seeking out the culprits.

He didn't have to look far. Of course, it had been Barbara and Jordan, the two hellions from his second marriage. He could tell by the proud but defiant grin on twenty-three-year-old Barbara's face and the go-to-the-devil expression on twenty-six-year-old Jordan's face. Either one of them was a menace, but when their objectives met regarding something like tonight, there was usually hell to pay.

"Paul, darling," said Margaret, his first wife, grabbing him by the arm, "Aren't children wonderful? Arleen's two got together with my five and planned the whole thing. All of the children have just been *dying* to meet their new stepmother."

Considering that Barbara was the youngest of his children and thirty-seven-year-old Frances was the oldest, the fact that they were dying to meet their new nineteen-year-old stepmother could only portend evil. Paul could feel a pressure building in his chest.

Arleen, his second wife, Jordan and Barbara's mother, took his other arm, and she and Margaret took him over to the table that held the enormous birthday cake studded with more candles than he cared to count. Nina, his third wife, was standing beside it, her eyes enjoying his discomfit. His divorce from Nina was still too recent and the break too acrimonious for the two of them to have drifted into the same easy relationship he had with his first two wives, although he realized that the generous amounts and promptness of Margaret and Arleen's alimony checks had something to do with that easy relationship, too. When he married Nina his lawyer had insisted that they sign a pre-nuptial agreement and Nina had reluctantly agreed. Vincent Tate had argued that Savannah should sign a similar pre-nuptial agreement, as well, Paul remembered uncomfortably. He'd only agreed to have Savannah sign it in order to secure Tate's assistance in dealing with Irene Royale, and the immediate change he had made in his will in Savannah's favor had made the pre-nuptial contract a joke, much to Tate's dismay.

Everyone sang "Happy Birthday," and Paul made a valiant effort to blow out the forest-fire blaze of candles, leaving only two. "I think someone may have exaggerated the number," he said with an attempt at lightheartedness.

"Nope, it's fifty-nine on the dot," Jordan called out loudly from across the room. "I counted them myself."

The cake was finally distributed and then someone took pity on him and pressed a drink into his hand. Paul recovered his wits enough to see that it was Garnet. "Darling girl," he said softly. "You always did know when I needed one of these. How in the world did you get roped into this?"

"Jordan, course." She grimaced. "I don't know if inviting me was his idea of an inside joke or if he really asked me just because I'd been your secretary for so many years."

"Do you think my other ladies knew about our relationship?" Paul had never wondered that aloud before.

"Margaret knows, of course." Paul wondered about that "of course" but decided to let it lie. "I'm not sure about Arleen, but I know that Nina had a detective follow us several times." The expression on his face made her pause. "You mean you didn't know that? I always thought you did."

"Ladies never cease to amaze me," he said with a shake of his head.

"And that's why you married so many of them?"

"Speaking of which, how's Savannah doing?" Just the thought of how she might be reacting to all these grown children of his was enough to bring the tightness back to his chest.

Garnet patted his hand. "She's fine, Paul. You worry too much."

"Keep her company, will you? Don't let them . . ." he couldn't quite put the thought into words. *Don't let them make me old to her,* was what he wanted to say.

"I'll talk to her," Garnet said soothingly.

"And I'll roast the hide off Jordan and Barbara," Paul promised grimly.

But Frances, his oldest daughter, intercepted him when he started searching for the two of them. "I know what you have on your mind," she told him. "But it was all of us, not just Jordan and Barbara."

"It was their idea," Paul countered. "And they were the ones who made sure everyone else went along with it, right?"

"We were all curious, Dad. How could we not be? Our staid, stolid pater marries a teenager? How could we let that lie without at least taking a look at her in person?"

"But it was Jordan and Barbara's idea to do it in a way that would emphasize my age to her in the worst possible way."

"Doesn't she know how old you are? I realize she's not known for her intelligence, but—" Something in her father's face made her break off abruptly. "I think I'll see if Mother's ready to leave yet."

"Do that," Paul said grimly. Over her head he could see Jordan and Barbara standing by the French doors, their faces alive with anticipation. They were just waiting for him to attack them, he realized. They planned to enjoy his discomfiture. He got another drink instead, and then made the effort to seek out Nina.

"You're keeping well," she said when he greeted her. "Marriage always did agree with you."

"You're keeping well, yourself, Nina," Paul said and meant it. He realized that Nina must be nudging fifty now, but she certainly didn't look it. After their marriage dissolved, she had returned to acting for a brief time, forced, she claimed, by financial necessity, but really because she missed the applause.

Happily, others claimed his attention before she could bring up the thorny subject of the pre-nuptial agreement again. When he found another moment to himself, Paul's eyes automatically searched for Savannah. He felt a little tremor of apprehension and his heart beat more quickly, then he spotted her beside Garnet, with the same placid, noncommittal expression he had seen on her face when Irene dragged her to parties.

He started over to her, but someone grasped his arm, detaining him. "She looks better than ever, Paul. Marriage must agree with her."

If it had been anyone other than Jeffrey Hanks saying those words, Paul would have searched them for a hidden insult. But Jeff's face, turned toward Savannah, was glowing with honest pleasure. "I've got a couple of picture ideas she might be interested in. I've just been waiting for you two to join the social swing again."

"Let's not talk business tonight," Paul said swiftly. "Give me a call at the office next week, okay?"

"Sure thing," Jeffrey said happily and went off to freshen his drink.

Paul felt like a man who had narrowly avoided an accident.

When they all left at last, he turned to look for Savannah, but she had disappeared. He hadn't had a chance to say a word to her all evening long. The last time he glimpsed her from across the room she had been listening to Jordan and somehow that upset him very much. Paul stared moodily at the remains of his birthday cake.

At the soft knock on the door, he looked up eagerly, but it was Carter, not Savannah, who stood there.

"I didn't know, Mr. Paul," Carter said, twisting his cap nervously. "I had no idea."

"Where is she?"

"In the pool, just swimming laps."

"Did she know they were coming?"

"The housekeeper said they just showed up and took over." Carter shook his head. "That Jordan always was a bad little boy, Mr. Paul." When Paul didn't reply, Carter left him alone with the remains of the cake.

After a long time, Paul went upstairs. From the bedroom window he could see Savannah relaxing in the pool. It was dark outside and the pool lights had been turned on. She was no longer swimming laps but was floating suspended on the glowing surface of the pool, her hair flowing out around her like a shimmering halo of silk. The water lapped up against her breasts, her torso. Little riplets of waves chased across the smooth, flat plane of her stomach. She looked so unbearably, so painfully young.

Damn Jordan!

When Savannah came up to bed, Paul was sound asleep. She stood over him for a moment, staring down at his face. She could see the lines and the signs of age so clearly tonight. Had they always been that clearly marked or was she just more sensitive tonight after meeting Paul's children?

Children.

She had known they were older than she. Paul had told her that the night he asked her to marry him. The night he bought her away from Mama's control.

But hearing that they were older and really understanding it had turned out to be two entirely different things.

They weren't just older—they were *old*.

His oldest daughter, Frances, was nearly forty, almost as old as Mama. And two of his sons, Elliot and Kenneth, were in their mid-thirties, balding, middle-aged men with round little pot bellies. She really hadn't figured out all the names and relationships yet, although Paul's youngest son, Jordan, had spent a lot of time coaching her, telling her all sorts of malicious but funny gossip about the other members of Paul's family.

She felt disloyal standing and listening to Jordan and yet fascinated by what he was saying. Her fascination ended when he asked her how come she and Paul had not started their own family.

"I'm surprised you're not already knocked up," he said, all his charm vanishing into crudeness. "That seems to have been his modus operandi in the past. At least until he got to poor old Nina."

She had moved away from him then, as quickly as possible, but the question he had raised kept returning to trouble her. Why hadn't she gotten pregnant? Looking around tonight, she could tell it obviously wasn't Paul's fault. It had to be something wrong with her. There was no one she could talk to about it either. The thought of going to a doctor made her cringe. Look what that doctor Mama sent her to had done: writing out the awful paper that swore she was a virgin. Had the doctor known at the time why Mama wanted it. She shuddered.

He had been holding her too tightly; Paul knew that now. Stifling her, suffocating her, not letting her see enough people. Hastily, he tried to right that all at once, accepting any and all invitations that came his way and setting up little parties of his own. The birthday party had broken the ice; Savannah had seen the worst of it. In the next few weeks, Paul made sure that she met all of his oldest and dearest friends.

The two of them rarely ate at home anymore, but that didn't decrease his compulsive gift-giving. Now she was apt to find something on her pillow when she awoke in the morning, or just as likely, on the seat beside her when she climbed into the Rolls at night. He had Garnet buy her other dresses and accessories and had them delivered to the house for her. He showed her off proudly to everyone, pleased at how well she handled herself at all the social functions.

And every time he looked at her, he saw how young she looked in comparison to his children.

He prayed she could not see it, too.

Savannah was used to being bored at parties—she had always been bored at the parties Irene dragged her to and she was bored with the ones Paul took her to now—and she had never really known why. It just seemed like the natural order of things. Or it had, until Paul's birthday party.

After that, she knew why she had been bored. There was never anyone present who was *her* age. She felt like a baby who should have been banished to the nursery instead of allowed to mingle with the adults. But how could she tell Paul that without hurting his feelings.

Now, along with the long empty days, she had long boring evenings to look forward to. It was only afterwards, in bed with her husband, that she felt truly alive.

Chapter 9

Paul watched her from across the gallery. Even after all these months, he still could not believe his good fortune. He hated going to functions like this art opening; he anticipating the smirks and knowing looks that would be turned his way. But if it gave Savannah this much pleasure, it was worth every sly glance and gossip column inch. Her face was glowing with excitement, and she examined the jewelry pieces before her with more interest than was fashionable at affairs like this, the champagne flute in her hand forgotten.

Marriage had agreed with her, he thought, very pleased with himself. That promise of further beauty he had glimpsed the first time he saw her in the flesh beside Jeffrey Hanks' pool had begun to blossom in the past few months, the angular model's curves giving way to a more sensual fullness. He wondered if others could see it as clearly as he—but then he was a connoisseur where Savannah was concerned, savoring every detail of her.

She needed more occasions like tonight, and fewer like the usual ones he was forced to take her to—where she sat surrounded by his friends and associates, all at least twice her age, bored to tears and too polite and well trained to show it.

She needed a hobby, he thought. Something to keep her occupied during the day. Until he saw her excitement tonight, he had not realized how very bored she must be.

The thought vanished as he watched her turn from the case before her and move to the next one. She was so beautiful that it almost made his heart stop to watch her. It took an effort, but he turned away before the sight could generate an arousal. There were enough whispers going around about the two of them as it was.

"Paul, could you unzip me?"

"Certainly, darling. Did you enjoy the opening tonight?"

"Umhumm," Savannah said softly, distractedly. She stepped away to pull the gown over her head. He tried not to let her see how much pleasure it gave him to watch her. At first, on the Island, she had insisted on dressing and undressing privately or in the dark. Only gradually had he been able to lure her into doing so in front of him. Now she was unclasping the tiny wisp of a bra. He turned away, ostensibly to brush his hair, but actually to watch her in the mirror as she stepped out of her panties. Nude, she walked to the bathroom, and in a moment he heard the shower.

Now his eyes were drawn to his own reflection and he found himself worriedly measuring the retreat of his hair from his temples. How much older than she would he look next year? he wondered sourly as he used her hand mirror to check the balding spot on his crown.

He put down the mirror hastily when he heard the shower cut off and was sitting on the edge of the bed when she same back into the room.

"Paul? Can I ask you something?"

"Of course, darling." He smiled at her fondly. Sometimes her questions were so naive they made him feel like a kindly old uncle.

"Why do you think I haven't gotten pregnant?"

It was a question designed to strike terror into his heart. "What?"

"I should have gotten pregnant by now, shouldn't I? Cara told me all about it. We're not using any kind of protection, so I should be pregnant."

She had sat down beside him on the bed, but he couldn't stand to look at her innocent face. He jumped to his feet and began to pace. "Not everyone gets pregnant, darling. Sometimes . . . sometimes there are reasons why . . . nature doesn't always . . ." He glanced her way and it was like an electric shock. How could he tell her that it was his own selfishness that was at work here?

"Are you saying that there's something wrong with me, Paul?" There was a tiny little quaver in her voice that almost broke his heart.

"No, no, of course not, darling." *Tell her, you old fool! Tell her about the vasectomy!* But he couldn't.

If he did, she would realize how selfish he truly was, and he couldn't bear to see that judgment in those clear green eyes.

"Nature," he muttered. "That's all."

He made love to her in a sweet tender way that made her ache with the desire to respond to him. But she couldn't, no matter how hard she tried.

At last she had to counterfeit her pleasure, something else she had learned from Cara, she thought bitterly, but had never had occasion to practice before. Just as Cara had promised, Paul had no idea that she had faked her response.

Long after he had drifted off to sleep, Savannah lay staring at the ceiling. Now that Paul had confirmed her worst fears, all she could think of was how terribly disappointed in her he must be. As she was in herself, she thought miserably. It was horrifying to realize that she was flawed in some way she could not understand. Sometime toward dawn, she forced herself to accept that it was just one more thing in her life she could not deal with—like a mother so immoral that she would try to sell her own daughter's sexual services, and a man dying because she had asked him to kiss her. She had put aside those things and refused to think about them, and she would do the same with this. That was the only way to survive.

In the light of day, though, it was a hard vow to keep. If she'd had a normal childhood, with a real mother instead of Irene, she could have talked with her mother about it—the terrifying feeling of emptiness that had settled inside her ever since Paul had confirmed her fears that it was her fault that she had not become pregnant. She put on a swimsuit and went out to sun beside the pool instead.

The gallery opening last night had reminded her of the jewelry maker on Antigua she had never gotten to meet, and she found herself wondering how the pieces she had seen last night were actually made. It seemed that the thought had no sooner surfaced in her mind than there was a stack of books on the art and craft of jewelry-making beside her lounger. "Mr. Paul said you might want these," the maid told her.

She spent the next week greedily devouring them one after the other, until she had read the whole stack. When she had read through the entire lot of them, she started at the first again and read through them more slowly this time, concentrating on each sentence, each illustration, until it was burned permanently into her brain.

She began to dream about jewelry, not the pieces she had seen in the books, but her own original designs. She would wake with an idea for a ring or a necklace clear in her mind in every detail.

She found her hands yearning for a sketchpad to capture her designs, and when she reached for it, it was there ("Mr. Paul said you might want this."), and with pencils, too, sharp and ready every morning.

Paul cut back on their social life and made an effort to take her to all sorts of jewelry exhibits at museums and galleries and to jewelry stores. She was exposed to every style and price range of jewelry:

from traditional Korean macrame jewelry of hand-knotted silk cord with gemstones woven into it, to fine Mexican silver jewelry from the thirties and forties, to the most innovative of modern art jewelry. They visited the glittering giants on Rodeo Drive and Wilshire Boulevard and prowled the shops on "little" Santa Monica Boulevard, Brighton Way, and Dayton Way. When he could not go himself, he sent her alone with Carter.

Savannah had grown used to Carter's taciturn treatment of her, and his unwillingness to focus on her face no longer bothered her. She forgot him entirely as she was caught up in the excitement of the jewelry she was seeing, the possibilities that were opening before her.

For his part, Carter found her indifference even more dangerous than her sweet nature had been before. He had to fight twice as hard to keep from falling under her spell.

Paul congratulated himself on introducing Savannah to jewelry-making. There was a separate artist's studio with a skylight beside the guesthouse. He'd had built it for Arleen just after they were first married, but she had never used it and it proved a nuisance when Jordan became a teenager, giving him and his buddies a place to bring their girlfriends without parental supervision. So Paul had closed it up. Now he had it cleaned out and repainted for Savannah, and she was delighted with it.

He had seen some of the sketches she had made, and they looked at least as good as any of the baubles he had bought for his female menagerie in the past. He ought to have some of them made up for her, he thought idly. He was sure that would please her. He made a note for his secretary to check with his favorite jeweler.

Paul gave her the box after dinner. It had been hard to wait that long. He had hugged his excitement to himself all day, anticipating her response when she opened it and saw what lay nestled on the midnight blue velvet inside.

He had anticipated every possibility except what actually happened.

When he came around to her side of the table and handed her the box, her eyes danced with delight. She tore into the wrappings like a child on Christmas morning while he leaned over her, watching. "What have you done this time?" she scolded happily. Then the box came open and she stared at what lay inside for a long stunned moment.

She thrust it away and burst into tears.

"Savannah?" he said uncertainly. "What's wrong?"

She simply cried harder, and when he tried to comfort her, she shoved away from the table and ran out of the room.

Paul sank heavily into the chair she had vacated and stared at the necklace he'd had made up for her, her own design, wondering what in the hell had gone wrong. After a moment he stuffed the box in his pocket and went in search of her.

He traversed nearly the whole house, panic rising in his chest, before he found her sitting in the dark living room. He thought she had stopped crying until he pulled her close and felt the dampness on her cheeks where silent tears were falling. He held her close for a long time, watching the moonlight. After a while the rigidness went out of her and she leaned comfortably against him.

He nuzzled her hair, enjoying the scent of it. "I was only trying to please you, darling," he said softly, his breath stirring the curls around her ear. "You know I didn't intend to upset you."

"I'm sorry, Paul." There was a small catch in her voice, and it made his heart break a little to hear it. "I'm such a baby!"

"Were you upset because I looked at your sketches?" That hadn't occurred to him at the time. He'd had no thought of invading her privacy, it was just that he enjoyed everything about her—from the tilt of her cheekbones, to the drawings she sketched, to the lovely faint smell of her that remained on the sheets in the morning, which he inhaled like perfume when he was sure she was not watching.

"No."

He kissed her softly on the smooth line of her jaw and let his lips trail down her neck. "They were such good designs," he murmured. "I thought—"

She yanked away, bursting into noisy sobs again.

Distress clutched at his heart. How could he have wounded her so badly and still not realize what he had done? "Please, darling! Tell me what it is."

"I thought they were so good!" she wailed. "All this time and I thought they were really good!"

"What was good? Your sketches?" She nodded

tearfully. "But of course they are. That's why I had that necklace made up for you."

"But it's all wrong, Paul. Can't you see that?"

"Because I had it made up in silver? That was what you had written on the edge of the sketch, darling. But I can have it made up in gold instead. . . ."

"It's not the gold or the silver—it's the metal itself. It looked all right on paper, but it doesn't do what it's supposed to in metal."

"And what's it supposed to do?" he asked fondly.

"You're laughing at me, Paul!" she accused.

"No, I'm not. I'm just trying to understand. You're not happy with your design now that it's actually made up?"

"I hate it!" She stood up. "I'm sorry, Paul. I have a headache. I'm going to bed."

She left him sitting there in the dark with his thoughts.

Paul put the necklace away in one of his safe deposit boxes with a few other treasured mementoes: a locket that had belonged to his mother, a stickpin of his grandfather's. Whether Savannah approved of it or not, *he* thought it was delightful. He was pleased to see that she had gone back to sketching, but not so pleased when the maid reported she had torn up every attempt and tossed them in the wastebasket. He told the girl to bring all Savannah's crumpled designs to him, and one or two evenings a week he would sneak into his study, smooth out the wrinkles, and leaf through her drawings with as illicit a feeling, as though he were looking at pornography.

After a few days she was crumpling only every third or fourth page, and he was certain the storm had passed. He was unprepared when she asked him if she could take lessons in jewelry-making from someone. It was a perfectly logical request. So how he could make her understand the fires of jealousy that flamed in him at the thought of her spending time away from the house wrapped up in her own private world. Jeffrey Hanks had called him twice after the party about roles for Savannah, and he had put Jeff off as he put Savannah off now.

"Work a little longer on your own," he told her. "I'll have some more of your designs made up. You pick the ones you want to see and tell me what metal you want to see them in. You'll learn much more that way than sitting in a crowded classroom somewhere."

"But, Paul—"

"Actually, you'll probably progress much faster this way," he said swiftly, not really caring if she did or not, as long as he could keep her all to himself.

At last she agreed, and he forced himself to ignore the twinge of guilt he felt, as he had ignored so many others since he had decided to make Savannah his wife.

"I have the new pieces," Paul told her. "Everything you wanted made up." He set her down at the table and opened the boxes for her, one after the other, and stood there proud as a new father, gazing at all the glittering evidence of her talent, some in gold, some in silver. "They're really wonderful, aren't they?" he murmured as much to himself as to her.

He was totally unprepared when she swept them off the table and onto the floor. "Savannah!"

"My God, Paul! Can't you see that these are crap?"

He was as stunned by her language as he was by her actions. He had never heard her swear before, and one corner of his mind was wondering jealously just where she had picked it up. "Savannah, I don't think you're—"

"You said I'd get better faster this way. I'm not. I'm getting worse!"

"I don't think you've given yourself a fair chance, darling." He knelt and began to pick up the pieces.

She stepped swiftly around him and began kicking the necklaces and earrings and broaches across the floor.

Paul scrambled to his feet and grabbed her arms. "Stop that. You don't know what you're doing."

"You're right. I don't. And you won't let me find out how to get any better. You don't care if I improve or not."

"That's not true," he countered, but he could feel the guilt-betraying blush sweeping up from his collar.

"If it's not true than let me take lessons."

"I've offered to have anything you design made up. What more can I—"

"You don't let me do anything!" she screamed at him. "You keep me here just like Mama did, all caged up with no one to talk to and no place to go. They only place we ever go is with *old people*!

Do you realize the only people I've met since we got back to Los Angeles who are even close to my age are your *children*?"

All the strength went out of him.

Savannah jerked free of his arms and ran from the room.

Paul clutched the edge of the table for support and then lowered himself to the floor slowly, like a very old man, and began to pick up the scattered jewelry.

He was still on his hands and knees when the maid came running in. "Pardon me, Mr. Paul, but Mrs. Marsdon . . . she . . ."

"She what?"

The woman was wringing her hands in distress. "She's upstairs tearing up all her sketchbooks and jewelry books. She told me to get a big wastebasket and take them outside and burn them."

Paul pulled himself up wearily. "Then do what she says."

By the time he got to his office the next morning there were already three separate messages from Jeffrey Hanks on his desk, each one more desperate and excited than the last. The last one summed it all up: "The perfect part for Savannah!!! The whole deal will be ours today if I get back to them by this afternoon with a firm commitment on Savannah as the star. You just can't turn this one down!"

"He dictated the exclamation marks, too," his secretary said with a grin.

Jeffrey hadn't seen her in months. He couldn't

know that she was becoming more beautiful every day, or that Paul was becoming more jealous.

Paul studied the notes, thinking of all that beauty back up on the screen for everyone to see and share. After a moment, he crumpled them up into balls and tossed them in the wastebasket.

"Mr. Marsdon! Aren't you going to—"

"No. And no calls from Mr. Hanks today."

In spite of his order, a call from Jeffrey came through that evening just as he was about to leave the office. "Paul! Why in the world haven't you gotten back to me? Didn't you get my messages?"

"Yes, I did, Jeff."

"Well, what's wrong with you, man? We've got to move!"

"Savannah isn't going to be doing any more movies, Jeff. Not for you. Not for anybody."

"You've got to be kidding! I can understand how you felt about those other parts, but this one is made for Savannah. It would be criminal not to—"

"I'm not kidding at all, Jeff. She's through with all that. She's my wife now. No more movies. No modeling. We're going to live sedate, private lives."

There was a momentary silence on the other end of the phone. "You selfish bastard!"

"I can afford to be, Jeff. She's mine now."

"Did you even say anything about this offer to Savannah?"

"I don't have to. She'll do whatever I decide."

"You're worse than that bitch of a mother of hers,

Paul. I thought you were a better person than this. What are you afraid of?''

That hit far too close to home. "Listen you old fag, I'm afraid of nothing. I just want my wife to stop being molested by creeps like you who only want to use her photographs and movies to make their own careers!" He slammed down the phone so hard that the receiver cracked.

He stared at it for a moment and then buzzed his secretary. "Get this replaced," he told her when she came in. "I'm not taking any more calls from Jeffrey Hanks. Now or ever. Call my staff at home and tell them the same thing. They're not to accept any calls from him. I don't want him bothering my wife."

She was looking at him strangely. "But Mr. Hanks is a friend of yours, Mr.—"

"No calls! And if you can't obey a simple order, you'll be replaced. Do you understand?"

"But Mr. Hanks said it was an emergency. You've never—"

"You're fired!"

"Garnet?"

"Is that you, Paul?" Her voice on the phone was warm and delighted. "How have you been?"

Miserable. Savannah had been as chill and formal as an iceberg ever since their argument. "Just fine," he said heartily. "I'm afraid I need a small favor, Garnet. I hate to ask it, but I need your help again."

"You only have to ask, Paul," she said gently. "You know that."

"Savannah has become interested in jewelry design.

She's been working on her own for a while, but now she would like to take some lessons. She mentioned classes at the university or an art school. . . ." His fist tightened around the phone. All those young men. "But I was thinking—"

"Private lessons, of course, Paul," Garnet said with the swift comprehension she had always shown. "I'll see what I can do."

When Paul hung up, he felt a little less guilty about not letting Savannah know about Jeff's movie offer. But only a little.

Chapter 10

Jordan Marsdon had discovered several interesting things about his new stepmother in the few minutes he had been able to speak with her alone at his father's birthday party. He had wasted no time in passing them along to his sister so Barbara could help him decide how best to use the information in the eternal war the two of them waged against the rest of the world in general, and their father in particular. Jordan had no idea when the war had started, except that it was long before Paul divorced their mother to marry Nina Grant. Sometimes it seemed to him that it had begun while he was in the cradle, and as soon as Barbara was born, she had become his instant ally.

It wasn't something the two of them had picked up from their older stepsisters and stepbrothers. The "Stodgy Five," as he and Barbara had dubbed the offspring from Paul Marsdon's previous marriage, were boringly content with the status quo and led lives dull beyond belief, each with a nominal position in their father's financial empire and none of them willing to rock the boat.

Nor was it something they had acquired from their mother. Arleen was as content now, with her divorced-Beverly Hills-matron lifestyle, as she had been with her pampered-Bel Air-wife lifestyle before that and was perpetually surprised that she had given birth to two iconoclasts whose supreme joy in life was to make everyone around them as uncomfortable as possible.

Jordan had realized early on, and passed the information along to Barbara, that great amounts of money would be at their disposal whether they worked or not—something that had apparently not occurred to the Stodgy Five, who had been laboring away in the Marsdon salt mines for years. So no matter how much Paul and Arleen had pleaded, threatened, and cajoled the two of them, Jordan and Barbara had refused to do anything of socially redeeming value—such as work for a living—and their father continued to shell out enough money to allow the two of them to live in a manner that wouldn't shame him. Jordan's only concession to the work-a-day world was the occasional claim he made to being an independent film producer—but that was only because it was such a wonderful way to pick up girls. Barbara had discovered that the words "my father is rich" had an equally salutary effect on males and kept her from having to pretend interest in an industry she found as boring as staid Bel Air itself.

The birthday party had been Barbara's idea, although Jordan was sure that the old man had given him the credit for it. No one realized what a great mind lurked behind Barbara's blonde California Girl exterior. One look at the old man's pallor as the lights came on and everyone shrieked "Happy Birthday" told Jordan that he and Barbara had scored big this time. Especially when he caught the stricken glance that his father flashed across the room at his new young wife.

However, until Jordan captured Savannah for a few moments of conversation, he had not imagined how extremely young and remarkably naive the most recent Mrs. Marsdon really was.

What a wonderful new weapon in the war, he realized at once, and concocted several plans for her immediate use.

But Barbara, strategist that she was, counselled patience. "He'll be watching us like hawks for a while. You'll see. He probably won't even let us near her for at least six months."

A year, to be exact. So now that their father's suspicions had been lulled by their inactivity, the demon duo was about to launch a two-pronged offensive.

Oh, what *fun* it was going to be!

Garnet called Paul. "I've taken care of that little errand you asked me to do."

"Savannah's jewelry-making lessons? You've found someone?"

"Someone very good. Leonardo."

"Leonardo? I've seen his work. It's very nice."

"He's agreed to give her a few lessons."

"A few lessons won't be enough, Garnet. He'll have to work her in as a regular pupil."

Garnet frowned at the phone. "I'm not sure he'll do that, Paul. His work is very much in demand, and he's only agreed to take her as a student on this limited basis as a special favor. And at a hefty fee."

"But you're sure he's the right one for her."

"Oh, yes. He's perfect. A wonderful artist."

"How old is he?"

"Twenty-four."

A pause on the other end of the phone, then, "Is he married?"

"No, single."

"What does he look like?"

"He won't offend her eyes if that's what you're worried about, Paul." Of course, she knew exactly what he was worried about. "He's quite handsome. Black hair, black eyes, a nice build, very intense looking."

A longer silence. "And he's the only candidate you've come up with?"

"The perfect candidate, not the only one," she told him. "He's gay."

She could hear him exhale in relief. "Well, I'll get in touch with him, then. Thank you, Garnet. I knew I could count on you."

Garnet hung up the phone and then opened the jewelry box in front of her. The necklace was very nice. Not the artist's best work, but good enough to bring a nice resale price. She'd only had to hint subtly before he was pressing it into her hands as an inducement to give his name to Paul Marsdon as a tutor for his wife. Clearly, he hoped Mr. Marsdon's wife would soon tire of her new hobby and become a good customer of his designs, and Garnet had led him to think his hope was a distinct possibility.

Leonard Zelinski had changed his name to Leonardo legally when he was twenty-one years old, three months after arriving in Los Angeles from Atlanta, Georgia. The name suited him. Teaching a rich man's wife the art of jewelry-making did not.

Leonardo had no patience with other people under the best of circumstances and especially not with dilettantes. He had agreed to the Hoffman woman's proposal in the first place only because he thought he might be acquiring a wealthy patron. However, when Marsdon himself called and heavy-handedly pressured him to agree to weekly lessons for his wife, for a period of time to be totally at the wife's discretion, Leonardo's blood began to boil. He knew he would not be able to control it for long. That his shop was on Brighton Way instead of Rodeo Drive galled him night and day. It was beside the point that on Rodeo Drive he would only have been able to afford a shop as narrow as a corridor in a cheap hotel. He longed for his own grandiose storefront, his own window onto the most stylish shopping street in the world. That was where he belonged, shoulder to shoulder with Bijan and Cartier, Gucci, and Hermes.

It was his unfortunate temper that had kept him from advancing as fast as his admirable designs would otherwise have assured, and while he knew that intellectually, emotionally he was a prisoner of his sudden rages.

When Savannah Marsdon showed up in person,

clutching a half-dozen sketchpads and accompanied by a bald-headed black giant who took up residence outside the door of his shop like a palace guard, Leonardo could feel his blood pressure rising. Everything about her irritated him. She was too young, too tall (towering over his own five-foot-six-inches even in her low-heeled shoes), and too eager to glance around his workroom rather than gaze respectfully at his designs. She was the kind of rich and beautiful woman who should be wearing his jewelry, not trying to create it herself. He decided, as he waved away the salesclerks and gave her a personal tour of the glittering cases displaying his work, to put her firmly in her place from the very first.

Once inside his studio, at the rear of the store, he reached for the sketchpads she clutched so tightly to her chest. "Let me just take a look at what you've done so far, love," he cooed at her in a tone that would have warned his intimates blood was about to be shed.

With his dark, intense eyes and his swift, graceful movements, Leonardo looked so much the artist that Savannah had frozen with fear as soon as she entered his shop. While he showed her his designs, she was wishing frantically that she had never set foot in this place. When he smiled and reached for her notebooks, she thought her heart would stop. How could she have been stupid enough to bring them with her! With a sick feeling in her stomach, she handed them over.

Leonardo made a production of cleaning off a

counter top and laid the notebooks in front of him. Then he went through them, page by slow page. Not speaking, not smiling. He scanned down each page and then gave one swift negative shake of his head before turning to the next one. When he finished, he stacked the notebooks neatly one on top of the other and handed them back to her. Savannah could feel her breath catch in her throat.

He leaned forward. "I wonder, Mrs. Marsdon, whatever made you think you had any artistic talent?"

"I . . . They . . . They're not any good?"

"No, Mrs. Marsdon. They're not. Anyone can see they are the feeble scratchings of an untrained amateur with more money than brains."

"I know I'm untrained," Savannah said defiantly. "That's why my husband—"

"Not just untrained, Mrs. Marsdon. Untalented Hopeless. Here," he said happily as he grabbed the sketchpads from her once more. "Let me show you." He had forgotten his hopes of acquiring a wealthy patron; there was nothing he loved better, absolutely *nothing*, than ripping a rival's designs to shreds.

Frozen-faced, Savannah bolted past Carter. When she reached the car, she yanked open the door without waiting for him and clambered inside. Then she gave an anguished little cry and looked up at him with stricken eyes.

"What's wrong, Mrs. Marsdon?"

"I left my sketchpads in there," she wailed. "He didn't like my work at all. I don't want to leave them here."

"I'll get them for you," Carter told her.

The studio door crashed open and Leonardo turned to see the Marsdon's big black chauffeur coming at him like a runaway freight train. Before he could move, the man had him pinned against the wall, with one huge hand pressing against his throat, cutting off his air.

"You want to die, Mr. Leonardo?"

"Here are your sketchpads, Mrs. Marsdon," Carter said when he returned to the Rolls. "Mr. Leonardo said he certainly hoped you didn't take his constructive criticism wrong. He's looking for you back in a week."

Her face was very white, very composed. "Are you sure that's what he said, Carter?"

"Oh, yes ma'am." Carter flashed a piranha smile in the rearview mirror. "He begged me to tell you that."

Leonardo dismissed the salesclerks who had come crowding into the studio after Carter left, and sat there gloomily massaging his neck. Who would ever have thought an old dude like that could move so fast?

He tried turning his head to the left and grimaced at the pain that little experiment unleashed. He would make sure the young Mrs. Marsdon never heard another unkind word from his lips; he would also be sure that every gossip monger he knew was alerted that the Marsdon marriage might be worth watching.

See how she liked being dissected in the press. Maybe Leonard Zelinski from Atlanta, Georgia, had to take whatever crap life dealt him, but nobody fucked with Leonardo of Beverly Hills.

The calls about Irene had been coming in with alarming frequency. Her drinking had worsened in the year since her daughter had escaped her grasp, and Paul knew if he didn't do something her escapades would wind up in the papers. He dispatched Carter to attend to it.

"Waste of good money to dry that woman out," Carter grumbled when he picked Paul up at his office afterwards. "She'll be drinking again as soon as she's out."

"You got her admitted all right?" Paul asked anxiously. "There weren't any problems?" He meant publicity and they both knew it.

"Why should there be any problems, Mr. Paul?" He decided not to mention the language Irene Royale had used, on him, on the admissions clerk, and anyone else who happened to be in sight. It would only raise Mr. Paul's blood pressure and it wouldn't help. He had also not mentioned Mr. Leonardo's initial uncooperative attitude towards Savannah— especially since that little matter was all straightened out now. As Carter turned through the East Gate into Bel Air, he felt particularly good about himself.

"What the—" Carter exclaimed. "How did he get in?"

Paul looked up from his *Wall Street Journal*. Jordan's Porsche was parked in in front of the Marsdon home.

"You want me to do something about him, Mr. Paul?"

"I should have let you drown him like a kitten when he was two," Paul said automatically, but he was thinking how handsome Jordan was, as handsome as he himself had been at that age. "I'll take care of it."

"Mrs. Marsdon shouldn't have to be bothered by the likes of him," Carter complained as he opened the door for Paul.

Paul found his aggrieved tone almost amusing. Evidently Savannah's charm had finally been too much for Carter. He, too, had fallen under her spell, and now she was under Carter's umbrella of protection as Paul had been for most of his life.

The French doors in the family room were open. Paul could hear the sound of laughter drifting in from outside. Jordan and Barbara, he identified immediately, and frowned in concentration. When he realized that the third voice was Savannah's and that he had never heard her laugh like that before, he stopped off at the bar for drink.

He drained half of it before he walked out onto the patio and saw the three young, gloriously tanned bodies basking in the sun beside the pool. He finished his drink in one gulp and had turned back for a refill when sharp-eyed Barbara spotted him and made a soft-voiced comment to Jordan.

"Dad, we've been waiting for you," Jordan called,

and Savannah turned and waved, so Paul had no choice but to join them.

Savannah smiled up at him and moved her legs so that he could sit down on the edge of her lounge. He averted his eyes from all that tanned, taut flesh beside him. If he looked her way he would be blushing. "What are you two hellions up to?" he said gruffly to Jordan and Barbara.

"We just wanted to visit with the two of you, Dad," Barbara said with an insolent grin that made him wary. Nothing the two of them did was ever without purpose. He had learned that long ago.

"I've asked them to stay for dinner, Paul," Savannah said.

It took every ounce of control Paul had acquired in his sixty years not to register surprise. That was the first direct action Savannah had taken. He was pleased and dismayed at the same time. Pleased that she was developing initiative and self-confidence; dismayed that it had to be wasted on Barbara and Jordan.

When he glanced up, he found that Jordan was studying him with a raised eyebrow. "That is all right, isn't it, Dad?"

He could feel Savannah's small start of surprise. Apparently she had no idea of the real relationship between him and these two. "Of course it is," he said heartily. After all, there was no way out of it now.

He enjoyed dinner more than he would ever have imagined possible—simply because Savannah enjoyed it. He had never seen her face look so animated and alive. Jordan and Barbara were knocking themselves

out to entertain her. They were kind, gentle, amusing—
everything he could have wished. By the end of the
meal, they had succeeded in lulling Paul's suspicions. He was totally unprepared when Jordan jumped
up and came around the table to take Savannah's
hands in his. "Barbara and I have a surprise for you,
Savannah," he said as he pulled her to her feet.

Savannah was laughing up into his face, waiting
for his next words, and Paul felt regret grip his heart
as he saw what a beautiful young couple they made.
Jordan was Paul thirty years ago. This was how it
should have been with Savannah and himself . . .
should have been and could never be.

"You told me when we first met that you had
never seen any of your own movies. And I'll bet you
still haven't."

Savannah was looking at him quizzically. "That's
right."

"Barbara and I are here to remedy that. We brought
one of your films with us. We can watch it tonight."

Paul wanted to leap to his feet and shout no. Only
the naked curiosity on Savannah's face stopped him.

They trooped to the projection room. He hadn't
run a film there since they had married. He hadn't
wanted to bring her films to her mind because he
hadn't wanted her to go back to making them. Now,
with his guilt over not mentioning Jeffrey Hanks'
recent offer to her, he couldn't bring himself to stop
the proceedings.

He didn't ask what film it was. It was only when
the titles began to roll that he realized Jordan and
Barbara had brought *Streets*. He had taken the seat

on Savannah's left and now he took her hand in his. But only a few minutes into the film, she jerked her hand away. In the flickering light, he could see she that she was hugging her arms tightly around her torso. Her face was steady, composed, so he didn't do anything. He turned back to the film, enjoying, as he always had, her beauty on the screen. Even at thirteen, in her first feature film, it was all there. He squirmed as he watched it, wondering if Savannah realized he was just as much her slave as the aging businessman had been the slave of the beautiful young prostitute.

When the credits came on, he turned to her and was amazed to see the hatred burning in her eyes. For a moment he thought it was for him, and he couldn't breathe. Then she said, "How could Mama do that to me?"

The relief that poured over him kept him from realizing that the credits had ended and something else had begun on the screen.

Then Savannah looked past him and moaned.

It was a montage of TV newscasts: Savannah dripping with blood on the courthouse steps, snips of her commercials and movies, Kit Nelson's photographs, and finally Nelson himself, dead in the Corvette, his face pressed against the steering wheel.

Savannah screamed.

She kept on screaming.

Paul scrambled on his feet and lunged at the projector. He lifted it over his head and smashed it to the floor.

Savannah continued to scream.

Jordan and Barbara were standing, idiotic smiles on their faces.

"If I had a gun, I would shoot you dead," Paul told them, shaking with rage he struggled to control.

He put his arms around her and pulled Savannah to her feet. For an insane moment the image of Jordan and Savannah in the dining room blazed back into his brain. "Get out of here," he told his children. "Don't ever come back. Don't ever come anywhere near us again."

Savannah was sobbing now, great rasping sobs that shook her body. All the strength had gone out of him and he could barely support her. Suddenly Carter was beside him.

Together they got her upstairs and Carter called the doctor. "Are they gone?" Paul asked him.

"Yes, Mr. Paul."

"I want the locks changed and a twenty-four-hour guard at the gate. Don't ever let them in here again."

Barbara hunched against the passenger door as Jordan took the Porsche down Bel Air Road at a reckless speed. She didn't trust herself to speak until he made the turn onto Sunset Boulevard on two wheels. "We went too far this time, Jordan."

"How did we know she was crazy?"

"He won't forgive us for this one."

"What can he do?"

Within a week they found out.

The money stopped.

They railed at their mother, but it did no good.

"He said if I give you one penny, he cuts off my allowance. You know he's always given me more than the court awarded me." Arleen shook her head. "And I can't let you move back here. He was very specific. You'll just have to wait until he cools off." She looked at her children curiously. "What exactly did you do?"

Their father's new secretary kept assuring them he was out of town. The security guard at the gate of the Bel Air home called the Bel Air Patrol every time he spotted them cruising by. Of the Stodgy Five, only Frances would take their calls, but instead of sympathizing or offering to help, she simply explained to them what fools they had been.

Barbara, the strategist, took over. "He's never going to cool off, Jordan. We'll have to get jobs."

"Doing what, for God's sake?"

"We'll make movies. You always said you were an independent producer. No one outside the family will know he's cut us off. We'll get projects just on the off chance that he'll put money into them. You'll see."

But first, they went to the newspapers.

Chapter 11

Paul kept the arrangements as quiet as he would a foray into adultery. Heaven help him if Savannah found out what he was doing! Just thinking about it at dinner the night before had caused him to break out in a cold sweat. If Carter let some word of it slip to Savannah, it would be a disaster, so to eliminate even that remote possibility, Paul called a Yellow Cab to deliver him to the Sunset Boulevard address.

He should have turned Irene Royale's request to meet with him down flat, but he found he could not. He was sure he knew what she wanted from him: money. He had sworn to Savannah he would not give her mother a penny more than they had agreed upon before their marriage, and if that was all there was to it, he would never have agreed to this meeting. But there were still things he yearned to know about Savannah, and the secrets lay with this woman who had shaped her daughter's life with such a powerful hand.

The restaurant where they had agreed to meet was,

appropriately enough, on the seedier end of Sunset Strip. The neighborhood matched his mood to perfection. He stood on the sidewalk for a few moments after the cab departed, debating whether or not to go through with it. In the end, it was his curiosity, about both Savannah and her mother, that would not let him back out.

When he joined Irene Royale at her table and she took off her sunglasses, Paul was shocked. That wan, drawn face now more than ever was a caricature of Savannah's.

"I don't look too good right now. I know that." As Irene picked up her coffee, the cup rattled in the saucer and coffee splashed over the sides. She gave him a humorless smile. "I suppose it would be indelicate to order a drink after you blew so many bucks getting me dried out?"

He waved away the hovering waiter. "I don't know why you wanted to see me. There's nothing for us to talk about."

She dug in her purse and pulled out a crumpled pack of cigarettes. "You should see the dump I've living in now." She lit her cigarette on the second try. "It makes Savannah look bad." She inhaled deeply and leaned back against the banquette.

"Why would you care?"

"I'm still her mother."

"A biological accident."

"You don't know where I came from, Marsdon. At least I kept her from that kind of life."

"Which was?"

Irene twisted around to stare at the bar. She turned

back and gave Paul a questioning look. He shook his head.

"Bastard," she said softly.

"Was Savannah?"

"Mother love is one of the strongest emotions, Mardson. You just want to fuck her. She's my baby."

"Look what you were going to do with her. You call that mother love."

"I call it survival, Marsdon. You've been a pampered rich kid from the day you were born. You don't know what it's like to be dirt poor. Neither does she. You don't know what it cost me to make sure she didn't know. Maybe you owe me something for that."

He took a deep breath, knowing how revolted Savannah would be if she knew where he was right now. "Who was her father, Irene? Tell me his name, something about him. That's the only way you'll get one extra cent out of me."

She shook her head.

"Then you'll just have to make do on what I'm already paying you."

"It's not enough."

"Not the way you're trying to live, no. I suggest you work on trying to bring your expenses in line with your income."

She leaned forward, fire in her voice for the first time. "I want to see her."

"She won't give you any more money, Irene."

"It's not the money." Still that same intensity. "I want to see her. Goddamn it! She's my child, Marsdon."

The group at the next table turned around to stare.

"She's not a child, Irene, and she doesn't want to see you."

"Do you love your children, Marsdon? And don't give me that 'of course I do,' crap. What would you have done for them?"

"Not what you did!"

"Men are bastards, Marsdon. I was younger than you want to know when I found that out. Maybe I made some mistakes with Savannah, but at least I kept her from that."

When he remained silent, she shoved the coffee away and stood up. "She's my daughter and I want to see her. You tell her that."

He watched her walk way. Such a plain-looking woman. Who would guess she had a golden treasure like Savannah for a daughter? Or that someone like him would have that same golden treasure for a wife? He thought for a moment of what his existence would be like without Savannah—and of all the selfish actions he had taken to bind her to him. Guilt hit him like a shock of cold water.

The Marsdon woman worked with a single-minded dedication that Leonardo found almost frightening. She seemed to be trying to pick every bit of knowledge out of his brain. She had learned more from him in the past six months than he himself had learned in several years of art school.

She wasn't afraid of anything, from working with sulfuric acid to soldering. She loved lost-wax casting, working for days on the wax models and then nearly driving him mad with her impatience while they waited for the castings to come back from the casting shop. She was far too critical of her work to be a success commercially, he decided. She destroyed as many models for pieces as she actually cast.

But Leonardo, never one to waste a thing, saved her crumpled sketches as he saved the metal filings and small cuttings of platinum and gold. He knew, if she didn't, that more often than not what the hands made was not true to the design in the head, and that there was only one real truth to adhere to: What the customer doesn't know won't hurt him. Only the artist knew the effect he was striving for and whether he had hit it or not; to maintain an address fashionably close to Rodeo Drive, one kept that kind of artsy-fartsy information to oneself.

Leonardo was a magpie—taking a stone setting from here, a design element from there. He never stole a whole design outright. Savannah might suspect, eventually, that he had incorporated some of her designs into his own work, but he doubted it. Better artists than Savannah had not been able to see themselves in Leonardo's display cases.

As he watched her preparing to join two pieces of silver, adjusting the torch to the correct mix of gas and air by the color of the flame and the sound as he had taught her, he found it hard to believe that this was the same woman he kept reading about in the papers. Girl, really, for she was still no more than that. He shifted uneasily in his chair. The enormous black chauffeur was guarding the door as he always did. Leonardo hoped the big bald-headed son of a bitch never found out about the careless things Leonardo had said to his friends after the first time Savannah came to his studio: the nasty hints he had made about a relationship between Savannah and the chauffeur. He had been furious, and his damnable temper had run away with him. His anger had lasted for the next two weeks, but by the third lesson he had softened. How could he help it? She was so serious about jewelry-making, as though there were nothing else in her life.

And she was so extraordinarily lovely. Those green eyes reminded him of immense flawless emeralds.

And innocent. He had not believed such innocence existed anymore. Maybe back in Atlanta, but certainly not in Los Angeles.

That was why he had been so stunned by the scandalous stories that were suddenly everywhere, in all the magazines, and the tabloids. He read far more outrageous things than those he had whispered to his intimates, even at the height of his rage. It had started with Marsdon's youngest children babbling on about how the new young wife had caused their estrangement from their father. But then it had suddenly escalated, booming out of all control, as the press realized what a prize they had on their hands in Savannah Royale Marsdon. Everything she did presented an opportunity for explosive headlines. Paparazzi followed her everywhere, sometimes half-a-dozen. The fact that she had become his pupil was widely reported, as was every other detail of her life the reporters could uncover, and the instant fame that brought made Leonardo's designs more in demand than ever.

That almost quieted the little twinge of terror he felt every time the big black chauffeur looked his way. If that old dude ever connected him with any of the gossip, he was a dead duck and he knew it. After that first day, Carter accompanied her back to the studio each time she came, and the sight of the immense chauffeur always made Leonardo's neck twinge.

As the stories continued, Leonardo found himself watching Savannah Marsdon with growing curiosity. How could she remain so calm in the face of such terrible publicity? One day, on a malicious whim, he had left one of the tabloids lying on the workbench, folded open to a story about her, and waited for Savannah and her huge black escort to arrive. She was barely in the studio door when Carter spotted the newspaper lying there. He had handed her sketchpads to her with one hand and picked up the paper with the other before she even saw it.

But Leonardo saw, and he knew why she never reacted to the publicity. Her rich old husband kept her wrapped in cotton, isolated from everything. He also saw the look that Carter aimed his way, a look that nearly made him pee his pants. He never tried any more experiments after that.

"How's this?" Savannah asked him.

The two pieces of metal were joined as neatly as he could have done himself, without gaps and without a noticeable soldered spot. It was going to be a very sophisticated design when she finished with it.

"Very good," he told her, already thinking of the intriguing variation he would make on it himself.

Savannah all but danced out of Leonardo's shop. "It's working," she told Carter happily. "I knew I'd get better." She held out the piece she had been working on and the gold caught the light. "Isn't that the most beautiful broach you've ever seen?"

The chauffeur tried to remain aloof, but her infectious grin was too much for him. "It is beautiful, Mrs. Marsdon. Mr. Paul will be so proud of you."

"He will, won't he?"

When she smiles like that it's as though the sun has come down to earth, Carter thought. Neither of them saw the lurking paparazzo as she threw her arms around Carter's neck in an exuberant hug.

"Let's not tell Paul yet," she bubbled. "Let's surprise him."

"Sure thing, Mrs. Marsdon," Carter told her. But as he opened the car door for her, his thoughts were dark. It wasn't right that a young girl like her should spend most of her time with only an old man for company. She didn't have a single friend to call her own. Her entire world was him, Mr. Paul, and that mincing little s.o.b. Leonardo. For the first time since Mr. Paul had come into his charge as a young boy, Carter was ashamed of his employer.

It was the last thing she ever expected to hear from Paul's lips. Savannah rolled away from him on the bed and clutched the sheet to her, staring at him as though he were a stranger, her eyes round with horror. "How could you even think of asking me that?"

"If you could have heard her, Savannah. She's . . . different."

"No she's not. She'll never change."

"She hinted to me a little bit about her past. There are things—"

"I don't want to hear it!" The sheet fell away as she clamped her hands to her ears, exposing her breasts.

He was swayed by the sight of them, but the pathetic picture of Irene Royale he had carried away from that meeting with her would not let him give in without a struggle. He pulled her hands away from her ears. "She just wants to see you, Savannah. She's your mother."

"When has she ever acted like it?" Tears were streaming down her face. "She's fooling you just like she fooled everyone after she murdered Kit!"

"That was a long time ago. She's different now. If you would only see her, talk to her, you'd—"

She rolled out of bed and stood there, defiantly naked, her face a mask of implacable fury. "I won't do it!"

He had indulged her in everything; he could not indulge her in this. It was his own guilt as much as anything else that made him refuse to say the words that would bring her back to bed.

Still naked, Savannah stalked out of the bedroom like a magnificent young valkyrie. For the first time since she had come to his bed on the Island, Paul slept alone.

*   *   *

The party dragged on forever. It was even more boring than usual. Savannah wasn't real friends with any of the women she met socially, but tonight they seemed even more remote from her than usual. If she and Paul were on speaking terms she would have gone to stand by his side, so she wouldn't feel quite so much like an awkward giraffe. But they had barely spoken since he had tried to argue her into allowing Irene back into her life, and Savannah's fury was still burning deep inside her.

She took a glass of champagne from a passing waiter and shut herself away in that insulated shell that had served her so well at endless boring parties in the past. She stood with a model's grace against the wall and studied the designs of the endless array of jewelry that surrounded her.

As soon as he realized what was happening, Paul tried to make a graceful exit. But everything and everyone was conspiring against him that night.

One person after another sought him out, and he could only watch Savannah's isolation from across the room. She had become a pariah without realizing it. How could she know that she was the target for such sordid speculation in the tabloids that it turned his stomach to read it? They made her sound like a nymphomaniac. To have had affairs with half the men she was reported to have bedded would have been a physical impossibility.

He blamed Jordan and Barbara more than anyone else. If it had not been for them, the furor brought on

by his marriage to such a young girl would have
faded in time. But when those two took their griev-
ances to the papers they unleashed a new storm of
publicity, more than they could possibly have imagined. Jordan and Barbara would suffer for that, he
vowed, just like the bitchy socialites who were so
gleefully snubbing his wife tonight. He could buy
and sell most of their husbands with a single phone
call, and tomorrow he would prove it. But tonight,
the most important thing was to make sure no one
said anything to Savannah to hurt or embarrass her.
And especially that no one who believed those ridiculous stories in the papers tried to proposition her.

Carter came to him in tears.

"Did you see this?"

Paul took the newspaper. The tabloid's photograph
showed Savannah reaching up to hug the chauffeur
around the neck. The headline implied she was having an affair with her husband's chauffeur.

"She didn't mean anything by that, Mr. Paul. She
was just being friendly. You know how she is."

Paul nodded.

He knew. Although the first sight of that photograph caused a jealous rage to rise up in him.

"And this isn't the worst of the stories. You can't
believe the things they're saying about her. It would
make you sick. What if she sees this trash?"

"I'll take care of it," Paul told him.

As always, it was Garnet he turned to. When he
phoned to ask her if she would consider coming back

to work for him as Savannah's secretary/companion, she agreed immediately.

"You've seen the stories in the tabloids?" The public image Savannah had acquired in the past few months was so far removed from the real Savannah, it was as if two different persons existed with the same name. "They're not true, none of them."

"I know that, Paul."

Her voice was so warm, and comforting that he relaxed immediately. "I don't want her to see them, Garnet. She has to be shielded from all this. She has no idea what they're saying about her and I don't want anyone to bring these ridiculous stories up to her."

"I'll take care of it," Garnet promised. "You know I was always good about managing your social life."

"It might be best if you moved in here for a while." The idea had just occurred to him. "That way we can make sure that . . ."

"That nothing troubles her. I understand. But my animals, Paul?"

He could picture the elegant shrug of her shoulders. "Bring them. I've missed them. And you."

When Garnet hung up the phone, she was shaking. She dropped down on the sofa and leaned over to put her head between her knees until the feeling of faintness passed. The dogs whined at her feet.

How could he be so cruel? Didn't he know what it would do to her to see him with that young girl day after day? Didn't he care?

Of course, he didn't know, she realized. And if he did, he wouldn't care.

She would have to be strong, Garnet told herself. The greatest opportunity of her life had just been handed to her and she intended to make the most of it. After all, she had others besides herself to think of. "Come here, my darlings," she said, and patted the cushion beside her. The Lhasas scrambled up beside her, both of them jockeying for position on her lap, and the cat leaped up on the back of the sofa to regard the three of them with icy disdain. "We're going to have a new home for a while, my pets. And then we're never going to have to worry about money again."

Why hadn't he done this sooner? Paul wondered. Garnet inserted herself so smoothly into their lives that she made barely a ripple in the household, and yet her influence was everywhere. She sifted through their invitations, selecting a few now and then, and calling to cajole the guest list from the hostess before accepting. There were no unpleasant surprises, no unguarded remarks to trouble Savannah with the truth of her public image. The best thing of all was that Savannah didn't realize how sheltered she was because she had always been sheltered. Garnet also took her shopping and out to lunch and all sorts of other womanly things that Paul was sure she had missed, taking the pressure off of him so that he could turn his attention back to business, which had been sadly neglected since his marriage.

It would have all been wonderful except for one

thing. Savannah no longer shared his bedroom. She had moved out the night he broached the subject of seeing Irene, and she had not returned.

But even that was not as painful as it might have been otherwise. On the nights they had no social engagements, Savannah went to bed early so that she could rise early to work on her jewelry-making while he remained in the study to work on whatever projects he had brought home from the office. Gradually Garnet fell into the habit of coming in to assist him as she had when she worked for him, and soon those long quiet evening hours with Garnet developed into his favorite part of the day.

Chapter 12

If Marsdon had asked *her* before he had his giant bastard of a chauffeur drag her off to that pricey sanitarium, Irene would have told him to save his money. She knew she'd never be able to stay off the booze permanently. Not as long as the hymns still played in the dark corners of her mind.

It would take more booze than the world could hold to blot out the sound of the choir singing joyfully of Christ's blood and the suffering sinners. Sometimes she heard the voices so clearly that she could actually feel the hard wooden pew pressing against her bony little bottom and breathe the hot stagnant air stirred only by the cardboard fans in the congregation's hands. She felt if she looked down she would see the toes of her patent leather shoes with the thin dusting of sandy loam she had picked up walking across the churchyard dulling the shine her mother had put on them the night before.

Sometimes, on a good night, she could remember the warm comfortable feeling of being wedged in between the solid bulk of her father and her slender wisp of a mother in the pew, watching the identical Jesuses with their upraised hands, one on either side of her, as her parents tried to introduce a breath of air with their fans—Mama's Jesus moving lightly and gracefully in front of her, barely stirring the air, and Daddy's Jesus pushing hard enough to churn up a whirlwind. She always ended up with her head leaning against Daddy's arm, her face turned toward his breeze until Mama yanked her upright again, hissing at her to sit up straight before the new preacher noticed.

There was always a new preacher. Theirs was a community of dirt farmers, a place for beginning preachers to start off or old preachers to come to die, but not a place for anyone with any ambition to be stuck in—or at least that was what Irene always heard Mama yelling at Daddy most nights after they thought she had gone to sleep.

Poor Mama, pretty and slim as a young girl, while all the other women her age were worn out by back-breaking labor and a houseful of babies, one after the other. Irene wondered about that. She liked to think it was because Daddy loved Mama and protected her. Just like he loved and protected Irene. With Daddy there, Irene believed there was nothing that could harm her.

Until the nightmares started.

She was nine that year. Another new preacher had come to the church, only this one was different from the rest. He preached fire and brimstone in a thundering voice that made her want to crawl under the pew and escape. His words painted such graphic pictures of the suffering of the sinners that she would wake up screaming at night. Even though she was nestled, safe and protected, on the pew between Mama and Daddy, she was sure that his hot black eyes were on her when he talked about the jaws of hell. The church was divided on the question of the new preacher. Half of them wanted to throw him out, and there were rumors that that was exactly what had happened to him with his previous congregation. The other half wanted to raise him to sainthood.

Mama and Daddy were squarely divided. Irene could hear them yelling at night about it. Mama thought he could walk on water and Daddy thought he should be lynched. They had a fight about Irene, too. Daddy said it was the new preacher giving her nightmares. Mama said that it was her own evil thoughts and that she should be spanked when she woke up screaming like that. Daddy said if Mama laid a hand on her, he would paddle Mama. When it was their turn to have the new preacher to dinner, Daddy made Mama pass and Mama refused to speak to him for a week. She made him live in a cold icy silence, his coffee and plate flung down before him without ceremony at the kitchen table and not a scrap of extra conversation.

Irene hated her for it.

She hated her even more when Daddy finally relented and let Mama take her next turn at having the preacher over for dinner. Mama cooked all day long, big fluffy biscuits and crisp fried chicken, green beans and new potatoes fresh from the garden, pick-

led beets from the pantry shelf and two kinds of pie.
Now that he had given in, Daddy was determined to
make Mama happy and he praised her to the skies as
they waited for the preacher to show up. Mama had
taken off her cooking apron and put on a fresh starched
one. Her cheeks were flushed with anticipation and
the heat from the stove, and little tendrils of her hair
clung around her face.

Irene had never felt so betrayed in her life . . . by
Daddy, not Mama. He was the one who agreed to let
the enemy come to their house. Irene was convinced
that the preacher was going to make sure she went
straight to hell. She couldn't forget the way his blaz-
ing dark eyes stared at her in church, and she daw-
dled over putting on her good dress until Mama came
and gave her a swat.

But when the preacher finally came, Irene saw that
she had been wrong. It was not her that his eyes
followed, but Mama. When he talked to Mama, his
voice was a warm caress that reminded Irene of the
hot stagnant air inside the church on a summer morning in July. During dinner he and Daddy got into a
fight over the sermons, and finally Daddy got so mad
he went slamming out of the house to do his chores,
not even waiting to taste the two kinds of pie.

Mama sat weeping silently and the preacher rose to
console her, patting her shoulder and leaning over
her to offer quiet words of comfort, too low for Irene
to hear. He stared at Irene at the other end of the
table and asked her if she wouldn't like to go outside
and play. But she was having none of that. She
knew—whether Daddy did or not—that someone

needed to be here to protect poor weak-willed Mama from this man, and so she shook her head stubbornly and said that she wasn't leaving until they had the two kinds of pie for dessert.

Mama remembered her manners, then, and leaped up to serve her guest; and the preacher laughed, a false hearty laugh, and sent Irene a look that promised her the jaws of hell would be snapping at her soul once again when he got back up in his pulpit on Sunday morning.

When Daddy's tractor rolled over on him and crushed him against the earth, it was the preacher who said the words over him.

Irene had fought and screamed against that with all her might, until Mama spanked her good and hard. Sometimes when the hymns came back to haunt her, she could see her daddy lying still and dead in the coffin and the preacher looming over him in the pulpit above, a triumphant smile in those black eyes. Irene was going to hell, those black eyes promised. He would see to it personally.

The nightmares came back, stronger and more vicious than ever, and with them came the preacher. She would wake to find him looming over her bed just as he had loomed over Daddy's coffin, with Mama or one of the neighbor ladies beside him. He would be holding their hand or patting them on the shoulder, telling them, "Don't worry about the child. She's in God's hands."

Only she wasn't in God's hands; she was in his.

That had to be God's will, because everything else

was. It was God's will that her father was taken from her like that. God's will that her mother had lost her husband. God's will that the preacher should come and comfort them each night. God's will that a new church should be offered to the preacher in Louisville; and of course, God's will that her mother should marry him and follow him to his new ministry, even though less than six months had passed since Daddy had been laid to rest.

Irene was beginning to hate God.

Especially after they moved to Louisville. Even though he was busy setting up his new parish and teaching her mother all the things a preacher's wife should know, the preacher still had time to give Irene private instruction in what God expected of her and what He would do to her if she failed Him.

She was terrified night and day that God would strike her dead for her real and imagined sins—she had never realized how many sins there were, how careful she would have to be not to fall from God's grace. There were so many ways she could fail Him. By failing Him, she failed the preacher and her mama and even her poor dead father. The preacher pointed out to both her and her mama that Daddy had been the heathen who would not sit down and break bread with a servant of the Lord.

Her biggest failure was the nightmares. Every time she woke screaming from her sleep, it was an indictment of the preacher. Soon everyone in the church knew that the preacher's stepdaughter was having nightmares. Mama grew pale and desperate as the church ladies whispered among themselves.

"We're going to lose the church," the preacher thundered at Mama. "The best church I've ever had and it's all because of her."

Mama, falling-down weary from lack of sleep after sitting up with Irene all the night before, told him to do whatever he could, to ask God's mercy on them all, because she could do no more.

That night when Irene's own screams woke her from her dream of the jaws of hell, dripping with the blood of sinners, it was not Mama, but the preacher standing beside her bed.

"Where's my Mama?" she sobbed.

He didn't answer as he climbed in beside her and pulled her to him. He was a big man, almost as big as Daddy had been, and for a moment it was so much like sitting beside the big comforting bulk of her father in church again that she relaxed against him and made believe her daddy had come back to her.

Only her daddy had never put his hands on her chest and rubbed the hard little nipples through the thin batiste of her nightgown. He had never touched her beneath the ribbed cotton of her panties.

When Irene tried to squirm away, the preacher thrust his fingers inside her so hard she would have screamed if his mouth were not covering hers. There was no way her child's body could fight his male strength when he pulled her panties off and put a knee between her legs to force them open.

Or when he shoved the hard male part of him, which she hadn't even known existed until that night, into the place where his fingers had already probed.

All she could do was scream for God or Mama to save her.

But nobody came, and he kept forcing himself into her, grunting and gasping like an animal as he crushed her against the mattress.

The pain went on and on until she couldn't scream anymore, until she could only whimper with the agony of it. Even after he finally rolled away from her, the pain was still there.

When he was through, he shoved her to one side of the bed and pulled the sheets off. He swabbed between her legs with them, mopping up the blood and semen. He took her nightgown and her panties and left her lying on the bare mattress ticking with a towel beneath her to catch the bloody mixture still seeping from between her thighs.

She always wondered if he had Mama wash the sheets.

The nightmares stopped.

When the next night passed without her screams, Irene's Mama fell to her knees and prayed her thanks to the Lord. The news spread through the church that the preacher had brought God's healing grace to his stepdaughter. Nobody asked why, if Irene was cured, the preacher still spent so much time alone in her bedroom with her, praying for her salvation.

Nobody asked Irene why the nightmares had stopped; but she knew it was because she was no longer troubled by the threat of God's vengeance or God's punishment . . . because now she knew, without a shadow of a doubt, that there wasn't any God.

She was eleven.

*   *   *

Irene was thirteen the summer when she got her first period, and not long after that a case of the flu so bad that it lingered on for two months, making her retch weakly into the toilet each morning. Mama wouldn't take her to the doctor. Instead, she treated her with folk remedies and drugstore medicines until Irene's body was so swollen and clumsy from the preacher's seed that even Mama could no longer deny it . . . and then Mama threw her out of the house.

Irene tried to tell Mama that it was the preacher's fault and not hers, but Mama turned a cold, hard face her way and never spoke to her again. None of the church ladies would take her in; they thought so highly of the preacher and his pretty wife. How terrible it was, they whispered to each other, that his stepdaughter would spread those awful lies about such a fine upstanding man of God.

The woman in that first foster home worked Irene like a slave, down on her knees scrubbing floors and up on a step stool washing windows. It was a blessing really, because she lost the baby, and if the preacher's seed had turned into a real live baby, she would have killed it.

After the fat her body had put on to nourish the baby melted away, Irene found she had a woman's figure. She also discovered that her body would buy her freedom from the grinding housework. She was placed in many foster homes over the years, but she never again had to work as hard as she had in that first one. There was always a man of the house to protect her, to indulge her, to use her, to be used by her.

At fifteen, when she ran away from the last of the foster homes, she knew all the ways a man could be manipulated by sex. She took that knowledge—and the hymns—with her.

Edward Harrison was the only one who had ever been able to blot out the sounds of the hymns. She was working as an elite call girl in New York City, making $100,000 a year in tax free income, when she met Edward's father at a party in an elegant and fashionable East Side apartment building, which also happened to be a very exclusive brothel. Even in the crowd of prosperous middle-aged men, which included some of the most prominent names in business and politics in the city, Andrew G. Harrison stood out. He was a powerful senator from California and used to getting what he wanted. What he wanted that night was for Irene to ditch the man beside her and go with Harrison back to his hotel room. The john, an assemblyman, had already paid for her services. He was more than a little drunk, and inclined to argue. Irene watched, amused, as the madam took the john aside and explained to him exactly who Senator Harrison was. Then Harrison paid the man double her price for the night and left with her.

He wanted to take her to his hotel room, but she demurred, insisting he take her back to her apartment. She had been twenty-four then and he was forty-nine.

She pleased him.

She was good at pleasing men. She had learned early that pleasing a man meant she could control him, and she had learned her lesson well. By the time Andrew Harrison left her apartment the next morning, she knew she had him hooked. For the next few weeks, he made sure that he had the exclusive use of her services during his frequent trips to New York. She continued to please him. Within three months he had moved her to Washington, into a lovely old row house surrounded by maples on a quiet street in Georgetown. She went with him on weekend junkets and an extended trip to Europe, all at taxpayer's expense.

She had never worried about achieving her own pleasure in bed. At the age of twenty-five she had never had an orgasm. In a way, she was grateful for that. If she had gotten any pleasure out of the act, she wouldn't have been able to manipulate men as coolly and carefully as she had to in order to get where she was now. She had never even come close to orgasm until she met the senator. A couple of times recently, however, she had hovered right on the brink, caught up in a painful urgent need for release—but the hymns were always there. Sometimes she wondered what things would have been like if the preacher hadn't come into her life, and if her father hadn't died beneath his tractor. Her feelings for Andrew became somehow mixed up with her feelings about her real father. Irene was more involved with Andrew than she had ever been with anyone in her whole life. By fall, when the golden maple leaves were everywhere, she would have done anything he asked.

*　　*　　*

Irene had been Andrew Harrison's mistress for a year when he first took her to his place, a horse farm in the Piedmont foothills near Charlottesville, Virginia. As the limousine followed the winding macadam road through acres of oak-fenced pastures, she could tell that Andrew was more keyed up than usual. Irene knew that the senator's wife lived here, instead of in the city, and she wondered if he was setting up a threesome with him, her, and his wife.

She turned to the window to hide a smile. One of her clients had worked for months to get his wife to agree to a threesome and then had been furious when Irene and the woman ended up concentrating on each other, forgetting he was even there. She would have to be careful that didn't happen today. Andrew was too big a fish to lose. Besides that, she needed him.

The main house was a huge Georgian mansion on a hilltop with a panoramic view of the Blue Ridge Mountains. In the elegant marble-floored foyer, Irene paused and looked up at Andrew Harrison. "Is your wife expecting us?"

"My wife is in California."

She pondered that as he led her up the graceful curving staircase to the second floor. She was still expecting some kind of group scene—a former mistress, another prostitute. When Andrew opened the bedroom door, Irene couldn't believe her eyes.

Standing by the window, looking out at the mountains, was the most handsome man she had even seen in her entire life. When he turned and smiled at her, her knees weakened.

Irene was bewildered. She had never thought of

Andrew as bisexual—he was too aggressively male—
but here was the evidence right in front of her, so
stunning in his blond beauty that she couldn't take
her eyes off of him.

"This is my son," Andrew said. "Edward. I want
you to fuck him."

Edward continued to stand there with the same
placid smile on his face, as though his father had not
spoken.

Irene had been involved in a lot of different scenes
in the past few years, but this was the weirdest one
yet. Normally, she avoided threesomes with two guys.
You never knew when that kind of situation might
turn violent. She had never even considered a father-
son act. "And what if I don't want to?"

"You don't fuck because you want to, Irene. You
fuck because I pay you."

"So why are you paying me to fuck him? He's
pretty enough. Can't he get his own girls?" She said
that for Edward's benefit, anything to shake the com-
placent expression on that handsome face.

"No."

The pain in that unadorned reply reminded her
fleetingly of the first night her stepfather had climbed
into her bed.

"Why not?"

"He was the best thing that ever happened in my
life. When he was twelve, he struck his head on the
diving board at a friend's swimming pool. He was
under water less than thirty seconds. We were so
relieved, his mother and I. It was a long time before
she would admit anything was wrong, but I knew. I
knew immediately that my boy had left me."

Edward was smiling.

"I had such plans for him. We could have started a dynasty."

Edward was smiling. He might as well have been alone in the room for all the attention he was paying to them.

"He lives entirely in the present. He doesn't remember anything in the past and he's not aware there's a future beyond this moment."

"You've brought him women before?" She was still thinking in terms of a business arrangement, an increase in her generous allowance from the senator if she pleased his son.

"When I can. His mother does not approve. She still thinks of him as that twelve-year-old boy. But he's a man. Twenty-eight. If the accident hadn't happened, he'd be married now with a son of his own. My grandchild." Irene was astonished to see that tears were streaking the senator's face.

Edward was smiling.

He was taller than the senator. When she crossed the room to stand directly in front of him, he towered over her. She reached up and took his head in her hands, turning his face to hers.

She received a physical shock when their glances met. She was drowning in the golden brown of his eyes. She knew that for him, at that moment, there was nothing else in the whole world except Irene Royce.

She had never been the total focus of a man's attention before. She forgot about Andrew, about the hymns, about everything but this beautiful golden man.

She undressed him slowly, letting her hands linger on his body, and then took off her own clothes. She led him over to the bed and stretched out on the satin coverlet, beckoning him down to her.

He explored her body with a maddening intensity, as though they were the only two people in the world and eternity was theirs. He stroked her between her thighs, rubbing the bud of her clitoris while he sucked her nipples with the greedy hunger of a baby. The first shattering orgasm, when it came, was more powerful than anything she could have believed possible.

He held her tightly until it subsided, and then kissed his way down the valley between her breasts and across the flat expanse of her stomach to her curly brown pubic hair, and then his hot breath was on her vulva and his tongue darted inside her.

Before he finally mounted her, she had two more orgasms and was weeping in delight.

She had sex with Edward twice more that weekend, long dreamy erotic sessions that seemed to go on forever. She had one shattering climax after another, and she could not believe what she had missed for all those years.

But even better than that, for the first time since the preacher came into her life, the hymns were gone.

In the limousine on the way back to Washington, Andrew said, "We've kept Edward in absolute seclusion since the accident. The full extent of his condition is not public knowledge. You'll keep everything that happened this weekend to yourself." There was no threat. There didn't have to be. She knew the extent of Andrew Harrison's power better than most people. She had seen him at work.

"Will I see him again?" She hadn't meant to say that. The words tumbled out by themselves.

Andrew looked at her. "You weren't faking with him, were you?" At her surprised expression, he said, "Oh, I've known all along I don't bring you to orgasm, Irene. But it doesn't matter, does it? Not when my money serves the same purpose. But he does?"

Reluctantly, she nodded, unsure what his response would be. She was relieved to see that it was amusement.

Although she continued to see Andrew on a regular basis—and he continued to pay all her expenses, giving her an extremely generous allowance besides—they no longer had sex. Instead, he either took her to see Edward at the Virginia farm or brought Edward into Washington. Her sexual encounters with Edward reached marathon proportions, and the senator's amusement faded into envy as he saw the passion his son aroused in Irene. Still, he continued to do everything he could to get them together on a regular basis without his wife discovering what was happening. He loved the boy more than anything in the world. If these encounters with Irene gave Edward pleasure, then he would move heaven and earth to see that they continued.

He grew increasingly jealous of Irene, checking up on her at odd hours, having her followed if she left the Georgetown house. While he had not been suspicious of her when she was his own mistress, now that she had become Edward's mistress, he was overwhelmed with the need to make sure his son was not being cuckolded.

Before she met Edward, Irene would have been furious—and frightened. She saw nothing wrong with turning a few tricks on the side as long as the john knew nothing about it. And she was very good at juggling johns.

But that was before she met Edward. It was as though she had fallen under a spell. She might have been a schoolgirl in love for the first time. She didn't have the slightest desire to see other men. Edward filled her thoughts constantly.

Irene turned the bottle of Jack Daniels around and around, staring at the unbroken seal. It wasn't going to work. She couldn't stay dry forever, not with the hymns swelling and pounding inside her skull. Soon she would be drinking again, and Marsdon would dry her out again, and then he would either wash his hands of her or stick her somewhere permanently. She shuddered.

She had tried her best to play on Marsdon's sympathy and work her way back into Savannah's life, but she could see that her efforts had led to nothing. Savannah was so protected there was no way Irene could get to her without Marsdon's consent.

But it wasn't a total loss.

Marsdon's damnable curiosity had given her an idea of what to do next, harping like he had on the identity of Savannah's father. Not that she intended to tell him anything. That little secret was one she intended to carry with her to her grave. Andrew Harrison had been a powerful, dangerous man when she knew him in Washington. Even though now he must be at least seventy, she had no doubt that he was still just as powerful—and as dangerous. He had made it clear to her what would happen if she revealed anything about Edward's condition, and she knew that had been a promise not a threat. However, that didn't mean she couldn't make a few threats of her own.

Irene broke the seal with her thumbnail and poured herself a water glass full of whisky. " 'The Old Rugged Cross' and 'Rock of Ages,' " she said and saluted the bottle.

She took one big swallow and let it burn a path to her stomach. "And to all the bastards in the world with outside plumbing," she added before she drained the glass.

Chapter 13

Senator Andrew G. Harrison was seventy years old and ready for a rest. The years he spent in the service of his country had taken their toll on him. He couldn't lay the burden down, though. Not yet. Not until he found the right person to take it up again.

He had the President's ear, and his congressional colleagues trembled when he frowned. He could launch a candidate's career by clapping him on the back or remove a man from consideration for an appointment with one phone call. He had dedicated the rest of his life to finding the one man best suited for the presidency, the man who could lead his country into the future it deserved, and he had the power to assure that man's success. But Andrew Harrison was a king-maker without a worthy subject.

If only his golden boy had lived. Not just lived, but been as strong and whole and brave as he was intended to be. How cruel fate had been to steal Edward from him, not once, but twice, leaving him a wasted old man without issue. That he had nothing of himself to leave behind on this earth was a loss that tormented Andrew Harrison every waking moment.

When the call came to his office on Capital Hill, out of the blue on a Monday morning, he recognized Irene Royce's voice at once. "Twenty years ago you weren't so easy to get in touch with, Andrew."

Blackmail didn't occur to him. There wasn't a man in Washington, from the President on down, brave enough to risk Andrew Harrison's wrath. "I'm sorry, Irene; I had no choice." It had pained him to send her away, not for her sake but for Edward's. She had been so good for the boy. But his wife had insisted and twenty years ago Claire's political connections had been stronger than his. One call to her father and he would have been ruined. "You were well paid."

"It wasn't enough to raise a baby on."

His heart thundered in his chest. "Edward's child?" he whispered.

"That bitch wife of yours wouldn't let me near you, Andrew. Your own grandchild, and she didn't want you to know anything about it. Did you know she had me arrested?"

"I didn't know. The child! Did it live? You didn't. . . ."

"Abort it? I should have, after the way you let her treat me, Andrew. I thought you loved Edward."

"The child . . . was it . . ."

"A girl. She's beautiful, Andrew. Edward's child. That's what your precious Claire didn't want you to know. How is Claire these days?"

"She's dead."

"I won't say I'm sorry. I had to change my name

and leave Washington because of her. And you, you could have known Edward's child all these years if it weren't for her." There was a pause and he could hear the long distance hum of the wires. Then she asked, "How is Edward?"

The naked hunger in her voice reminded him of how he had watched the two of them making love, two fine young animals rutting. His groin tightened at the memory. "He's dead, too, Irene."

When she did not reply, he grew frantic, thinking they might have been cut off. "Irene? Irene? Where are you calling from?"

"Where you'll never find me, Andrew."

"Irene, please. The child . . . What's her name?"

"I can't tell you that. I won't make it easy for you to find her. You weren't there when she needed you. She was abused, Andrew. Her own stepfather took advantage of her. She was only eleven."

"No," he moaned.

"How could you have let that happen to Edward's child? Do you think he would forgive you for that?"

"For God's sake, Irene! I had no idea—"

"We've had a hard life, Andrew. Your wife made sure of that."

"Irene, you've got to let me make it up to her. Let me see her."

"Why, Andrew? So you can turn her against me. What will she think of me when she finds out how much money you've got? She'll blame me, not you. We're barely making it, Andrew. You should see the dump we're living in. Pretty soon I'm going to have to put her to work. At least we'll have a nice apartment that way. Remember that apartment I had in New York? Edward's daughter is a real beauty. With her earnings we should be able to afford an apartment twice as nice as—"

"Irene, please! You can't—"

"I've got to go now, Andrew. It's been wonderful talking to you."

Although the connection was broken, he continued to clutch the phone, as though hanging up the receiver would break the only link with his granddaughter.

A physical piece of himself to leave on this earth. Proof that his life had not been in vain.

Edward's child.

It was Claire's fault that Edward had been taken from him. She was the one who allowed him to go swimming at his friend's house that fateful day when he was twelve. Then, for months afterward, she had blithely insisted that nothing was wrong with the boy.

He had forgiven her for the accident and for her steadfast refusal to admit the truth of Edward's disablement because of the way she had devoted herself heart and soul to their son's care. When she found out about Irene, she had confronted him in front of the boy and demanded that Irene never be allowed near Edward again. "I've put up with your women," she told him. "But I will not have my son molested by that slut."

"Claire, be reasonable. Edward is twenty-eight-years old. He's a man. And a man needs sexual release." Edward sat beside her on the sofa, calm as a golden Buddha. To look at him broke Andrew's heart. There was no sign in his outer appearance of the void within.

"I'm warning you, Andrew. Don't bring your whores in here again." She put an arm around Edward and pulled him closer to her. "I'm his mother. I'm all he needs." She reached over and unzipped Edward's fly. As Andrew watched in stunned disbelief, her hand disappeared into Edward's trousers.

He had forgiven her for that, too, eventually, because he finally understood that it was only another way she was devoting herself to Edward's care. But he would never forgive her for not telling him that Irene was pregnant with Edward's child. What right had she had to keep that kind of revelation from him? What right had she to take Edward from him as she had done?

Three years after she forced Andrew to break off Irene's visits to Edward, Claire learned she had cancer. Two weeks later, she and Edward were dead, drowned in a boating accident. Only it wasn't an accident, and Andrew knew it. The selfish bitch had killed his boy, had murdered him as surely as if she had put a gun to his head. She knew she was going to die and she had chosen to take Edward with her, rather than let him live without her.

Now this foul whore proposed to keep his granddaughter from him. Threatened to condemn a Harrison to a life of prostitution. Had allowed the child to be sexually abused at the age of eleven. As he thought of all the care and attention he would have lavished on Edward's child, he could taste the salt of his own tears.

It was fifteen minutes before he could compose himself enough to question his secretary. She had no idea where the call had come from, but he made damned sure she would try and find out where the next one originated—and *please God* let there be a next one. Within the hour, he had hired a private detective agency who held out exactly zero hope as they took his check. By the end of the day, he had called in a handful of political debts to try and trace Irene's twenty-one-year-old tracks. As, one by one, his sources reported negative results, he spent the next forty-eight tortured hours wondering if he had learned of his granddaughter's existence only to lose her.

He had almost given up hope of hearing from Irene again when the second call came to his home.

"I've been thinking it over, Andrew," Irene said without preamble. "It's only fair that I give you a chance to help me support Edward's child."

"Anything, Irene," he said, almost babbling in his haste. "Only don't—"

"Don't let her be a prostitute like me?" Irene's chuckle sent a chill down his spine. "Anything but that, right? A fate worse than death. So what does that make me, Andrew?"

"For God's sake, Irene, I didn't make you what you are! You were a grown woman when I met you. We're talking about a child—"

"A woman, Senator. A twenty-year-old woman."

"Edward's child. My granddaughter. Just tell me what you want, Irene. Anything. It's yours."

"I know how you work, Andrew. I want you to call off whatever bloodhounds you've unleashed. They'll never find me, and I promise you if they get close enough for me to spot, I'll make sure you never hear another word from me or your granddaughter."

"What else?"

"Money. Twenty-five thousand dollars. All cash. Unmarked bills." She gave him a post office box number in Pasadena. "You mail it to me. And if you hope to hear from me again, you better not have that box watched. Do you understand?"

Andrew G. Harrison, one of the most powerful men in the United States Senate, who had made a career out of crushing his opponents' balls to get what he wanted, knew that his own nuts were in the cracker. "I understand."

As soon as she hung up, he called everyone, beginning with the detective agency, to tell them to forget he had ever wanted to know about a woman named Irene Royce.

When Garnet Hoffman became Savannah's secretary/companion, she realized at once that, for the sake of her own future, she had to educate Savannah in the art of living life as one of the wealthiest women in the country, the role to which Savannah's marriage to Paul Marsdon entitled her. Savannah spent far too much time alone in her studio, working feverishly on her jewelry designs, leaving the Bel Air mansion only for her lessons with Leonardo or to attend functions with Paul

What a waste of Paul Marsdon's largesse, Garnet

thought. He would have gladly paid for anything his young wife desired, and what she appeared to desire was to be shut up in her studio for twelve to fourteen hours a day.

All that was about to change.

Swiftly and efficiently, before Savannah quite realized what was taking place, Garnet had turned her whole life upside down.

First there were the tennis lessons. Savannah hadn't set foot on the tennis court since they moved into the house. Garnet arranged twice-a-week lessons with a tennis pro, a female tennis pro to quiet any objections Paul might raise. Then there were the exercise sessions the other three days of the week, and the afternoons of shopping at Giorgio, Cartier, Hermes, and Bijan's—where Savannah and Garnet were always instantly admitted without the bother of making an appointment—and all the wonderful stores at the new Rodeo Collection. They bought mountains of clothes and hundreds of accessories from purses (which Savannah still forgot to carry) to scarves, all chosen with Garnet's impeccable taste. Savannah was never tempted to return anything whether she ever had occasion to wear it or not. It was an absolutely perfect situation as far as Garnet was concerned. Savannah never looked at prices or totaled the bills the salesladies held out to her before she scribbled her signature across the bottom. Paul gave Garnet whatever amount she claimed was on each store's statement that month with an equal lack of attention, so that Garnet could make any adjustments she pleased, and her bank account prospered.

She increased the amount of entertaining and travel Paul and his young wife did, teaching Savannah the art of giving a dinner for two hundred people and how much to tip bellhops. She meshed their frequent trips in so well with Paul's necessary business traveling that he had no cause for complaint, but instead praised her for her resourcefulness.

Much as Garnet enjoyed traveling, she enjoyed staying at the Bel Air house more, especially the long evenings alone with Paul in his study after Savannah had retired to her room. She knew that Paul was no longer sleeping with his young wife, although she had no idea what the problem was. Whatever it might be, she was glad for it, because in a strange way it made her feel as though she and Paul were finally married, and that Savannah was not his wife, but their daughter. It was an almost perfect existence.

Except for two small things.

Garnet found she was growing to hate Savannah. Not for the girl herself, but because in educating Savannah to live as her position as Paul's wife entitled her, Garnet realized just how much she had lost by being Paul's lover and not his spouse. They had agreed, Paul and Garnet, that she must never leave Savannah alone—not at her tennis lessons, her exercise classes, her lunches with other women, at her own large elegant parties, or even in the dressing rooms of the stores they visited. There was too great a chance that someone might say something to Savannah that would expose her to the shattering truth of her public image.

That meant Garnet shared all the luxuries with

Savannah. Jealousy overwhelmed her half-a-dozen times a day as she realized the opulent existence even Paul's ex-wives led compared to her spartan life all these years in her Malibu hideaway.

Garnet became more determined than ever to secure her financial future. It was not enough that she amass adequate funds for simple subsistence. Now she wanted more, much more. And she was determined to get it, whatever the means.

The other flaw in Garnet's existence was her relationship with Paul. The fantasy of marriage that she cherished each night as they worked together in the study, the dogs at their feet and the cat prowling the room restlessly, was wonderful. However, it was hard to sustain the illusion after she retired alone to her bed. She began to wonder what it might take to make the fantasy fact. After all, Paul had married four women, and now it was obvious that the newest and youngest of them no longer aroused him enough to seek her bed. Who was to say that another divorce might not be imminent? If it was, why couldn't Garnet herself be a candidate for Mrs. Marsdon number five?

She knew how tortured Paul was over the reports in the papers that Savannah was seeing other men. While she continued to guard Savannah like a duenna, Garnet began to leak small items to the newspapers, so that now it might almost seem to Paul that the reports could have a basis in fact. Anything that widened the schism between Paul and his young wife could only help her cause.

*   *   *

When Irene picked up the package at the Pasadena Post Office, her hands were trembling so badly that she dropped it twice on her way out of the building. She hadn't realized it would take so much out of her to talk to Andrew after all these years. Finding out about Edward's death was a shock, but it was more than that. When she had the inspiration of substituting her own childhood experiences for Savannah's, she knew that would move Andrew. What she had not realized was how vulnerable to those memories she still was herself.

But this, she thought, hugging the package to her as she hurried through the barrel-vaulted gallery and down the post office steps, this was the cure. Cold hard cash.

Screw the preacher and Mama and even Daddy for deserting her. Screw Savannah and the old bastard who married her. All the happiness she ever wanted was wrapped up in this box. As soon as she got home and unwrapped it, her new lifestyle would begin. After that, the first thing she wanted was a drink, and, come to think of it, the second thing she wanted was a drink.

Savannah watched idly as Garnet pawed through a stack of scarves and emerged victorious with the right one, the perfect scarf to complement the suit they had just bought. Her modeling days had made her accustomed to having people fuss over her, and now she stood patiently while Garnet held the scarf up to her face to assure herself that it was indeed the ideal shade of green to match both Savannah's eyes and the suit.

Savannah had realized the very first time they went shopping together that Garnet Hoffman was the mysterious someone who had selected all of the perfect, beautiful clothing for her when she married Paul. Then, as now, she had the feeling that Garnet knew her sizes and her preferences better than she did herself. She had also realized, just after Paul hired Garnet to be her companion and secretary, that the small, poised woman also knew her husband better than she did, and she wondered what that meant.

Sometimes in the midst of rushing frantically here and there in the new life Garnet had introduced her to, Savannah forgot that she and Paul no longer shared a bed. She had moved into another bedroom on impulse, never considering what might happen next. When she might have moved back, Paul made the mistake of bringing up the subject of Irene again, of increasing Irene's allowance. Savannah had raged at him until he promised not to give Irene anything beyond the amount he was already sending her. She could not believe that the man who had rescued her from Irene could be so insensitive.

Then Paul hired Garnet Hoffman.

Savannah suspected the two things were connected. She couldn't shake the feeling Paul had been disappointed in her when he found out there was some defect in her which kept her from getting pregnant. Or perhaps he had realized, in spite of what Cara told her, that she had been counterfeiting her pleasure when they made love. It had began the night he let her know that it was her fault she could not have children. Ever since she had realized that she was flawed in a way so terrible that he could not even bring himself to discuss it, she had been totally unable to derive any pleasure from their lovemaking.

The argument about Irene could have been just a ploy. Maybe Paul had intended to move Garnet into the house all along. All Savannah knew was that she felt very strange each evening as she went up to her separate bedroom all alone, leaving the two of them downstairs together. Yet she couldn't figure out what to do about it. Paul seemed content with the situation— even happy.

And herself?

She was, if not happy, then content, Savannah realized. She had added the unpleasant facts that not only did she no longer derive any pleasure from making love to her husband, but that he had stopped even wanting to sleep with her, to the list of things she refused to think about.

She had her jewelry-making to occupy her, and all the diversions Garnet had introduced into her life. If it were not for the empty aching hollow inside her where a child should have been growing, she might even have been happy.

Still, leaving the two of them alone together each night troubled her. She could not force herself to return to Paul's bedroom, or even to linger with them in the study, not when their mutual contentment in each other's company was so obvious. Instead of retiring when she left them each evening, Savannah took to returning to her studio instead. There was more comfort in the glowing perfection of gold than in the lonely solitude of her empty bed.

*   *   *

Irene's calls always came at night, and they made Andrew Harrison's life a living hell. After a while he didn't know which was worse—when she called or when she didn't. It was three long weeks after he sent the first money when he heard from her again. When she made that third call it was obvious that she was either drunk or out of her mind on drugs. She raved on and on about how the stepfather had molested Edward's daughter, until he thought he would go mad hearing it. When he hung up the phone at last, he went into the bathroom and retched. She had asked for no money that night, and just before she hung up she was crying so hard her voice was unintelligible.

It was a week before he heard from her again, and then she asked for more money. She was sober that night, and the catalogue of violations that had been inflicted on his grandchild sounded even more appalling recited in that cold colorless voice.

After that he heard from her almost every week, although sometimes two weeks would go by, and, once, three agonizing weeks crawled by before the phone rang, just past midnight, and he heard her whisky-roughened voice.

He forked over the sums she asked for willingly, just to keep her calling. She refused to tell him anything that might help him to locate her or his granddaughter. He had her calls traced, but all he learned was that she was calling from a variety of pay phones in the greater Los Angeles area. He wanted desperately to hire a detective firm in L.A. to

find her, but she threatened that at the slightest hint
he was trying to track her down she would vanish
again.

So Andrew waited for her calls, waited to hear the
catalogue of indignities and perversions that had been
visited upon Edward's daughter, and cursed Claire
anew each time he hung up the phone for keeping the
existence of Edward's child from him. It was ironic,
he thought. The most powerful man in Washington
and there was no way he could use that power to help
Edward's child.

Or himself.

Paul had sadly neglected his business interests from
the moment he married Savannah, and he was still
paying the penalty for that disinterest, working ten
and twelve hour days at the office some weeks, and
bringing a bulging briefcase home each evening. His
doctor told him he should slow down and watch his
diet more closely, but he had never been a man who
delegated authority well, and there were too many
things that simply could not be delegated at all. But
more than that, he didn't want to make any changes
in his lifestyle which might indicate—either to himself or to Savannah—he was growing older.

He should have been upset that Savannah made no
move to come back to his bed; however he found, to
his amazement, that he was relieved. He still cared
about her, but the intense infatuation was gone. Instead, he felt like a father toward her, protective,
benevolent. He was more worried about what she
might do with the rest of her life than anything else.

He had a nagging suspicion that he had protected her too much, made things too easy for her, but he wasn't sure what to do about it. The guilt that any of his dealings with her seemed to rouse was there stronger than ever. It was only with Garnet that he could relax and be himself, his own age and guilt-free.

Paul was not a man who could live without sexual release. Garnet knew that well, had in fact been counting on it. As the months stretched out and he still did not return to his young wife's bed, she knew that victory was within her grasp.

It wasn't just that marriage to Paul would end her desperate search for financial security. It was more, much more. When she wed him, she would have stolen him away from a young woman less than half her age—and not just any young woman, but Savannah Royale, whose beauty was beyond compare.

That knowledge burned within her, giving her an energy and vitality that made her seem thirty instead of almost fifty. Her cheeks glowed. Her eyes sparkled. Every movement she made was filled with zest and spirit. Paul's glance followed her everywhere, and Garnet knew it was only a matter of time.

Chapter 14

It had been one hell of a night, starting when Nick Savidge, the muscular young man with the bronze surfer's tan she had met a month ago at a West Hollywood bar, showed up at Irene's door with two bottles of champagne and a lid of grass. She had made a lot of new friends since the senator's money began flowing into her account. Life was a constant party, and she almost never heard the hymns anymore. When things got dull, she called Andrew.

God, but it was satisfying to make him squirm!

It wasn't hard either. All she had to do was take the most painful episodes of her life and tell them as if they had actually happened to Savannah. It was as though by making Andrew suffer, she was actually paying back all the bastards who had abused her so many years ago.

Just the thought of it made her horny, and halfway through the champagne and pot, she adjourned to the bedroom with Nick and let him pound away inside her as she planned what she would say to Andrew tonight. The thought of Andrew's torment brought her to a gasping, shuddering orgasm almost immediately, and she waited impatiently until Nick finally exhausted himself.

When he rolled to the other side of the bed, his penis draped across one tree-trunk thigh like a wilted flower, and began to snore softly, she reached for the telephone and called the number in Washington, D.C., that she knew by heart now.

Nick Savidge woke from a sound sleep to find the crazy broad he had just fucked hovering over him with glittering eyes like a demented vampire. Only instead of blood, she was trying to fit his diminished self back inside her: an impossible task when a man had just come as hard as he had. When he objected that she was trying to raise the dead, she applied her mouth to the task in a way that would have seemed like paradise only half an hour ago, but was now torture.

When he protested, she called him a fag, which really hurt since he prided himself on screwing twice as many women as men, and he could have sworn he had given her a good pop.

He pushed her away but she crawled right back, fondling his shriveled prick until he shoved her again, more violently this time, and told her to get dressed. He didn't know who it was she told her dirty stories to over the phone, but whoever it was, she always turned into a real sex machine afterwards and this time he planned to make a little spending money off of it.

While she struggled into her clothes, he had time for a quick phone call to make sure the party was still on in Marina Del Rey, and then he stuffed her into her brand new Jaguar and drove her there.

One quick snort of coke and she was really flying. She disappeared into one of the bedrooms with the first couple of guys and Nick, having collected his payment in advance, wandered out to find a comfortable chair by the pool and smoke another joint or two while she balled her frenzy away.

Irene shook him awake sometime near dawn, and he could tell by her eyes that she was still wired. When they got to the Jaguar she demanded the keys.

He refused, and she let loose with a string of abuse that would have made a cesspool look like a crystal-clear spring.

Reluctantly, Nick handed them over. But he wasn't stoned enough to climb back in the Jag with her.

He stood with the ocean at his back and watched her lay streaks of rubber right down the middle of the street as she headed into the dawn.

Paul caught the report of the spectacular crash on the San Diego Freeway on his way to work, but he paid no particular attention to it. It wasn't until Carter called him at 10 A.M., that he found out it had been Irene Royale in the airborne Jaguar. His first thought was that he had to be the one to tell Savannah before she heard it from anyone else. He instructed Carter to come for him and spent the half hour waiting for Carter to arrive trying to find out Irene's condition.

It was not good.

When he got home, Garnet met him at the door. "What's going on, Paul? Carter said we weren't to go anywhere and I couldn't get another word out—"

"Where's Savannah?"

He looked past her into the living room, as though she had ceased to exist. He missed the expression of pain that flashed across her face at his inattention.

Garnet had composed herself by the time his glance returned to her. "She's in the studio. She was quite irritated with you when she found out we were not to leave the house. She was to go to Leonardo's for a lesson this morning."

Paul realized with a little shock of surprise how far apart he and Savannah had grown these past few months. He had no idea what her schedule was these days.

He found Savannah bent over her workbench. When she did not look up or acknowledge his presence in any way, he walked closer, so that he could see the piece she was working on. It was a pendant—an octagonal topaz caught in a web of gold—and so sophisticated in design he would not have recognized it as her work. One more indication that he had lost track of what was going on in her life. "Savannah? I'm afraid I have some bad news."

"What's wrong?" she asked, her eyes still on her work.

"Irene has been in an accident. A car wreck."

"Is she dead?" The conversational tone of his young wife's voice surprised him more than the fact that she still did not glance his way.

"Not yet. I'll take you to her."

Now she did look up, and the emerald coldness of her eyes was like a physical blow. "Why?"

"She's your mother, Savannah! She's dying. Your place is—"

"I'm not going!" She stood up so abruptly that her stool went crashing to the floor. "You may have forgotten what she did to me, but I haven't, Paul. *You* go visit her!" She darted past him and out of the studio door.

Slowly, he walked over and picked up the stool and set it upright once more. He had made a terrible mistake with Savannah; he could see that now. He had sheltered her too much and led her to believe that she wouldn't have to face anything she didn't want to face. That would have to change. Starting today.

Savannah huddled on her side of the Rolls, as far away from Paul as she could get, still stunned by the way Paul had marched into her bedroom and told her she was going to the hospital to see Irene if he had to have Carter pick her up and carry her. She had never seen him like this before, and she found herself wondering if this was what he had been like to Jordan and Barbara. Maybe they had a reason for trying to strike out against him.

But she had no time to worry about her stepchildren's problems. The thought of seeing Irene blotted out everything else.

She didn't know exactly what she had been expecting—perhaps the mythic mother monster that

Irene had grown to be in her dreams. But the woman on the hospital bed was a pathetic shrunken stick figure, so swathed in bandages that it could have been a stranger lying there.

The figure mumbled something.

"What did she say?" Savannah asked the nurse.

"She's just rambling," the nurse told her.

The nurse left the room. Savannah walked over to the bed. Irene's eyes were closed. She put her hands on the rails and leaned closer. "Mama? It's Savannah."

"Are you washed?" Irene mumbled.

"What, Mama?"

"Are you washed in the blood of the lamb?"

"Mama, I don't—"

"Mama washed the sheets. I know she did."

"What sheets?"

"Why didn't she stop him? I screamed and screamed and nobody came. I was just a little girl. Why didn't somebody stop him?"

Savannah clung to the rails. "Stop who, Mama?"

"It hurt so bad when he put it in me," Irene whimpered. "Make him stop, Mama." Her eyes opened. She stared straight at Savannah. "Please make him stop!"

"It's Savannah, Mama."

The nurse was back.

" '. . . cleft for me . . .' "

"What, Mama?"

" '. . . let me hide myself in thee . . .' "

Savannah couldn't see through her tears. She reached blindly for her mother's hand.

" '. . . let the water and the blood . . .' "

"The old hymns," the nurse said. "She knows them all." She adjusted the IV. "They must be such a comfort to her."

Paul took her arm as they left the hospital. "I was very proud of you, darling. I know it was hard for you, but—"

"You don't know anything!" She jerked free of his grasp and plunged ahead of him to the Rolls where Carter stood beside the open passenger door.

Paul caught up with her at the car. "Savannah—"

"You know what she was like!" She was trembling with emotion. "My God, of all people, *you* know! You know what she tried to do to me!"

Paul reached for her arm. Savannah slapped his hand away. "You have to face certain things in life," he said. "You can't always—"

"I was safe! Do you understand that? I could look at her and not feel anything but hatred! I could shut her out of my mind! I didn't have to think about her! About Kit! About any of that!"

People were staring.

"Savannah, get in the car. We'll discuss this when we get—"

"I didn't want to feel *sorry* for her!" Tears were rolling down her cheeks. "You did that, Paul! Why couldn't you leave it the way it was?"

"She was your mother. You have to understand—"

"I hate you!" she screamed at him. "Do you understand that? I hate you for making me feel this way!"

*   *   *

Carter drove with one eye on the rearview mirror. Mr. Paul had stayed at the hospital to make the arrangements. The little girl was all alone in the back seat, hunched over and bawling her eyes out.

It was all he could do not to cry, too.

How could you know a man and not know him at all? He would have staked his life on Mr. Paul's love for that little girl—and yet, look what he had done to her.

And for what?

Irene Royal was the scum of the earth. He had seen her drunk and filthy. Heard her lewd language. And worst of all he knew what she had tried to do with her little girl. She wasn't fit to have a daughter like Savannah.

Mr. Paul wasn't fit to have her for a wife. Not after what he did today.

Carter gripped the wheel so hard his knuckles whitened. For forty-eight years he had put Mr. Paul's well-being above his own.

No more.

From now on, his first loyalty went to that little girl in the back seat.

The calls stopped.

At first Andrew lived by the phone, certain that Irene would call at any minute. But when three weeks turned into six, he forced himself to face facts. Irene had milked him as much as she intended to and then moved·on. He wondered if she realized she could have had everything he owned if she had just continued to call. He made a few halfhearted efforts to have her traced, but he knew it was in vain.

How cruel life was.

He would have preferred never knowing about Edward's child to this.

Damn all women anyway!

Paul gave the matter plenty of long, hard thought. He wasn't going to be around forever. That fact was becoming clearer to him with each passing day. He had been in for his annual physical the week before and his doctor had been more vehement than ever about slowing down and watching his diet. There was a tiredness in his bones these days that warned him the doctor just might be right. It was time he took some steps to insure Savannah's future happiness.

Having had her life arranged for her for all these years, being as sheltered as she had been, had led her to believe she didn't have to face anything she didn't want to face. Whether she hated him for it or not, that would have to change.

It never occurred to Paul that he was still doing the same thing—trying to arrange Savannah's life for her.

The problem, as he saw it, was that he had far too much money. If she inherited the bulk of his fortune, it would be a barrier and not a shield—that kind of wealth would cut her off from normal relationships and make it impossible for her to remarry. Although Paul had revised his will to make Savannah his primary heir, he intended to change that now. He would see that she still had enough money to live comfortably, more than enough, and of course there would be the movie and modeling money which had been held in trust for her—but she would not have the kind of great wealth she would have had as his widow under his present will. The pre-nuptial agreement she had signed at his lawyer's insistence would make sure she could not challenge his will. He would give Vincent Tate a call this afternoon.

Vincent Tate had been waiting for this day for four years, ever since Paul Marsdon had made a fool of himself by marrying an eighteen-year-old girl. The pre-nuptial agreement he had worked up for Marsdon had been a jewel. Marsdon could do anything he wanted with his money and she wouldn't have a legal leg to stand on.

Tate genuinely liked his client, and he had been horrified when he met the girl's mother. To think that a man as fine as Marsdon had fallen into the clutches of women like that.

Of course, you couldn't warn someone when they were suffering from the malady known as true love. But Tate had shuddered every time he saw Savannah Marsdon's photograph in the papers or a headline with her name.

But at last, Marsdon had come to his senses. Vincent Tate followed his client's instructions to the letter, with a few extra legal twists added to make sure that promiscuous bitch didn't get her fingers on a single cent more than Paul Marsdon intended for her to have.

Paul was acting strangely these days, Garnet thought.

She couldn't quite put her finger on it, but something about him had been different in the weeks since Savannah's mother died.

Garnet had been hurt, deeply hurt, by his inattention while Irene Royale was in the hospital. He and Savannah had quarreled, and the air remained cool between them. But to Garnet's dismay, her relationship with Paul seemed to have floundered. He no longer seemed interested in her sexually, although she was certain he still was not sleeping with his wife. Had she been `outflanked once more? Garnet wondered. Was there yet another woman in Paul Marsdon's life?

It was the suspicion she might have an unknown rival that made her take to prowling through Paul's things while he was at work and Savannah was locked in her studio. That was how Garnet found his notes for a new will.

She had to admire the beauty of it. Vincent Tate was a genius. Everyone would get a share of Paul's money, a small share. There was even a tiny bequest for Garnet herself. However, the majority of Paul's fortune would go into various trust funds and charities. She crumpled the notes in disgust before she realized what she was doing.

Quickly, she smoothed them out and put them back where she had found them. Her attempts to rekindle an affair with Paul met with defeat, and Garnet finally realized she had no hope of becoming his fifth wife. But she had expected he would be more generous than this in his will. Once more, she had been shortchanged.

That evening, when the three of them sat around the dinner table, Garnet viewed him with a more jaundiced and critical eye than she had in some time, and what she saw, she did not like. The active antagonism between himself and Savannah since Irene's death had taken its toll on him. His color was bad. He looked old, far older than his sixty-one years, and very tired.

Savannah, at the other end of the table, fairly glowed with health. The gap between them seemed more than forty years. Tonight Paul looked old enough to be her grandfather, and Garnet wondered how she herself looked to Paul. Had she aged as badly as he had? Was that why she had not been able to snare him again?

Savannah left them to return to her studio as soon as dinner was finished, and Paul strolled into the next room. Garnet drifted over to the antique mirror above the sideboard to check her reflection in the glass. She was caught up in the contemplation of the faint networking of wrinkles at the corners of her eyes when she heard Paul's footsteps. He called her name.

"I have a little errand I need to do tonight," he said with uncharacteristic hesitation in his speech, as though he were forcing each word out. "Would you mind driving me out to the Malibu house?"

She looked at him curiously. "Me?"

"I . . . I'd rather no one else knew I was going out there. Even Carter."

Her curiosity was running rampant, but Garnet merely said, "Of course, Paul. I'll just get my purse."

* * *

The Malibu house was dark when she pulled into the drive. She looked across at Paul and was alarmed to find him slumped against the seat. "Are you all right?"

He straightened with an effort. "I'm just tired. It's been a long day."

"Couldn't whatever you're doing have waited until morning?"

"I don't know," Paul said softly.

She sat behind the wheel for a moment until she realized he was not going to get out first and open her door. Instead, he waited for her to come around and open his for him. He took her arm and leaned on her heavily as they walked into the house. "You're not feeling well, are you?"

"I think I've got a touch of something," Paul told her. "Just help me into the study."

She assisted him into the chair behind his desk, and he asked her to open the safe, calling out the combination to her. When she did, she found that there was only one object inside: a thick file stuffed with papers, photographs, and newspaper clippings.

"Lay it in the fireplace," Paul told her.

When she had done so, he rose with an effort and went over to kneel beside the fireplace. He looked through the file for a moment, and then, taking a matchbook from his pocket, he struck one and held it to the edge of the file.

"Paul! Are you sure you know what you're doing?" she asked as it began to blaze.

He didn't answer. He stood up slowly, grabbing the edge of the fireplace for support and started back toward the desk. Halfway there, he gasped and clutched at his chest.

"Paul?"

He reeled against the desk and fell heavily.

Garnet stood where she was for a moment, watching his still body, face down on the oriental rug. Then she rushed to the fireplace and tried to stamp out the fire he had set there.

One photograph, untouched by the flames, went flying out of the file and she stooped to retrieve it. It was of a beautiful nude child of three or four who could only have been Savannah Royale Marsdon. It was so beautiful and so terrifyingly sexual that Garnet very nearly threw it back into the flames. Had it not been for the price she knew she could get for it, that was exactly what she would have done.

Instead, she slipped it into her purse. Then she reached for the phone to call the paramedics, although she already knew their trip would be in vain.

BOOK III

Lucette

Chapter 15

The golden vision miraculously appeared on the sand below on the evening of the second day.

Above the beach, on the redwood deck, Devon Blake halted, mid-motion, the act of removing his T-shirt as the cotton cleared his eyes and he caught sight of her.

Transfixed, his arms still entangled in the fabric over his head, he watched her jog past, leaving graceful narrow footprints in the wet sand beyond the surf's reach, and it seemed to him that he had forgotten the simple mechanics of breathing until she was out of sight. He had never considered himself a romantic, but as he stared at the delicate tracery her bare feet had left along the beach, he wondered if he shouldn't try to preserve it in some way before the waves could erase it—as evidence that a fantasy creature had really passed this way.

When Devon realized his brain was actually dwelling on the logistics involved in acquiring a sack of plaster of Paris before the tide came in again, he decided that the golden beauty had been sent by some higher being to save his sanity. He shrugged the rest of the way out of the T-shirt and tossed it onto the railing. Popping inside only long enough to get himself a cold beer, he settled down on the lounger to watch for her return.

Two weeks to himself in a friend's house at Malibu to repair mind and body after eighteen months nonstop work on the Colvin project—the offer had seemed like heaven at the time. But it had taken only twenty-four hours before Devon (at twenty-eight, California's fastest rising young architect—at least that's what *California Magazine* had called him last month) was ready to climb the walls.

He had been angered to discover, when the *California* article came out three months after the interview, that the writer had labeled him a workaholic. Almost as enraged as he was by the articles that appeared every time his mother cajoled him into attending a political fundraiser or campaigning for a candidate—articles that kept raising the question of whether he was finally ready to follow in his father's footsteps.

But as the afternoon crawled by, minute by excruciating minute, and Devon found himself calculating and recalculating how much "enforced rest" time he had left to serve before he could return to his office again, he reluctantly conceded that the interviewer might have been right after all.

Unfortunately, he had expressed his objection to the term vehemently to everyone in his firm when the article came out; if he cut his vacation as much as five minutes short, he knew he would never hear the end of it. He was doomed to suffer through the remainder of the two-week sentence without reprieve.

Until the golden beauty appeared.

It was half an hour before she made the return trip along the sand, walking now instead of jogging. A huge black man, his bald head shining like a beacon in the dying light, followed twenty feet behind her, and something in his posture or stride proclaimed, "I am here to protect this woman."

Devon realized with a little shock of astonishment that the man must have been with her the first time she passed by, but Devon had not registered his presence. The golden beauty had captured his attention completely.

A couple appeared from between the next two houses and started purposefully across the beach toward her. They had the look of autograph hunters after their prey, and Devon wondered if she was an actress. Movies were something he'd had no time for since high school; in fact, high school was the last time he'd had an interest in any activities that didn't touch on architecture. He had begun to wonder lately if that was—and continued to be—a reaction to his mother's urgent desire to push him into politics.

The black man quickened his pace so that the couple's path would intercept his before they could reach the beautiful woman. The couple caught sight of him and turned away abruptly. From his vantage point, Devon could read the embarrassment on their faces as they walked quickly back the way they had come.

His duty done, the black man slowed his pace,

dropping back until he was again following her at the precise distance as before. The woman continued to stroll along the edge of the surf, head down, studying the rippled patterns left by the waves on the sand. She gave no sign she was aware that the little drama had been played out between her bodyguard and the couple, or that she had an appreciative audience on the redwood deck above.

Devon, standing now, put both hands on the railing and leaned forward into the breeze off the ocean, watching the woman and her companion continue down the beach.

When he could no longer see them, he went down the stairs to the beach. Turning in the direction she had been jogging when he first saw her, he followed the double set of footprints she and her bodyguard had left on the sand. Two miles down the beach, he found the spot where she had turned around. The sun had long ago dipped below the ocean, but the moon was up, and by its light he could see where the two of them had stood and talked.

He wondered what they had talked about.

He wondered who she was.

When he, too, turned back, the tide was coming in, erasing her footprints from the sand. Before he drew even with his own deck, every trace of her had vanished.

He put Mozart on the stereo—*Eine Kleine Nachtmusik* and the *Clarinet Quintet*—and sat on the deck for a long time watching the black waves rolling in out of the night before he finally went in to bed.

*   *   *

The next two evenings he watched from the deck as she walked or jogged along the beach, just at the edge of the water, letting the surf break over her bare toes. The bodyguard was with her, always the same twenty feet behind her.

On the third evening, he nearly panicked when she did not appear at the same time. He was berating himself for not trying to find out who she was, not trying to introduce himself to her there on the beach, bodyguard or not, when he suddenly caught sight of her.

Her golden brown hair was bathed in the warm red glow of sunset when she passed below him on the beach. For once, her gigantic bodyguard was not in attendance. When he realized that, Devon was galvanized to action. By the time he dashed down the steps to the sand, she was two hundred feet away, jogging into the fast-approaching night.

He sprinted after her.

By the time he reached her, she had slowed to a walk again. The conversational opening he'd been perfecting as he pounded down the beach after her vanished from his mind when she turned and he got his first glimpse of her eyes.

For the past two nights he had lain awake wondering what color they were. Now he couldn't understand how he could have considered anything but clear green flecked with gold. In the end, all he could think to say was, "I'm Devon."

She hesitated, as if she were searching his words for some double meaning. Finally she said, "I'm Savannah."

This close, he was mesmerized by her beauty, the creamy ivory skin with its golden undertones, the mane of champagne curls surrounding her face like a halo, the proud thrust of her breasts beneath the thin fabric of the maillot. He wanted to drink her in, every bit of her.

"Did you want something?" she asked finally, when he did not speak. Her puzzled frown made a tiny little wrinkle between her eyebrows. He wondered what it would be like to put his lips on that spot.

To carry you off on a white stallion. To marry you and lock you away in my castle for the rest of my life. "Will you have dinner with me tomorrow night?"

She was frowning now and he cursed himself for a fool. Why couldn't he have started off with something more subtle, before blurting out his dinner invitation like that? He stood there stoically, like a condemned prisoner, waiting for her to refuse.

Instead, she said, "I'm Savannah Marsdon," and waited for his reaction.

"I'm Devon Blake."

She was still frowning as she lifted her left hand to shove her hair away from her eyes, and he realized the heavy gold band she wore was probably a wedding ring. The thought hadn't even crossed his mind; now it hit him like a poleax. "You're married?"

"I'm a widow."

His relief was so great that he had blurted out, "Oh, good," before he realized what he was saying, and he found himself blushing like a boy. "I didn't mean that like it sounded. It was just that . . . I've been wanting to meet you ever since the first evening I saw you jogging along the beach and . . .''

She was smiling at him. "I'd love to have dinner with you."

His elation at her acceptance vanished as soon as he realized how many hours lay between now and tomorrow night. "What about breakfast?"

He felt like a gauche teenager as she gave him a puzzled look. "Instead of dinner, you mean?"

"No, plus dinner. Plus lunch." His heart pounded. "Plus, can I walk you home?"

Savannah darted an occasional sidewise glance at Devon Blake as they walked along in silence, but mostly she kept her head down, hoping he wouldn't see how nervous she was. His shadowy presence beside her in the darkness reminded her for the first time in ages of the Prince, the childhood fantasy figure who had sustained her for so many lonely years. Devon Blake had appeared out of nowhere with his black eyes and his black hair to charm her and make her laugh. He was handsome enough to be the Prince, and there was something about him that made her think he was used to telling other people what to do. The Prince would have that air of authority.

It was hard to relax. Just being around people frightened her now. Six months ago, when Paul died, all the solid supports of her life had come crashing down around her. Everything she thought was real had vanished with the phone call that told her Paul was dead. She learned, that night, that no one was what they seemed. No one was to be trusted. Not

Paul. Not Garnet. Not his friends who had pretended to accept her while he was alive. Not even her own perception of herself.

She had experienced at the funeral, with the intensity of a bomb burst, just what the public thought of her, as hordes of bystanders shouting insults and accusations vied with reporters, cameramen, and photographers for a glimpse of Paul Marsdon's young widow. When the graveside service ended, she was almost trampled in the crush. Paul's children were there, all of them, and Savannah could still remember the scornful looks on their faces as they watched the crowd surge around her. None of them made an effort to pull her free of the mob. Her veil was torn away, her hat trampled, her dress ripped. Only Carter's strong shoulder had saved her from physical harm by clearing a path from Paul's grave to the limousine. She carried the bruises the crowd's grasping hands had left on her body for weeks. The bruises had long since faded, but six months had not stilled her distrust of people—former friends and strangers alike. She had learned to watch for the look of disgust that flickered over a stranger's face when she gave her name, the sign that she had been judged on the evidence presented by the media and convicted without a trial.

She hadn't seen that look in Devon Blake's eyes, not yet, but she could feel her shoulders tensing as she waited for the blow to fall. The fact that he hadn't reacted to her name had thrown her off guard. Now she was regretting her impulsive acceptance of his invitation to breakfast. At the stairs to her deck, she paused and turned to face him squarely.

"You're sorry you said yes," he blurted out before she could speak. "You don't know anything about me. I could be a really horrible person. But I'm not, I promise you." His boyish smile made her heart beat faster. "I'll bring references. I'll introduce you to my mother. Anything you ask. Only please have breakfast with me."

Savannah realized that, in spite of everything that had happened in the past six months, that was exactly what she was going to do.

Carter watched from the darkened house as Savannah turned to the man beside her and laughed, a wonderful musical sound that he hardly ever heard and had despaired of ever hearing again. Theodora had called him several times since Mr. Paul had died, asking what he was going to do with himself now. She couldn't or wouldn't understand how much Savannah still needed him.

That poor little girl had been thrown for a loop when Mr. Paul died. Carter still couldn't understand how Mr. Paul could have done some of the things he did. Why had he made her visit Irene in the hospital? And why in the world would a man married to Savannah want to have an affair with Garnet Hoffman? Carter knew they had been lovers before, but he had thought that particular flame had burned out long ago. Only he couldn't ignore the reality. Mr. Paul had died in Garnet's arms at the Malibu house, and Garnet had wasted no time giving out interviews about her relationship with Mr. Paul.

The funeral had been worse than anything he could possibly have imagined. He had never realized people could be such savages. Savannah was so shaken by the experience that she refused to set one foot out of the house. That was when Mr. Paul's lawyer had let her know that Mr. Paul had changed the terms of his will so that not even the house was to be hers. Carter could have sworn the man took a vicious pleasure in being the bearer of bad news.

He still couldn't understand why Mr. Paul had changed his will, making it look to all the world like he had cut his young wife out of his life. Oh, she would still have money, but not the great wealth that would have been hers as Paul Marsdon's heir. To the public it looked as though Mr. Paul were punishing her for her supposed unfaithfulness. The details of the pre-nuptial contract had been printed in every paper along with the provisions of the will.

Carter tried his best to shield her, but suddenly Savannah was bombarded at every turn with the vicious rumors that had circulated during the three years of her marriage. The truth of her negative public image shattered the protective shell Paul had placed around her during those years. In the space of a few short days, she found out that the public believed she'd had multiple affairs both before her marriage and during it. She was an old man's darling, a vicious little gold digger. Now she understood why people had reacted to her the way they did, and she was devastated. When she found that Paul had deeded a house in Malibu to Garnet, an action that seemed to bolster Garnet's claim that she and Paul had been lovers for longer than Savannah had been alive, that was the last straw. She could have stayed in the Bel Air house a few more weeks, but instead she had gone to Carter in tears and asked him to find her somewhere else to live. She could no longer stay there, reminded as she was at every turn of how much she had misjudged Paul Marsdon. Her hurt and bitterness was almost more than Carter could bear.

Now, watching the couple on the sand below, he was glad he had chosen this Malibu beach house. He had seen the man watching them from his deck as they walked along the shore each evening, and he had recognized the look in the man's black eyes as they followed Savannah. It was the same look he'd had himself, so many years ago, when he watched eighteen-year-old Odessa Williams walking down the street. He had purposely stayed at the house tonight, knowing the man couldn't resist the opportunity to approach her. He had been right, and as he watched Savannah's joyful face, glowing in the moonlight as she looked up at the tall man beside her, Carter smiled.

"But this restaurant is closed," Savannah said, perplexed, as Devon Blake opened the door of his car for her. He had picked her up at seven A.M.

"Not for us."

"But . . ." In spite of the empty parking lot, he was whisking her inside the big double doors. The headwaiter ushered them into the dining room and

Savannah saw that one table—and only one—was elaborately set for breakfast, garnished with a dozen red roses.

She laughed delightedly. "But why?"

"I thought we might have more fun this morning *without* my mother here to vouch for me," he said as the waiter brought champagne and orange juice. "This seemed like the next best thing."

They talked about everything. Or rather, he talked and she listened. He knew so much more than she did. He talked about books, music, and architecture . . . about how his mother wanted him to be a politician like his father, and how sometimes he almost thought it wouldn't be such a bad idea. She listened, enthralled, and wished that she didn't always feel so stupid, so childish. Not that it was his fault, of course. It was just that every day it became more apparent to her how little she really knew. Between Mama's strictness and Paul's protectiveness, she had missed out on so much of life. She feared that she would never catch up.

"You're too good a listener," he said at last. "I've never told anyone all this before."

She dipped her head shyly. "Thank you for sharing it with me."

"But I want to know about you."

She had opened like a rose while he talked, and now she could feel herself closing up into a tight bud of resentment. Was this the way the most wonderful morning in her life was going to end? Was the Devon Blake she thought she had glimpsed during breakfast as much of a mirage as everyone else? "What do you want to know?"

"Don't," he said softly, reaching across the table to take her hand. "I'm not trying to pry open your innermost secrets. Not yet."

He said it with a wry little grin that almost made her laugh, and then the weight of the past six months settled down on her once more. What was there about her that hadn't already appeared in the newspapers? Thinking of what *had* appeared there, all the awful lies, she colored. "I design jewelry." That seemed like the most innocuous topic she could bring up about her life.

"Do you sell your designs?"

"I— No— Not yet. They're not good enough yet. It's just a hobby. My husband used to have my designs made up for me at first. And then I took some lessons."

"Could I see some of your work?"

She was startled by the apparent sincerity of his interest. "I haven't done anything in a long time." She hadn't realized that until now. "Not since . . . not since my husband died."

"When did he die?"

"Six months ago," she said slowly. She had assumed everyone knew that. Just as everyone knew who she was without being introduced. Just as no one really knew her at all. Tears spilled past her lashes suddenly, and she turned away.

He came around the table to her and knelt beside her chair. "Savannah? Look at me?"

She shook her head, biting her lip to keep the tears from overflowing again.

He took her chin in his hand and gently turned her face to his. With the other hand, he took her napkin and dabbed at the tears. Then he leaned forward, touched his lips to hers for just the briefest moment, and everything in the room stopped.

As Devon rocked back on his heels, he found himself without words. For the son of one of the congressional masters of filibuster and an accomplished public speaker in his own right, that was an unheard of state.

He stood up and pulled her up beside him.

They left the restaurant without speaking, ignoring the stares of the waiters. No one else existed on earth as far as Devon was concerned. He helped her into the car and drove without thinking. He had parked the car and slipped the key from the ignition before he realized that in his dazed state he had brought her directly to his beach house.

Getting out of the car first, he pulled off his jacket and his tie and opened his shirt collar. He stepped out of his shoes and tossed them and his socks into the backseat with his jacket and tie.

He came around to her side of the car and opened the door. But instead of taking her arm to help her out, he knelt at her feet and pulled off the little high heeled sandals she was wearing. "You have elegant feet," he murmured. "I followed your footprints all the way down the beach."

"I never thought about my feet being elegant,"

she said with an expression of great wonder in her eyes.

"What about these?" he said, stroking the back of his hand down her right leg.

"I'll do that."

She reached under the full skirt of her dress and removed the pantyhose with lithe grace.

"You do that like a model."

She looked at him, startled.

"Should I know who you are?" he teased. "Fashion is not my strong suit. I never read *Vogue* or *Woman's Wear Daily*."

"I've been on the cover of *Vogue*," she admitted. "Yesterday, I thought . . . I thought you recognized me."

"I did," he said, leaning forward to touch his lips to hers again. "You're the woman I've been waiting for all of my life."

When Savannah didn't return, Carter broke out in a cold sweat. She had told him breakfast and here it was nearly noon. Had he made a terrible mistake last night, bringing her together with that man? His heart told him no, remembering her happy laughter in the moonlight, but he no longer trusted his impulses, not after he had been so wrong, so tragically wrong, about Paul Marsdon.

He got out the car and drove down the highway toward the man's house, frustration mounting with every mile. When he drew within sight of the house, he saw the man's car sitting in the driveway.

Carter pulled over to the side of the road and

parked. He had no desire to go bursting in on something that was none of his business. But, then, Savannah Marsdon's safety and well-being *was* his business. He debated with himself for several minutes, before he finally got out of the car, slamming the door with unnecessary vigor. He stomped around to the back of the car and took out the pair of binoculars he kept in the trunk.

Climbing up on the hood, he trained the binoculars on the beach house. There wasn't a sign of life anywhere. He sighed, wondering what he should do, when a movement in the surf caught his glance. He swung the glasses that way and adjusted the focus.

Savannah and the man were frolicking in the surf, splashing water on each other, running and tumbling in the waves like happy children. Carter spent a few seconds calculating the cost of the man's suit and Savannah's silk dress, and shook his head. Then he focused the glasses on Savannah's face and the look he saw there made him laugh out loud with pleasure.

The temptation to continue watching was strong, but Carter forced himself to slide down off the hood and put the binoculars back in their case. He might wax the car this afternoon, he thought as he put the glasses back in the trunk. It didn't look like Savannah would be needing him for some time.

They were standing in the living room, just inside the glass doors. The bedroom lay beyond, with its king-sized bed, but they hadn't gotten that far yet.

Devon unbuttoned the front of her dress, pushing away the soaked silk. He touched his lips to the tops of her breasts showing above the lace of her bra and found them chill to the touch. He reached behind her to unfasten the bra, and then leaned forward to warm them with his face. He turned his head slightly and took her nipple between his lips, caressing the tip of it with quick, darting motions of his tongue.

She gasped with pleasure and held him close. There was an answering throb in his groin so strong that he could barely discern it was pleasure instead of pain. *Patience*, he told himself. He had always been a patient and considerate lover, and it was more important to him than ever before in his life that he be so now.

He forced himself to remain motionless for a moment, allowing himself only the pleasure of his cheek against the cool, firm globe of her breast, until the urgent desire to take her, to lose himself in her exquisite flesh, was controlled again. "Do you want to shower first?" he whispered into the damp gold strands of her hair. "It will warm you."

"I'm so warm, I'm burning," she said. She touched his bare chest with her long cool fingers and he knew he was lost.

Chapter 15

"Devon, darling, when are you going to bring your new friend to meet the family?" his mother asked one afternoon when he had come by for tea in response to her invitation. "Charles saw you whisking her into a limousine somewhere up the coast last week." Charles was his uncle, Congressman Lewis. "According to Charles, she's quite beautiful. In fact, he said if looks counted for anything, she would be a great asset if you ever decided to run for office."

"I'm delighted to have Charles' opinion of her political value. As far as I'm concerned, having someone like Uncle Charles in office is a good argument against the democratic form of government," Devon quipped, trying to avoid the little flurry of guilt his mother's words stirred in him. The truth was Savannah hated going out, and he had forced her into that little excursion very much against her will. He was ready to show her off proudly to his family and friends, but she balked every time the prospect came up. When it finally occurred to him she was worried

about seeing people, about being recognized, he realized she must still consider herself in mourning for
her husband. He had the impression it had not been a
happy marriage, but she obviously preferred not to
talk about it. For his part, he didn't like to think of
her with somebody else—making love to someone
else—not even the husband who had died before he
met her.

His mother refilled his teacup. Tall and slender,
with iron-gray hair, she looked so perfectly at home
surrounded by her fragile French antiques in the spacious living room of her Beverly Hills mansion that it
was hard to imagine she had any existence outside it.
Yet she was a tireless campaigner and fundraiser, on
the road for her candidates for weeks at a time. She
sat the teapot down and confronted him with her
calm gray glance. "I do hope you took the time to
check her out before you became too involved with
her."

Devon bristled and tried to hide it. Amanda Lewis
Blake's grandfather had been a congressman, as had
her father, and her husband. She had never given up
the idea of having her son run for political office, and
heaven help him, occasionally he considered it. He
knew he could do a better job than Uncle Charles—or
half the other candidates he had met through his
parents. But he knew, too, that it had to be his own
idea. He had seen her take his father, a man with no
political ambitions of his own, and push him into a
lifelong career in Washington, just to satisfy her own
longings. She should have run for office herself, he
thought. But he would wager the thought had never

occurred to her. Devon's father had achieved her ambition for her; he had made her the wife of a congressman and given her twenty years in Washington before he died. Robert Blake had punished her, too. The two of them had ended up with a marriage in name only, more concerned with appearances than actualities. That thought opened too many old wounds and unleashed Devon's temper. "Since I'm not going to run for public office, I didn't see any need to 'check her out.' Did it ever occur to you that two people could fall in love and not give a damn about how it might look to their constituents?"

"Don't swear, darling," Amanda said automatically, but Devon was already on his way out of the house.

No, she answered his question to herself, it had never occurred to her that two people would do *anything* without wondering how it might look to their constituents.

She wondered if Devon knew how much he frightened her with his uncompromisingly honest approach to life, his annoying preoccupation with the truth. He had judged her very harshly for putting up with his father's little peccadillos, but he had judged his father even more harshly for living a lie. No doubt he would chastise her even more strongly if he found out she'd had discreet entertainments of her own on the side. Unfortunately, he wasn't mature enough yet to realize that in politics, discretion was more important than honesty.

She frowned as she considered Devon's annoyance at her maternal questioning. He seemed far more

protective of this mystery lady than he had of past
conquests. She wondered just who his new friend
might be. Her brother had been so struck by the
beauty of Devon's girlfriend that he had babbled on
about it for a good quarter of an hour. It was too bad
that Charles, and not Amanda, had been their father's
son. Both Amanda and her father had realized how much
better suited she was for public office than poor,
foolish Charles. And, of course, how impossible it
was for a woman of her generation and breeding to
even consider such a thing.

Amanda sighed. The only useful information she
had gotten out of Charles was that he was sure he
recognized the young woman, although he could not
recall who she was. But, Charles had added, Devon
seemed enchanted by her—something both Amanda
and Charles had found startling. Not that Devon had
ever lacked for girlfriends. It was just that none of
them had ever managed to hold his attention for any
length of time.

Actually, she was pleased that Devon had been
caught up too intensely, first in school and then in his
own architectural firm, to become deeply involved
with anyone until now. A handsome bachelor could
present a very attractive image to the voters.

Amanda drummed her fingers on the table. She
was rather annoyed with her son these days. She had
given him the five years since his father's death to
come to his senses. Her own father had insisted that
was the best course of action. The boy would come
around, her father had told her in the weeks after his
son-in-law's death. However, Devon still continued

to resist his natural call to the political arena, and Amanda knew that her father, now eighty, longed to see some sign that their family dynasty would continue. She also knew that the burden lay solely on her. Charles' son was as foolish as his father, but without the charisma that attracted voters to his elder.

Devon was the family's only hope. Unfortunately, he had either laughed at or ignored her attempts to exert a little maternal pressure. She was frankly at a loss as to what to try next.

Would his new friend be a help or a hindrance?

Some women loved the thought of being married to a powerful politician. Others, for whom Amanda had no empathy at all, shrank from it.

Which was Devon's mystery woman?

Amanda knew she would have to see the lady for herself to judge.

Meanwhile, there was another tack to try. There was one old friend she knew she could count on to nudge Devon in the direction he should go, a man Devon really admired. She reached for her ever-present notebook and jotted his name at the top of the list.

She thought for a moment and then swiftly added half-a-dozen others, men whose assessment of Devon's potential she could count on—and whose own interest in him as a potential candidate would be aroused by that same question. Amanda was not her father's daughter for nothing.

She went upstairs to make her calls.

Devon let himself into his Hollywood Boulevard

condominium and went in search of Savannah. She hadn't moved in with him as yet, but she might as well have. They spent most of their weeknights here, although she still refused to stay the entire night. She insisted that Carter take her home to her Malibu beach house each evening. She would call Devon as soon as she got there, and sometimes he would fall asleep with her soft sultry voice whispering in his ear, just as though she were still in the bed with him. Weekends, they spent at her beach house. He would arrive late Friday night and leave after six on Sunday evenings. The nights he wasn't able to see her at all, he found himself missing her more than he thought humanly possibly.

He found her on the terrace, sketching something on a drawing pad. She was working on her jewelry designs again, although she refused to show him anything yet. "I've gotten rusty," she had complained. "I've forgotten everything I learned."

"Are you going to let me see that?" he asked, leaning forward to kiss her on top of her head. The mass of golden hair smelled as good as a summer meadow.

She had stuck the pad behind her back as soon as he spoke, and now she shook her head mischievously.

"Never?"

"How about when it's made up?"

He grinned with delight. "You've come up with a design you like?"

Excitedly she began to tell him about it. Silhouetted against the Hollywood Hills, she was glowing with such beauty and vitality that all he could think of was sweeping her off her feet and into bed. "You're not listening," she accused suddenly.

"I was thinking how beautiful you are." He pulled her back into the apartment and began to unbutton her blouse. He loved the little shiver of delight that she gave when it came open and he kissed the lovely ivory valley between her breasts. "You would make a wonderful politician's wife," he said lazily, letting one hand trail up her long sensual leg, beneath her skirt, until his fingers found the warm moistness of her. She squirmed against him with a moan of delight. "There isn't a man in the state who wouldn't vote for me if they could see you like this."

She tried to move away, but his hand refused to give up the prize. "You're an architect, not a politician," she protested.

"It was just something my mother mentioned today," he said soothingly, while his fingers probed deeper. She arched against him then, and he forgot everything else but the need to bury himself in her.

Carter picked her up outside Devon Blake's condominium building just before midnight. Savannah had a warm contented look on her face that made him feel good. He had done a fine job bringing those two together. He could tell Devon Blake wasn't the kind of man to let his woman keep running off from his bed each night for much longer. If things kept going the way they were, there would be wedding bells before long. It was time he stopped thinking of those two and started thinking about Nolan Carter.

He had plenty of time to himself to think things

over these days. He knew he could stay on as a
driver for Devon and Savannah if that was what he
wanted, but he'd been thinking a lot lately about
retiring. Maybe even trying to get back with Odessa.
After all, he was sixty-six years old now. He had
mentioned to Theodora last week that he was thinking about hanging up his chauffeur's cap, but he
hadn't let on to her that he'd like to get back together
with her mama. That gal's steamroller tactics wouldn't
work on Odessa, and he didn't want her getting
Odessa's dander up before he had a chance to sweet
talk her himself.

Theodora had hidden her feelings with her usual
gruffness, but Carter could tell that she was really
pleased at the prospect of having her daddy to herself
for a change.

Savannah's periods had always been erratic, so at
first she didn't realize that they had ceased entirely.
When it finally occurred to her that it had been at
least a month and a half since her last menstrual
flow, she was elated. After the four years of her
marriage to Paul, she had given up hope that she
might ever have a child of her own.

She slipped off her dress and peeled out of her
underthings and regarded herself in the mirror of
Devon's dresser.

Were her breasts fuller? Was the curve of her
stomach less flat?

She turned this way and that, but she could see no
outward sign of what she suspected.

The click of Devon's key in the lock was followed by his voice calling her name.

Leaving her clothes where they lay, she went to welcome him home, hugging the happy possibility to herself like a treasure.

Amanda Blake clenched the phone with white-knuckled hands, listening to the calm voice of her father on the other end of the line. She had waited for her son to bring the lady in question to meet her, but despite hints, pleas, and suggestions, Devon proved to be intractable, as usual. She had had no alternative but to investigate the woman's character on her own. Especially since she had received positive feedback to the feelers she had put out regarding Devon and politics.

At least Robert was no longer alive to stand between his son and a political career, she thought and sighed heavily. Although, heaven knows, that would have been the last thing Robert intended. But Devon had become so fixated on what he termed his father's hypocrisy that Amanda knew there would have been no chance of talking Devon into what she had in mind if his father had not died. Thank God she had her own father to lean on. Edwin Lewis, even at eighty, had few peers in the art and craft of American politics. He was convinced his grandson would go far, perhaps even as far as Pennsylvania Avenue, if they could simply channel him in the right direction. Above all, Edwin had impressed upon her, outward appearance was the most important thing. Devon had already developed a fair reputation for honesty in his business dealings. That would be extremely useful as they helped him take his rightful place in politics.

When she received the report on Devon's new girl-friend, Amanda's immediate reaction was that all was lost. How *could* Devon have been so stupid as to involve himself with that kind of woman?

Luckily, her first move, as always, had been to consult her father, and Edwin's stern voice over the phone quieted her tears and went far toward allaying her fears. "It's all in how you approach him," Edwin told her. "We're lucky that he's been so secretive up until now." And that the woman, apparently weary of the notoriety she had received after her husband's death, had not tried to publicize this relationship with Devon.

Amanda's heart fluttered as she thought of her son's photograph appearing on the front page of some of the tabloids the investigator had shown her. She began to cry again, but silently, so that her father did not realize it as he gave her detailed instructions on how to present the matter to Devon.

"The test result is positive. You're definitely pregnant, Mrs. Smith. I'll transfer you to the receptionist so that you can set up your next appointment with the doctor."

Savannah caught sight of her face in the mirror as she waited for the receptionist. She was grinning like an idiot. Now that her suspicions were confirmed, she felt like dancing in the street. She had wanted a baby for so long, had felt so incomplete, and now she was finally going to have one—and not just a baby, but Devon's child. Her happiness was complete.

She would tell him tonight.

Devon sat down so heavily the gilt Louis XV chair creaked, the stack of newspaper clippings still clutched in his hands and a shell-shocked expression on his face. It was obvious to Amanda that he had suspected nothing like this of the woman he had been dating. Her heart sunk when she also realized from his despair how serious the relationship must have become.

"I'm shocked that she didn't tell you any of this herself." Amanda considered carefully and then spoke the words that she and her father had agreed would wound him above all else. "I'm afraid she's not a very honest person, Devon."

There was so much raw pain in the look he gave her that she regretted for an instant that she had been the one to shatter his illusions about this woman.

But only for an instant.

Devon was late, today of all days.

Savannah closed the vertical blinds in the living room, shutting out the view of downtown Los Angeles and Century City, along with the late afternoon sun. Then, too nervous to sit inside, she carried a stack of magazines out onto the terrace, where she sat flipping through them without seeing the pages, until she heard the sound of his key.

She jumped to her feet, scattering the magazines, and hurried back inside. "Devon?"

He did not answer. She found him sitting in one of

the black satin armchairs. There was something strange
in his face. Something cold and hard and icy, like
concealed rage. What could be wrong? Her only
thought was that someone must have died. Only a
terrible loss could give a man that kind of look.

He still did not speak. He simply looked at her as
though he had never seen her before in his life. She
couldn't imagine what was wrong. She clutched her
stomach protectively. All day she had waited, bubbling with anticipation, to tell him her news, and
now, much as she longed to, she knew it was not the
right moment. She had to wait, to wait until he got
whatever was troubling him off of his chest.

Savannah sat down across from him, primly, like a
little girl, back straight, knees together, hands clasped
in front of her, and waited for him to say whatever it
was aloud, so that they could both deal with it. When
he finally spoke, what he said was the last thing she
would have imagined.

"I've seen the stories in the newspapers."

Her heart lurched and faltered. It had been eight
months since Paul's death. Why were they attacking
her again? Her eyes flew to the morning paper lying
on the black marble tabletop. "I didn't see—"

"I was working so hard about the time your husband died that I didn't have time to keep up with the
news," he said. She realized he was not talking
about the current papers and began to relax a little.
"Before that I never read the kind of trashy tabloids
where someone like you would be featured."

It was as though he had struck her. She knew what
he was talking about. After Paul's death, Carter had

been forced to tell her what was happening and to show her some of the terrible stories so she would understand why people were reacting to her the way they were. "You know those stories weren't true."

"Do I?" He said it so calmly, so smugly, that she was stunned.

"Of course you do. You know I'm not that kind of person, Devon. Not the kind of woman who—"

"Who would marry a man forty years older than she was and torment him with a string of lovers?"

She was standing with the certainty of her innocence, her fists clenched at her sides. "I didn't do that!"

"Then explain one thing to me, Savannah. If you didn't, why did your husband cut you out of his will?"

Savannah shook her head in confusion. He had hit upon the one thing she could not explain. Not to herself, not to him. Why *had* Paul done what he had done? Was it to punish her for her obstinacy where Mama was concerned? Was it because he had fallen in love with Garnet Hoffman? She turned away, as defeated by her own suspicions as by the look of disbelief on Devon's face.

Before she realized what he was doing, he was beside her. Grabbing her roughly by the arm, he swung her around to face him. "Don't you walk away from me. I want to know the truth."

She tried to pull away and he yanked her back.

"Don't do that, Devon! I'm pregnant!"

He released her at once and stepped back. She couldn't tell if the disgust she saw so clearly on his face was for his own roughness or for what she had just said.

"When had you intended to make that little announcement?" he said after a moment.

"Tonight. I was going to tell you tonight. I just found out for sure today and—"

"I suppose you're going to claim it's mine."

She couldn't believe this was happening. How could he be so cruel? She knew this was not the real Devon. Not the man she had come to love. "Of course it's yours. You know it is."

"When did you start planning this little entrapment? When we first met? Or did you check out my credit rating first? I understand your husband left you a little short of funds when he died."

"I didn't plan anything. It just happened!"

"It doesn't just happen, lady. Not in this day and time. Did you forget your pills accidentally on purpose?"

The look of confusion that washed across her face gave him pause.

"You weren't using anything!"

"I didn't think I could get pregnant. All the time we were married I tried but—I wanted a baby so badly, but nothing happened—and when I asked Paul he wouldn't tell me—I thought there was something wrong with me. . . ."

"You really expect me to believe that, don't you?"

"If you love me . . ."

"How many times did you use that line on that poor old man you were married to?"

There was something about Devon now that reminded her of the young man who had tried to pick her up on Antigua. Finally she understood what that stranger had thought of her.

When she did not answer, Devon said, "I suppose you think I should be gallant at this point and offer to marry you."

She simply stared at him.

"None of your other lovers will step forward, I suppose?"

"I don't have any other lovers." It was barely a whisper and yet the effort of speaking the words aloud nearly crushed her.

"I believe even Carter was on that list. It was such a very long list that I can't remember everyone's names. I wonder if you can."

"I can't believe you are being so cruel. You know Carter. You know he's not my lover. He has been a wonderful friend to me. He has stood by me."

"I suppose you mean unlike me. Oh, I'll stand by you, Savannah. I wouldn't abandon a child of mine to the kind of life you would give it. But don't expect me to love you. I couldn't love someone who had deceived me the way you have."

"I don't want to marry you," she lashed out at him.

"Then what was this little charade about? Are you saying that you're not really pregnant?"

"I'm pregnant, but that's not a permanent condition, I assure you. I intend to do something about it."

He reached for her again, but she eluded his grasp. "I don't want you to have an abortion."

"But you don't want to marry me, either, do you? I'm sure this will be the best thing for both of us."

"Don't do something you'll regret," he warned her.

"I already did. I fell in love with you."

The tears were streaming down her face but her voice was calm.

He slumped back wearily. "I'll make the arrangements tomorrow. We can be married this weekend."

"I told you I don't want to marry you."

"You don't have any choice."

He insisted she spend the night there. Since he gave her no option, she made up a bed for herself in the guestroom and lay there wide awake, listening to the sounds of Devon moving around the apartment.

It was so clear to her now. She had let herself be seduced by a fantasy, not a real man. She had believed with all her heart that after all these years the Prince had finally come. Only Devon Blake wasn't the Prince. And she was no longer a child. She carried a real child in her body now; the fantasy was over.

She waited until the sounds ceased, until she was sure he had fallen asleep, and then she dressed quickly and let herself out of the apartment.

When Savannah called she was crying so hard that Carter couldn't make out what she was saying at first. Nothing but the fact that she wanted him to come for her right now. He recognized the address as an all-night coffee shop a few blocks from Devon Blake's Hollywood Boulevard address, and when he reached there and saw her looking so frail and lonely, peering through the plate glass window at the parking lot, his heart ached for her.

She rushed out to the Mercedes, and he saw that her face was streaked with tears. She sagged against him as though she had lost the will to stand. "What's wrong, Savannah?" He called her that now, but only when no one else was around. Otherwise it was "Mrs. Marsdon."

"Just take me home," she begged him.

Quickly he bundled her into the car and drove skillfully through the night streets, grateful for how little traffic was out at this hour, so that he could keep one eye on the rearview mirror. Had she had a fight with Devon Blake? Had someone attacked her? Had she gotten ill? She had seemed perfectly fine this afternoon, even exuberant, when he had driven her to Devon Blake's home. So why had she been all alone in that coffee shop, blocks from Blake's apartment? He had no idea what had happened, but he intended to find out.

She cried all the way to the beach house, and by the time they got there she was totally exhausted. Carter helped her into the house and then left her in the living room while he made coffee. When he came back with two cups of coffee and a damp cloth to bathe her face, he found that the tears had slowed.

Gently, as though she were a young child, he

wiped her face with the cloth, erasing the tear tracks and streaks of mascara while her breathing gradually smoothed. He waited until she had finished half the coffee before he asked her again what happened.

In broken little sentences, she told him, and he could see that each word inflicted new pain as she spoke it. Carter felt his anger for Devon Blake growing. He might be sixty-six now but he was still capable of beating the shit out of a sorry bastard like that.

Savannah sensed his rage and laid her hand on his arm, as if to restrain him. "It's not really Devon's fault," she said slowly. "I thought he knew about me. I thought the whole world knew about me! I should have told him about myself instead of letting him find it out like that. All of those awful stories . . ."

"He should have believed you," Carter said, unwilling to admit that she could have done something wrong.

"Why?" she countered. "It all sounds so ridiculous. I still don't understand why Paul did any of the things he did. Sometimes I wonder if he really did believe all those terrible things in the papers. Maybe that was why he changed his will. Maybe that was why he and Garnet . . ." She shook her head, unable to go on for a moment. She took a deep breath and shoved her hair back from her face. "When I told Devon I was pregnant, he wanted to know if he was the father."

Carter's fists clenched as he saw the pain that caused Savannah.

"I don't really think he meant that part of it. But then he said . . ." She faltered, and then turned away as she spoke, unable to meet Carter's eyes. ". . . he couldn't believe I hadn't gotten pregnant just to trap him . . . because I hadn't . . . hadn't used anything." She was blushing now, a bright furious red. "He didn't believe me, but I didn't think I could get pregnant. All the time with Paul, nothing happened. Paul said sometimes nature just doesn't . . . I didn't know what was wrong with me. I never went to a doctor to find out. But—"

She broke off, staring at Carter. "What is it? What's wrong?"

He felt as though someone had struck him. "He didn't tell you?"

"Tell me what?"

"He didn't tell me either, but I was the one who drove him to the doctor, so I knew what he had done." A sick feeling of betrayal was welling up inside him. How can you know a man for forty-eight years and still not know him at all?

Savannah was staring at him blankly.

"He had a vasectomy. Right before you two got married. That's why you never got pregnant. He was the one, not you."

The coffee cup slipped from her hand and shattered on the floor. Her face was so pale beneath her tan that he thought she was going to faint. "How could he do that to me?" she whispered. "How could he let me go on thinking that there was something wrong with me? He *knew* that was what I thought!"

Now Nolan Carter was crying, too, mourning the man that he had thought he knew for almost half a century but had never really known at all.

By the time the sun rose, they had made their plans. At six, Carter fielded a call from Devon, telling him Savannah was still asleep and promising to have her call as soon as she woke up. Devon called back at eight and again at ten and received the same message. When he called once more at noon, the phone rang and rang unanswered.

Chapter 17

He should have insisted that they fly, Carter thought. Not that Savannah could have asked for a smoother ride as the Mercedes sang along Interstate 10 in his skillful hands, but he wasn't sure that a lengthy automobile trip, even in the powerful and comfortable Mercedes, was a good idea in her condition.

A glance in the rearview mirror told him she had finally stopped crying. She was calm now, and composed, but every drop of color seemed to have drained from her face. It frightened Carter to look at her.

Their hastily concocted plan had been to drive to Dallas. Not that Savannah had any special reason for choosing that destination, except that she had a modeling assignment there once and it seemed a long way from Los Angeles. It was not a very sensible reason for relocating, but Carter had not argued. He knew that it was tremendously important to get her out of California right now.

The lawyers could handle closing up and selling the beach house and transferring monies to wherever she decided to settle. Before leaving the city, she had called the new firm Paul's lawyer had turned her over to after Paul's death. They would take care of everything. They would also refuse to give out any information about her whereabouts without checking with her first. Devon Blake would not be able to track her down and prevent her from doing whatever she wished about the child she carried. The question was: Exactly what did she intend to do about it?

When Carter finally posed that question, he thought for a moment that the tears would start again. Then Savannah steadied herself. "I'm going to have the baby," she said with a quiet firmness that thrilled him. He was no believer in abortion, but if she had decided on that course he would have helped her. He felt guilty over paving the way for Savannah to get involved with Devon Blake, especially for having misjudged the man so badly. He would give her any assistance he could, now.

However, in a funny way, he found himself blaming Mr. Paul rather than Devon Blake for what had occurred. He could see how devastating it must have been to the young man to have all those terrible stories dropped on him without warning. Whatever the madness was that had possessed Paul Marsdon when he changed his will, and when he got involved with that Hoffman woman, those actions had only added to the problem. Carter could almost forgive Devon Blake for reacting badly—if only it had not hurt Savannah so much.

The important thing now was Savannah's health and the health of her baby. If they drove the rest of the way to Texas, he was afraid she might lose the child. When they reached Phoenix he would find some place for her to eat and rest while he made reservations for a flight to Dallas. He didn't dare let Savannah travel alone right now; he would accompany her on the plane and arrange for someone to drive the Mercedes on to Texas.

It wasn't until he saw the Phoenix skyline that Carter realized he had not let Theodora know he was leaving California.

Savannah stared out the Mercedes' window, but she was too numbed by what had happened to register anything of the passing landscape. She had discovered last night that she had a deadly enemy, and that enemy's name was Savannah Royale Marsdon.

How could she ever have any kind of normal life as long as people connected her with that awful woman whose exploits were familiar to everyone in Los Angeles? That woman who looked like her and used her name, but had no connection with the real Savannah. She could see now that the only hope of normalcy she had was to put both that woman and that city as far behind her as possible.

She did not understand how her public image and her private image had diverged so sharply, but last night they had come together with a resounding crash. She still loved Devon, loved him with all her heart. But she knew she could not marry him for the sake of the child. Not when he felt about her as he did. She wouldn't be the cause of one more child growing up as unloved as she had been.

Tearing herself away from Devon was like tearing off a piece of herself, but it had to be done. Savannah curved her arms around her still-flat belly protectively and stared blankly at the Arizona landscape.

The sleek Mercedes in the restaurant parking lot, with the California license plates, caught Lucette Edwards's eye as she lit a cigarette. Thirty-one years of Arizona sun had dried her skin and baked the fat from her flesh so that she was as lean, brown, and supple as worn saddle leather, but the one thing that the Arizona sun had not done was rid her of the urgent desire to be somewhere—anywhere—else. The people in the Mercedes were on their way to that mythical Somewhere Else, and Lucette longed with all her heart to go with them.

Instead, she was stuck in Phoenix, teaching third-graders and treating herself to one luxury a month—a gourmet meal at an expensive and plushly elegant restaurant on East Camelback Road. A costly extravagance she couldn't tell anyone about because they wouldn't understand. Not even her husband. Jerry would only have berated her about the money, not realizing how much good it did her soul to sit there eating fine food and drinking fine wine, dreaming that she was in Los Angeles or New York.

Not that Jerry was any great shakes with money himself. She kept telling herself that it was because he was so much younger than she was, and that she was expecting too much out of him. But the truth was, he loved to gamble. Lucette's father had been like that; he was the kind of gambler who would put a bet on which of two raindrops would roll down a windowpane the fastest. She had mothered her father for years, and now, when she was honest with herself, she admitted she was doing the same thing with Jerry. He had just started teaching when they met, and she had been surprised and pleased that a good-looking man, who was so much younger than herself, would take an interest in her.

It was only later, after they had been married for six months and Jerry had traded teaching for a traveling salesman job that gave him several days a month in Las Vegas, that she realized what she represented to him: a steady source of financing for his habit. Of course, by then it was too late. She had already fallen head-over-heels in love with him—and she still was.

Lucette watched the Mercedes in fascination as the driver, a huge bald black man in a chauffeur's uniform, got out and walked around to open the passenger door. She realized she was holding her breath in anticipation, as though a play was about to begin or something momentous was about to happen. The chauffeur's body blocked her view briefly, and then he stepped back and she could see the passenger emerge.

It was a young girl, perhaps ten years younger than herself, realized Lucette, and she had the polished look of luxury that Lucette had longed for all of her life. She was everything Lucette had ever wanted to be, and yet there was a frailness there, a vulnerability, that Lucette could never have tolerated in herself.

That kind of frailty couldn't have survived the emotional sterility of a life like Lucette's, and Lucette was, above all, a survivor.

Yet, what an exotic creature the girl was. Lucette read all the fashion magazines, another extravagance she didn't dare let Jerry know about, and she recognized the style and presence of the Bill Blass outfit the girl was wearing.

As the chauffeur lead the young woman across the parking lot, Lucette realized something was not quite right. The girl's pale color, her hesitant steps, made Lucette wonder if she had been ill. The black giant hovered over her like a sultan's harem guard, Lucette thought, engrossed in the scene.

She had a wonderful table for the unfolding drama, as the girl and her chauffeur paused just before reaching the maitre d' and had a lengthy, low-voiced discussion. Lucette finally realized that, incredible as it might seem, the girl was actually urging the chauffeur to eat with her. Fortunately, the black man had the sense to refuse. He turned her over to the maitre d' and departed.

The young woman was shown to a table near Lucette's, where she spent an inordinate amount of time gazing at the menu and then ordered hesitantly. By that time Lucette's entree had arrived. She stubbed out her cigarette and ate heartily, keeping an eye on the other table. When the salad came, the girl barely touched it, merely moving it around on the plate with her fork. Then, when the entree arrived, the girl took one look at it, shoved back her chair, and hurried toward the restrooms.

Lucette followed more slowly, but purposefully. As she expected, she found the young woman throwing up.

This is a situation Lucette dealt with, sometimes daily, on a third-grade level. She found that this exotic creature was just as grateful as one of her students to have her face bathed with a damp towel and receive a few words of comfort.

"I knew I wouldn't be able to eat anything," the girl said weakly when her retching had ceased.

"When is your driver coming back for you?" Lucette asked. At the startled dismay in the girl's brilliant green eyes, she explained, "I saw you arrive. My table is by the window."

"I've interrupted your dinner," the girl said miserably.

"Don't worry about it," Lucette told her. "I know you don't feel like eating anything else, but why don't you join me at my table." As the girl started to demur, she added, "It will be a perfect place to watch for your chauffeur."

At that, the girl acquiesced and followed Lucette back to her table. However, one glance at the remains of Lucette's meal, and the pallor in the girl's face became more pronounced.

Quickly, Lucette signaled the waiter to clear the table and had him bring hot tea with lemon for the girl. She didn't regret not finishing the meal. What were a few bites of food, even at these prices, compared to the fascinating creature seated across from her? Lucette chattered gaily about her life, the children she taught, Phoenix and Scottsdale, anything to distract the girl, but she could tell it was not working. The emerald glance would not be directed away from the parking lot.

"There he is," the girl said at last with great relief and stood up.

Lucette rose reluctantly to follow her, not eager to have this adventure end so suddenly. She was dying to know who the expensively dressed young woman was, where she had come from, and where she was going. As for the girl's malady, Lucette suspected she knew the cause of that, even though the young woman wore no wedding band.

The chauffeur met the girl at the entrance, took care of the bill with money from his own pocket, and then held the door open for her.

Lucette quickly paid her own check and hurried out the door as well, just in time to see the girl suddenly sway, as though her knees had turned to rubber, and then faint dead away in the parking lot.

Carter glanced around the motel room that was beginning to seem like a prison after a week's occupancy. He wasn't sure exactly how it had happened. One moment he was ushering Savannah toward the car and then scooping her up into his arms when she fainted, and the next a leathery little woman had descended upon him, snapping orders like a drill sergeant.

If the orders had not been to Savannah's benefit, he would have squashed the woman like a troublesome bug. But truth to tell, he was frightened. Savannah had been suffering for some time as they drove, and he had hoped the restaurant stop might refresh her. However, he returned from making the arrangements for the flight to Dallas and delivery of the Mercedes only to find her looking like death warmed over. His heart nearly stopped when she fainted in the parking lot. He was certain it had something to do with the child she carried, and he felt absolutely helpless faced with such female mysteries.

The woman had him put Savannah, not into the Mercedes, but in her own aging gray Chevrolet and then follow her to her own doctor's office. Once there, she had him carry Savannah inside and after a few hurried words with a nurse, into an examining room. Then he was banished to the waiting room, leaving Savannah alone with strangers.

Clutching his cap in his huge hands and too nervous to sit, he had stood just inside the door, trying not to show his awareness of the covert stares of the other patients, and the surprised, shocked look of each new patient as she opened the door of her gynecologist's waiting room and caught sight of a huge uniformed man in this female place. It seemed like hours before the Edwards woman emerged with a shaky, but conscious, Savannah and ordered him to follow them to her house.

He had been allowed to do no more than carry her bags in the house before he had been banished to a nearby motel while Savannah remained in the care of this strange woman, forbidden by the doctor to travel. Every time he tried to speak to Savannah about her plans or find out what she required, the woman shooed him away, telling him he was only making her condition worse. The thing was, he knew the woman was right. He could see the pinched pale look leaving Savannah's face as the woman fussed over her.

Lucette Edwards had taken a week of sick leave from her elementary school to nurse Savannah. Carter had expected that when the week was over and the woman returned to her teaching, Savannah would be ready to continue their journey. This morning had dashed that hope.

Savannah refused to leave Phoenix. She was terrified she might lose the baby she carried, and at the moment Lucette Edwards appeared to her to be her only hope. The Edwards woman and her doctor had convinced Savannah that she would be imperiling the health of her unborn child if she did any more traveling, whether by car or plane. This morning Savannah had asked Carter to find her someplace to live in Phoenix until the baby was born.

Carter knew he should have been grateful to the Edwards woman for stepping in. Savannah's health had improved and she had not lost the child. Instead, he resented Lucette Edwards's hold over Savannah. She was a pushy, controlling woman who disguised her petty tyrannies as being all for Savannah's benefit, and she disgusted him.

Unfortunately, he wasn't too happy with himself at

the moment either. He had finally gotten around to calling Theodora this morning and letting her know where he was. After he hung up, he wasn't sure that had been a good idea. She was furious that he had left town with "that Marsdon woman." She told him just the fact that he was employed by Savannah Marsdon was causing her problems at the university—although he found that hard to believe. More likely, she was still jealous of Savannah. She couldn't bring herself to understand how much that little girl needed him.

Not that he had tried to explain the whole situation to her over the phone. He could just hear Theodora's delight if she found out that Savannah was going to have a baby fifteen months after her husband's death.

He hadn't smoked for nearly twenty years, but the strain of this week and watching Lucette Edwards puff away like a smokestack had brought his old habit back. Now, he reached for a cigarette, lit it, and leaned back against the headboard, as he considered the situation.

Unfortunately Theodora's reaction wouldn't be much different from that of the public at large. Maybe it was best, after all, that Savannah stay here in Phoenix until after her child was born.

Even if it did mean continuing to expose her to the Edwards woman's influence.

Savannah had never felt so safe and secure in her entire life. Or so blessedly normal.

She could tell that Carter was utterly baffled by her dependence on that wizened little monkey of a woman with her leathery skin, and she really couldn't explain it to him. She just knew, with absolute certainty, that this Arizona city was where she had to stay until the baby came.

When Lucette Edwards put her to bed in the spare bedroom that first day, Savannah had been quaking with terror. The doctor had told her there was a real chance of losing the baby if she kept on traveling as she had planned.

Devon's child.

She had clutched her belly and shivered beneath the cool sheets, tears trickling down her cheeks. Lucette sat beside her, wiping her face occasionally with a cool damp cloth until at last, bone weary, she had drifted off to sleep.

When she awoke, Savannah found herself in another world—the, to her, exotic world of suburban America: children on skateboards and bicycles shrieking outside, a totally inane situation comedy blasting out on the TV in the other room, and the smell of something absolutely delicious wafting through the open door into the bedroom. It was as though one of her fantasies had suddenly sprung to life.

After a week of Lucette's constant nursing, she had regained some of her color. She had morning sickness every day, though, and Lucette fell into the habit of bringing her a small snack of crackers each morning to settle her stomach before she tried to get out of bed. She had lost a little weight, but the doctor didn't seem to be as alarmed about that as Lucette was.

Lucette's principal refused to let her have the next

week off from school. So, reluctantly, Lucette went back to her third-graders, although she still fixed Savannah's breakfast before she left for school. Since Savannah was out of bed now, Lucette prepared a lunch each morning that only required warming. Savannah appreciated all the fuss, although most of the time she could barely eat half of the huge meals Lucette had cooked for her.

Lucette kept pressing her to stay on in the spare bedroom, but Savannah told her new friend she didn't dare impose like that. The truth was that Lucette's husband, Jerry, made her nervous. Even though he wasn't home very much, when he was home, he made her feel like an intruder. So although she would have loved nothing better than to den up like some animal mother in Lucette's spare room until the baby came, she had Carter search for a house.

Carter found the perfect place, a large spacious house in Scottsdale, but it was Lucette who took care of the thousand-and-one details of furnishing it, and hiring a girl for the cooking and housekeeping. When Lucette finished all the preparations, it was as easy for Savannah to move from the spare room to her new home as stepping into a favorite pair of shoes.

When Jerry was out of town on one of his nearly constant business trips, Savannah would have Carter waiting with the Mercedes to pick up Lucette at the grade school and bring her straight to the house. Lucette loved the way her students stared in awe at the big shiny car and the uniformed chauffeur. "They think I'm someone important," she told Savannah with an unaccustomed shyness.

Savannah hugged her. "You are!"

"She's bleeding," Carter said hoarsely. "I don't know how bad it is."

The call came right before lunch. The school secretary had come to Lucette's classroom to tell her and was watching her pupils right now. "Have you called the doctor?" Lucette asked him.

"She wanted me to call you first."

"Go ahead and call him and tell her I'll be right there."

Lucette hung up the phone and turned to find the principal regarding her with a steely glance. "I assume you're leaving for the rest of the day, Mrs. Edwards."

"I'm sorry, Mr. Boggs. It's an emergency."

"You've had a lot of emergencies recently, Mrs. Edwards. I would suggest that you try and get your personal life straightened out."

Carter met her at the door. "The doctor told her to go to bed."

"You go have Rosa make some tea and I'll see how she's doing." She made her voice as calm and confident as if she were talking to a roomful of her students. She could see Carter visibly relax.

Savannah was lying in the center of the big bed, her knees drawn up to her stomach. "Oh, Lucette," she cried. "I'm so afraid."

Lucette smoothed her hair back from her face. "Tell me what happened."

"I just started bleeding. At first, it was only some

reddish-brown spots on my underwear. But then when I went to the bathroom it was just bright red blood." She started to sob.

"Don't do that, Savannah. You're only going to make things worse."

Carter brought the tea and Lucette managed to get a few sips down her. Then she left him sitting with her while she went out to call the doctor herself.

When she hung up, she was frowning.

She didn't realize Carter was standing there until he spoke. "She finally went to sleep."

"We've got to try to keep her calm and off her feet."

"He said she might lose it, didn't she?"

She nodded. She didn't feel like repeating the calm clinical instructions abut fishing whatever tissue Savannah might pass out of the toilet and bringing it down to the doctor's office for a pathological exam.

Carter looked at her helplessly. "It will kill that little girl if she loses that baby, Mrs. Edwards. We've got to do something."

Lucette knew that he had been just as jealous of the attention Savannah paid her as she had been of him, but suddenly they were partners. She reached out and patted him on the arm. "It's going to be okay," she told him.

She wondered if it really was.

"You've gone completely off your rocker." Anger was in Jerry Edwards's voice, but his head was busily trying to figure the angles. Jerry was *always* trying to figure the angles. That was what had brought him an almost perfect life. Some of his buddies here in Phoenix didn't understand why he had married a woman ten years his senior, a woman who looked even older than that. But as he set his empty beer can down on the counter and Lucette scurried to the refrigerator to bring him another cool one, he knew he'd made the right decision.

With Lucette, he had everything he wanted at home, plus no questions asked when he was away. It was true what they said about older women. Lucette was *always* grateful as hell.

Actually, it might not be so bad having some of her attention diverted to this Marsdon woman, he thought. But before he agreed to this setup, he had to take a good hard look at it and see what was in it for Jerry Edwards.

"Let me get this straight. You're going to give up a perfectly good job to be this rich bitch's personal servant?"

Lucette flinched as she put the beer can in front of him with a coaster under it, just the way he liked it. "It's not like that, Jerry. She really needs me. The doctor says there's a good chance she might lose her baby. She's going to fix up a room for me there, and when you're out of town, I'll stay over. But I'll be here when you're home, Jerry. Just like always. And I'll make more than I was making teaching."

She stood there nervously twisting her hands, waiting to hear what he would say. Jerry wasn't about to be rushed into making a decision, though. Not till he had all the facts. "How come she needs you so much? Where's the father?"

"I told you, she's a widow," Lucette said quickly.

Something about the way she said that didn't ring true. There was a secret there, Jerry thought, and where there were secrets there was always the possibility of making some money. He had a real skill with cards, with almost any dance with Lady Luck, in fact. The thing that had always held him back was that he could never get together enough of a stake at one time to make a real killing. This Marsdon woman with her fancy car and her big black chauffeur and her new house, she represented big bucks. The question was how to get some of those dollars into more deserving hands. Jerry Edwards's hands, to be more specific.

"I guess it would be the charitable thing to do," he said piously.

Lucette was so thrilled she didn't even notice the mocking tone in his voice. She hurried into the living room to phone Savannah and give her the good news.

Jerry leaned back in his chair. If Lucette was going to be making more money, maybe he should spend a little more time in Las Vegas each month. No telling when you might parlay a few hundred dollars into the kind of stake that really meant something. Then, too, if Lucette was staying at the Marsdon woman's house most of the time, he wouldn't always have to let her know immediately when he got back in town from one of his trips. That would give him some extra time here alone. Well, not entirely alone. There was a cute little waitress in a downtown cafe, he'd been thinking about asking out. And who knew when another lovely like that might turn up out of the blue.

If she noticed the picture of him and Lucette on the bureau, he'd just say it was his mother or his older sister. He'd used that line before, and it had always worked. Women never believed someone as young and good-looking as Jerry would be hitched up to someone as old and weather-beaten as Lucette. That was another little plus that made for an almost perfect life.

He had a feeling the Marsdon woman represented a plus, too. He only had to figure out what it was.

Chapter *18*

"You what?" Lucette stared at Savannah in amazement.

Savannah hung her head, feeling like a two-year-old. "I never had a chance to learn," she defended herself.

"Everyone learns how to drive when they're teenagers!"

"Obviously not everyone, or I'd know how," Savannah countered. Actually the whole subject was beginning to amuse her. Somehow, with Lucette, she didn't feel quite so inadequate, even when a great big glaring inadequacy like not knowing how to drive showed up. "Why should I know how to drive, anyway? I have Carter."

Lucette shook her head firmly. "That's not good enough. Everyone should know how to drive."

"Then teach me." Savannah stroked her swelling belly. It really didn't show yet, but she could feel the subtle difference. "If the doctor says it's okay," she added softly. The last time she was in his office, he had heartily assured her that she wouldn't have any more problems, and she hoped he was right. She wanted this baby more than she had ever wanted anything in her life. But the thought of learning to drive thrilled her.

Ever since she met Lucette she'd been experiencing a life that was totally alien to her, but absolutely normal for everyone else. Lucette's surprise that she didn't know how to drive was nothing compared to her astonishment a week ago when she found out Savannah had never been inside a grocery store. Lucette had risen to the occasion, giving Savannah a quick course in housewifery and bargain hunting, showing her how to cut coupons from the newspapers and taking her from store to store, teaching her how to shop for the specials. To Savannah it had been high adventure.

Life was so strange, Savannah mused. She supposed to an outsider it would seem as though she'd always had everything anyone would want, and yet, until she met Lucette, there were so many simple things she could not do. Now, for the first time in her life, she felt as though she were just another person, and not a freak.

Carter had been mortified when he drove the two of them to the grocery store and realized that Savannah actually intended to go inside. He seemed to think it was an indictment of him, an indication that he was no longer able to take care of her. He was just as mortified when Savannah told him that afternoon that Lucette was going to teach her how to drive if the doctor approved.

"But why?" he wanted to know.

It would have been funny to hear that whine in the big man's voice, Savannah thought, if those two words weren't his automatic response to everything she proposed these days. "Because I want to," she explained patiently.

"I can drive you anywhere you want to go."

"That's not the point. All my life, everyone around me has made sure that I didn't do anything for myself. I'm tired of living in a cocoon. If it hadn't been for everyone from my mother to Paul doing my thinking for me, Devon might not have—" She broke off, unable to go on. The sense of loss that swept over her was overwhelming.

"If you're determined to do this, why don't you let me teach you?" Carter asked her.

Savannah shook her head. Lucette had such an easy way about her, always teaching you things without your even realizing it. She knew she would be relaxed and confident with Lucette coaching her. The threat of a miscarriage, of losing Devon's baby, had shaken her to her very foundations. Although the danger had apparently passed within a week, it was a whole month before Savannah felt safe moving around. Hiring Lucette had been the best thing she had ever done. Ever since the day Lucette moved into the house, she had felt stronger and more in control of herself. Especially since the doctor had seemed so cold and unfeeling. "If you lose the baby, then it wasn't meant to be," he had told her. "It's nature protecting the species. You're a young woman. There's plenty of time for you to have other babies."

Only there wasn't. Not without Devon. How could she explain that to the doctor, to Carter, to anyone?

Carter felt a little shudder of fear. What was he going to do when Savannah didn't need him anymore? He thought about all the things he had given up, first for Paul and now for Savannah. His wife, his marriage, his daughter. Suddenly, he felt very old and very tired.

Theodora was so cold on the phone that he seldom called her anymore. He wrote her a letter at least twice a month, and sometimes more, telling her about Arizona and the trivial details of his life, but never the big secret of Savannah's pregnancy.

Theodora never wrote back.

When he couldn't stand it anymore, he would give her a call and then squirm as his phone bill mounted while she pointed out with cool logic how ridiculous it was that he was living so far away from his real family, subjecting himself to a rich woman's whim.

She was right, of course, but then she had never met Savannah. If she had, maybe even Theodora's cold heart would have been moved by that little girl's plight. Time and time again, he was tempted to tell her why he had helped Savannah flee Los Angeles. But—and it was a terrible thing to say about your own daughter—he didn't trust Theodora to keep it to herself.

The California press and the scandal sheets had lost interest in Savannah. But news of her pregnancy—long after her husband's death—would revive all that. After the heartbreak she had suffered over Devon

Blake, he didn't think she would be strong enough to face that now.

Much as he wanted to confide in Theodora, he kept everything to himself. Once a month he called and let her torture him with her scorn, never offering a defense or rebuttal.

At four months, Savannah suddenly developed a desire to buy maternity clothes, although she really didn't need them yet. The doctor had told her that, because of her height and the small amount of weight she had gained, it would be some time before her waistline expanded. He was concerned about her weight, since he considered her model/actress build underweight by normal standards. She would have to gain twenty pounds to bring her up to what she should have weighed to start with, he complained. Lucette was constantly nagging at her to eat. She tried forcing herself to eat all the nutritious meals and healthy snacks Lucette fixed for her whether she had any real appetite for them or not. That was for the baby's sake. The maternity clothes would be for her. The doctor told her she could do anything within reason as long as she didn't let herself get too tired out, so she and Lucette haunted the Scottsdale shops, looking for maternity outfits. She came home with armloads of things. Lucette claimed Savannah was singlehandedly responsible for an upturn in the Arizona economy.

Savannah didn't care. She was having a wonderful time. The best part was trying on her new outfits with a pillow stuffed under them to see what she would look like when the baby really started to show.

Her morning sickness had finally disappeared and life was really wonderful—except for the days when Jerry Edwards was back in town, which thankfully was not too often. It wasn't Jerry himself—although Savannah didn't really like him—but his effect on Lucette that made Savannah so uneasy. She could tell Lucette was crazy about her young and handsome husband. Jerry didn't return that affection. He was distant with his wife. Almost cold.

Savannah didn't like the way he looked at *her*, either. It wasn't a sexual thing. It was something else. Something she couldn't quite put her finger on. When she mentioned it to Carter, he muttered a curse word under his breath, which shocked her since Carter never swore. He apologized immediately, but he wouldn't tell her what he thought about Jerry.

Aside from that one small annoyance, life was perfect. It was almost like having a real family at last, she thought. With Lucette and Carter there taking such wonderful care of her, nothing could possibly dampen her spirits. Not even Jerry Edwards.

It wasn't until the sixth month that Savannah's pregnancy really began to show. She had only gained twenty-two pounds in all. She had more energy now, and she and Lucette spent a lot of time talking about what she would do after the baby came. At first, when Lucette brought up the subject, Savannah couldn't think beyond the actual event, but gradually she came to realize that life would indeed go on after the arrival of her little bundle of joy. It seemed impossible to imagine at this point, but Lucette assured her she would need something to occupy her time besides her child, cinching her argument with examples of the mothers of her third-graders. It was better for the child, Lucette insisted, when the mother had her own activities to occupy her, instead of trying to relive her life through her offspring.

It was then that Savannah shyly confessed her interest in jewelry-making. At first Lucette seemed only mildly enthusiastic about the subject. But when she heard that Savannah had taken lessons from a well-known jewelry designer with a Beverly Hills' address, she insisted on seeing some of Savannah's own designs. Savannah protested she hadn't brought any, but then she found that Carter had packed them for her, after all.

When Lucette saw them, she became wildly enthusiastic, spinning plans of a studio and shop they would run together, with Savannah doing all the designing and Lucette doing all the selling. Even Carter had to admit the idea sounded good, on the surface, at least. Savannah was bubbling with energy, so she and Lucette spent a lot of time letting Carter drive them through Phoenix and Scottsdale, looking at jewelry shops and scouting possible locations for a shop of their own.

Lucette came back from every excursion brimming with ideas. She had Carter purchase Savannah all new drawing supplies and then pestered Savannah until she reluctantly started sketching once more. At first, she was shy about showing her designs to Lucette.

Then she found that not only was Lucette good about giving uncritical but helpful advice, she also had a very artistic eye. Savannah herself was more pleased with her sketches than she had been in the past. The realization that another human being was growing inside her had changed her outlook on the world. She felt more mature and capable and that seemed to be reflected in her designs. She was happier with what she had done in the few weeks since she had taken up designing again than with anything she had done in the past.

Lucette's idea of a shop still seemed like a fantasy, but Savannah enjoyed discussing it. Lucette knew a lot about her now, not everything, of course, but she knew that Savannah had been a model and actress.

Lucette loved the name "Royale." "That's what we'll call the store," she told Savannah. " 'Royale' in your handwriting will be our logo."

Lucette waved her hands around so enthusiastically that Savannah could almost see it, too.

At seven months, Savannah started childbirth classes. She was the only woman in the Lamaze class who did not have a husband with her. It was Lucette who assisted her while the other couples performed the exercises. At first, Savannah was embarrassed. If it had been anything else, she would have dropped out immediately. But not this. Having a healthy baby was the most important thing she could do, and she was determined to leave nothing to chance. She read everything she could find on nutrition for pregnant women and quizzed her doctor at each office visit.

Now that her belly had swelled enough for her to really need the maternity clothes she and Lucette had bought in their first flush of shopping, she was already tired of them. Although they shopped more, she no longer got as much pleasure from looking for clothes for herself. Instead, she discovered a new pleasure.

Baby things.

Diapers and tiny undershirts. Crocheted sweaters and caps. Kimonos and saque sets. It was like playing dolls, and in a strange way it reminded her of all those button-eyed stuffed animals that inhabited her pink room when she was a teenager. That troubled her, and she pushed the thought away as quickly as she could. The baby was no fantasy. She had first felt it move at five months, and her shriek of joy had brought both Carter and Lucette running through the house to see what was wrong. Now it tumbled and turned, making her belly jiggle like a plate of Jell-O, and she loved it.

Carter had painted the room they had set aside for the nursery a cheerful pale yellow. The baby furniture was delivered the following week, and now the room was just waiting for its new occupant. When Carter presented her with a tiny rubber duck for the baby's bath, Savannah had been so touched that tears sprang to her eyes.

Lucette scolded, but Savannah settled down into a placid waiting after the nursery was completed. The last big decision she had made was selecting a pediatrician. Now she was content to drift through the days, more concerned with the new life inside her than with anything in the outside world. She sat with her sketchpad on her lap for hours without putting a single line on the blank paper.

She had continued her Lamaze exercises even though she felt odd lying on the auditorium floor with her pillow and practicing her panting with a room full of couples. She and Lucette stood out as the only exceptions, and there were whispers and stares when they came in each Monday night. Finally it began to bother her so much that she insisted on hiring one of the instructors to come to her house once a week for private lessons. When Lucette was unable to be there because Jerry was in town, Carter would take her place, coaching Savannah with her breathing. At first, the instructor, a tall, energetic woman named Myra, seemed shocked to see the immense black man helping her client huff and puff her way through the exercises. But gradually Myra relaxed. After a couple of sessions, she was calling Carter "Coach" and joking with him.

For Christmas they had a small tree, which Carter and Lucette decorated while Savannah, stretched out on the sofa, gave her opinion of where each decoration should be hung. The ornaments were Lucette's, a diverse mixture of fragile glass balls she had inherited from her mother and paper snowflakes and bread-dough snowmen from her ten years of teaching elementary school.

They opened their gifts on Christmas morning and Savannah was touched when she found that both Lucette and Carter had given her things for the baby;

a wonderfully embroidered christening dress from Lucette, and a tiny gold ring from Carter.

She had been unable to go shopping without one or the other of them accompanying her, so Savannah had done pencil sketches of each of them for their present. Carter had insisted on baking the Christmas dinner by himself, and it was a wonderful success. Savannah ate so much she couldn't breathe and then stretched out on the sofa while Lucette and Carter cleaned up. It was a perfect day and it ended far too soon, in the late afternoon, when Jerry Edwards called to tell Lucette he was home. She scurried around gathering up her things, promising she would be back as soon as she could.

Then Carter disappeared to make a phone call, and when he returned he looked so gloomy and dour that Savannah had to ask him if something was wrong.

He shook his head and went outside. When she heaved herself up off the sofa, she saw that he was polishing the already spotless Mercedes.

Was it something to do with his family? she wondered. She knew he had a daughter in Los Angeles, but he seldom mentioned her.

She stood by the window for a long time. It was silly, after Lucette and Carter had gone to such lengths to pamper her today, but she felt very lonely and deserted. She couldn't help thinking about Devon. Had he tried to find out where she had gone? Or had he cared enough to even inquire?

Self-pity washed over her and tears spilled out of her eyes as she stood there.

Then the baby rolled over in her belly, as though it

had decided to be a tumbler in the circus, and Savannah smiled through her tears.

She cradled her huge stomach in both hands, enjoying the liquid movements of her tiny acrobat. In just six short weeks she would never feel lonely again.

"I promised my daughter that I'd fly back and spend New Year's Day with her," Carter said the next morning as he brought Savannah's breakfast to her. Lucette still wasn't back yet. "I'll only be gone overnight if I fly there and back."

"That's silly," Savannah said as she sat up in bed so that he could give her the breakfast tray. "Why don't you take a week off and relax? You could take the Mercedes if you wanted to. I won't be using it, and Lucette is terrified of driving it."

"I wouldn't want to leave you alone that long."

"I'm doing fine. There's plenty of time before the baby is due." She smiled at him cheerfully. "You might as well get your rest while you can. I'll bet you never thought your job was going to include being a nursemaid."

He smiled shyly. "I'm looking forward to it. I didn't get to see enough of Theodora when she was a baby. I've always regretted that."

"Spend the time with her now," Savannah told him softly. "It'll be good for both of you."

When Lucette came back the next day, she told him the same thing Savannah had. He caught her alone later and asked her if she was sure she could manage without him there. They had become allies ever since Savannah's near miscarriage, and he knew she would tell him the truth.

"Nothing's going to happen until February 6th," she assured him. "Go ahead and take a week off. Just leave me your number so I can get in touch with you if I need to."

Theodora was bubbling over with plans for the two of them when he called her. "I'll even cook you a big New Year's Day dinner," she promised. "You can put your feet up and watch football all day long if you want, Daddy."

In spite of Savannah's offer to let him take the Mercedes, he decided to fly back to Los Angeles. He told her it would be too much like a busman's holiday if he chauffeured himself, but the real reason was that he could get back to Phoenix faster by plane if he needed to. Not that there was any reason to worry, he assured himself. Savannah looked healthy and happy sitting in the front seat as Lucette drove him to the airport on December 30th. He intended to call a cab, but Savannah had insisted they take him. Lucette flatly refused, as always, to drive the Mercedes, so it was her little car that delivered him. He refused to let Savannah get out and go inside the terminal, though, and he made Lucette promise to take her right home and put her to bed so she wouldn't get over tired.

Lucette got a little huffy at that, as if he was suggesting that he didn't trust her to look after Savannah while he was gone.

Savannah thought their clash was funny and he carried the memory of her laughter all the way to Los Angeles with him.

*   *   *

Savannah groaned as the phone rang early the next morning. The trip to the airport yesterday had been harder on her than she expected. She'd had a difficult time sleeping last night and she still felt lousy. Before she could heave her huge self across the bed and reach the phone, the ringing stopped, and she assumed that Lucette had picked it up.

Lucette herself appeared in a few minutes with a strained, apologetic smile on her face. "That was Jerry," she said. "He's going to get into town about six tonight and he wants me to go out with him to celebrate New Year's Eve. I don't want to leave you, but he's never asked me before. He's going to bring me back here after the party, probably about 2 A.M. Do you think you'll be all right until then?"

Lucette's eagerness was almost palpable, and although Savannah felt an instant dread at the thought of being alone for any length of time, she hid it well. "Of course I'll be all right."

To prove it, she spent the morning with her sketchpad, and even managed to come up with a new design for a ring that she considered the best she'd ever done. Lucette was obviously pleased that Savannah was designing again after such a long lapse. When Savannah stretched out on her bed after lunch, Lucette brought her hair rollers and sat in front of Savannah's dresser, babbling on about the shop they would open—Royale—while she rolled her hair.

Savannah tried to listen, but her attention kept being drawn back to her huge belly and the small, tightening feelings that swept across it every so often. She drifted off to sleep at last, and when Lucette woke her at five with her dinner tray, the strange sensations had almost stopped. Still, she had no appetite, which dismayed Lucette. She threatened not to go at all unless Savannah finished everything on her plate, and Savannah made a valiant effort to do so.

Thank heavens Lucette left the room for a few minutes and gave her a chance to sweep the remains of her food into the wastebasket beside her bed. She was able to accept Lucette's praise with a straight face and see her off to her party without a cloud of guilt hanging over her. She wanted Lucette to enjoy her evening out with her young husband tonight. It pleased her that both Carter and Lucette, who had devoted so many long hours to her benefit, were finally enjoying some time to themselves.

If only the house didn't seem so empty with both of them gone.

Savannah spent the evening lying on the sofa, watching the televised New Year's Eve celebrations from all over the country and sipping apple juice from a crystal flute. It was twelve minutes to midnight when the little twinges she had been feeling all afternoon suddenly resolved themselves into a full-blown contraction. Her first thought was that it couldn't be happening. Not now. Not when she was still six weeks away from her due date.

Then the full realization of what this might mean hit her, and she struggled to sit up.

She waited, terrified, to see if there would be

another one. It came in exactly eight minutes by the
New Year's countdown on the television, and she
clung to the arm of the sofa, whimpering, until it
passed—not from pain, but from fear.

As "Auld Lang Syne" began on the television,
she felt a sudden gush of liquid between her legs.
Her water had broken.

"You can't do this to me!" Theodora looked like
a wild woman with her hair writhing around her face.

"I'm not doing anything *to* you," Carter said
patiently, although what he longed to do was give her
a good hard slap and stop this ridiculous argument
that had been going on since 2 A.M.

"The hell you're not! Rushing off to take care of
that goddamned white woman when I need you here!"
She shoved her hair back viciously. "What has she
got that makes you jump every time she cracks her
whip? Are you sleeping with her, Daddy? Is that why
you're so concerned about that bitch?"

He stopped in mid-motion, as shocked by her pro-
fanity as anything she called Savannah. "Try to understand, Theodora. She's just a little girl. She needs
me there."

"Teddy, Daddy. Everybody calls me Teddy. Even
the president of the fucking university calls me Teddy!"
Before he realized what she was doing, Theodora
reached in his suitcase, grabbed all the neatly folded
shirts, and threw them on the floor. "She's a twenty-
two-year-old woman who's probably been fucking
half of Phoenix! Are you on her stud list? Is that why
she's called you back in the middle of your holiday?"

He wanted to tell her why he was going back, but he didn't dare. While she watched with her arms crossed defiantly, he stopped and picked up all the shirts and replaced them in his suitcase. He snapped it closed and straightened. "I've called a cab. I'll just wait outside until it comes."

Theodora's face crumpled like a child that's just been told there won't be any dessert. "But what about Mama? What am I going to tell Mama?"

"Odessa? What about her?"

"She was coming for New Year's Day dinner. I told her you wanted to see her. Goddamn you, she was so pathetically *glad*!"

He almost weakened. If there was anyone who could have kept him in Los Angeles, it was Odessa. His blood sang at the thought of seeing her again. But the early morning phone call from Lucette Edwards had cancelled out anything else. "I'm sorry, baby. You tell your mama there's nothing I would have liked better than seeing her today, but there's an emergency in Phoenix and I have to get back."

"You stupid son of a bitch! You're walking off from two women who love you more than anything else in the world for some white cunt who—"

He slapped her.

It wasn't a hard slap. He could have taken her head off if he had wanted to. It was just enough to shut her up. To keep her from saying the words that would cut him in two. He snapped the suitcase closed and started outside.

"Goddamn you, Daddy," Theodora said. "When

are you going to remember that *I'm* your daughter. Not her.''

He didn't have any answer for that. Not there. Not on the way to the airport. Not as the plane covered the distance between Los Angeles and Phoenix.

"She's still in labor,'' Lucette told him when he reached the hospital.

"Since when.''

"Sometime last night.''

"Can't they give her something? Stop it?''

She shook her head. Her eyes were on the door to the labor room.

"When did it start?''

"I don't know. When I got back there was an ambulance in the driveway—''

He grabbed her by the shoulders. "You weren't with her?''

She looked up at him, her eyes wide with fright. "I was out with Jerry. She said it was all right. She said—''

"You left her alone.''

She twisted out of his grasp. "I don't have to answer to you,'' she said, but in a high, panicky voice that told him she was just as upset as he was. "She was six weeks from her due date. There shouldn't have been any problem. Jerry called—''

"Jerry!'' The way he said it was a curse.

"Yes, Jerry. My husband.''

"So you left her all alone?''

"It should have been all right!''

She was right. It should have been. But it wasn't.

* * *

The labor went on and on. She had forgotten, finally, why she was there at all. The only thing that mattered now was that the pain should stop.

She begged them for something to end the pain, but no one replied. No one talked to her at all.

She couldn't understand what had gone wrong. It was supposed to have been painless, natural. Lucette was to have been at her side coaching her.

Instead there was the pain. On and on. Only the pain.

They wouldn't let Lucette back in the delivery room and they wouldn't even consider the possibility of Carter coming in. So the two of them sat and smoked in silence. Waiting for God knows what.

The doctor will come out any minute, Lucette thought. Any minute, and he'll say, "It's a girl," or "It's a big strong boy," and Savannah won't remember any of this. That was what the mothers of her third graders had told her.

Nobody came.

Every time a nurse or orderly went through the door, they could hear Savannah screaming.

It was half an hour after Carter arrived before the doctor finally emerged. Lucette scrambled to her feet and looked at him expectantly, ready to rush to Savannah's side, but he shook his head. "We're going to have to do a Cesarean."

"But the baby's too early," Carter protested.

"The baby's heartbeat is slowing down. We don't have any choice."

*   *   *

She was aware only of bits and pieces of reality through the groggy haze of the anesthesia. The pain had disappeared, but she was aware of pushing and pressing sensations on her abdomen, and the comments of the doctor and the anesthesiologist. It seemed like the operation had barely begun before someone muttered, "It's a boy," but not with elation. She strained to hear the baby's cry, but there was only the background conversation for what seemed like far too long. The cry, when it came, was not lusty, but weak and faint. No one asked her if she wanted to see the baby.

She tried to ask what was wrong, but the anesthesiologist was saying something to the doctor about blood pressure dropping, and then she wasn't aware of anything at all.

It was two days before she could see the baby. A nurse had helped her walk down to the neonatal intensive care unit. She had already received all the information about his low birth weight, only five and a quarter pounds, but she was still not prepared for how small and skinny he was in his glass and metal womb. Surrounded by the humming machines and blinking lights, he looked even tinier, and as she watched him struggle for each breath, Savannah understood for the first time that he was going to die.

Benjamin was the name she had chosen for him before she left the hospital. At home, she would sit in the rocking chair in the pale yellow nursery for hours. Sometimes she talked to him aloud. "What did I do wrong, Benjamin? Why did you come so early?"

She kept imagining it wasn't really Benjamin in the hospital incubator with the wires and the tubes. Benjamin wasn't that lean, fragile-looking infant with the matchstick arms and legs. Benjamin was the fat, cheerful baby in the baby-food commercials. This was some imposter who had taken his place.

She wondered if she was going crazy.

Six days after his birth, she made Carter and Lucette take her back to the hospital, and she made the slow painful trip down the hospital corridor, favoring her stitches.

Outside the infant-care unit, she scrubbed up, and then, with a deep breath to steady her nerves, she went inside.

He looked like a small wild bird caught in a nest of tubes and wires. She stood there wondering what it would be like to touch his frail little arm.

After that she came every day at the visiting hour. She was never allowed to touch or hold him. Sometimes she was not even allowed to enter the infant-care unit and had to watch from outside the window. But she came every day.

On the thirteenth day, she saw Benjamin's eyes open for the first time. Before that, he had always been asleep.

But this time they were open, and she saw when she gazed into them that he had his father's eyes.

Devon's eyes.

He died at 5 A.M. on the morning of the fourteenth day.

All of them, Carter, Lucette, and the nurses, tried to talk her out of it, but Savannah insisted on making the funeral arrangements herself. There had been so little she could do for Benjamin; she had to do this one thing for him herself.

At the funeral home, she realized that she had never known that a coffin could be so small.

At the graveside service, she learned just how much of oneself such a tiny box could hold.

Chapter 19

The tall, elegantly dressed woman, her golden brown curls tangled by the chill November wind, darted through the Manhattan traffic with an assurance that earned her a respectful salute from one passing cab driver and a chorus of honks and curses from everyone else.

"You shouldn't do that," Carter scolded as he held the door of the limousine for her. "You're gonna get yourself flattened one of these days."

Savannah laughed, her face glowing with vibrant color. "You're turning into an old fogy."

"I'm old enough to be one," he agreed. "I'll be seventy-three next month."

"I don't believe you." Her astonishment was not feigned. Carter had a timeless quality about his face that made it difficult to realize that he was old enough to be her grandfather. "Besides, I'm getting old myself." Her twenty-eighth birthday had been in August and they had celebrated by moving into a new shop, their second expansion since they moved to New York five years ago. It still thrilled her every time she saw "Royale" scrawled across the door in her handwriting—Lucette's doing.

The thought of Lucette brought a frown to Savannah's face. "Jerry's back in town," she told Carter when he had slipped behind the wheel. "He picked up Lucette at the shop at lunchtime."

"That trash! Why doesn't she just throw him out?"

Savannah had wondered that herself. Lucette seemed so strong in so many ways; how could she let herself continue to be a victim of Jerry's gambling? On the generous salary Savannah was paying her, plus her share of the store profits, Lucette should have been well-off. Instead, she was forced to scrimp and save and make all sorts of ridiculous compromises so that Jerry could continue to squander her money on horses, cards, cars— anything on which he could place a bet.

What a difference between those two, Carter thought as he angled the limo through the traffic. Savannah was a new woman now, while Lucette . . .

After the baby died, Savannah had gone into a depression that lasted for months. She looked like a walking ghost instead of the vibrant woman his rearview mirror reflected back at him now. In those first painful months it hadn't helped her to see that flood of articles in the newspapers about Devon Blake running for the California Senate. Every time she saw his name, her spirits plummeted even lower. The only thing that seemed to rouse the slightest spark of interest from her was her jewelry designing.

If it hadn't been for Lucette Edwards, he wasn't sure what would have happened. Maybe Savannah's spirits would have just sunk deeper and deeper until she grieved herself to death over that baby.

Lucette had turned Savannah's interest in jewelry-making into a business. She had become Savannah's business partner, confidante, and substitute mother. For all his initial dislike of the woman, Carter had to admit she had done wonders for Savannah. First, there was the exclusive shop in Scottsdale, and then, only a year after it had taken hold, the move to New York City.

Savannah fought that move tooth and toenail, but Lucette had refused to give in until she got her way.

Carter hadn't wanted to make that move either. He knew Theodora would protest it to high heaven, and she had. Once again, though, he had to admit Lucette was right. Savannah's innovative designs had been a great success. Since Savannah had insisted on giving both him and Lucette a piece of the business, they had shared in that success financially as well as emotionally.

But for all Lucette's spunk and fire, she couldn't seem to do anything with that husband of hers. It was her being older than Jerry that was the problem, Carter thought. She treated him too much like she was his mama instead of his wife. Most men wouldn't like that, but Jerry Edwards's reaction went beyond dislike. He felt perfectly justified in milking every last drop of Lucette's money and every ounce of her energy in his behalf.

Savannah looked better these days, more healthy and more beautiful than Carter ever remembered seeing her. But Carter could see that Jerry's manipulations

were taking their toll on Lucette. These days, she
looked like a tired old woman.

Savannah stared out the window at the crowded
sidewalks as Carter maneuvered through the traffic.
Moving back to New York had made her come alive
again. Carter disapproved, but she had discovered
how much fun it was to walk in the city, especially in
the winter. This was her favorite time of year, when
the icy winds blew between buildings with what
seemed like hurricane force and rattled the leafless
branches of Central Park trees. The colder it got, the
more alive she felt. She loved walking along Broome
and Greene streets in SoHo and peering through the
frosted windows of shops and galleries. Or along
quiet Harrison Street in TriBeCa. Or on Madison
Avenue from 60th to 72nd, shopping the opulent
offerings of the international boutiques, or stopping
in to browse through the Ralph Lauren collection in
the Rhinelander mansion. It was especially wonderful
when a white snow blanketed the city and everything
looked so clean and fresh and new.

But most of all she loved New York's chauvinism
where the rest of the country was concerned. New
Yorkers believed that the world ended at the Hudson
River. No one cared who she had been or what had
been said about her on the West Coast. What she was
here was all that mattered, and here she was Savannah Royale, jewelry designer, nothing more.

Aside from Carter and Lucette, she had no close
friends, but that didn't seem to matter as much in
New York City as it had in Los Angeles. In New

York, she never felt alone. Everywhere she looked there were people just like her, caught up in their own private thoughts, working out their destinies with only the city itself for a companion.

No one ever approached her, not with Carter, huge and unsmiling, just behind her everywhere she went, so she was free to think whatever solitary thoughts she wished without being disturbed. Free to sample all the city sights and sounds as though she were enclosed in her own protective bubble. If it weren't for Lucette's problems with Jerry, life would be perfect.

Or almost perfect.

Her jewelry was a success, no doubt about it. However, there was still an elusive something Savannah was seeking that she hadn't managed to capture yet. Commercial success had nothing to do with that something; it was a quest carried on deep inside her. When she found whatever it was, Savannah knew it wouldn't show up in those neat little rows of black figures Lucette always stuck under her nose when Savannah tried to discuss how she felt about her jewelry designs.

She made a futile attempt to smooth her wind-blown hair. It was no good trying to talk to Lucette about anything these days. Sometimes she seemed determined to turn Savannah into a one-woman factory. They had already been approached several times by companies wanting to mass-produce Savannah's designs. To Lucette's chagrin, Savannah always turned them down flat.

"I don't want to be a cookie cutter," she had told Lucette.

As always, the explanation fell on deaf ears. Lucette saw everything in terms of the bank balance. A piece of jewelry was a commercial product and the only thing about it worthy of contemplation was how to increase the price it would bring from Royale's customers.

After the baby died and Savannah was finally on her feet again from the Cesarean, Lucette had not begrudged her the time she had spent prowling through the museums and galleries in Phoenix and Scottsdale. Then, Lucette had seemed to understand Savannah's need to fill the empty place in her soul with things of beauty. She had spent hours and hours studying the silver and turquoise Indian jewelry at the Heard Museum, and had gone back day after day to lose herself in the paintings at the Phoenix Art Museum. However, it was the contemporary sculpture she found in some of the Phoenix and Scottsdale galleries that stimulated her the most, pieces so exciting that she could have spent the rest of her life gazing at them.

Savannah came away from each outing newly inspired and anxious to try and incorporate the things she was feeling into her own jewelry designs. Lucette's understanding extended until they opened their first jewelry store on Scottsdale's Fifth Avenue. After that, Lucette had expected her to stop searching for further inspiration and keep turning out variations on what was selling. Savannah had heard the words "cost effective" over and over until she could have screamed in frustration.

Lately, Savannah had been spending more and more time at the Metropolitan Museum of Art, the

Guggenheim, the Whitney, the Frick, and especially
the Museum of Modern Art, looking for that something to which she couldn't put a name.

Just as she had in Arizona, Lucette was once more
complaining that Savannah spent too much time searching for inspiration and not enough time producing.
She refused to listen to Savannah's argument that her
work was going stale. How it could be going stale
when it was selling as fast as Savannah could produce it, was the question with which Lucette kept
attacking her.

It was, though, and Savannah knew it. Was it
because she was too insulated here in New York—
too cozily caught up in her own little world? Or was
it due to something else? To a need for a change of
direction in her work? Or was it because she still
hadn't been able to capture that elusive something for
which she had been searching for so long?

Savannah knew, *knew*, that when she finally identified that unnamed quality, she would know what it
would take to revitalize her work.

Lucette would just have to be patient until then.

Lucette looked at the photographs and then at the
sleazy little man who had handed them to her. ''This
isn't much for seven hundred dollars.''

''It's a bargain. Your husband has eyes in the back
of his head. Most husbands, I can snap the good
shots the first day. This guy's careful.''

''Not careful enough,'' she said bitterly. She took
out her checkbook and wrote out the check.

''You gonna get a divorce?'' the detective asked

her. "Or are you just gonna hold this over his head till he straightens up?"

She looked down at the top picture—Jerry and a blonde young woman, a woman his own age. "I don't know." The camera had caught him with his hand down the front of her dress, his tongue in her mouth. *Maybe I'll just blow my brains out.*

After the sleazy little detective left, Lucette pulled out the checkbook again and did what she hadn't dared to do while he was there, totaled the balance. When she saw the figure, she panicked. The rent was due, she had nothing to eat in the apartment, and Jerry would be wanting money for this weekend.

Wanting money, but never wanting her.

Lucette slipped the checkbook back in her purse and pulled out her compact. She opened it and stared at her face, calmly and without emotion, for the first time in over a year. As she glanced from the mirror to the photographs the detective had brought her, she could see how hopeless the situation was. She was only thirty-eight, but she looked closer to fifty thanks to her years in the Arizona sun. The lines those Arizona years had weathered into her face made her skin look like sand-scoured granite. The old woman in the mirror did not belong with that young vibrant man in the photographs.

But what could she do? She wasn't strong enough to break free of him on her own, not as long as she stayed in New York. Even though she knew how Jerry was using her, had known it for years, all he had to do was turn that handsome face her way and she was willing to give him anything he wanted.

Lucette snapped the compact shut. Somehow, she had to get out of this situation. Out of this city. Otherwise Jerry would continue to feed on her like a parasite, while giving nothing in return.

And she would let him.

Lucette always got to Royale earlier than anyone else. She loved this time of the morning best, when she had the store all to herself. For an hour or so, she could pretend it was all hers and hers alone. She would wander through the showroom, replacing the jewelry in the cases, making notes about new arrangements, suggestions to Savannah for other designs. Then she would occupy herself until Savannah and the salesgirls arrived by going over the books, watching the black totals grow larger while the red ones shrunk.

But not today.

Today she went straight back to her desk to think. Over the years, she had pieced together the details of Savannah's life, merging little things Savannah had told her with the information gleaned from articles in back issues of newspapers and magazines. She had known the private woman for seven years. Now she knew the public woman as well. The only thing she had not been able to learn was the name of Savannah's mystery lover. According to the background information she had gathered, it could have been any of a number of men. But somehow Lucette didn't think so. Savannah still had an almost virginal air about her. She had refused the advances of more men than Lucette could count over the past few years. If she were the nymphomaniac the papers described, she would have shown some sign of it. A person didn't change *that* much. Look at Jerry! He hadn't changed a bit in all the years they had been married.

Whoever Savannah's mystery lover had been, it was unimportant now. No one need ever know about the baby who died. Lucette wasn't cruel enough to use that information, even to save herself from Jerry, and besides—it wasn't necessary. There was more than enough scandalous information about Savannah's past already on public record for what Lucette had in mind—and that would assure that Savannah never suspected *her* as the author of the publicity campaign Lucette intended to launch.

Lucette had turned out to have a natural genius for publicity and promotion. That was what had made Savannah's first shop in Scottsdale an overnight success, and what had made their New York debut a smash, as well.

Not that the best promotional ideas were worth a damn without the talent to back them up. Luckily, Savannah had that talent. Lucette only had to walk among the cases out front or look at the photographs of Savannah's award-winning designs on the wall behind her desk to reassure herself of that.

Success, though, the kind of success that Lucette had yearned for all of her life, took more than talent. It took the kind of publicity that money couldn't buy.

The notoriety of Savannah's past would provide that publicity.

Savannah would never cooperate or consent, but she wouldn't have to. Lucette had something in mind which would assure publicity, whether Savannah co-operated or not.

Savannah looked so different now from the frightened girl she had taken under her wing in Arizona that Lucette almost faltered. It wasn't just her surroundings, the living room of Savannah's spacious West Village townhouse with the strange, Lucette thought, collection of art Savannah had accumulated over the past five years: black and white photographs of unrecognizable geometric forms, African masks, works of abstract expressionism —it was also Savannah herself. She had acquired a silky patina of sophistication, the exquisite polish of a true New Yorker that was forever beyond Lucette's reach. If Savannah were the woman she appeared to be, then Lucette had no hope of success.

But of course Savannah wasn't that cool sophisticate, Lucette reassured herself. Lucette knew better than anyone else, with the possible exception of Carter, the secrets lurking beneath that elegant surface, the little girl who still lived behind those clear green eyes. That knowledge gave Lucette the wedge she needed. She set her glass of Chablis aside. "I want to move Royale to Los Angeles."

Savannah stiffened as though Lucette had struck her. "Move? But why? We're so happy here."

Lucette let tears come to her eyes. It wasn't difficult. All she had to do was think of Jerry with that young blonde and she was practically bawling. "*You're* happy," she pointed out.

"I thought we were both happy."

"I want to get away from Jerry."

"Why don't you just divorce him?" Savannah asked reasonably.

"You don't understand!" Now the tears were real. "He's like a drug. I'm addicted to him. All he has to do is snap his fingers and I'd come crawling to him on my hands and knees. How can I have any self-respect?"

"But California . . ." Savannah was near tears herself. "I can't— You just don't know what you're asking, Lucette. The publicity . . . They'll put everything in the newspapers again. All those lies about me. I can't do it."

"It's been seven years, Savannah! No one will care anymore. You're just being paranoid."

"No," Savannah protested. "I won't go back. If I could do it for anyone, I'd do it for you, Lucette." She reached out for the other woman's hand.

"I can't live here anymore. I can't!" Lucette was shaking with sobs. "If you make me stay here I'll kill myself! I swear I will!"

When Savannah finally agreed, Lucette felt such a release that she knew everything she said had been the absolute truth.

Chapter 20

"Miss Royale? Just a few more questions, I promise."

Savannah shook the golden brown tangle of curls back from her face and looked down at the female reporter from her model's height, gold flecks of annoyance glinting in her clear green eyes.

By anyone's standards, Royale's Los Angeles opening was a huge success. Half an hour ago, Lucette had sought her out to assure her that everyone who counted was there, and Lucette was never wrong about those things. Savannah should have been able to relax and enjoy her moment of triumph. Instead, she was backed up against a jewelry case by a redheaded reporter half her size and tenacious as a bulldog, who refused to be satisfied with the banalities that were all Savannah proposed to give her.

The shimmer and flash of the brief metallic-mesh gowns the hostess/salesgirls wore as they drifted through the black-tie crowd like silvery moths distracted Savannah. She missed the reporter's next question as her gaze lingered on the showroom.

It was a work of art. Her eyes had not yet tired of it, although she had spent every day for the past month within these walls. Other Rodeo Drive shops might be painfully narrow, but no artifice was needed to make Royale wide and spacious—a hefty chunk of Savannah's personal fortune had gone into assuring adequate floorspace and an interior to lure the most jaded of Rodeo Drive regulars. The results were on a par with the best this glittering street had to offer.

Freestanding jewelry cases rose like burnished black obelisks out of the dark chocolate-brown of the thick carpet, each case terminating in a bottom-lit Lucite pyramid. Each of the glowing pyramids held a matching set of jewelry or else a splendid solitary piece, all Savannah's own innovative designs. Inscribed across the gleaming black base of each obelisk in the silver script was Savannah's own distinctive signature, the single word, "Royale."

Lucette's idea.

Just as moving back to Los Angeles had been Lucette's idea. The past was forgotten, Lucette insisted. Yesterday's news. So for the woman to whom she owed so much Savannah had let herself be talked into returning to the state she had sworn she would never set foot in again—and returning in style, if tonight's preview party were any indication.

Savannah clasped her hands together in a futile attempt to warm them. It was crazy, but ever since she left chill New York for balmy California, her hands had been like ice.

"Miss Royale? If we could just—"

"Let me call Mrs. Edwards over," Savannah told the diminutive redhead. Faye Johnston, that was her name. But Savannah had forgotten which newspaper she was from. "Lucette can fill you in on the details of Royale's operation, Faye, and—"

"Actually, what I'm looking for is some personal angle on you, Miss Royale." Faye Johnston smiled with an ingenuousness that was out of place on her forty-year-old face.

Savannah felt her face tighten into a mask. "I don't see what my personal life has to do with the store or the jewelry I create."

"It has everything to do with the store," the reporter scolded. "When a customer buys an exclusive design by Savannah Royale, she is buying a piece of you as well. Don't you see that?"

"I'm afraid I don't," Savannah said bluntly. "You see, I don't consider myself for sale."

The reporter relaxed into a chummy manner that didn't fool Savannah for a second. "We're all for sale, honey. The price is just a little higher in your case than most."

A stray shaft, Savannah thought desperately. She doesn't know anything about Mama and how she tried to sell her own daughter. No one knows that!

Miraculously, Lucette was at her side, saving her from the necessity of a reply. Savannah almost sagged with relief. "Where have you been?" she asked, her voice sharpened by panic.

"Circulating. Where you should be." Tonight Lucette resembled a wizened little monkey in her pearl satin sheath banded with black and the ridiculous little poof of a hat poised like a butterfly on her silvery gray hair. She was a genius with everyone and everything except herself, Savannah thought fondly. When it came to her own personal appearance, Lucette had no taste at all. Savannah had spent the past week trying to argue Lucette out of wearing that outfit tonight, even though she had known from the beginning it was a lost cause. But somehow Lucette managed to carry it off, where a lesser woman would have been laughed from the room. "There are some more people you simply must meet, Savannah. If you'll excuse us, Ms. Johnston. . . ."

The reporter held her ground. "I was just trying to find out something about Miss Royale herself. Her customers will want to know—"

"Miss Royale doesn't like to talk about her past life," Lucette said with a tight-lipped smile that made her look more like a sad little monkey than ever. "If you'll excuse us."

"My God, Lucette!" Savannah whispered when she caught up with the other woman. "You don't have to be so heavy handed. You make me sound like . . ."

"Like what?" Lucette stopped and faced her belligerently, but to Savannah's relief, she kept her voice low. "You don't like to talk about your past and you know it. You'll barely talk to me about it. Why shouldn't I—"

"Telling a reporter something like that is . . . It's almost guaranteed to make her try to dig something up about me. You don't know how reporters are."

"You're right," Lucette snapped. "I don't. I don't have your background. I've never had to deal with reporters before. If I weren't trying to help you with Royale, I wouldn't be dealing with them now."

"I'm sorry," Savannah told her friend. "I don't mean to upset you. It's just that—"

"Come along." Lucette took her by the arm and guided her through the crowd toward the back of the showroom, through the mauve and silver opulence of the private sales rooms, and into the gray and bone elegance of their shared office. "You're still sorry that I talked you into coming back to California, aren't you?" she said when she had closed the door behind them.

Savannah hugged her icy hands to her sides. "We were doing all right in New York. I don't understand what you think this will accomplish."

"Trust me," Lucette told her firmly. "Everything else has worked out okay, hasn't it?" She gave Savannah no chance to reply. "Let's take a few minutes to ourselves. A crowd this size is enough to frazzle anyone's nerves."

Savannah managed a grin. "But it means we're a success, right? Even the persistent Ms. Johnston means we're a success."

"For now." Lucette's gray eyes narrowed, considering. "It's a beginning, anyway. Something we can build on. There are a lot of important people out there. A lot of good contacts. We don't want to let them get away without being exposed to your charms."

"Then I'd better do some repairs on my makeup," Savannah murmured. "Or they're more likely to run screaming into the night than buy a piece of jewelry." She went into the washroom, leaving the door ajar.

Lucette followed. Closing the commode lid, she sat down and lit a cigarette.

Savannah coughed meaningfully, but Lucette ignored the hint. She inhaled deeply, eyes closed, and then expelled the smoke in an abrupt explosion. "I think you should reconsider about the modeling, Savannah."

Savannah's creamy ivory skin paled beneath her makeup. "You promised you wouldn't bring that up again."

"But can't you see how perfect it would be?" Lucette's cigarette dangled from her lips as she sketched a headline in the air with exuberant hands. "Savannah Royale models her own creations!"

Savannah's eyeliner slipped and left a shimmering silver streak across her temple. She sighed as she reached for a tissue to wipe it away. "I won't do it, Lucette. The business can go bankrupt, but I'll never model again."

"That's a very selfish attitude, young lady," Lucette said primly, sounding like the third-grade schoolteacher she had been when they first met.

"You can call it that," Savannah said calmly. "I call it survival instinct. I won't do it, Lucette. Not even for you."

"It's not just for me," the other woman said impatiently. "It's for both of us."

Savannah met her glance in the mirror. "I'm sorry."

Lucette stood up and opened the lid of the commode far enough to drop the cigarette butt in. She let it close with a snap. "Don't worry about it tonight," she told Savannah as she stretched lazily. "Lord, I can't wait to get home and get these shoes off. Ready to face your public again?"

"I need a few more minutes," Savannah said without turning around. "You go on ahead."

"All right." A frown deepened the wrinkles in the tanned leather of Lucette's face. "But don't sulk back here all night or I'll come and get you."

"I'm not sulking," Savannah protested. "I'm just . . . recharging. I'll be there in a few minutes."

"Right." Lucette nodded emphatically. The little hat lifted up, looking for a moment as though it might flutter away.

Savannah held back her grin until Lucette had gone. Then it faded as she confronted herself in the mirror. The modeling question would come up again. They both knew it. But for once Lucette wasn't going to be able to talk her into something.

She shook the golden brown curls away from her face. "Not this time," she promised her reflection.

Savannah strode back into the showroom like a swimmer plunging into the icy depths of unknown waters. No one watching her graceful entrance could have judged the effort it took. She was everything Lucette could have wished for, mingling, laughing, constantly moving. Let everyone have a piece of her tonight, she thought. When this opening was over, she would be safely locked away in the solitude of her workroom where no one could touch her.

At Lucette's insistence, Savannah wore no jewelry at all tonight—whether her own or anyone else's design. Her dress was a dazzling chemise of black silk georgette iced with silver bugle beads and sequins that captured the light and glittered seductively at her slightest movement.

The glistening chemise was a great success. Lucette had chosen it with almost as much care as she had the furnishings for the store, explaining her reasoning to Savannah at the first fitting. "You see, you have two groups to satisfy. Your female customers want you to exhibit your fashion sense so that they'll know they can trust your jewelry designs. But they don't want to be afraid they might lose their man when he comes in to buy them a little trinket."

"Wise of them." Savannah grinned at her over the fitter's head. "And the men?"

"They just want to see some skin," Lucette told her with a world-weariness she found appalling. But Lucette had been right.

As usual.

Savannah could see, this evening, that the chemise satisfied them all. The midnight silk georgette covered her completely from collarbone to ankle, and the neckline was high enough to reassure the most nervous female customer of Savannah's good intentions. For the males, there was a tantalizing, peekaboo view of her long slim legs, a glimpse of the softness of her upper thighs through the high slit in the glistening skirt as she moved through the showroom. Everywhere she turned, she met only approval and admiring glances. After a while, Savannah relaxed her guard and allowed herself a glass of champagne.

Smile. Laugh. Swirl away with a shimmer and flash of sequins and beads. It was just like modeling, except that when she modeled she had the Prince to get her through the long, boring sessions, and now she had nothing but nervous energy and champagne to sustain her. She took another sip of the sparkling liquid in her glass and smiled at the group she had just joined. *Lick your lips*, the memory said. *That's it, darlin'*.

Her stomach lurched. She thrust the nearly full glass into a passing salesgirl's hand and began to make her way through the crowd toward the rear of the showroom.

"Savannah!" Lucette was beside her. "I thought you were coming right out. There's someone you simply must—"

"I can't right now," she said with quiet desperation. "I need some air."

"Don't pull that. Not now. This is too important." Lucette pulled her toward a group of four men and two women on the far side of the showroom.

She felt a little like an ocean liner being pulled by a small but determined tugboat. She clenched her teeth against the threat of nausea. Five minutes, she promised herself grimly. *Five more minutes is all they get.*

When they reached the group, Lucette took the arm of the tall, black-haired man who was its focal point and half-turned him toward Savannah. "Here's the designer herself," she told him heartily. "I promised I'd bring her over. Savannah, let me introduce you to everyone.''

Her voice droned on, but Savannah no longer heard the words. The shock of meeting those black eyes as the man turned had frozen her where she stood. It might have been this morning that she had left his bed for the last time. The only change in him that she could see was a faint frosting of silver at his temples and a slight hardening of the determined line of his jaw.

"Devon?"

"Savannah." His voice was deeper, richer than she remembered. He was staring at her, his brows drawn together in a frown. "So you came back."

"I shouldn't have!" The words were torn from her heart.

"No," he agreed. "You shouldn't have." His lips curved upwards into a bland social smile, but there was a quick flash of real pain in his eyes.

She reached for him. It was instinctive. All the years, all the bitter words that had passed between them, couldn't quell her desire to comfort him.

He turned on his heel and strode away before her outstretched hand could touch his sleeve.

A murmur of confused comments rose from the group that had been with him. Three of them, two men and a short, pretty brunette, followed him. A third man and another woman stayed to watch. Like curious bystanders at the scene of an accident, Savannah thought numbly. Belatedly, she realized that the remaining woman was Faye Johnston.

"So," the reporter said. "You know Devon Blake?"

The glitter of interest in the redhead's eyes made Savannah's stomach churn. "We . . . We've met. It was a long time ago."

Lucette swung back from watching the group depart, and her bewildered glance landed on Savannah. "You look like you're coming down with something," she said abruptly.

Savannah managed a trembling smile. "I told you I needed some air."

"Next time I'll believe you. You look like death warmed over."

Faye Johnston moved closer. "Miss Royale—"

"Not now," Lucette told the reporter. "Can't you see she's not feeling well."

"Perhaps she should lie down," Faye Johnston said. She took Savannah's arm. "Let me help you get her back to—"

"No." Savannah stepped back out of the redhead's grasp. "I can manage, thank you."

She turned and walked swiftly through the crowd with Lucette trailing after her. At the door to the private sales rooms she paused and looked back across the showroom. The third man had disappeared, but Faye Johnston still stood where Savannah had left her. The reporter was scribbling rapid notes in a tiny black notebook.

"Savannah?"

She ignored Lucette and kept going until she reached the office. Once inside, she dropped down into the gray tweed chair behind her chrome and glass desk.

Lucette closed the door and locked it.

Savannah glared at her. "I'll never be able to work

in this office. It's too sterile. There's no color anywhere!''

"You wouldn't work here anyway and you know it,'' Lucette said absently. "I decorated it for me, not you. You'll spend all your time hiding out in your workroom.'' She crossed over to her own desk, and perching on the edge, lit a cigarette.

"Do you have to smoke so much?''

Lucette exhaled noisily. "Yes, I do.''

Savannah found she was gripping the chill glass top of the desk with frantic pressure, as though she feared she might fall if she released it. She let go and rubbed her hands together to warm them. "I'm exhausted, Lucette. If I leave now, you'll be able to—''

"What was all that about?''

She didn't even try to pretend that she didn't know what Lucette was talking about. "I told you. I needed some air. You know how I feel about crowds.''

Lucette studied her with the calculating glance Savannah had come to know so well. "Was he the one?''

Savannah nodded.

"Oh, my God!'' There was a rising note of exultation in Lucette's normally dry voice. "Devon Blake!'' She hugged herself and the little black hat tipped forward. "You had an affair with Devon Blake? They say he'll be the next governor of California. In a few years he could be President!''

Savannah sucked in her breath. She had a terrifying feeling that she might faint. Too many ghosts had returned to haunt her tonight. "I should never have come back! I should never have let you—"

"Get hold of yourself!" Lucette said sharply. "You're not a child anymore. Women meet their ex-lovers every day."

But that was the problem, Savannah thought as she lowered her head and laid her cheek against the cold glass top of her desk. She might look like a woman, but somewhere deep inside her woman's body, a wide-eyed little girl still waited for the Prince to come and rescue her. Despite all the years. All the pain. All the sorrow. Nothing had changed at all.

Lucette's chuckle drifted into her awareness. "Don't worry. I'll keep Ms. Johnston off your back tonight." Savannah turned her head slightly so that she could see the other woman's wiry silhouette through her lowered lashes.

"Devon Blake!" Lucette paused, her hand on the doorknob as a thought struck her. "Did he know you were pregnant?"

"Yes. But he thought I was going to have an abortion." Savannah jerked her head up. "And you won't tell him about the baby! You don't tell anyone anything about me!" She barely recognized that nearly hysterical voice as her own.

"Are you kidding? After that scene outside, I won't have to." Lucette slammed the door behind her.

Savannah stared at the bone-colored walls as she hugged her icy hands to her body, seeking warmth in the rough texture of the beaded fabric of her dress.

So cold. She didn't remember California being so cold.

It only took Faye Johnston one day to uncover the story she knew was there. It took an additional day of the best writing she'd ever done to phrase it carefully enough, with a deft mixture of fact and innuendo, so that any lawsuit brought against the paper by Savannah Royale Marsdon or an unnamed candidate for governor of California would be a waste of time. Then it took one more day of fast talking and arm twisting to convince her editor that he should run it exactly as written.

So it was Tuesday morning when Savannah opened the newspaper and found the headline she had begun to hope would not appear. But there it was in bold black print: *California's Bad Girl Returns*.

The paper slipped from her trembling hands section by section and fluttered to the terrazzo of the entry hall. Behind her, the phone began to ring.

BOOK IV

Savannah

Chapter 21

Lucette leaned back in her chair, ignoring Savannah, who was pacing back and forth across the width of their shared office. Instead, Lucette ran her hand along the top of her desk, enjoying the cool, elegant feeling of glass and chrome beneath her palm, and thought, I love this room. Who would ever have believed that a schoolteacher from Arizona would end up owning a store on Rodeo Drive? Especially a store as successful as Royale.

Well, not exactly owning, Lucette qualified, but close. She took care of everything except the actual designing, and with the share of the business that Savannah had given her, the distinction between owning and managing wasn't worth quibbling over. So the little thrill of ownership she enjoyed every time she glanced around the gray and bone room she'd had designed especially for herself was perfectly justified.

It almost made up for the empty spot in her life that Jerry had left.

"How can I make you understand?" Savannah burst out. "I've been on public display all of my life. I'm not going through it again. You don't know what it's like!"

"You're right. I don't," Lucette snapped back. "Some of us poor mortals haven't been able to live on the same plane as you have. You've always had it better than the rest of us."

"Sure. With people pointing and staring at me all of my life. Letting me know how different I was. You think that's so wonderful?"

Savannah turned away wearily, ready to give up the fight, but Lucette wasn't through with her. "There's only one thing to do and you know it. You have to meet this bad publicity head-on. You can't show any weakness in public."

Savannah finally seemed to be listening, and Lucette pressed her advantage. "You've been sulking for a week and it hasn't done any good, has it. There's more publicity than ever. It's time you got out in the world and showed your face. I'll arrange it."

It took a long time to get Savannah calm enough to return to her workroom. It was all Lucette could do to keep from glancing at her watch. Faye Johnston was meeting her at the Beverly Wilshire for lunch. The reporter had been pestering her ever since the night of the opening for additional information.

Not that Lucette was going to give her anything that could actually hurt Savannah, but she was learning to play the game with a vengeance. She had spoken to at least one reporter or columnist every day since the opening, and she had already noticed that even a denial brought reams of publicity ". . . a source close to Savannah Royale Marsdon today denied rumors that . . ." Every time there was a new story, traffic in the store doubled.

And no wonder.

The contrast between the vile insinuations in the newspapers and Savannah in person was so startling that people kept coming back just because they couldn't believe their eyes.

And when they came back, they bought. Royale was already a success by any standard, and Lucette planned to do anything she could to keep it that way. This was what she had dreamed of all her life.

She refused to feel guilty about how she had achieved that success. It wasn't her fault that Savannah was already notorious in California. Lucette was just using a preexisting condition for the good of Royale.

When Theodora called Carter, her voice was so strained he didn't recognize it at first. "I've been reading in the newspapers that you're back," she said.

"I didn't think you wanted to hear from me again." It was true, he thought guiltily, but he knew he should have made the effort.

"I don't need you, Daddy, but Mama does," and then her voice faded away, choked off by tears.

Carter gripped the phone with all his strength. "What is it, Theodora? What's happened?"

"Oh, Daddy . . ." The only word sandwiched between her sobs he could make out was "cancer."

He sat down heavily. "Theodora . . ."

"It's really bad, Daddy. She didn't want you to know about it, and I promised her I wouldn't tell. But, oh Daddy . . ." and now her voice sounded like a little girl's voice and not that of the cool, sarcastic forty-two-year-old college professor. "Oh, Daddy, she looks so bad!"

"It's all right, Theodora. You did right to tell me."

She looked so tiny in the hospital bed, so much smaller than he remembered her. For a moment he could almost believe that he was in the wrong room. That all of this was a mistake.

"Odessa?"

"Nolan!" Odessa's voice was weak but astringent. "What are you doing here? I'll give that Teddy the rough side of my tongue."

"Don't you go scolding Theodora. She did right to tell me."

He eased himself down on the edge of the bed and Odessa's black eyes snapped at him in a way that made him remember all the things that had been between them. "I should never have left you," he said brokenly. "I've been such a fool." He leaned forward and laid his massive head on her frail sunken chest and wept for all the years that had vanished.

Odessa caressed his head with a trembling hand. "Don't, baby. Don't," she murmured. "We were both hardheaded fools. Me as much as you. I knew how much that man meant to you—how much of your life you put into taking care of him. I shouldn't have tried to make you choose between your work and us. A man's work is important to him. I understand that now."

"It shouldn't be more important than a man's family," Teddy said angrily from the door.

"You hush, Teddy," Odessa said. "Your daddy and I understand each other now."

Carter gathered her into his arms.

After a long moment, Teddy walked across the room, and Carter gathered her into his grasp, too.

"I'm home," he told Odessa. "I'm going to help Theodora take care of you."

Teddy burst into noisy tears of joy.

"Why in the hell did he have to call today?" Ramsey Porter groused. "Driving to Santa Barbara will play havoc with your schedule for the next couple of days." The primary campaign was heating up, and they were all tired and irritable. Ramsey pointed out frequently that if Devon *did* decide to run for President, running for governor of California was the best training ground there was for a presidential campaign. California's population centers were scattered all over the state, making for the kind of long days a presidential candidate put in on the campaign trail. Jumping from Los Angeles, to San Francisco, to Oroville, to Oakland in a single day was a distinct possibility, depending on what was scheduled. When the campaign really got hot, Devon would be making four or five speeches a day.

Devon shrugged. He and his campaign manager both knew that there was no way around it. When the old man summoned you, you showed up. The former senator from California was the strongest of Devon's political friends and his most ardent supporter. It would be political suicide to ignore one of his politely worded requests.

"At least take Maggie with you," Ramsey pleaded.

"Right," Maggie agreed. "That will give us time to go over the notes for your speech at the Beier dinner." The brunette was on the campaign roster as public relations adviser—she should have been listed as PR genius. Having her on his campaign staff was a sign to those in the political know that he was going to be a winner. She knew that, too, and it meant that Maggie usually got what she wanted to keep her happy and on the campaign.

"I wish I could. But Senator Harrison said to come alone."

Ramsey threw up his hands in disgust. "So he pulls the strings, we jump, and a day and a half of scheduled appearances bite the dust."

"That's about the size of it." Devon grinned. "But I could take all this bellyaching from you a lot more seriously if I didn't know you'd be arguing exactly the reverse if I said I wasn't going." Devon had worked with Ramsey long enough to know that the lanky campaign manager was a born complainer, nagging until every detail connected with the campaign was perfect. That was one reason everything had run smoothly this far.

Ramsey grinned back. "So I love to complain. So sue me."

Actually, Devon wasn't that unhappy about the

senator's summons. It would give him a chance to get out of L.A. overnight. There was a restlessness eating at him, a dissatisfaction with everything around him, a malaise that he could not shake. To be honest, he had to admit that Savannah Royale Marsdon was the cause.

During the drive to Santa Barbara, Devon pondered the problem of Savannah. Seeing her again after all those years had been a shock. He'd had no idea that Maggie Evans had wrangled him an invitation to the opening of Savannah's new jewelry shop—not until the limousine pulled up in front and he saw "Royale" scrawled across the glass of the door. Even then, he wasn't sure, not until he saw her coming toward him in a beaded black dress that left nothing to his imagination.

Devon gripped the wheel, remembering.

He hadn't been able to get that image of her out of his mind since that night. It hadn't helped that Ramsey and Maggie kept trying to pump him about any past relationship with Savannah. Or that the newspapers were hinting at the same thing. But hint was all they could do; there was no proof of any ties between them. If he were being honest with himself, he might have admitted that was exactly what troubled him. At any rate, Devon knew that a meeting with the old man would get rid of his restlessness if anything could. You came away from an encounter with Senator Andrew G. Harrison as though you had been forged in a hot flame.

As he made the one-and-a-half hour drive along Route 101, he found himself enjoying the solitude.

He liked going alone to Santa Barbara. It always gave him a chance to get his head straight before he met with Andrew. The senator was a wily old fox, and one needed every ounce of brains on the ready. Devon enjoyed sparring with him. If it hadn't been for Andrew, he'd never have gotten into politics in the first place. After his breakup with Savannah, he'd been at loose ends, unsure what he wanted to do with himself. Architecture no longer interested him, in spite of the years of schooling and the long hours he had put in establishing himself in his own business. Yet, nothing else appealed to him.

Andrew had succeeded in doing what Devon's mother could not, convincing him that a political career was what he wanted most in life.

Or perhaps I already knew that, Devon thought, and it just took Andrew to make me admit it to myself. After seven years in political harness, there was no longer any doubt in his mind. This was what he wanted to do with his life, and he was damned good at it.

As he drove down the long, winding private drive of the senator's six-acre Santa Barbara estate, past avocado and citrus trees and acres of rolling lawns, Devon could feel the adrenaline start to flow as it always did at the prospect of a meeting with Andrew. He parked his car and strode toward the house without pausing for the admiring glance he usually gave Andrew's magnificently designed brick, glass, and wood masterpiece of a residence. The senator's man was waiting for him at the door.

The senator himself sat sternly erect on one of the

massive leather sofas in the high-ceilinged living room with its Italian-tile floors. "There have been reports that you're interested in a woman who is not of the caliber to be a president's wife," he said without preamble.

The statement caught Devon off guard and he found himself reddening. "My private interests are no one's business but my own," he said bluntly. "Although I can assure you that the papers are entirely wrong about any sort of current relationship between myself and Mrs. Marsdon."

"So there was a past relationship between you and this woman?"

"That falls under the heading of private business, Senator," Devon warned.

The senator went on as though Devon had not spoken. "I can understand that a man might be fascinated by a certain type of woman, but you have a career to think of. A brilliant career ahead of you."

"I told you there's no—"

"But there was once. Am I right?"

Feeling like a swimmer in deep water who has just encountered a shark, Devon admitted warily, "Once. But I had no idea who she was then."

"And when you found out?"

"I appreciate your support, Senator. Just as I appreciate all the political advice you've given me over the years. But my private life is my own and I don't intend to discuss it with you or anyone else."

"Just tell me this one thing. Have you seen her alone since her return to California?"

"No."

"Will you?"

"No."

The senator leaned back with a sigh. "You have to forgive an old man, my boy. I don't want to see you making the kind of mistake that would cripple all our efforts when we've barely started."

"I understand your concern, sir," Devon said stiffly.

"You'll be staying the night, won't you? I'll have your room prepared."

"I'm sorry," Devon said, although he had planned exactly that. "I have to get back to L.A. tonight."

"Then have a safe trip and I'll see you next week after the Beier dinner."

Devon was in his car before he realized he'd driven all the way to Santa Barbara for an interview that lasted less than three minutes.

Wouldn't Ramsey love that?

As Andrew stood at the window and watched Devon's BMW speed back down the drive, he could feel the irregular flutter in his heartbeat that worry produced these days. That Devon had been involved with the Marsdon woman before made this a much more serious situation than he had first suspected.

When Devon's mother called upon him seven years ago to nudge Devon toward the political career he was destined for from birth, Andrew had done so willingly, wondering why he had not realized sooner that this tall, strong young man was the clay he had been seeking. For seven years he had put everything— all of his hopes, all of his dreams—into Devon Blake's political efforts. Devon had truly become like a son to him, the son that Edward would have been if not for that cruel trick of fate. Devon had a keen mind that, combined with his charisma and good looks, would take him far in politics—if Savannah Royale Marsdon did not destroy him first.

He wondered if Devon's mother had known about his involvement with the Marsdon woman and then decided she must have. Amanda Lewis Blake had been too good at the art of politics not to have known a vital piece of information like that.

Too bad Amanda had not been born a man, Andrew mused. She had her father's political savvy, something her husband, Robert, had lacked in spades. Andrew had been surprised that she hadn't taken a bigger part in her son's political career over the years. But when her father died, at eighty-three, Amanda had seemed to lose all interest in politics, dropping all the campaigning and fundraising efforts she had formerly devoted herself to like a super woman. Without her assistance, her brother Charles had been defeated when he ran for reelection. But, then, the man had never served on an important committee all the time he'd been in Congress. No, that family's political spark had missed Charles and come through Amanda to her son. Amanda had asked Andrew to nurse that spark to life, after her husband's ineptitude with his son had almost extinguished it, and Andrew had succeeded better than either he or Amanda had expected.

Now he had an even bigger task confronting him. If he failed, Devon's political future, as well as Andrew's own dreams, would be lost.

Upstairs, in his safe, was a thick folder of private investigators' reports, newspaper clips, and photographs—evidence of the sordid life the Marsdon woman had led. He had decided at the last minute not to show the folder to Devon—you never knew how a man might react when he was ruled by his testicles instead of his brain.

He was going to do everything in his power to prevent a relationship between Devon and the Marsdon woman, and power was something he had a great deal of—more than even his enemies might suspect.

Odd. Andrew had thought he would hate the woman for threatening all he had worked for. But, surprisingly, he felt a different emotion when he leafed through the photographs of her in that file. There was something about the Marsdon woman that frightened him, although he could not put his finger on it. That she appeared to be, at least in her photographs, a woman of strength and character, a woman he would have loved to see at Devon's side under any other circumstances, was not the source of the almost unreasoning panic he felt every time he saw that lovely face. He had been the destruction of more good men than he cared to remember, when their destruction had served the greater needs of the people.

No, it was something else, something he couldn't explain to himself. But whatever it was, he would not let it sway his actions toward her. She was a threat to Devon and must be removed by any means, fair or foul.

The first action he took would be to make sure the amount of negative publicity the woman was receiving tripled. That, in itself, should be enough to turn a rational man like Devon away from her, knowing what he would lose by being linked with her publicly.

If that didn't work, there was a final solution, one that he had been called upon to use only three times during his fifty-four years of political life. But, time enough to consider that when all else had failed.

Wearily, Andrew climbed the stairs, knowing that tonight, as every night, he would lay awake until midnight, waiting in vain, as he had for more years than he cared to remember, for the phone to ring and the whisky-roughened voice of Irene Royce to torment him.

Maggie Evans was thrilled when Devon showed up after all instead of spending the night in Santa Barbara. Naturally, there was a party he just had to attend, and naturally, when he arrived, he found that Savannah Royale Marsdon was there, too. He could tell by the sly sideways glance his hostess gave him that she had seen the speculation in the paper about a relationship between the two of them and had arranged the seating purposely so that he and Savannah would be thrown together. Of course, that little item would make tomorrow's papers.

He'd have to remember to give Andrew a call in the morning and warn him, Devon thought resignedly, as he gave Savannah the briefest of polite social greetings and turned his attention to the stout matron on his left. As he made idle dinner conversation, he tried not to think about Malibu seven years ago and the roar of the surf filling the bedroom as they made love.

*   *   *

It wasn't working!

Savannah bent over her workbench, her mind not really on the delicate pattern she was fashioning from wax. When she finished this gold brooch, it would hold a three-carat Columbian emerald of magnificent clarity and color, a stone so fine Lucette would be able to get any price for it she wanted to ask.

But, impatient as Lucette was to get her hands on the finished piece, Savannah was not in the mood to create it. She had spent two weeks following Lucette's advice to confront head-on the negative publicity that welcomed her back to California. She attended a potpourri of social events at Lucette's urging. Unfortunately, at more of them than she cared to remember, Devon Blake was also present.

The reason why was no secret, of course. Not with such a large percentage of California voters living in Los Angeles, Orange, and San Diego counties. Without strong support in Southern California, he wouldn't have a chance in the governor's race. Naturally, he'd spend a lot of his time wooing the same wealthy and influential people that Lucette kept wrangling invitations from in hopes they would buy Savannah's designs. That had to be why she and Devon kept turning up at the same functions over and over.

But *God* how it hurt to see him standing across the room and remember how tenderly he had made love to her seven years ago. Or how much his eyes looked like his son's.

She was careful to give no sign of the pain she felt, just as he was scrupulously polite when they met, making small jokes about his supposed "relationship" with her for the sake of the other guests. They both knew they were being watched—and she had no more desire to be linked with him than he with her.

Still, every glimpse of him was agony.

Bad as that was, it wasn't the only thing. As the weeks dragged by, it had become obvious to Savannah that a new wave of vicious publicity about her was surfacing in the newspapers, and she had no idea why. Every old story about her was disinterred and retold in the most damaging manner possible. Paul's children, Garnet Hoffman, people in Hollywood, even Paul's lawyer—everyone who might have something ruinous to contribute to the systematic destruction of her had granted interviews.

The crazy thing was, it was great for business. The more stories that ran, the more of Southern California's elite appeared at the store, anxious to talk to her about commission work and custom designs or ask her advice on resetting stones.

Savannah wanted to shrink away from the unwanted attention, but she tried not to show it, calling on every ounce of her acting experience to see her through. To make matters worse, Carter had come to her telling her he had decided to retire. She and Carter had been through so much together, she was reluctant to let him go, even though she knew she had no right to ask him to stay any longer than he wished.

"Don't worry, Savannah," he whispered as she threw her arms around him. "If you need me, you just let me know and I'll come back."

It was hard to believe Carter was seventy-three. She had never thought of him as any particular age. He had simply been *there* whenever she needed him. It made her wonder what her life would have been like if Paul had lived? He would be sixty-eight now, she realized. Would they have continued to live together like the strangers they had become? Or would he have divorced her to marry Garnet Hoffman as Garnet claimed he had intended?

Just the thought of Garnet—of Paul sleeping with Garnet while he was married to her—unnerved her so much that she unwittingly crushed the small wax model.

She stared down at the ruined hours of work somberly. She had felt so *flawed* when she was married to Paul, so tormented by her inability to conceive. If only she could have explained that to Devon. If only she could tell him how wrong he had been about her. Let him know that she understood why he had reacted to the news of her pregnancy—and the dreadful stories about her—as he had. If only she could tell him how fragile Benjamin had looked in the nest of wires and tubes that had kept him alive for fourteen days.

But that was fantasy again, and fantasy belonged with the Prince, in the lost world of her childhood.

Her child's death had been reality, and she would never be the same innocent girl again.

Angrily, Savannah brushed the tears from her eyes and began to model the brooch again.

Lucette was alternating between highs and lows.

On one hand, everything she had ever wanted was coming true. The onslaught of new publicity had made the store a wild success, with no signs of lessening. Savannah's designs were good enough to keep customers coming back, even after the novelty of her notoriety wore off.

And the customers!

How could she have ever dreamed in Arizona, standing in front of a rowdy roomful of third-graders, that she would be talking to Middle Eastern princesses, Hollywood stars, and senator's wives. Men and women both jockeyed for her favors, thinking they could get to Savannah through her, and Lucette loved every minute of it. She lunched every day at the best restaurants in Los Angeles, and she never paid for her own meals.

Things were going her way at last. Even Carter had finally chosen to retire, thank heavens. In spite of their uneasy alliance formed during Savannah's pregnancy, Lucette had always considered him a rival. Savannah was too prone to listen to his advice over hers. However, Lucette realized that his mere presence, huge and black, looming over Savannah as he treated her like royalty, had only added to Savannah's publicity value. For that reason alone, she had given up trying to dissuade Savannah from keeping him on.

Even the pain of leaving Jerry had finally eased. Oh, it was still there. She probed it now and again, like touching a sore tooth with her tongue, just to see if it still ached.

It would always ache.

But she was surviving.

Everything would have been wonderful if it were
not for the stories about Savannah that were suddenly
everywhere. Not the hints of old scandal that Lucette
had dropped to a few reporters, but a full-blown
attack painting Savannah as a heartless whore who
had preyed on an old man for his money and been
roundly punished for it in his will. The viciousness of
the stories appalled her.

The worst part was—it didn't end. Day after day
the attack continued. As Savannah grew thin and pale
and nervous, Lucette was tortured by the knowledge
that these ruthless attacks were her fault. When Savannah came to her in tears after one of the more
vicious stories, it was all Lucette could do not to
blurt out what she had done, then and there. She
would have to tell her soon, Lucette realized. And
when she confessed, she knew that Savannah would
want to abandon the whole project. Maybe they would
move somewhere else.

But not New York. She was never going back to
New York again. She was finally free of Jerry's
influence on her, but she knew the only way she
would be able to maintain that freedom would be to
keep half a continent between them.

Chapter 22

The doorman called up at five minutes past midnight. "I hate to bother you at this hour, Mrs. Edwards, but there's a man down here who insists he's your husband. His identification—"

Lucette had already dropped the phone and was on her way downstairs, with only a pause to throw her robe over her nightgown. It never occurred to her not to answer the summons.

The first wild, frantic joy that swept through her when she got downstairs and saw Jerry standing beside the uninformed doorman crested abruptly as she reached him.

He was a mess. A black eye, clothing torn, a sheepish expression on his handsome face.

Lucette assured the nervous doorman he had indeed done the right thing, and she bundled Jerry into the elevator. As soon as the door closed, she was kissing him hungrily.

He responded for a moment and then flinched and turned away.

"What's wrong?" she demanded.

"They beat me up pretty good, Lucette. I was lucky, though. This time it was only a warning."

"How much do you owe them?" she asked dully.

"Five hundred thousand dollars."

The elevator door slid open behind her.

"You can't be serious," she squawked.

"You have to help me, Lucette. They're going to kill me if I don't pay off." He reached over and caught the door before it could slide shut again.

Lucette walked numbly down the hall to her apartment. She had left the door ajar in her haste. Jerry walked in first and looked around. She felt a little thrill of pride as she followed him inside.

The same decorator who had done the store for her did this room, too, in the same mauve and silver scheme as the private sales rooms of Royale. Lucette had okayed far more expensive furnishings for the room than anything she could have afforded herself, telling Savannah that it would serve as an adjunct to the store, a place where she could have private showings for special customers. Of course, Savannah had readily agreed to anything that would protect her from the drudgery of dealing with the people who paid the bills.

Lucette's pride in the room vanished abruptly when she realized Jerry's only interest in his surroundings was to judge her current standard of living, to see how much he would be able to prize out of her this time. "You're making plenty of dough, that's obvious."

"But not that kind of money," she said frantically. "Not five hundred thousand dollars. What have you gotten yourself into, Jerry?"

"I made the mistake of betting with some very rough players, baby. And they won't take, 'I don't have that kind of money' as an excuse. They're going to nail my ass to the wall."

He walked over to where her purse lay open on the table and pawed through it for a cigarette and a light. He inhaled deeply, savoring the smoke, and then he turned the purse upside down and went through the contents, counting the bills in her wallet, flipping to the last balance in her checkbook, stacking up her credit cards.

"Jerry. . . ."

He shoved it all off onto the floor.

"This isn't enough," he snarled at her. "I'm not going to be able to stall them for long." With a vicious gesture, he stubbed out the cigarette he had just lit, but she could see that his hands were trembling.

He was really frightened.

She stood there, wanting desperately to stop this before it started. To throw him out of the apartment. To do anything rather than become his slave again.

Only, the battle had been lost earlier, when she darted out to the elevator in answer to the doorman's call, and now, no matter how disgusted she might be with herself, Lucette knew she was going to do whatever Jerry asked her to do. No matter what the cost.

She went to him and put her arms around him. Jerry began to make love to her in that sweet, tender way that he had not done since they were first married. When he finally plunged inside her on the mauve damask of the sofa and brought her to the first shuddering orgasm that she'd had in five years. Lucette knew she would sell her soul to save him.

Lucette laid her head against the cool glass of her desk top and tried desperately to think of what she could do. She knew that Jerry was telling the truth. He would be killed if she couldn't help him come up with the five hundred thousand dollars.

She was willing to do anything to save him. even divert funds from the business. Savannah wouldn't notice. She seldom bothered to glance at the books, leaving all that to Lucette, which was exactly how Lucette had wanted it.

But Lucette had been going over Royale's financial situation in her head all night long as Jerry slept beside her, and there was no way to squeeze that much money out of the business quickly enough to do Jerry any good. Only, she couldn't tell Jerry that this morning. Not when he was treating her so sweetly, making tender love to her once again in the early morning hours, rising before she did to fix coffee for them both. It was like a dream come true, and she would do anything to keep it from ending.

Anything.

Her gray eyes narrowed suddenly. There was a way. A way that she wouldn't dream of using if it were not for Jerry's life hanging in the balance.

Devon Blake's supporters had that kind of money.

Lucette knew a lot about Devon Blake, more than Savannah realized. She had been bowled over to learn that Savannah's mystery lover was such an important politician. She was sure, from watching the two of them at the social events where they were thrown together, that Devon Blake was still fascinated by Savannah. She was equally sure that Savannah was still in love with Devon, although Savannah acted like a sulky child and refused to discuss the subject any time Lucette brought it up.

Lucette had enjoyed watching Devon Blake's supporters agonize every time their candidate's glance strayed in Savannah's direction, or a hostess seated him beside her. What she was planning wouldn't hurt Savannah, at least not much. Otherwise, she wouldn't even dream of doing it. It couldn't hurt because there was no hope for Savannah and Devon Blake to make it as a couple, and the sooner Savannah realized that the better. But the mere possibility was guaranteed to make those stuffed-shirt hypocrites around Devon Blake squirm! God, how she would enjoy watching that.

Lucette reached for a cigarette and then for the phone. Eleanor Goodwell, wife of Judge Goodwell, was fast becoming one of the store's best customers. Lucette had done her a small favor recently, making sure she got a coveted piece of jewelry before one of her rivals. Lucette was certain Eleanor wouldn't mind doing her one small favor.

Jerry would be so happy with her!

Savannah gave her hair one last glance in the mirror. Tonight she was wearing a severe black dress in silk crepe that skimmed closely over her body to

the black satin evening sandals held on by the nar-
rowest of diagonal ribbon straps. The sleeves were
long and narrow, ending just at her wrist bone, while
the neckline veed to a point just below her midriff.
The only jewelry she wore with it was a heavy
sculptured cuff in eighteen-carat gold on each wrist,
her newest design, which Lucette had urged her to
unveil at this party. Her hair tumbling loose past her
shoulders did away with the need for earrings, and
the bare valley between her breasts needed no adornment. "You'll be a walking advertisement for the
shop," Lucette had assured her when she first had
Savannah try on the dress. Savannah wondered, now,
how being a walking advertisement differed from the
modeling that she had steadfastly refused to do. Somehow she had the sinking feeling that Lucette had once
more outflanked her.

Just as Judge Goodwell's wife had outflanked her
on the matter of an escort. Although Savannah had
protested that she was perfectly capable of arriving at
the Goodwell's on her own, Mrs. Goodwell said she
was sending an escort for her. By the woman's arch
air, Savannah was sure it would be some eligible
bachelor. She had tried to forestall another ridiculous
attempt at matchmaking, since each one inevitably
ended with her having to fight off an escort who had
swallowed her public image without a second thought
and was determined to be the next lover of the infa-
mous Mrs. Marsdon. But Mrs. Goodwell had remained impervious to her objections. Savannah had
been irritated over the woman's stubbornness all
afternoon.

However, when the doorbell rang, she couldn't help feeling a little flutter of anticipation. If only those awful stories would fade away again and she could be just like any normal person. If only her escort would be some tall, handsome man, ready and willing to whisk her off her feet and onto his white charger. The ironic little smile that thought brought to her lips still lingered when she opened the door and found Devon Blake standing there.

"Aren't you going to ask me in?" he said when she remained frozen in position.

"What are you doing here?"

"I'm your escort tonight."

She started to shove the door shut and he caught it with one hand and pushed it open. "What do you think you're doing?"

"I'm not going with you."

"Don't be stupid. If you refuse to go with me, everyone will believe all those stories about us are true."

"And you wouldn't want that, would you?" she said bitterly.

"No, I wouldn't. Neither would you. Now invite me in before someone drives by and sees us acting like idiots."

Savannah stepped back away from the door and walked into the living room. She turned and surveyed him with a calmness she didn't really feel as he followed her.

"A big house," he said, his swift glance taking in the big square room with its rough-hewn wood and warm brick, white linen sofas and sleek lacquered tables. "You live here all alone?"

When she didn't say anything, he asked, "Are you taking a wrap?"

"I'm not going, Devon."

"Oh, yes you are, Mrs. Marsdon," he said grimly. "I don't know how you managed to arrange this little set-up, but since you had me show up like a trained monkey, you're definitely going with me."

"I didn't arrange anything!" Savannah cried. "Now get out of here and leave me alone."

"If I thought you were telling the truth, I would be very curious to find out just who *had* arranged this little farce. But right now, all I'm worried about is getting you to this dinner on time, so that we don't start any more rumors about ourselves."

"This is ridiculous, Devon! You know you don't want to go anywhere with me. And I certainly don't want to go anywhere with you!"

"Ah, but you, or someone, made sure I had no choice, Savannah. I can't refuse a directive from Judge Goodwell's wife. If I did, I could just kiss all my Los Angeles support good-bye. Now come on."

She could see by the stern line of his mouth that it was no use arguing, and besides, he was right. Not showing up would be worse than whatever indignity she had to suffer on the way. She could just see the speculations that would be in the papers tomorrow.

The evening dragged on and on, and Savannah was frantic with weariness by the time the party was over. Devon hadn't spoken on the long, silent drive to the party, and once there, he made only what conversation was necessary for politeness' sake. She had thrown herself into circulating at the party with a vigor that would have made Lucette proud. Lucette had been telling her she was her own best advertisement for her jewelry, and tonight she could see the truth of it. Several women asked her about the gold cuffs she wore and made a point of telling her that they would be stopping by to see her collection later in the week.

The low point of the evening, however, came as they were leaving. Mrs. Goodwell patted her on the arm and gave her a conspiratorial look that all but said: Aren't you glad I arranged Devon Blake as your escort? Savannah could have screamed, especially since she knew Devon also saw the woman's expression and would immediately jump to the wrong conclusion.

Savannah braced herself for some further nasty words on the way back, but Devon was lost in silent introspection. Gradually, she too relaxed, staring out at the city speeding past in the darkness and occasionally catching a glimpse of Devon's reflection in the glass.

When he pulled his BMW into her drive, she threw her own door open without waiting for him to stop the engine. "Thanks for a wonderful time," she said quickly and dashed into the house. She stood with her back against the door until she heard the BMW disappear down the drive once more.

She was still standing there when the phone rang ten minutes later, her head thrown back against the wood, tears trickling down her cheeks and splashing down her neck into the bare valley exposed by the vee of her neckline.

She let it ring three times before she heaved herself away from the door and stalked across the foyer to answer it.

"Hello," she said, her voice husky with tears.

"I'm coming back."

Her heart fluttered wildly in her chest at the sound of his voice. "Why?"

"You know why."

He broke the connection, but she still stood there, clutching the receiver, until she heard the sound of his engine outside, terrified that if she put it down the eggshell of reality would shatter into a million pieces. Carefully, oh, so carefully, she put the receiver back in its cradle then and went to open the door.

He stepped inside and closed the door behind him.

They did not speak.

She took his hand and guided him upstairs to her bedroom. Without turning on the light, she pulled him inside. He took her in his arms, and they stood quietly like that, letting the pain of seven lost years dissipate, allowing each of their bodies time to remember the magic of the other.

Devon let his lips drift down the finely chiseled line of her jaw, the elegant column of her neck, to the hollow between her breasts that he had longed to kiss all evening long.

Her deep husky moan brought him instantly, painfully erect, and seven years was no more than a second compared to the eternity it took for them to undress each other and tumble onto her bed.

Exploring her body—which was at the same time both familiar and new—released the most intense flood of sensations he had ever known. His lips trailed over her, measuring her skin, while his hands reassured him of the curves of her breasts. Only when he would have stroked the smooth satin of her stomach did she catch his hands and push him gently onto his back, fitting herself down over him with a groan of triumph, and riding him like a magnificent huntress.

She shook him awake at two in the morning. By the light from the lamp beside her bed, he could see the ivory skin and lapis lazuli veins between her breasts where her emerald silk kimono had fallen open. The warm, fragrant scent of her and him was all mingled together, and inhaling it was like taking the most powerful aphrodisiac in the world.

He reached for her, and she came willingly, pausing only long enough to switch off the light. She kissed his ear, and the hollow at the base of his throat, and his eyelids. "But you have to leave before dawn," she murmured. "Think of your reputation."

"Dawn," he agreed as he rolled her over onto her back, although at the moment he hadn't the slightest worry, and leaving was the furthest thing from his mind.

He phoned while she was still in bed, sprawled

across the emerald bedcover of Siamese silk that was surely ruined after their night of delicious debauchery. Just hearing his voice made her glow with pleasure.

"You can't do this," Ramsey Porter said. "Not on the spur of the moment, Devon. You've got too many—"

"I am doing it." Devon continued to throw clothes into the open suitcase on his bed. "I need a few days off. A little time to myself." He grinned at the man who was both his campaign manager and his friend. "Four days. And you're going to cover for me. Otherwise, I'll go crazy and you won't have a candidate for the governor's race."

"But what will I tell everyone?"

"Tell them anything you like." He snapped the suitcase shut. "Tell them I've gone fishing. That's exactly what I intend to do."

Savannah had called Lucette with trepidation, stumbling over the story she had prepared of a sudden virus. What if Lucette wanted to drop everything and come rushing over to check on her?

To her vast relief, Lucette simply told her to take two aspirins and try to get some rest. "In fact, why don't you take a week off?" Lucette offered. "I think you've been working too hard recently."

"You don't mind?"

"Of course not. What do you think I am—a slavedriver?"

*   *   *

They arrived at Devon's mountain cabin, with the furtive air of truants, in the early afternoon. Savannah was busy unpacking when she realized with a rush of horror that she would not always be able to make love to Devon in the dark. Not for four whole days.

He would see the scar across her belly, the scar which seven years familiarity had made her forget. What would he think when he saw it, the horrible line running from her navel to her pubic hair?

Savannah sank down on the bed, stunned by the nature of the catastrophe she had stumbled into unaware. That horrible feeling of being blemished, of being flawed in some way—was she never going to be free of it!

Devon called her out to eat the quick lunch he had thrown together from the supplies they brought, and she went obediently, but the spark had gone out of her.

Devon sensed the change in her mood immediately, but he was unwilling to confront it just yet. He had no idea what it might be, but whatever it was, they would overcome it. Maybe she was remembering how horribly he acted when she told him she was pregnant. He cringed at the thought.

He had even, God help him, come to terms with the fact that she'd had no other choice but to have an abortion when he turned her away like that. Whatever she had done had been as much his fault as hers. He could no longer blame her for destroying a life he had not been quick enough to try and save.

The two of them sat there moodily, toying with

their perfectly scrambled eggs and nibbling at the triangles of toast, until their food grew cold. Together they cleaned up the small kitchen in a silence that would have been companionable an hour ago, but now was terrifying.

Savannah was so overcome with dread that she was afraid she was going to throw up. When Devon suggested a walk, she all but bolted from the house, striding through the woods ahead of him.

He followed her, unsure whether she wanted to leave him behind or was daring him to catch up to her. He had waited too long for this moment to destroy it by making the wrong move, so for now, he kept a precise six feet behind her as she forged her way down the trail.

He was unprepared when she suddenly halted in a slight clearing between the towering trees and pulled her sweater over her head. She wore nothing beneath it, and the dappled sunlight on her ivory breasts was the most beautiful thing he had ever seen.

He started toward her, but she held up one hand in an unmistakable gesture for him to halt.

When he did, she knelt to remove her shoes and socks and then stood once more. Mesmerized, he watched her unzip her jeans. With tantalizing slowness, she pulled them down over her slim thighs and kicked them aside. Now, only the thin nylon of her panties covered the golden brown of her pubic hair.

Devon found himself trembling, not with desire, but with the sensation that something momentous was about to happen. He couldn't understand what it was, but he felt that, whatever it was, it would change his life forever.

Savannah slipped her fingers under the elastic of her panties, pulled them down over her hips, and let them fall like a brightly colored leaf to the ground.

She stood there like some ancient goddess of the forest, defiantly naked, clothed only in her glorious golden beauty, and Devon sensed he was being challenged in some inexplicable way.

Looking straight at him with those clear emerald eyes, she delicately traced a line from between her breasts down over her stomach. Only then did he see the faint scar on the ivory of her belly . . .

. . . and the stricken look in her eyes when he raised his glance to hers once more.

Without speaking, he removed his jacket and laid it down on the leaves. He pulled her to him and laid her down there, letting her hair spill out around her in golden brown waves, and then, slowly, as if it were the most treasured part of her, he kissed every inch of the faint line all the way down her stomach until it was lost in the rich profusion of her pubic hair.

"Our baby?" he asked when he raised his head.

Tears were leaking from beneath her closed eyelids. "He came too early. They tried to save him but he only lived fourteen days."

"What was his name?"

"Benjamin, his name was Benjamin." She reached up and clasped his head to her, fiercely. "Oh Devon!" She was nearly choking with her sobs. "He had your eyes."

*   *   *

Jerry Edwards was too far away to hear what the couple was saying. But he had gotten great shots of the impromptu striptease in the woods with his new Nikon and the zoom lens.

Then things got boring. She started crying for some reason, and then he could almost swear that Devon Blake was crying, too, if that weren't such a crazy impossibility.

Things got so dull that he almost drifted off to sleep as the couple just lay there holding each other. He was beginning to wonder if Blake might be impotent when the politician finally removed the rest of his clothes and began to make love to the golden goddess beneath him.

It was the best set of photos he could have asked for, Jerry thought, snapping away, and this was only the first day.

Chapter 23

Devon was in the best of moods, humming as he drove in on the freeway, an utterly mad thing to do. But then, after the past weekend, he felt like doing all sorts of utterly mad things. If the old man weren't scheduled to come in from Santa Barbara this afternoon, he would have played hooky one more day.

Unfortunately, the thought of Senator Harrison reminded him of the senator pumping him for information about his relationship with Savannah—a relationship that hadn't existed at the time but most certainly existed now, with a vengeance. Every muscle in Devon's body seemed attuned to a higher order of existence after four days of indulging in her exquisite flesh. If the subject came up again, he would simply tell Andrew that there was now a relationship, a relationship he certainly planned to continue, as he had whispered into Savannah's ear on the pillow this morning before he left her—but in no way was that relationship going to affect his campaign. Devon began to hum again.

Christie, Ramsey Porter's cheerful blonde assistant, met Devon at the door of campaign headquarters. "Senator Harrison got here early," she said with something approaching reverence. "Ramsey said for you to go straight to your office."

Was the old man going to rake him over the coals for taking a few days off? Devon managed to hold back a grin. Nothing could destroy the memory of the last four days, not even a flogging by a master like Andrew. He found Andrew, Ramsey, and Maggie Evans waiting in his office, their faces long enough to suggest that the candidate had just died—only the candidate was in the best of health.

"What's wrong, people? I know I didn't miss any major dinners or public appearances."

It was Senator Harrison who pointed to the large manila envelope on the desk. "Open it."

Devon didn't like the tone of his voice, but he decided not to make an issue of it. After all, if you're older than God and almost as powerful, you can talk to the underlings any way you please on a Monday morning.

Still, he was mulling over the response he might have made if anyone other than Senator Andrew G. Harrison had spoken to him that way instead of paying much attention to the envelope—until the first photograph came sliding out.

An eight-by-ten glossy of Savannah, nude beside the cabin, and himself, equally nude, reaching out for her.

Even though Devon understood immediately what was happening, the sight of her magnificently naked, with her proud breasts thrusting forward and pubic hair curling in ringlets, was so powerfully arousing that his breath caught in his throat.

He slid the rest of the photographs out of the envelope. It was all there, every moment of the four days he had just spent with Savannah, and each picture was a gem—clear and perfect. There was no doubt who the couple was in any of the photographs.

"Thoughtful of the lady to provide you with souvenirs," Senator Harrison said dryly.

"You don't know that it was her," Devon protested automatically, but his mind was turning over the possibilities, and at the moment, he couldn't think of any alternatives. No one else had known they were going off together or could have known where they were going once they decided to leave Los Angeles.

Only he and Savannah.

And the photographer.

He looked up and found Ramsey and Maggie staring at the photos, too. He shoved them back in the envelope. "What's the asking price?"

Ramsey answered. "Five hundred thousand dollars for the negatives."

"If I'd known my photograph could bring that much, I'd have become a model myself."

No one laughed.

Devon laid the envelope down on his desk. "How long do we have?"

Ramsey had jammed his hands in his pockets the way he always did when he was nervous. "They want the money by midnight, Wednesday."

Devon looked around at them: the senator leaning on his cane, Ramsey with his hands in his pockets, Maggie nibbling on her lower lip. "That's easy enough, then. We won't pay."

The group erupted in protest. Andrew Harrison's voice drowned out everyone else. "Don't be stupid, boy. We have to keep your association with this woman from becoming public knowledge."

"You let me handle this, Senator. It falls under the heading of private business." Devon picked up the manila envelope and left.

This time when he hit the freeway, he was no longer humming.

"What are we going to do now?" Ramsey Porter said when the door slammed behind Devon. "If that bitch's name is linked to his with any solid proof behind it, we're ruined."

"Watch your language!" Senator Harrison said sharply. "There's a lady present."

Maggie Evans grinned. "Don't worry about me, Senator. I think Ramsey is pulling his punches because he's hot for her himself. Otherwise he'd have called her a cunt."

Harrison frowned at both of them. "This is no joking matter, and Devon is too emotionally involved to handle it himself. I'll be staying in the city until this thing is settled. Call somewhere and get me a room. Then we can start figuring out how we're going to raise five hundred thousand dollars without arousing any suspicion."

Ramsey Porter shook his head. "Devon said we're not going to pay it."

Senator Harrison glared at the campaign manager. "Devon is a fool!"

When one of the clerks came running back and told Lucette that someone was demanding to be put through to Savannah in her workroom against Savannah's express standing-orders, Lucette knew at once who it was.

"I'll handle it," she told the girl and wiped her suddenly damp palms against her skirt. The phone on her desk rang almost at once. "I'm sorry, sir. Mrs. Marsdon never takes calls in her workroom."

"I have to talk to her right away."

It was Devon Blake's voice on the other end of the line, just as she had suspected. Lucette gripped the phone so hard it almost shot out of her slippery hands. "Of course, sir. I'll put you through immediately."

As soon as she transferred the call, she ran into the bathroom and threw up. When her poor heaving stomach had settled itself, she washed her face and brushed her teeth, and then went to call Jerry and tell him it looked like everything was going to work out all right.

Savannah couldn't figure out what was going on, but she followed Devon's instructions to the letter. The car was waiting outside Royale and she slipped into it quickly. They had gone a block down Rodeo

Drive before she realized it was Devon himself driving, a cap jammed down on his head, and not a chauffeur. "What is this?" she asked delightedly. "Are you spiriting me away to ravish me again?"

He didn't answer.

"Devon?"

"Just hang on for a few minutes," he told her without glancing over his shoulder. Finally, he pulled the car over, parked, and turned around to face her.

Savannah was beginning to tremble. For some reason this whole thing reminded her of the night he had found out about all those awful stories about her. There was the same uncompromising look in his black eyes now. "I don't understand what's going on."

"This was waiting at my campaign office this morning." He tossed the manila envelope to her and she caught it awkwardly. "Everyone was standing around looking at it when I came in," he added cruelly as she opened it and the photographs came sliding out into her lap.

She took one look at the nude photos and moaned softly. "They were *looking* at these?" She wasn't ashamed of their lovemaking, but the thought of a roomful of strangers pawing through these pictures made her sick.

"They want five hundred thousand dollars for the pictures, Savannah."

She looked up in confusion. Her mind had ceased to work for the moment. "Who does?"

Devon's black glance bored into her. "I thought you might know the answer to that."

Someone rapped against the closed driver's window.

Devon turned to roll it down and a policeman said, "Any trouble, buddy?"

Devon shook his head silently.

"Then move along."

"Sure, officer."

He started the motor without looking back at her and pulled out into the traffic. She realized he was taking her back to Royale. "We have to talk, Devon."

"We have talked."

"I don't have any idea who took these photographs."

He didn't answer.

"You don't believe me, do you?"

"Who knew where we were going besides the two of us? Who knew we were involved again besides the two of us?"

"I don't know. All I know is that I don't know anything about this."

He changed lanes with a vicious jerk of the wheel and gathered a chorus of angry honks from the other drivers. "What proof do you have?"

"I don't have any proof. How could I have any proof? You just have to trust me, Devon." She had the sudden awful feeling that she was fighting for her life and her happiness in these few seconds.

Devon pulled over to the curb across from Royale. When he turned around to face her, she could see by the indecision in his eyes that she had lost.

Lost him. Lost her happiness. Lost everything.

Silently, she handed the manila envelope to him.

When he said nothing, she bolted out of the car

and dashed across Rodeo Drive while car brakes screeched and horns blared. When she reached the door of the shop and looked back, he was gone.

For the first time, Andrew felt that he really understood Claire and her obsessive desire to protect Edward from Irene. For years, that awful picture of his wife masturbating his son had remained in his brain, and nothing he could do would dislodge it. But, now, he finally understood. Somehow, with a woman's intuition, Claire must have known what an awful person Irene really was. Must have sensed that she would be the kind of person who would take a poor innocent little girl and force her into prostitution.

Edward's daughter.

When he thought of what must have become of his grandchild, his blood ran cold. It had been eight years since Irene's calls stopped as abruptly as they had begun, and yet, every time the phone rang late at night, Andrew still expected to hear Irene's voice on the other end of the line, telling him the awful stories about what she had let happen to the girl. He had thought that nothing could be worse than the psychological torture of those phone calls.

Then they stopped.

Until he began to groom Devon for the boy's rightful place in politics, the place that would have been Edward's, Andrew had found nothing to fill the terrible hollow in his soul that Irene's calls had left there.

Now this Marsdon woman was threatening to undo

everything, and Devon was playing right into her hands.

Well, like Claire so many years ago, Andrew recognized the enemy, and like Claire, he knew he would be justified in whatever action he was forced to take to protect his boy. All those years in Washington made him a master at the slick handling of campaign contributions. All he needed to do was make two phone calls and the five hundred thousand dollars would materialize in plenty of time to make the deadline.

Andrew waited impatiently in his luxurious suite at the Bel Air Hotel until nearly five for Devon to call him. At last, he gave up and called the boy himself, unable to wait any longer. To his mounting irritation, it took three tries before he finally tracked Devon down at a fundraising dinner. "What in the hell are you doing there, boy?" he growled when Devon came on the line.

"Working. I am still a candidate, you know."

"There are more important things to be doing with your time today."

"Such as?"

Andrew hesitated. Who knew about a telephone line these days? However, his rage overpowered his prudence. "Lining up the money," he thundered.

"I told you I'm not going to pay."

"You don't have any choice."

"You're wrong, Andrew. A man always has a choice in a situation like this. The choice I'm making is to face it head-on. The pictures aren't faked. I was there and so was she. If the blackmailer chooses to publish them, then—"

"Don't use that word over the phone!" Andrew's heart was pounding in his chest. "You saw her, didn't you?" he accused.

"Of course I did. You think I wouldn't tell her what's going on. She's involved, too."

"I know that. I just wondered if you realized it."

"You're dead wrong, Andrew. She's not part of *that*. She was as shocked as I was."

"Have you forgotten that she's an actress?"

A silence, then, "She said she wasn't involved in this and I believe her." But the pause told Andrew there was now a chink in Devon's armor that hadn't been there this morning.

"You just stand back, boy. Let me take care of it. This is my kind of business, not yours."

"It's none of your concern, Andrew. Stay out of it."

When the line disconnected, it took a moment for the fact to register on Andrew. Not even the President of the United States had the guts to hang up on Andrew G. Harrison, not even now that he was semi-retired from the political arena. No one but his boy.

Andrew leaned back and smiled proudly. What a President Devon would make. It was Andrew's job—his duty—to see that Devon made it all the way to Pennsylvania Avenue.

Before midnight, Andrew had made both calls and finalized all the arrangements. The five hundred thousand dollars would be in his hands by tomorrow night, in plenty of time for the Wednesday deadline.

It was the worst week of Devon's life. Half-a-dozen times he picked up the phone to call Savannah, and every time, he put it down again before he could dial her number.

Was she involved?

If she wasn't, how in the world was she going to feel when those photographs appeared in print? The blackmailers had said that if the money weren't delivered, every newspaper, and the television and radio stations, would have copies of the prints in time to make the Friday morning news.

Devon woke up two hours early on Friday morning and lay in bed, dreading what was to come. But when he turned on the television, there was nothing about a gubernatorial candidate and a very notorious lady. Nor was there anything in the copy of the *Times* he picked up on the way to headquarters.

Devon found the senator, Ramsey, and Maggie all crowded into his office. A bottle of champagne was iced down in a silver bucket on his desk. "What are we celebrating?" he asked warily.

Only Andrew was drinking. He lifted his glass in a toast. "I saved your campaign, boy." He motioned to a manila envelope on the desk. "The negatives."

"You paid them," he said flatly.

"Of course, I paid them. There was no alternative."

"And where did the money come from?"

"Pour him a glass of champagne," the senator told Ramsey.

Ramsey glanced across at Devon.

"Don't bother," Devon told him. He reached over and knocked the champagne bucket to the floor. "Goddamnit, I asked you a question, Andrew! Where did the five hundred thousand dollars come from to pay those bastards?"

"You don't want to know the answer to that, boy." The senator looked very old and weary. "It won't show up anywhere, believe me. There's nothing to worry about. No one will know."

"I'll know! And someone, somewhere, thinks they own a piece of me for that little favor, right?"

"You'll never know that officially, I promise you. They believe in you and what you stand for. They know you'll make the kind of decisions that will help us all."

"You bastard!" He wheeled around and stared at Ramsey and Maggie. "Did either of you know what was going on?"

Both of them shook their heads silently.

"What are you trying to do, Devon? Of course, they didn't know. They're only—"

"They're my campaign staff and they'd damned well better know the meaning of loyalty! Or they're out. Just like you, Senator." He turned back to Ramsey and Maggie. "As of right now, Senator Harrison is no longer welcome in this campaign headquarters. I want his endorsement stricken from every piece of my campaign literature. If you two can't deal with that, you're both out, too."

"Don't be ridiculous, Devon," Andrew said. "You know you don't have a chance without me behind you."

"No, I don't have a chance *with* you behind me, Andrew. This is it. We're finished. I don't want to find you here when I get back."

"Goddamnit, boy, even the President himself listens to me!"

"Fine. Go talk to him."

Lucette had called in sick for the second day in a row. Much as she worried about Royale without herself at the helm, she was terrified to leave Jerry alone with the money.

"You've counted that for the hundredth time," she told him while she fixed coffee. He looked awful, eyes bloodshot, a two-day growth of beard masking his face. She was sure he hadn't slept since they picked up the money where the campaign people had dropped it. "When are you going to pay off your friends?"

Jerry snapped the suitcase shut and shoved it back in the closet. "We should have asked for more," he said dismally. "If I had realized how easy it would be. . . . At least I kept a few negatives for a rainy day."

"We don't need them." She went and knelt in front of him. "We have your life, Jerry. That's all I care about."

She reached up to kiss him, but he shoved her away. "That's not all I care about. This is enough money to really make something of us, baby. If I bet it right—''

''Jerry, no! You're not going to gamble that money! Are you crazy? You said those men would kill you if you don't pay them off!''

''But if I put this on a sure thing . . .''

Lucette ran to the closet and started to yank the door open.

Jerry bounded after her and slammed his shoulder against the door, thudding it shut. ''What do you think you're doing?''

''I'm not going to let you do this, Jerry. It's crazy! Do you realize what I did to get this money for you? Not only did I commit a crime, I betrayed my best friend in the whole world because I thought I was saving your life. Now you want to throw all that away on one of your sure things! Well, not this time!''

She yanked at the doorknob again and he slapped her so hard that her head struck the doorframe.

Half-stunned, she slid down the wall and slumped against the door like a doll with the stuffings gone. He shoved her aside roughly and yanked open the door. As she stared up at him with fear-glazed eyes, he grabbed the suitcase. He paused at the door and said, ''I'm doing it for us, Lucette. You'll see. It really is a sure thing.''

The door slammed behind him, and in a minute she heard the front door open and close. She felt totally alone, and she realized for the first time that was exactly what she had been ever since she married him.

*   *   *

The boy hadn't realized what he was saying. He was confused, that was all. A woman could do that to a man. Claire had known that, and now Andrew knew it, too. If Claire had only confided in him, told him what she suspected of Irene Royce, he would have tried to help her.

He had been so furious when Irene told him about the child, his granddaughter, and how Claire had refused to let her tell him about it before. Now he understood. Claire had only been protecting his boy, his wonderful golden boy.

But she hadn't gone far enough. She had hounded Irene from Washington and prevented her from contacting Andrew, but her womanly nature had prevented her from taking the final step. Had he been in her place, knowing what he knew now about Irene's true nature, and the suffering and degradation she would inflict upon Edward's daughter . . .

Now the same decision faced him. This woman, this Savannah Marsdon, was clouding Devon's brain and causing him to act in ways that would end any chance of a political future for the boy. He had to make a decision about her and he had to make it fast, before any further damage could be done.

But it was too important a decision to make here in Los Angeles. He had to go back home, to Santa Barbara, so that he could weigh the consequences of his action in peace. There, he had the file on the Marsdon woman locked in his safe, the file he had been gathering ever since the first reports of her involvement with Devon had come to his ears. There, he would sit in judgment on Savannah Royale Marsdon, and what he decided would affect not only her life and Devon's and his own, but also the future of his country.

Removing her and the filthy scum who had used her to blackmail his boy from this earth might possibly be the most important thing Senator Andrew G. Harrison had ever done for the United States of America.

Chapter 24

Savannah dialed Lucette's number for the third time that day, and then slammed the phone down in frustration when she got the busy signal again.

How could Lucette do this to her?

Two of the salesgirls were threatening to quit because everyone who came into Royale and saw Savannah on the floor, instead of lurking in her workroom, wanted her to attend them personally, and the girls were afraid their commissions would suffer. For Savannah's part, she was tired of the sidelong glances from women who had come only to see the notorious proprietress of Royale and not to buy her jewelry designs.

Lucette *knew* she hated this and she had sworn— *Sworn!*—that Savannah would never have to do the actual selling, and yet here she was forced to deal with the public for the third day in a row. When word spread that Savannah herself was accessible, store traffic tripled. Today, like yesterday, Savannah had missed lunch, running on caffeine and nerves,

and now, twenty minutes to closing, both were beginning to give out.

She couldn't help but wonder what would happen
if the story of the four days she had spent with Devon
became public knowledge. Then they would come
swarming into Royale in even larger numbers, all the
crepey-skinned ladies with their hard sharp eyes. The
thought of anyone seeing those photographs of her
and Devon made her squirm inside. She hadn't asked
Devon what he planned to do about the photographs,
but somehow she just couldn't see him paying blackmail money. So she might as well get ready for
another siege of awful publicity. Surely, one of these
years it would cease to hurt so badly. But then, she
had thought the same thing about her love for Devon,
and look what happened.

If only Lucette were here!

Savannah dialed the number again and received the
same frustrating busy signal.

By the time she was able to shoo the last customer
out the door, soothe the ruffled salesgirls' feelings,
and prepare the next morning's deposit, it was nearly
seven. And by the time she got home and threw
herself down wearily on the sofa, it was eight. She
was almost too tired to answer the doorbell when it
sounded, and only the thought that it must be Lucette,
risen from her sickbed at last, made her get up.

When she saw that it was not Lucette but Devon
who stood there, she was dumbfounded.

"Savannah?"

"What are you doing here?"

"I don't know."

"Honest as always." She tried to smile, but the effort was too much for her.

"Will you let me come in?"

"Do you think there's really any use?"

"Savannah, please. We have to talk."

She stood aside and let him enter.

"Savannah," he said, and then he was gathering her in his arms and kissing her with an intensity that took her breath away.

For a moment she responded, and then, ever so gently, she disentangled herself. "I have to know something, Devon. What are we going to do about us?"

"If you've forgiven me for being such an idiot, we can adjourn to your bedroom."

She shook her head. "I'm serious, Devon. There's something about me you have to understand." She paused, trying to find the words. "Did you know that until after Paul died I didn't know how to cook?" she said after a moment. "I didn't even know how to drive a car. All my life I've been a frightened little child, manipulated by other people. I don't intend to live that way anymore, Devon. When I was a little girl, I used to dream the Prince would come and make everything all right." She looked at him steadily. "That's not good enough anymore. I love you with all my heart, but I won't hide or lie for you. I'm through with fantasy. I won't be two people: the real me and the one the public knows."

He took her hands in his. "What do you want me to do?"

She took a deep breath. They would be the hard-

est words she ever forced herself to utter. "Your
senator isn't going to like this, but either our love is
public knowledge or we don't see each other again."

For a moment she thought she had lost.

She tried to jerk her hands free of his, but he held
on tightly. "I love you, Savannah," he whispered,
as he pulled her close. "Not Senator Andrew G.
Harrison, or the thought of being governor, or even
President. Just you."

Who would have thought that Ramsey Porter would
turn out to have principles, Andrew fumed. The campaign manager was following Devon's instructions to
the letter, refusing to even talk with him on the
phone.

Maggie Evans was a different story. He understood her well. Her kind was turned on more by
power than by sex, and even though he was a sick
old man, she was drawn to him. She would tell him
anything about Devon's plans he needed to know. He
could stay here in Santa Barbara, and she would be
his pipeline into Devon's campaign.

He had already alerted his man Quinn—it amused
Andrew to call Quinn a spot remover—that there
might be several spots that needed removing. That he
would have the blackmailers eliminated was certain.
Andrew's investigators were already working on their
identities.

But the Marsdon woman was a different proposition. He could not make up his mind to give the final
order on her. Once it was given, there would be no
turning back. Quinn was absolutely devoted to him;

when he received the order to eliminate the Marsdon woman, she was dead, wherever she might be, whatever she might be doing.

Ramsey Porter had a way of filling a room with his presence. He did that now, in Savannah's big square living room, as he and Maggie Evans waited to hear what Devon wanted to say to them. Both of them were obviously confused by being called to Savannah's house, but while Maggie's glance darted around as though she were memorizing the furnishings and trying to locate the wall safe, Ramsey's eyes remained glued to Devon, who was mixing their drinks at the bar. Savannah wondered if he was simply trying to ignore her existence.

Devon must have been reading her mind, because when he handed his campaign manager the Martini he had ordered, he said, "It won't work, Ramsey. She's not going to vanish. The two of you might as well get used to that now."

Maggie Evans's bright-eyed glance swung her way. "Is that really a good idea, boss."

"Savannah and I don't care if it's a good idea or not. We're tired of hiding what we feel for each other." He came over and took Savannah's hand, and smiled down at her in a way that warmed her to her toes. "If either of you can't deal with that, you might as well resign now."

Ramsey shifted restlessly and drained the rest of his Martini. Maggie simply watched them. As though, Savannah thought, they were characters on a soap opera and she couldn't wait to find out what was happening in today's episode. She remembered the polished little brunette now. Maggie and Ramsey had been with Devon that night at the opening of Royale. The realization that they had witnessed her confrontation with Devon that night, had seen him walk out on her, made her uncomfortable.

"I assume your silence means you're still with me, then," Devon said at last.

Ramsey stood up. "For as long as you last," he said as he ambled over to the bar and mixed himself a second Martini.

"Neither of us has any illusions about how difficult this is going to be, I assure you. But we've come up with a plan we think might work. Savannah's negative image is what we're fighting against. Before we confirm our involvement with each other publicly, we're going to try a public relations campaign to moderate that image." Devon ran one hand through his hair. "The two of you don't know Savannah, so you will have to take my word for this. The image of her in the public's mind is a totally false one. But it's so deeply ingrained that we may not be able to erase it. We know it's a gamble, but it's one we're willing to take. A carefully orchestrated series of print interview and talk shows just might swing public opinion in her favor. If not . . ." He shrugged. "Then the campaign is dead before it begins."

"This is crazy," Maggie said sharply. "It will never work. You're giving up an almost sure shot at being governor and a real good chance at the presidency."

Savannah's heart plummeted. They had talked this over for hours last night, but to hear it put so bluntly aroused all her apprehensions once more. She could not, absolutely *could not,* be a secret mistress. But the thought of the sacrifice Devon might be making for her sake was horrifying.

Before she could speak, Devon's arm was around her. "But look what I'm getting," he said, and there was so much love and warmth in his voice that she was certain they had made the right decision after all.

"Maggie's right," Ramsey said gloomily. "It's totally hopeless."

"So?" Devon prompted.

"So we go for it." Ramsey gave a gale-force sigh. "What else can we do?"

"How about you, Maggie?"

"Oh, I'm in, boss. You couldn't do it without me, anyway."

"She's right," Devon told Savannah. "She's an absolute genius at public relations."

Savannah smiled tentatively at the two campaign workers, still overwhelmed by the magnitude of what they were trying to do. "I want to thank you both," she said. "I . . . this means a lot to both of us."

"We're not doing it for you, lady. We're doing it for Devon," Ramsey said gruffly.

"Ramsey!"

"It's all right, Devon," she said swiftly. "They don't know me, yet. You said so yourself."

"Besides," Maggie piped up, "you won't be thanking us after you've been on half-a-dozen talk shows and had your bones picked over by reporters."

"I'm not looking forward to it," Savannah admitted. "But I don't see that I have any choice."

"You don't," Devon told her.

"But until we see some moderation in that image, I suggest that we keep this relationship totally under wraps," Maggie said swiftly. "We're all big boys and girls, so we won't pretend you're not sleeping together, but don't get caught. Don't be seen in public together. Don't send her flowers, Devon. Anything that could link you together before we've done some cosmetic surgery on Savannah's image could be a big mistake. Only the four of us know what we're trying to do, so let's keep it that way."

"Yes, Mother Maggie," Devon said lightly. "Now, maybe you'll get busy earning your keep and let Savannah know what kind of information you're going to need for the PR work."

"He's a slavedriver," Maggie told Savannah. She pulled a notepad out of her purse as the two men moved out to the terrace with their drinks.

Half-an-hour later, Savannah was exhausted and the notepad was overflowing with illegible scribbles. "My own shorthand," Maggie had told her. Savannah didn't delude herself that the other woman's brittle cheerfulness was actual friendliness. That was too much to expect from someone as loyal to Devon as these two appeared to be. Savannah knew she presented an almost insurmountable threat to Devon's career, and it was only with the help of Maggie and Ramsey that there was the slightest chance of victory. She was a little disconcerted that Ramsey seemed even more dejected than he had been at first as the two made their preparations to leave. She wondered what he and Devon had been discussing so intensely, out on the terrace.

Maggie recaptured her attention by waving her notepad. "Don't think you're home free, yet. This is only the beginning. I'll be in touch."

When the door closed behind them, Devon took her in his arms. "We're going to make it," he told her. "You'll see."

"I know we will," she murmured, but in her heart she knew that he wasn't the Prince who could make everything all right. He was just a man—a man she loved with all her heart and soul—and they could be heading straight for disaster.

"What were you and the boss talking about while I was interviewing the lady?" Maggie asked Ramsey as he drove her home.

"Did you get anything we can use?" Ramsey countered.

"If we were the *National Enquirer*, yes. If we're trying to turn her into Snow White, I don't know."

"I've heard you claim you can make a candidate out of a good head of hair."

"She's not running for office," Maggie protested.

"Sure she is."

"Which one?"

"The President's wife."

When he dropped her off, Ramsey considered trying to invite himself up, but Maggie didn't give him an opening and tonight he wasn't really up to the effort of trying to convince her. He liked Maggie, liked her a lot. More than was good for him, in fact. But even though they had worked together on several different campaigns in the past, he'd never been able to get her interested in him. She only liked to fuck candidates. She was as bad as a rock and roll groupie or a Hollywood name-fucker. She had balled him exactly once, when she was trying to get him to hire her on to the first campaign he ever managed. Since he was only a campaign manager and not a candidate himself, he hadn't been able to talk her into a repeat performance.

Tonight, though, it was easy to put Maggie out of his thoughts. Devon had handed him a much tougher assignment than turning Savannah Royale Marsdon into a Girl Scout on the public opinion polls. All the time that Maggie had been pumping Savannah for something to make her palatable to the public, Devon had been pumping *him* for every scrap of information about how Senator Harrison had handled the blackmailers.

"I don't know how the old man collected the money," Devon had told him, "but I'm willing to bet there was some sort of campaign funding involved, with a promise of future consideration for some special interest or another."

"But you had nothing to do with it," Ramsey said desperately, knowing where the conversation was going as surely as if he had a road map. "It wasn't your decision."

"It's my campaign. We're not going to have any coverups. Not now. Not ever. If you can't deal with that, then you can't deal with me, Ramsey. We're going to find out everything we can on the blackmailers and then we're going to turn that and Andrew over to the authorities.''

"Jesus Christ, Devon! You throw the most powerful politician in the country off your campaign, refuse his endorsement or support, and now you want to turn him in for screwing around with your campaign contributions?''

Devon grinned wryly. "That's about the size of it, I guess.''

"Christ, an honest candidate! I may vote for you myself.''

Andrew was dozing when the phone rang sometime in the early morning hours. He slept by fits and starts now, a full night's sleep was a thing of the past. But each catnap left him briefly groggy when he awakened, and when he picked up the phone and heard the husky female voice on the other end, he thought it was Irene at last. It was a moment or two before he realized that it was the sleek little brunette, Maggie something-or-other, Devon's campaign person, telling him she had found his call on her answering machine.

"I'd like to talk to you, Miss Evans. Privately, if possible.'' He paused and instinctively chose the tack he thought would work with her. "I think Devon is making a mistake aligning himself with the Marsdon woman, when there are other women more suitable to be a companion to a man like him.''

Her swift intake of breath told him he had judged her correctly. One whore was bound to be jealous of another.

"You realize Devon and Ramsey would toss me off the campaign in a minute if they knew I was even talking to you."

"But I need your advice, Miss Evans. You would be making a more valuable contribution to your country's future than you realize."

"Do you want me to come there? To Santa Barbara?"

"I'll send my car for you tomorrow evening . . . this evening," he corrected himself after a glance at the clock beside his bed.

"Better not, it might be recognized. I'll drive down, myself. I'll see you tonight, Senator."

Maggie didn't know where she had gotten the urge to collect politicians like scalps, but there was no denying she had it. Not that she wasn't good at her job, too; but this other was like a holy calling. The opportunity to add Senator Andrew G. Harrison to her collection was just too good to be true.

It wasn't a sexual thing, she admitted to herself as she drove to Santa Barbara. She'd have a real hang-up if a seventy-nine-year-old walking cadaver turned her on with his looks. But all she had to do was picture the senator standing before a bank of microphones, and some over-manicured, over-styled newsman introducing him as one of the most powerful politicians in the country, and she was so hot she was writhing against the car seat in frustration.

As she eased her hand down between her legs, she wondered what the record was for the fastest trip between L.A. and Santa Barbara, because she knew she was going to break it.

*   *   *

Andrew was aghast as the girl told him what Devon was planning to do. The boy had completely lost his senses. How could he think there was any way in the world that he could transform that whore in the public's eye? The public was unforgiving; Andrew knew that well enough. He had seen a lot of men go down because they couldn't control their desires.

"You're sure no one else knows about this yet?" he asked Maggie Evans.

"No one. And we're going to keep it that way. As I understand it, if we can't get her reputation retooled, the romance is over." Actually, that was more her fantasy than anything Devon had said in front of Savannah, but she had known too many politicians not to know how they thought. Anyway, the Senator seemed satisfied.

She wasn't.

Maggie reached down and grasped the hem of her dress and pulled it straight up over her head.

"What are you doing?" Andrew demanded with something like fright in his voice.

"What does it look like, Senator?"

He was grasping the edge of his chair with gnarled fingers. "I'm afraid you're going to be disappointed, young woman. That part of me is dead."

Maggie unhooked her bra and stepped out of her panties. "I've been responsible for raising the hopes of more politicians than you can imagine."

He protested faintly, but her fingers were already undoing his fly, and then her lips were on him, teasing his flesh back to life. She was skillful, he acknowledged that with some far corner of his brain, but even if she brought him to erection, he feared he would not be able to sustain it.

Then she was in his lap, straddling him, pumping against him with such vigor that he was involuntarily reminded of Irene and Edward making love, and he exploded into her with a fury that left him gasping for breath, his heart pounding erratically.

She brought towels and washcloths from the bathroom and cleaned both him and herself efficiently, and helped him back into his clothes. He was almost certain the pleasure of that act had been his alone but she dressed with a dreamy introspection that seemed to argue otherwise, and then she left to drive back to Los Angeles in the dawn.

It was close to noon before Andrew could bestir himself enough to get the Marsdon woman's file from his safe and nearly one o'clock before he had gone through all the information again and looked at each photograph one last time.

There was no choice.

Savannah Royale Marsdon must be eliminated before she could destroy Devon's political hopes forever.

Andrew G. Harrison made the call that condemned her to death as surely as if he had put the bullet through her brain himself.

Chapter 25

Ramscy watched Maggie prancing around headquarters with that look on her face that told him she had just bagged another political prick for her collection. After three campaigns with the little bitch, he knew that look well. So why the hell did it still bother him to see it? There were plenty of other women in the world; why did he want one that would never in a million years be interested in *him*?

He flipped through the list of suggestions she had turned over to him this morning for Devon's public appearances next week, not really seeing what was written there. Instead he was watching her as she leaned over to retrieve something from the very back of a file drawer. The way her skirt tightened over her trim little ass held his glance riveted.

Suddenly, she straightened and turned around so quickly that he thought he'd been caught eyeing her. Then he realized she had heard the sound of Devon's office door opening. She watched with a hungry look in her bright eyes as the candidate wandered over to

the coffeemaker and poured himself a cup. There was
no doubt in Ramsey's mind that Devon was one
political trophy Maggie was still dying to collect. Not
that there was much chance of that. Not when you
saw Devon and Savannah together. Ramsey guessed
he must be a romantic, after all. He'd like nothing
better than to see those two kids get a break.

Then an unpleasant thought struck Ramsey. Maggie
had given up on small potatoes long ago. So if it
wasn't Devon she had laid last night, just who was
it?

Frankly, Maggie didn't think Savannah would be
able to hold her own with the media. Eveything
about the Marsdon woman screamed that she had
been sheltered and pampered all of her life. She
wouldn't stand a chance up against the big fish in
their own pond.

But Maggie was going to do her job and do it well.
The sooner she showed Devon Blake how unsuitable
Savannah Royale Marsdon was for a man with his
political possibilities, the sooner she could carve another notch on her bedpost. Only with Devon, she
wasn't sure whether it was the collecting impulse or
something else.

She had to be careful, though, because Ramsey
was watching her like a hawk, and Ramsey knew
her far too well. He would scrutinize anything she
turned in to see if she was trying to use it to get to
Devon, to get Devon into her bed.

Too bad about Ramsey, she thought. The only
reason she had ever balled him in the first place was

to have a chance at the city councilman candidate he was managing at the time. She knew the effect she had on him, and sex with him had told her that he could be a sensitive, caring, passionate partner, more than capable of satisfying her physically.

Only for her, that wasn't enough.

He didn't have the kind of power it took to really turn her on. Not like that old man in Santa Barbara. She had to work like a fiend with her hands and her mouth to bring Senator Harrison to an erection and then she had sacrificed all her own pleasure to make him come.

Yet that meant more to her than the kind of long-term loving relationship she could have had with Ramsey. Maggie had given up trying to understand herself a long time ago. At least she wasn't a teenage groupie chasing after rock stars, to be used and discarded like Kleenex. She was widely respected in her chosen profession, and sometimes it seemed to her that her dedication to collecting political bedpartners was no more bizarre than anything else connected with the crazy world of politics.

She had given Savannah's public relations campaign a great deal of serious thought. There was really only one place to start: Gary Winding's show. She knew that both Ramsey and Devon's immediate reaction would be a resounding negative, but she also knew that they would have to reconsider, and would realize that she was right.

Maggie realized that Ramsey's eyes were glued to her from across the room. She stretched lazily, like a cat, letting the material of her blouse tighten across her chest and show her nipples. By accident, he would think. She half turned so that she could see Ramsey's reflection in the coffeemaker beside her, and for a moment, she was the victim of a wave of sorrow.

Too bad; he would never be anything.

Too bad; she could only come with gentlemen who had a great deal of influence and political power. Otherwise she would have been quite happy going to bed with lanky Ramsey Porter. She blew him a kiss in the coffeemaker, a kiss he would never see. Then she turned to her typewriter and started composing the memo detailing just why Savannah Royale Marsdon should make her kick-off appearance on television by letting herself be assassinated by Gary Winding's venomous tongue.

Lucette was terrified, and even sitting in her lovely gray and bone office with a cup of tea brought by a solicitous salesgirl couldn't calm her. Jerry wouldn't tell her what he had done with the money. Surely he couldn't have gambled it away already. Not all of it. Not five hundred thousand dollars.

He told her that she got on his nerves hanging around the apartment, so she had reluctantly gone back to the shop, claiming she'd had some sort of virus, but was over it now. No one had doubted her story. She knew she looked awful. She had aged considerably in the past few days.

The salesgirls fussed over her, glad to see her back in charge, but Savannah was remote. At first, Lucette was afraid that Savannah suspected what had happened, but then she realized Savannah was distant with everyone, not just her.

Once, she would have made it her business to worry an explanation out of Savannah and try to fix whatever it was—for the sheer joy of being in control, she admitted to herself as she looked at her gray face in the washroom mirror. Now she was too frightened about Jerry, wondering what he had done with the money . . . wondering if the men who were after him would catch up with him . . . or if she and Jerry would be caught and imprisoned for blackmail: wondering, wondering. She threw up everything she tried to eat. All she could do was drink coffee and chain-smoke.

And worry.

"I won't do it!" Savannah thrust the memo from Maggie Evans aside and glared at the three of them. "I've seen Gary Winding's show. He loves carving people up. The man should have been a butcher."

"We have to start somewhere," Devon told her.

"But why there? Why can't I start with someone who doesn't get his kicks by humiliating his guests." She glared at Ramsey. "Was this your idea?"

"No, it was mine," Maggie said quickly, before Ramsey could reply. "They both turned thumbs down on it. I had a devil of a time getting them to even consider mentioning it to you."

"What changed their minds?" Savannah didn't like the aggressive little brunette, and she knew Maggie didn't like her, not really, whatever Devon and Ramsey might say. But there was something about the woman that convinced Savannah that she was being quite honest in this case.

"They know I'm good at what I do. The best. I'm probably the only person in the country who could actually turn your image around."

"But you don't think I'm likely to succeed, do you?"

Maggie shook her head. "Maybe one chance out of a hundred."

"And the Gary Winding Show might be that chance?"

"It could be," Maggie said slowly. "Depending on how nasty he is and how you handle yourself. Sometimes the public goes for the underdog—and believe me—you don't have a chance in hell of being anything else with Winding, at this point. His own nastiness might gain you some sympathy that would carry over. But that's not why I suggested that you start with Winding."

"You don't have to do this, Savannah," Devon said quickly. "Not if you don't want to."

She reached up and touched his cheek. "But Maggie thinks I do, right? And you and Ramsey agree, at least enough that you let her bring it up. So why, Maggie? Why do you think I should start with Winding?"

"Because," Maggie said, "you'll have to face Gary Winding sooner or later. If you can't get past Winding, we won't be able to turn your image around. We might as well find that out now, rather than later in the game."

Savannah looked at their faces. They were all so

sure she wouldn't do it, and she knew they were right. So she couldn't understand who the stranger with her voice was who said, "How soon can you get me set up for Gary Winding's show?"

Ramsey called Devon at Savannah's house. "It's all set up. She's scheduled for Friday. Maggie will come by and brief her on the details and give her some help preparing for it."

"Did you have any trouble getting her on?"

"Oh, no. Winding leaped at the chance." *Like a goddamned piranha*, he thought, and wondered uneasily if Maggie was really right about this being the best chance for Savannah. "As soon as the first hint of this gets out, you're going to have reporters crawling all over her looking for a story. Better move her to someplace safer right now."

The experience with Maggie Evans had drained and exhausted Andrew, but then so had his decision to eliminate the Marsdon woman. It was strange, because never in his political life had he looked back or second-guessed himself, even the few times it had been necessary to order a "final solution." But this time he was troubled, and he was not sure why.

He felt a compulsion to keep going back through the photographs, looking at them again and again, but for what purpose, he didn't know.

There would be no report from Quinn, no contact at all until the call came, and then there would be a single word. "Done." With that word, Andrew would know that Savannah Royale Marsdon was dead and that his boy was safe at last.

That was the way Quinn worked. Once unleashed, nothing would stop him until he accomplished his task. There was nothing for Andrew to do but wait and try to put the entire matter out of his mind.

When the housekeeper brought in the day's mail and laid it on the table beside his chair, he saw that there was an Express Mail package from his investigator in Los Angeles. When his man called, he had given Andrew a thumbnail sketch of the contents: birth certificate, school records, more photographs, including one of the girl's mother, but none of the father. Andrew had suspected that the girl was illegitimate, and his investigation had seemed to confirm that. No trace of the father existed except for his name on the birth certificate.

Andrew started to open the package and then hesitated. Would the contents have changed his decision if they had arrived before he called Quinn?

He doubted it.

So let it go, he thought, and tried to rest before the weariness in his soul overwhelmed him.

He waited until the housekeeper had left, then he rose slowly, feeling the weight of his years, and took the unopened package to the safe. He wanted nothing lying around that might reveal his interest in the woman to the servants. Her's was the kind of sensational personality that lower class mentalities fixated on. While they might not remember his interest in a congressman or a governor, they would certainly recall any scrap of information regarding a woman who appeared so frequently in the tabloids.

How could Devon be so *goddamned* blind!

The surge of rage that coursed through him settled like a fist around his heart, and he had to lean against the wall for support until the pressure relaxed.

This week had been hard on him, too hard for a man of his years. He would give Dr. Laire a call later, have himself checked into the hospital for a rest. In view of what was to come, that might not be such a bad idea.

His breathing steadied, and he made his way over to the safe and opened it. To his irritation, he found that the unopened package was too large to fit in this small safe, and he was too weary to go downstairs to the larger safe in his office. Reluctantly, he opened the package and took out the folders and manila envelope inside. As he did, a note fluttered to the floor.

He stuck the folders and manila envelope inside the safe and bent to retrieve the note, clasping the wall for support. For one agonizing moment, he thought he might not be able to rise again without calling for the housekeeper, and he knew that fat cow would be in the kitchen by now, watching her soap operas. When he finally pulled himself erect, it seemed to him that every joint in his body creaked.

He had crumpled the note, and now he smoothed it out. *Had a devil of a time locating any photographs of the mother,* it said. *The woman was notoriously camera-shy. Also have not been able to find out anything about the mother and her family before she turned up in California just before Savannah Royale's birth. Looks fairly certain at this point that mother was unmarried. There is a strong possibility Royale*

*is not mother's real name, nor father's name. Do you
want me to pursue this?*

Andrew found that he was intrigued in spite of his
exhaustion. What kind of a family would produce a
whore like this Marsdon woman?

He braced himself against the wall and opened the
file folder. The birth certificate lay on top. His glance
went first to the father's name: Edward Royale. Andrew found himself thinking of his own Edward, his
golden boy, and the grandchild that had been lost to
him. Tears blurred his vision for a moment and when
they cleared he was finally able to focus on the
mother's name: Irene Royale.

A little tremor raced through him at the coinci-
dence. How could this whore's parents have the
same first names as the parents of his own grandchild? The bile rose in his throat as he read her date
of birth. Even in that detail, fate was mocking him.
She could have been Edward's daughter, the daughter Irene Royce had thrust into a nightmare existence.

He snapped the file shut and thrust it back into the
safe, unable to read any more.

He should have locked the safe then, but the same
strange compulsion that had lead him to go through
Savannah Royale Marsdon's photographs over and
over, drew him to the manila envelope his investigator had sent.

Just a quick glance at the new photographs, he
promised himself, and then he would close the safe
and call Dr. Laire. He opened the envelope and slid
the photographs out into his other hand.

There was a hodge-podge of images: the public

and private Marsdon woman in shots both amateur and posed. He examined her face in each photograph, not knowing what he was searching for, only that he sought it.

It was near the last of the stack that he found the lone photograph of Savannah Royale Marsdon and her mother that his investigator had mentioned, and his heart thundered in his chest when he realized the identity of the woman standing beside the teenage Savannah.

Now he knew why he had been drawn to examine the photographs of this young woman over and over. It was his own dear Edward that he saw captured in her face. And he knew, too, in that horrifying moment of realization as the blood thundered in his temples, that he had arranged for the murder of the only piece of himself left on this earth.

Desperately, he shoved the photographs back into the safe and slammed the heavy metal door shut. Rage was rising in him like a black tide: rage at the unfairness of life, the capriciousness of fate, the deviltry of women.

He clung to the wall as the tide closed around his heart like a huge fist, mercilessly squeezing until he gasped with the pain. He knew what it was, had expected it for so long, that he was not frightened, but even more enraged.

Not now!

Not when he was the only man on earth that could keep the assassin he had unleashed from murdering his grandchild.

Savannah!

Edward's child!

Edward! My golden boy!

His own fury whipped about him like a whirlwind, intensifying the crushing pain in his chest as he
stumbled forward toward the desk where the phone
sat. When he could no longer see, he could feel, and
when he could no longer walk, he could crawl, but
despite the most superhuman effort, he was not able
to defeat the weakness of his own worn out body.

His hand was still six inches from the phone, from
Savannah's salvation, when he died.

Lucette felt like she really was coming down with
the flu. Her joints ached and her skin looked gray in
the washroom mirror. She couldn't keep anything in
her stomach. The salesgirls kept asking her if she
didn't want to go to the doctor, and she had to keep
making up excuses. There was absolutely no one that
she could confide in. For more years than she liked
to think about, her life had revolved around first
Jerry and then Savannah. Now Jerry wouldn't tell her
what he had done with the money, and Savannah had
left at noon without a word to anyone. Lucette had
finally gone home an hour early, leaving the salesgirls
to close up. But she still couldn't eat, and all her
energy was gone. When the doorbell sounded, she
was too apathetic to even ask who it was.

She answered the door and found Jerry standing
there with two bottles of champagne, beaming at her.

"You didn't believe me, did you?" he said as he
went on into the kitchen and put the champagne in
the sink. He opened the refrigerator door and emptied

the entire contents of the icemaker into the sink around the bottles.

"What did you do?" Lucette asked him, a curious mixture of fear and exhilaration bubbling through her.

"I told you it was a sure thing!" He struggled with one of the bottles. "I doubled the money. We're going to have enough to pay those bloodsuckers back and still have five hundred thousand for ourselves."

"Jerry! You haven't paid them yet?"

"Don't worry about it." The cork came free suddenly, and champagne gushed upwards. "They won't care as long as they get it."

He poured out two glasses and handed one to Lucette. "Here's to us, baby," he toasted.

"To us," she echoed weakly.

He reached over and patted her on the bottom. "Now go get dressed. We're going out for dinner. This is going to be the biggest night of our lives."

Quinn was doing his calisthenics when Will burst in. At fifty-two, he was as lean and trim as a marine, and he intended to keep it that way. Unless there was a hit squad at the door, Will knew better than to interrupt him.

He finished the last of the exercises and rubbed his face with a towel. "What is it?"

"Senator Harrison is dead. It just came over the radio."

"Dead, how?" The Old Man hadn't said anything about his life being in danger on this one.

"Heart attack."

Quinn nodded and picked up one of the weights. The muscles stood out like cables in his arms. "Too bad."

"So, do we call it off?"

He lifted the weight up over his head. "Call what off?"

He knew what Will meant, but he liked to give a man enough rope to hang himself.

"The operation. The senator is dead. We have our money. Why—"

Quinn dropped the weight back in the rack and swung around to face Will. "Because it's our job, asshole. Because we do our job and do it right."

"Hey, don't get riled! I just thought—"

"Don't think, Will. That's my job. You have any word on the Marsdon woman's location yet?"

"Not yet. I'm starting to think she's gone to ground. You think she knows she's a target?"

"Unknown. What about the other two?"

"Spotted. Anytime you're ready."

"Good."

From Quinn, the slightest praise was like a medal of honor. Will glowed with pleasure.

Quinn turned back to the weights, Will forgotten. He'd do a good job on this one for the Old Man's' sake. Whatever it took.

He owed the old bastard that.

Chapter 26

"Now what?" Ramsey stabbed the headline on the Los Angeles *Times* with a blunt forefinger. "Do we drop our investigation?"

"Why would we?"

"The man is dead, Devon. We're going to look like we're trying to cover up by dumping on a dead man."

"That's a chance we'll have to take. I refuse to go into this campaign with some unknown son of a bitch thinking he owns me because of Andrew Harrison's underhanded financial deals."

"I assume that means you're not going to his funeral," Ramsey said, rubbing his forehead wearily. It had been a long day. Word had leaked out last week that Devon and Senator Harrison had parted company politically, and reporters had been harassing Ramsey for some kind of statement from the candidate other than Devon's tight-lipped, "No comment." Since the news of the senator's death broke, the phones were ringing off the walls.

Devon sighed. "I don't know. I was absolutely furious at the way he handled that blackmail thing, but I really liked the contrary old bastard. You know, whatever he did, he thought he was doing what was best for me."

"Yeah, that's what my old man used to think when he beat the hell out of me." Ramsey paused, distracted by the sight of Maggie wandering across the outer office. "But how will it look, you going to his funeral, when this blackmail payoff thing comes out?"

"I'm getting tired of worrying how things look."

"Then, you're in the wrong business, buddy. When you become a political candidate—anything from dog-catcher to President of these United States—you move into a glass house. You're going to find out that every so-and-so on the street has a stone in his fist."

"That's what I like about you, Ramsey. You're a real optimist."

"So that means you're not going to the funeral?" Ramsey asked hopefully.

"No, that means I am going."

It was the fairy tale night to end all nights. Stuck in Arizona, Lucette had dreamed of magic evenings like this with Jerry at her side, but she had never thought it would happen. Jerry had thought of everything, from the rented limo that picked them up at her apartment, to dinner in a fine French restaurant with champagne and caviar and the waiters bustling over every few minutes to check on them.

During dinner, Jerry leaned over and pressed a key into her palm.

"What's this?" she asked him.

"A key to a safe-deposit box," he told her. "It's all in there. Enough to pay off those bloodsuckers and then live like kings. You keep the key, baby, and I'll go back to my nickel-and-dime bets."

When he smiled that boyish smile at her, Lucette could feel her heart melting. She knew it wouldn't last. That much money would draw him like a magnet. But just for tonight, she could let herself believe it. Let herself think there was going to be a happily-ever-after for both of them.

"What about the rest of the negatives?" she asked him.

"They're in the safe-deposit box, too."

"Why didn't you destroy them?"

"They're insurance, baby. We might still need some spare cash. You never know."

Lucette looked around the restaurant at all the people living the life she had longed for all these years. It was wrong to buy her happiness with Savannah's. She knew that. But just for tonight, she would say nothing. She had the key to the safe-deposit box. Tomorrow or the next day, before Jerry could do anything with the negatives, she would get them from the bank and destroy them. "What about those men?" she asked suddenly. "Have you paid them off yet?"

"I told you not to worry about that, Lucette. I'll take care of it. I'll take care of everything. I'm the breadwinner now."

Lucette hid her smile in the champagne. She had suspected that her new earnings from managing Royale had irritated Jerry, but this was the first time he had said so. He waved to the waiter for more champagne, while her mind began to turn busily. What if she could get Jerry to let her invest some of their five hundred thousand in the business? She could open a Royale in Palm Beach and one in Dallas. When Savannah got over her snit, Lucette knew she could talk her into expanding. Maybe they could do a line of mass-produced jewelry, even . . .

Jerry leaned across the table and gave her arm a shake. "Come back to me, Lucette. I can see the dollar signs in your eyes. Forget about that damned business tonight. In fact, forget about it forever. You don't need that stupid bitch anymore. We're flying high, baby. Tomorrow morning I want you to call her and tell her you resign."

"Jerry, no! I can't!"

He had been half-joking, but at the sound of alarm in her voice his face hardened. "What's the matter, Lucette? Don't you think I can really take care of you?"

"Of course I do, Jerry, but—"

"But nothing. Tomorrow, you call her and tell her you quit."

Savannah was the only chance she had at the gold ring, and now he was telling her to give it up!

Well, she couldn't. She wouldn't. The thought of giving up everything she had worked for while she watched him squander his winnings was more than she could bear.

Lucette shoved back from the table.

"What do you think you're doing?"

She bolted from the restaurant.

He caught up with her at the door and grabbed her arm. The grip was so painful that she stood still beside him as they waited for the limo.

Too much champagne, she thought miserably, too much for both of them. She should have handled it differently. Shouldn't have made an issue of it tonight while he was drinking. He hadn't thought of the safe-deposit key yet, but he would, and when he did, he would take it away from her. She'd be lucky if he didn't go out and blow the whole amount someplace tonight.

The limo pulled up. Jerry opened the door to the passenger section without waiting for the chauffeur and shoved Lucette inside so roughly that her head hit the doorframe. The doorman protested, and Jerry turned to curse him.

Her head was swimming with pain, but Lucette took the opportunity to dig in her purse for the safe-deposit key and stuff it in her bra. Then she leaned back against the seat, eyes closed, and tried to ignore the throbbing in her temple. Jerry climbed back in the car and roughly ordered the driver to take them home.

He was going to beat her when he got her back up to the apartment. She knew that without a doubt. Sometimes when he was like this, he didn't know his own strength. She had to do something, she thought desperately, had to get away from him before then.

She lay there, feigning unconsciousness as the driver pulled up in front of her apartment building. "Come on, Lucette," Jerry said roughly. "I'm not going to carry you."

The driver came around and opened Jerry's door. "Is she all right, sir."

Lucette kept herself still, holding her breath for as long as she could.

"You really hurt her," the driver said and turned around to yell at the doorman to call the cops.

Jerry came bursting out of the limo and went after the driver, shouting at him to mind his own business. Through her lashes, Lucette saw the driver turn and punch Jerry as the doorman ran up, and she knew it was now or never.

Without sitting up, she opened the door on her side of the limo and, clutching her purse, snaked her way out onto the pavement. Crouching behind the car, she peeked over the trunk. Jerry was struggling with the doorman and the driver.

And then she saw the two men with automatic weapons come out of the shadows. The doorman and the driver were holding Jerry between them, one on either arm, pulling his arms out as far as they could from his body in order to avoid the kicks he was aiming at both of them. None of them saw the gunmen.

Her scream caught in her throat. When it finally came out, the automatic weapon fire drowned it out. The bullets laced through Jerry with precision, without touching either of the other men.

"Check the car for the woman," one of the gunmen called to the other, and she dived away from it, kicking off her heels, and ran.

Lucette called Royale as soon as it opened, but

Savannah wasn't there. "She's on vacation," said Penny, the oldest and most level headed of the salesgirls. "She won't be back for at least two weeks."

That was why Savannah hadn't answered her home phone all night long. "Where did she go? I've got to talk to her today. This morning!"

"I'm sorry, Lucette. She didn't leave a number where she could be reached. She said I was in charge of the store until you got back. And brother, do I wish you'd come back. We'll have a rough time with both of you gone. What are you up to, anyway?"

"A . . . A second honeymoon . . . but don't tell anyone, okay? Jerry and I just needed a little peace and quiet to get our marriage back on track. You understand."

"How romantic. Why don't you get Savannah to design you matching wedding rings? You should have seen the set she designed last week." Penny burbled on while Lucette hung on to the phone and looked around the motel room desperately, as though she could find some help there. Why hadn't Jerry paid off his gambling debt as soon as they got the money? My God, everyone knew those kind of men were vicious killers. He had just kept laughing it off and laughing it off, and look what happened! She choked back a sob.

"What did you say, Lucette?"

"Nothing. Look, if Savannah should call in, tell her I need to get in touch with her. Tell her to leave a number for me to call."

"Don't you want to leave a number for her?"

"I . . . I can't." Lucette hung up the phone before Penny could ask any more questions.

The key was lying on the nightstand beside the phone. A key to a safe-deposit box with one million dollars in cash and the rest of the negatives of Savannah and Devon. The key that might as well be her death sentence. She had no idea who Jerry owed the debt to or how to go about paying them. Or even if it was already too late to pay up. Those men hadn't even tried to ask Jerry if he had the money before they killed him. She knew instinctively they wouldn't give her any more of a chance than they had given him.

It was really ironic, but there was only one person in the world she could turn to. She had to get to Savannah some way.

Had to.

Before the killers got to her.

The "safe house" was what Ramsey Porter called it, like it was something out of a spy movie. They had agreed that Savannah was to be unavailable to the media except on her own terms, so through a third party, she leased a furnished house on Nimes Road in Bel Air, which she moved into immediately and anonymously. Hidden away in the Spanish-flavored mansion, protected by an iron gate and vine-covered walls, it seemed to Savannah that she had come full circle. Once more she was isolated from the world—insulated from daily life—just as she had been during her marriage to Paul.

Most of the time she was alone. Maggie Evans showed up in the mornings to go over the questions Gary Winding might ask her and a variety of possible responses to them. Devon was there each night as soon as he could tear himself away from whatever political function Ramsey Porter had scheduled for him. But the rest of the time she was alone, trapped in a terribly elegant prison with nothing but time on her hands.

The enforced solitude reminded her mostly of the early days of her marriage, when she and Paul had first come back from Antigua, and she had nothing to fill her time. Jewelry-making had been a godsend then. It had gotten her through the boredom and then through the heartache when she found that there was nothing between herself and Paul. She no longer found that release in her workroom. Now she had long periods of time to wonder why.

Eventually the answer came to her. She knew what had changed. She was no longer designing out of a desire to express something within herself. Instead, she was struggling to meet Lucette's criteria of what would sell in Beverly Hills. The more she thought about it, the more she realized that Lucette was selling, not her jewelry designs, but her image, at Royale. And that image was false. It was not the real Savannah, but the "bad girl" manufactured by the media.

She had not called Royale for a week, and now she realized she had no desire to. Royale was not her store; it was Lucette's. Just as the designs she was coming up with were not her designs, but someone else's.

For the first time since the knowledge had come to her in New York City that her designs were going stale, Savannah found that her fingers itched for a sketchpad. Suddenly, she was brimming over with new ideas. These were not stale designs. Oh, no. The furthest thing from it! Not one of them would please Lucette or the bright, brittle ladies of Beverly Hills who were thronging into Royale for a glimpse of Savannah Royale Marsdon.

But they would please her.

Savannah hugged herself with delight. For the first time in her life, she was not going to worry about what other people thought. And she knew, with a deep-down gut feeling that she had never felt before, that these designs were going to be *good*.

In fact, they might even be that terrible menace that Leonardo used to complain about so bitterly: Art.

Christ, Andrew, Devon thought as the service dragged on, *if you only knew how much I looked up to you. Why did you have to go and make such a dirty deal behind my back?*

Looking at Andrew's shriveled form in the powder blue casket, it was hard to believe just how powerful and influential a person he had been. What a lonely life the man must have led. Devon had known that Andrew was a widower, but he hadn't realized there had been a son. Or that both wife and son had died together in an accident almost twenty-six years ago. Suspected murder/suicide, the paper had reported this morning. What secrets had been in Andrew's closet, Devon wondered. Had the decision to hide them led to that tragedy?

Devon's mother sat beside him, ramrod stiff in her black silk dress, without a sign of emotion behind her veil. It hadn't occurred to Devon that she would expect him to escort her to the senator's funeral. He was briefly puzzled, but then he realized that even though she had left politics behind, she was still keeping up appearances. It had been instilled in her from the cradle to worry about what the voters would think, just as she had tried to instill that same viewpoint in him. As far as Amanda Lewis Blake was concerned, she was carrying the political torch for both the Blakes and the Lewises by being here today.

He hadn't said anything to his mother about Savannah yet—but that was at Maggie's urging. She wanted everything about him and Savannah kept totally under wraps until Savannah's appearance on the Winding show. Since she was getting a huge chunk of his campaign budget for her PR expertise, he would have been a fool not to listen to her, no matter how much what she said galled him.

Was he doing the right thing by exposing Savannah to Gary Winding's talons? Or was he being as self-centered as Andrew? He thought he could make a difference in politics, but was that difference worth the pain Savannah might suffer?

Devon tried to slip out of the church without arousing any attention, but of course it was a hopeless cause. Ramsey had warned him that the reporters and newsmen would be after him like vultures, and he was right. Amanda nodded graciously, like the Queen Mother, but said nothing as he steered her through the throng. Devon's clipped "no comment" answers to their probing questions drove them into a frenzy.

It was over an hour before they could get away from the church. Even then, a particularly dedicated news team followed him as he took his mother home and then all the way back to campaign headquarters. They set up a command post across the street, obviously prepared to tail him everywhere he went.

There was no way he would get to the Bel Air house to see Savannah tonight, not without leading those jackals straight to her. The schedule Maggie shoved under his nose when he got to headquarters didn't improve his temper any. "This has me in San Francisco on the same day Savannah does the interview on the Gary Winding Show," he pointed out.

"I know," Maggie said complacently. "I designed it that way."

"And just why the hell did you do that?" he asked with such anger that she blinked.

Ramsey cleared his throat. "She's afraid you might try to turn into a white knight when Gary Winding unsheathes his claws."

Devon forced himself with a very great effort to sit still and consider the prospect rationally. He knew they were right. He knew that he wouldn't be able to keep from jumping in if something went wrong. And of course, that would blow Maggie's carefully laid plans and his political career as well. Reluctantly, he nodded. "But make sure I'm back that night."

"No can do," Maggie told him. "You'll have to settle for the next afternoon."

*   *   *

When Devon had slammed out of the office, Ramsey said, "You don't want him there because you think she's going to go down in flames." It wasn't a question.

"Without even a parachute," Maggie said cheerfully. "I'm trying to prepare her, but the lady's never been up against a heavyweight like Gary Winding. He'll rip her to shreds and gnaw the bones. If Devon stays overnight in San Francisco, he may calm down long enough for us to talk some sense into him. He could drop her now without smearing his reputation publicly. That's what we have to convince him to do."

"I suppose you're right," Ramsey said slowly, not pleased with the vibrations he was getting. "Think I better fly up there with him?"

"No need for that," she said quickly. "His reservations are all set. The tickets and all the information are in his top desk drawer."

"You're really great, Maggie," he said heartily. "What would we do without you?"

"If you feel that way, give me a raise."

When she had gone, he went back into Devon's office and found the tickets. A quick call to the hotel in San Francisco turned up a reservation for Maggie Evans as well as for Devon Blake. A check with the airline told him she was flying up on an earlier flight. Devon wouldn't even know she was in town until she turned up in his hotel room.

It was too much all at once. It was bad enough that Devon wasn't going to be able to make it out to see

her tonight, but when she found out he was scheduled to be in San Francisco the afternoon she was to
appear on the Gary Winding Show, it was more than
Savannah could bear. She had watched the show that
afternoon, against Maggie's express orders, and she
had been appalled. The man was totally unfeeling.
She was very much afraid that she wouldn't be able
to pull it off. Only the realization of what her failure
would mean, to herself and to Devon, kept her from
confessing her fears to him.

He seemed to sense that something was wrong.
"I'll be back the next afternoon." His voice over the
phone was so warm and comforting that it only made
her feel worse. "I'm sorry, but they . . . Maggie
and Ramsey . . . think it's best that I not be there."

"So do I," Savannah said quickly. She knew
why Maggie didn't want him there. It was going to
be a debacle, and Maggie didn't want him tainted.
"I'll be all right."

"Ramsey will drive you to the show, if you want."

"I don't think that's a good idea, either, Devon.
I'll get myself there." That way, if something went
wrong, she would have had no connection with Devon
or Devon's campaign.

"Savannah," he said desperately. "However this
interview turns out, it's not the end for us. You know
that, don't you?"

"Of course I do, darling," she told him, although
she was terrified that it might indeed mean just that.

"I love you, Savannah."

"I love you, too, Devon."

So why am I asking you to sacrifice your whole

political future because my mother and my husband gave me a public image that no one should ever have to life with?

It was a question that kept her awake most of the night.

When Theodora handed him the phone, she said scornfully, "It's that woman. I told her you were busy, but she insists on speaking to you."

Carter took the phone from her and waited pointedly for her to leave the room before he said, "Hello. Nolan Carter speaking."

"Carter! I'm so sorry to . . . I had to talk to you. I didn't know who else to call. I need you, Carter!" She broke down in sobs.

"What's wrong, Savannah? What's happened?"

He listened as she poured out her story. When she had finished, he said, "Don't worry. I'll be there."

Odessa was lying on the hospital bed that they had bought and installed in her room. It had been so good to get her home from the hospital to Theodora's house in Westwood. But at the same time, he knew it meant that she wouldn't be with them much longer.

Looking at her eyes, it was hard to believe that she would never get up from that bed again. Those eyes reminded Carter of the saucy teenager he had married, but the poor body was just yearning for release now. The end was nearer than he liked to think. He hoped she would understand.

"Savannah Marsdon called me," he told her when her eyelids fluttered open. "She's going to be interviewed on the Gary Winding Show day after tomorrow and she wants me to drive her there.'' There was no question in his voice, but they both knew he was asking Odessa's permission.

''It's because of Mr. Paul, isn't it?''

''How can you work for a man for that many years and not understand him at all? I saw him grow from a little boy and I would never have thought . . . I've got to do it, Odessa.''

''You feel like you're making up to her for what he did?''

He nodded. ''Maybe if I hadn't been there for him all those years, he would have had to do things differently. Maybe he would have treated *her* differently, I don't know. All I know is, I've got to do this for her. I've got to be there for her.''

Odessa's hand rested on his arm, light as a butterfly. ''I know that, Nolan. It's all right.''

Carter gathered her into his arms, gently, so as not to make the pain worse, and he held her close while the tears ran down his face, tears for all the years he had wasted on a man who turned out to be less of a man than he had thought. Years that should have belonged to Odessa and Theodora.

Well, the three of them were suffering for it now, and there was little enough he could do about it. But maybe, just maybe, there was something he could do for Savannah that would ease his guilt where she was concerned.

Theodora was waiting in the hall, her face filled with fury. ''I can't believe it. Mama is dying and you're going to desert her for that white woman. You've never cared about us, Daddy. You've never cared about either one of us."

"Keep your voice down," he told her and pulled her across the hall into his bedroom. When he let her go, she jerked away from him and stood glaring, hands on her hips.

He had missed so much of her life, he thought sadly, and now he had to miss a little more. "I'm sorry, Theodora, but this is something I have to do."

"What about Mama? What about easing her dying moments? Isn't that important?"

"Your mama and I have made our peace, honey. She knows what I have to do and why I have to do it."

"Well I goddamned sure don't!"

"Theodora!"

"What are you going to do, Daddy? Wash my mouth out with soap? It's a little late for that, don't you think?" She turned and stormed out of the room.

He sat down on the edge of the bed. It was a little late for everything.

"Two women and you can't find either one of them?"

Will's face remained carefully blank. Only the muscle jumping in his jaw gave him away while Quinn raged at him.

Quinn was pacing the room like a big cat in a cage. He had always served his country faithfully and well, and he had transferred that loyalty to the senator. He couldn't bear the thought of failing the senator, not this one last time.

"They've both gone to ground. The Edwards woman made a withdrawal as soon as the banks opened the day after we hit her husband, and then she dropped out of sight. We think she's still in the city. The Marsdon woman seems to have dropped out of sight before that, but we can't figure out why. Her house is vacant. No one answers the phone. Neither one of them has been back in touch with the shop. All we know for sure is that the Marsdon woman is going to be on the Gary Winding Show, Friday afternoon." Will shook his head in disgust. "Too bad we can't hit her there. We'll have to try and spot her coming or going."

Quinn stopped in mid-stride. "Why can't we hit her there?"

"On live TV? In front of a studio audience?"

"Why not?" It would be a tribute to Senator Andrew G. Harrison. No one would know it but him, Quinn thought, but he was the one that mattered, anyway.

Chapter 27

Lucette clutched the newspaper and read the item again. "Friday's guest on the Gary Winding Show will be Savannah Royale Marsdon."

She had hibernated in this motel room while she tried to get in touch with Savannah, watching television and ordering room service, afraid to venture out of her room except at night, and even then, terrified that those men might appear out of nowhere and murder her like they had Jerry.

It was hard to believe Jerry was dead, and harder still to realize how little she cared. For so many years she had worried about him and catered to him, babying him, and always welcoming him back when he blew their savings. Now he was gone and all she could feel was anger.

Why hadn't he paid those men? Why had he put both of them in danger like that?

She was certain the police must be looking for her, and yet there had been nothing in the papers. Jerry's death had rated exactly two paragraphs on one of the inside pages. For that, she was grateful. She dialed the number of the wife of the producer of Gary Winding's show. Catherine had been a constant customer at the shop ever since it opened, and Lucette was sure she could talk her out of a ticket to Friday's show. If she could just see Savannah, talk to her, she knew that Savannah would help her, would figure out some way to keep those men from murdering her like they had Jerry. Seven years of friendship wouldn't disappear just like that.

She thought about the way Jerry's body had jerked and danced as the bullets hit him.

Oh, God! Savannah had to help her.

Devon woke Friday morning long before dawn and lay there, his head resting on one hand, watching Savannah sleep. Why had he let Maggie talk him into taking this damn trip to San Francisco when he should be here with Savannah? He couldn't fault Maggie's logic, but damn it, there was more to life than logic. He had watched Gary Winding's show yesterday, and the man was even worse than he remembered. Winding would make mincemeat out of Savannah, and since his show was live, the extent of the disaster would be immediately apparent. He should never have agreed to this, Devon thought. Maggie's sink-or-swim philosophy might prove too costly.

He leaned over and kissed Savannah gently.

Her eyelids fluttered open. "What a lovely good-morning," she said as she stretched.

"I've decided I can't live without you. Why don't you come with me to San Francisco today?"

"What about the Gary Winding Show?"

"He'll have some young actress waiting as a backup. You'll make her career."

"You don't think I'll be able to do it, do you?"

She rolled away from him and got up. Throwing on her robe, she went over to the dresser and began to brush her tousled hair with long vigorous strokes.

"Of course I do, but—"

"You'd better sound more sure than that when you make your campaign promises. Otherwise you won't get any votes."

"Savannah, I only—"

"It's a little late to start worrying isn't it? Besides, you're safe, whatever happens."

"What's that supposed to mean?"

"It means that I noticed Maggie Evans has set up everything very carefully so that whatever happens to me, it won't touch you. If I go make a fool of myself, you're still home free. I was an actress, remember? I know an audition when I see one. Who's the next candidate for the future President's wife? Maggie?"

"That's ridiculous!" He reached for her, but she eluded him.

"You'd better get dressed," she told him. "Maggie won't like it if you miss your plane."

Before she could move away again, he took her in his arms. "Don't do this, Savannah. You're just nervous. So am I. It's going to be all right."

It's got to be!

"You didn't have to do this," Devon said when

Ramsey picked him up at the Bel Air house. "I could have driven myself."

"I wanted the chance to talk to you," Ramsey told him, but he waited until he had driven through the iron gates onto Nimes Road before he added, "I think you're making a big mistake."

"If it's about Savannah, I don't want to hear it."

"It's about Savannah."

"Look, Ramsey, I love the woman. At this point, I'm not sure I even give a damn about my political prospects. Not if it means giving her up. Right now I feel like I'm throwing her to the wolves and leaving town in the bargain."

"So do I."

"This whole thing was your idea!"

"No, it was Maggie's. And I think she was wrong. Oh, she's a brilliant public relations person, and for anybody else this would have been the right way to go. But not for you, Devon. We both know Gary Winding is going to demolish Savannah when he gets her on the show. There's too much in her past for him to play with. It's not her fault, I grant you that. But it still makes it open season on her as far as Winding is concerned. It's going to be a disaster."

"So what do we do? This morning I tried to get her to call it off. She won't even consider it."

"It's too late for that. She'll have to go on."

"And let Winding use her for a punching bag?"

"If you go on with her, it might not be so bad."

Devon digested that for a moment in silence. "What about my great political career we were trying to save?"

"Screw the career," Ramsey told him. "This is the woman you love. Besides, it's all going to come out anyway. You're too honest to keep dodging for much longer. The media's going to nail you, and when it comes right down to it, you're not going to deny the relationship. So why put her through this alone when it's only a matter of time before the whole thing is out in the open."

"What do I do about San Francisco?"

"Put me on the plane and I'll take care of it."

Devon chuckled.

"What is it?"

"Maggie's going to blow a gasket when she finds out what we're planning. I'd hate to be the one to tell her."

"Don't worry about that," Ramsey said. "I'll tell her myself. I'm looking forward to it."

When she recognized Ramsey's car outside, Savannah took the stairs two at a time. Ramsey had never shown up alone, and she was terrified that this meant something had happened to Devon. She couldn't believe her eyes when she threw open the door and saw Devon standing there.

"Why aren't you in San Francisco?"

"Because the woman I love is in Los Angeles."

Carter dressed slowly. It seemed like centuries since he'd last had his chauffeur's uniform on. It reminded him so strongly of Mr. Paul and all the wrong Mr. Paul had done, that he felt like bursting into tears. Why was life so unfair? He had made such a rotten choice, sticking with Mr. Paul over the years when he should have been with Odessa. How come Odessa couldn't have stayed with him instead of giving him that ultimatum? Why was he compelled to do this one last thing for Savannah before he could be free of the guilty feeling that had descended upon him after Mr. Paul's death?

The questions went on hammering at his brain, but he had no answers for them.

When he was completely dressed, with his cap on his head, he went into her room to let her know he was going.

"Odessa?'" he said softly.

When she didn't respond, he leaned over frantically to check her breathing.

"I'm still here, Nolan," she said softly, her breath brushing his freshly shaven cheek. "My, you look handsome. I always thought you were the best-looking man I'd ever seen in your uniform."

She looked so tiny and fragile lying in that big bed, like the slightest breeze would blow her away. All of a sudden he was more frightened than he had ever been in his life. "Maybe I shouldn't go," he said.

"You've got to go," Odessa told him. "That little girl needs you. And you've got a lot to undo, Nolan. You couldn't live with yourself if you didn't try to undo it."

The limousine had been delivered earlier that morning. Carter took a minute to buff a few spots from its shiny finish. Old habits die hard, he thought. Old habits. Old loyalties. Maybe he wasn't trying to undo what Mr. Paul had done, after all. Maybe he was continuing to do what he had done ever since he was eighteen years old: doing what Mr. Paul wanted him to do.

He heard the whisper of footsteps on the grass behind him and turned to find Theodora standing there, glaring at him. "How can you do this, Daddy? How can you turn your back on us, just because that white woman snaps her fingers?"

"Your mama understands."

"Well, I don't!"

"This is the last time, Theodora. This one thing more, and all the old debts are paid." He knew in his heart that it was true.

"Sure, Daddy," she mocked. "I believe you. The last time." Tears glittered in her eyes. "Until the next time, right?"

"I've got to go." He was pleading with her for her approval, knowing all the while he wouldn't get it.

She just shook her head, not trusting herself to speak. When he drove off, he could see her, still standing in the yard, arms crossed in front of her chest, staring stonily after him.

"This really is the last time, Theodora," Carter told the empty car. "The last time. I promise you."

Ramsey let himself into the suite that had been reserved in Devon's name. Upstairs he could hear the shower running.

He dropped the garment bag by the door and went over to the bar. A bottle of Devon's brand of Scotch sat beside a full ice bucket. The tiny refrigerator beneath the bar held mixers. He shrugged out of his jacket and loosened his tie, and then attended to the serious business of fixing himself a drink.

Upstairs the shower stopped.

Ramsey carried his drink around to the sofa and put his feet up on the coffee table. The drapes that blocked the view of the open bedroom-loft area upstairs were pulled shut. He sipped his drink and watched the stairs.

"Devon?" Maggie called down. "I had to fly in early to take care of a few things. My room wasn't ready yet, so I borrowed your shower."

In a moment she started down the stairs, dressed only in a towel, her hair flowing free, with that eager anticipation on her face that he had always dreamed of seeing there. When she caught sight of him, she stopped abruptly. "What are you doing here?"

Ramsey grinned at her. "I would think that should be my line, Maggie."

"Oh, no! Oh, shit! Ramsey, you didn't let him stay there with her?"

"Let him? I advised him to. In fact, I told him to get on the show with her if he could manage it."

"You stupid asshole!"

"I love it when you talk dirty, Maggie." He saluted her with his glass. "Want a drink?"

She stomped the rest of the way down the stairs and marched over to the bar to fix her own. Ramsey watched, fascinated as the towel fluttered open and shut along one side, revealing the sleek line of her torso.

"Do you really think it would have worked?" he asked her as she came over and sat in one of the armchairs, curling her legs beneath her.

She gave him a dark look. "What would have worked?"

"The man is madly in love with another woman. What makes you think he would crawl into bed with you?"

She shrugged. "It was worth a try."

Ramsey started to unbutton his shirt.

"What do you think you're doing?" Maggie snapped.

"No sense wasting your trip up here."

"Get your shirt back on." She was all business now. "You need to call down to the desk and see about getting a VCR and some tape up here."

"Why am I going to do that?"

"Because we're going to have a fiasco on our hands, and I plan to play it over and over for you until you're sick of it." She got up and started back toward the stairs.

"What are you going to do?"

"Get dressed, and then start trying to figure out how to get our campaign out of the toilet."

"Come on, Maggie," he said plaintively. "Have a heart. Isn't there any way I can get you to go to bed with me?"

"Sure," she said as she walked upstairs. "Run for office."

It took some fast talking to get past the first two underlings, but once word got to Gary Winding's producer that Devon Blake had shown up with Savannah Marsdon and was asking to be allowed to go on this afternoon's show with her, the red carpet was rolled out. Carter was introduced as her bodyguard, and the flunky who had balked at even letting Carter into the studio in the first place was delegated to stand beside him in the wings and act as his gofer.

When Devon and Savannah were shown to the Green Room from their dressing rooms, Devon saw that a buffet had been catered for Winding's guests. He glanced over at it and wondered if any of Winding's victims were ever relaxed enough to eat before going out to face him in front of the cameras.

"What do you think of this outfit?" Savannah asked him, once Winding's people had left. "Maggie helped me pick it out."

"Gorgeous," he said, and it was, but tasteful, too: a severe high-necked dress in a clear bright blue that was perfect for television. It clung to her torso but flared out into a graceful swirl at mid-calf. With it, she wore a sterling silver necklace, cast and forged into a high-standing collar in back and dropping to a vee between her breasts. Like a dramatic exclamation mark, it ended in a point from which hung a large tear-shaped diamond.

"One of my wilder pieces," she said, touching it. "Maggie hoped it would get him off on the subject of my jewelry. Do you think he'll find the lost wax process as intriguing as all those lovers I was supposed to have had while Paul was alive?"

"Let's hope so," Devon said fervently.

Half an hour before showtime they received a

quick visit from Winding himself, who pumped their hands enthusiastically and accepted their gracious thanks for offering to rearrange the guests booked for today's show and letting them appear together.

Rather like the French aristocracy thanking the executioner for moving them up in the guillotine line, was Devon's thought, but he wisely kept it to himself. Savannah's face was like white porcelain beneath her makeup, and her hands, when he took them in his own, were icy. "It's going to be all right, darling." He didn't dare kiss her and destroy the makeup man's work, so he contented himself with holding her hand.

"He doesn't look the same in person," she said faintly.

"He doesn't have his makeup on yet," Devon said. *Or his killer instinct unleashed.*

"That bastard!" Maggie screamed at the television.

"What is it?" Ramsey called down from the bedroom.

"They just announced that the whole show is going to be devoted to Savannah and Devon. The son of a bitch canceled his other guests. He's going to crucify them! Get your ass down here, Ramsey. I want to watch you squirm!"

Lucette hunched down in her seat, trying to ignore crowd noise around her. She was afraid she was going to pass out. Bright lights danced in front of her eyes and the sound of the crowd kept fading away as though someone had stuck cotton in her ears. Those gunmen couldn't have followed her here, she kept telling herself. It was just nerves giving her that prickly crawling feeling between her shoulder blades, as though someone was drawing a bead on her with a rifle. Just nerves. Who wouldn't have nerves after watching Jerry get killed like that?

The producer's wife had gotten her a good seat, on the aisle, close to the stage. She was determined not to faint, or worse, throw up. If she did, the ushers would either make her change seats or remove her from the audience entirely, and she wouldn't get to see Savannah.

Without Savannah there was no one between herself and those murderers.

The lights flared up like starbursts inside her head, and she leaned forward and gripped the seat ahead of her, willing them away.

"Hey!" said the man ahead of her. "What are you doing "

"Sorry." She leaned back in her seat and stared at the chairs on the stage where Gary Winding and his guests would be seated in a few minutes.

Beneath his bulky jacket Will was damp with sweat, even though the temperature in the television studio was a cool sixty-seven degrees to keep the audience alert. He was desperately afraid that the man beside him had finally lost his marbles. Quinn was acting like this was a life-and-death deal, instead of a simple monetary proposition.

If it had been him, Will would have simply pocketed the money and forgotten about the hit. The old bird was dead. Who was to know?

But Quinn, like a dog grieving on his master's grave, was determined to carry this out if it killed him. It had been bad enough that they couldn't locate that Edwards woman after they took out her husband. How could she have slipped through their fingers like that? And why had the Marsdon woman hidden out all week? Did she know she was a target?

Will had argued that they should wait for a better shot at the Marsdon woman, but Quinn turned thumbs down on that, afraid she'd go into hiding again once the show was over and they might not get another chance at her.

Getting tickets to the Winding Show and getting into the studio with their armaments was the easy part. Quinn was a master when it came to logistics. Waiting was the hard part, although you couldn't tell it by Quinn's calm face. Ten to one the bastard hadn't even broken a sweat.

Will watched the empty seats on the stage where their quarry was about to appear, feeling the cold hard bulk of the Uzi strapped to his chest beneath his loose fitting jacket, and prayed that it would be a quick, clean kill, with plenty of time to get away.

Maybe the son of a bitch beside him was ready to die, but he damned sure wasn't.

She was going to fail!

As soon as the audience lights went down and Gary Winding walked out on stage, Savannah knew that she had lost the battle. The jovial look was gone; this man was the beast she had seen on the TV screen earlier in the week. He looked at her with such scorn and loathing in his eyes that she wanted to sink back into her seat, to crawl away.

But she didn't. She threw her head back and regarded him with a haughty dignity that she was far from feeling while he introduced her as the "notorious" Savannah Royale Marsdon.

"We've put together a few highlights of Mrs. Marsdon's life for you," he said to the camera. "Just in case those of you who aren't regular readers of the tabloids might have forgotten exactly who Savannah Royale Marsdon is."

Savannah found herself watching the monitor along with the studio audience, as her life flashed by with Winding's malevolent narration. Although the first row of the audience was only ten feet away, she couldn't make out any individual faces. But she heard the murmur of disapproval ripple through the crowd like a wave when the most provocative of Kit Nelson's photographs of her as a teenager flashed up.

"I understand you even did some nude modeling when you were three years old, Savannah," Winding said. "Too bad we couldn't get our hands on any of those photographs."

"Obviously, I had no say in what photographs were taken of me at that age," Savannah said desperately.

Her words were drowned out by the moan from the audience as the photograph of Kit, slumped against the wheel of his Corvette, flashed up on the monitor.

Shock held her immobile for a moment. Then, thankfully, her brain began to work once more, and she managed to fight down the impulse that would

have sent her fleeing from the stage. As long as there
was the slightest chance that she might still hold her
ground, she would stay and battle her nemesis, that
other Savannah, the one that the public believed was
her true identity. There was too much to lose if she
did not.

"I think we can safely say that yours was not the
ordinary teenager's life," Winding said and drew a
ghoulish chuckle from the audience.

She could feel Devon's rage as though it were a
physical substance. The pressure of her hand against
his arm kept him from rising to the bait as she
followed Maggie's instructions to try and turn the
questions into an opportunity to say something about
child actors and their problems.

Winding bulldozed right over her amateurish attempts to change the direction of the interview and
went for the jugular time after time.

At last Gary Winding's attention shifted to the card
in the stage manager's hand. Savannah was shocked
to realize they had only been on for a few minutes,
although it had seemed like an eternity. The first
commercial was about to run.

"Stay tuned," Winding told the camera. "We'll
be right back after these messages." He sat back in
his chair, waiting for the stage manager's signal to
resume.

Devon leaned forward and said clearly, "Why
don't you try me for a while, you son of a bitch?"

Someone in the studio audience gasped, and then a
smattering of applause broke out.

"Oh, I intend to Mr. Blake," Gary Winding promised. He turned to the audience. "Now, now," he told them. "No need for applause. I know you're all here because you love me dearly."

Scattered laughter, and then the camera light was on again.

Winding looked straight at Devon and said, "Devon Blake, you're well known to most of our local audience and perhaps some of our national viewers as a strong candidate for the position of governor of this great state of California. There's even talk that you might be willing to fill a vacancy on Pennsylvania Avenue in a few years. Just what is your relationship with this fascinating woman, Mr. Blake?"

Devon took Savannah's hand in his and smiled at Gary Winding. "Savannah and I are engaged to be married."

"Jesus!" Ramsey said fervently.

Maggie whirled to face him, rage in her eyes. "I hope you're satisfied. He's as good as dead politically."

Lucette scanned the aisles, trying to figure out how she could get close enough to the stage to get Savannah's attention without the ushers cutting her off, when she caught sight of *them*, one section over and a row down. The two men who had murdered Jerry were there, looking for her.

She shrank back against the seat like a frightened rabbit. A whimper escaped her lips, and the man in front of her turned around and glared.

On the stage, Gary Winding said, "Right after this

message, we'll give our studio audience a chance at you two lovebirds.''

Savannah slumped back in her seat, too weary to even dread what was coming next. How could she have been so naive? That negative image built up for her by Irene and Paul and all the other people who had manipulated her since she was a child was too strong to overcome.

That powerful nemesis, the public Savannah, had destroyed Devon's love for her once. Now it was destroying his chances for a political future.

"Thirty more minutes," Devon said quietly. "Think you can make it?"

She smiled brightly at him, trying to look calm and confident.

Gary Winding switched off his mike and leaned close enough so that just the two of them could hear. "Thirty more minutes in politics for you, Mr. Blake." He smiled nastily. "How does it feel to be a has-been?"

He stood up before Devon could reply and took the hand-mike that someone extended to him. The camera caught him striding down into the audience. "All right, audience," he said jovially. "Have at 'em. Who wants to ask the first question?"

Savannah looked down at her hands, at Devon's and clasping hers; and then he was squeezing her hand to get her attention. She glanced up and saw that he was staring out into the audience, at the gesturing woman in the aisle seat that Winding was making his way toward.

Lucette! What in the world was she doing here?

"I can tell you're an eager beaver." Winding smiled at the camera. "What's your question for Savannah and Devon?" He extended the microphone.

Lucette clasped it with both hands. "Savannah! They're here."

"A UFO nut," Winding joked as he struggled to pry the microphone from her grip.

Still hanging on to the mike, Lucette screamed, "Help me, Savannah! They're trying to kill me!"

She cried out as Winding elbowed her viciously.

"Don't hurt her," Savannah shouted, leaping to her feet.

Winding jerked the microphone away and scuttled backward, out of Lucette's reach.

"There!" Lucette screamed. "Over there!" She tried to point as two ushers pinned her flailing arms.

"Are you getting this?" Winding screamed into the microphone. "She tried to attack me! Keep the cameras rolling!"

He didn't know if Lucette had gone insane or what, but Carter saw the two men she had been gesturing at rise from their seats and start down the aisle toward the stage with a purposefulness that made him straighten and step forward himself, earning a yell from one of the cameramen.

Someone grabbed his arm and Carter shook free.

The men were running now, toward the stage, toward Savannah. Carter saw the glint of metal in their hands and realized they were carrying automatic weapons.

He lunged forward, but everything had gone into slow motion except the two men rushing the stage. He tackled the smaller of the two like a linebacker and sent him flying into the other man just as they opened fire.

Bullets sprayed across the set.

Carter punched the man beneath him in the face, feeling the jawbone crack beneath his fist.

The other man was trying to roll free of his partner and scramble to his feet, the Uzi still clutched in his hands.

Carter clipped him behind the knee and he staggered and went down. An usher piled on top of them both and caught the toe of the man's shoe in his teeth. The man rolled away and lifted the Uzi, pointing it at Carter's face.

They hung in a frozen tableau for an eternity that could only have lasted a second. Carter could feel the blood congeal in his veins. Slowly, never taking his eyes from Carter's face, the man swung the carbine toward himself, opened his mouth, stuck the barrel inside, and pulled the trigger.

Blood and brains sprayed everywhere.

The audience was screaming.

Carter stumbled to his feet and looked back toward the stage.

Savannah and Devon lay there, a bright pool of blood welling out around them.

Chapter 28

"Charter a plane if you have to," Ramsey yelled from downstairs where he was firmly planted in front of the big television set.

Maggie held the phone to her ear with her shoulder waiting for the airport to answer while she finished buttoning her jacket.

On the small TV set beside the bed, the announcer's voice was saying, "We continue to bring you live coverage of an on-the-air shooting on the Gary Winding Show. For those of you who are just joining us—A few minutes ago while Winding was soliciting questions from the studio audience, a woman appeared to become hysterical and tried to wrestle the microphone away from Winding. Studio personnel think this may have been a ploy to allow two gunmen . . ."

She reached over and turned the volume down as the airport answered. While she made the arrangements, Maggie stepped into her shoes and slammed the suitcase shut. When she hung up, she turned the sound back on.

". . . at least one fatality, and several people have been rushed to area hospitals. No names are being released at this time, although people in the studio audience say Winding's guests, Savannah Royale Marsdon, former model and actress, and Devon Blake, considered the front-runner in next year's California governor's race, were injured, and one of the gunmen committed suicide. The extent of those injuries is not know at this time. Blake and Marsdon had just announced to the Winding Show's national audience that they were engaged to be married. Rumors of a romance between Blake and the notorious Mrs. Marsdon have been circulating for—"

Maggie switched off the television. She knew politics inside and out. No matter how seriously wounded Devon was, his campaign was dead. In the space of one hour he had gone from first place to dead last.

"Aren't you ready yet?" Ramsey called up to her.

"Coming. The plane will be waiting for us." Maggie picked up her suitcase. By the time she reached the bottom of the stairs, she had made her decision.

Maggie left him at the airport, saying she was going to the campaign headquarters to field calls. Ramsey told her he would let her know what he found out.

He had a hell of a time getting in to see Devon, even after he showed all of his identification. All he could find out was that Devon had been shot. No one would give him any information at all about Savannah or the extent of her injuries. It was over an hour before he was allowed to go up to Devon's hospital room.

When he turned the corner in the corridor, he saw Savannah, her dress stiff with dried blood, standing beside a closed door. She glanced up and saw him.

Without thinking, he held out his arms, and she came to him and wept on his shoulder.

When her sobs quieted, he asked her softly, "How bad is it?"

"He's going to be all right," she said quickly. "I'm sorry. I was just so relieved to see you. The police took Carter with them to identify the other gunman, and Devon just got out of the recovery room a few minutes ago, and when I saw you . . ."

He could see embarrassment flooding over her. "Hey, none of that." He gave her a friendly hug. "We're family now."

Her smile made the sun come out. Then it faded as she glanced over his shoulder. Two men in suits and a uniformed policeman were coming down the hall. The uniformed policeman took up a stance outside Devon's door.

"What's going on, officer?" Ramsey asked him.

One of the men in suits answered, "We need to ask Mrs. Marsdon and Devon Blake a few questions. Are you her lawyer?"

"I'm Ramsey Porter, Devon Blake's campaign manager . . . and Mrs. Marsdon's friend," he added firmly for Savannah's benefit. She flashed him a small, worried smile.

"Could we talk in the waiting area, Mrs. Marsdon? You come, too, Mr. Porter."

Ramsey tried to tell himself that last remark had only been a polite request, and not an order.

"Were you present at the shooting, Mr. Porter?" the detective asked him.

"No, I was in San Francisco on campaign business. I was watching the interview on television there. I chartered a plane and flew back as soon as I could."

The detective's attention shifted to Savannah. "Do you have any idea why someone would hire those men to murder you, Mrs. Marsdon?"

Savannah stared at him, shock draining the color from her face. "Me?"

"They were specifically hired to murder you, according to the surviving gunman. Lucette Edwards . . . Your business partner?" Savannah nodded. "Mrs. Edwards claims that the same two men murdered her husband three days ago. She was also to be a target, but you were the primary."

"Jerry . . . Jerry is dead?" Savannah looked as though she might faint. "Poor Lucette," she whispered.

Ramsey reached over and took her hand and squeezed it. She squeezed back with surprising strength.

"Who hired these men?" Ramsey asked.

"Andrew G. Harrison," the detective said.

"Senator Harrison?" Ramsey was stunned. "That crazy old . . . Was Devon a target, too?"

"We don't think so at this point. According to the man we were questioning, the senator hired these two just before his death. They had done other jobs for him in the past. They were waiting for a chance at Mrs. Marsdon, and when they found out she was going to be on the Gary Winding Show, they thought that might be the only opportunity for a while.''

"But why would Senator Harrison want to murder me? And Lucette? And Jerry? I don't understand it! I've never even met the man.''

"Mrs. Edwards said that she and her husband were involved in blackmailing Devon Blake. Something about photographs of you two together?''

"Not Lucette! She wouldn't! We've been friends for seven years.''

"Mrs. Edwards said that the blackmailing attempt was to get money to pay off her husband's gambling debts. Apparently, he ran up a five hundred thousand dollar tab with some very rough characters back east. They were threatening to kill him if he didn't come across with the money. However, the husband appears to have been a compulsive gambler. When Blake paid them off, instead of settling his gambling debts, he gambled that money. He won. In fact, the wife says he doubled his money and came away with a cool million. She has the key to his safe-deposit box. She thinks these birds were enforcers trying to make him pay the gambling debt. The one we caught says no.''

Savannah was staring at them with a look of stubborn disbelief, but a nurse interrupted them before she could speak. "Mrs. Marsdon? Mr. Blake is asking for you.''

Savannah hurried after her without waiting to ask the detective's permission.

Ramsey cleared his throat. "There's something Savannah . . . Mrs. Marsdon . . . doesn't know about."

The detective turned his way. "You have some information for us, Mr. Porter?"

"You'll need to talk to the D.A.'s office about this before you let out any word to the press. Devon and I have been working with them on this blackmail thing."

"And?"

"It wasn't Devon who paid those turkeys off. It was Senator Harrison. Against Devon's express orders. The old man was batty on the subject of keeping Devon and Mrs. Marsdon from being linked publicly, so he went ahead and paid. We think Harrison made some sort of campaign promises to some big spenders in return for the five hundred thousand. Devon runs a clean campaign. We didn't want any coverups. When he found out what Harrison had done, he told the old man he was no longer welcome as a supporter."

"The guy must have a lot of balls to dump someone with as much political clout as that old bird had," the other detective said.

"He does," Ramsey said proudly. "We gave all the information on this to the D.A.'s office and they were looking into it. I don't know how far the investigation has gone at this point."

"We'll check with the D.A.'s office, and we'll want to question Mr. Blake as soon as he's up to it." The first detective glanced at him curiously. "How

about Mrs. Marsdon? Think she was in on the blackmail with the Edwards woman and her husband?''

"No way," Ramsey told them. "She had nothing
to do with it."

"Are you certain of that?" the other detective
said.

Ramsey thought about his first glimpse of Savannah a few minutes before, when she was standing
beside the door to Devon's hospital room, her dress
stiff with his dried blood. He remembered the expression on her face just before she caught sight of him.
"I'm certain."

The first thing she did was smother Devon's face
with kisses. "You're crazy," she told him.

"For being in love with you?"

"You could have been killed." She leaned forward gently, so as not to cause him any pain, and
held him. Their lips touched.

"Just what the doctor ordered," Ramsey said from
the doorway.

"What are you doing back here?" Devon said
weakly. "You're supposed to be in San Francisco
giving a speech for me."

"Planes fly both ways. You think I'm going to sit
up there dangling my toes in the bay not knowing if
you and Savannah are dead or alive. They just kept
training their cameras on that stage with blood all
over it and refusing to give out any information."

Savannah looked down at the front of her dress as
if she had just noticed for the first time that she was
covered with blood. She touched the largest of the

spots and then looked at Devon, her eyes like stark emerald pools in the dead white of her face.

"The lady needs to go home, Ramsey," Devon said quickly. "Could you drive her?"

"There's really no need . . ." Savannah began faintly.

"No problem," Ramsey told him. "And then I'll be back to keep you company for a while."

On the way downstairs, darkness closed in around her, and she swayed against Ramsey. He flagged a passing nurse and they helped her to a seat. The nurse had her bend over for a few minutes and put her head between her knees.

"Would you like to see a doctor?" Ramsey asked her when she finally straightened up.

"No, I'm okay now," she told him. "It was just remembering all that blood. Blood everywhere. And Devon was so still. I thought he was . . ." She paled again, and he took her arm.

"Do you have a woman friend who can stay with you tonight?"

"I . . . Lucette was the only . . ." She paused and looked at him, her cheeks flaming. "I don't have any women friends in Los Angeles now."

"Don't worry. I'll have someone from Devon's staff meet us at your place. Just until you're feeling a little more steady." He soothed her protests before she could voice them. "We don't want Devon worrying about you."

"But—"

"You're our responsibility now. Just like Devon."

He had her wait in the lobby while he called campaign headquarters. Maggie wasn't there, he was told. Hadn't been there all day. He asked one of the girls to have Christie meet him at Savannah's. The bouncy little blonde would be good for Savannah. Christie had never met a stranger in her life.

The phone was ringing when they reached the house. Ramsey answered it for her. He covered the receiver with one hand. "A reporter," he explained and cut the caller off with a few quick sentences. When he hung up, the phone rang again almost immediately. This time he listened to a few words and said, "Hang on a minute." He turned to Savannah. "Nolan Carter?"

She reached for the phone. "Carter? Are you all right?"

"I'm all right. How about you? Is there someone there to take care of you, Savannah, or do you need me to come by?"

"Devon's people are going to be here," she said with a shy sideways glance at Ramsey. Being adopted by Devon's campaign staff was still too new a thing to cope with after everything else. "I'll be all right."

"Then I'm going to go along home," Carter said.

"Home? Where are you now?"

"The police station. They just this minute finished up with me. This is getting too hard for an old man like me."

"Nonsense," she said fondly. "But you go on home. I'll be fine now."

When she replaced the receiver, the phone rang

again before she could remove her hand. She looked at Ramsey.

"Let it ring," he told her. When it stopped, he took the receiver off the hook. "Let Christie answer it when she gets here."

He waited until Christie showed up at the Bel Air house. She was friendly and animated, just the right combination, as she shooed Savannah upstairs to shower and change. But when they were alone, she told Ramsey, "The vultures are gathering. You better have a couple of the guys come out and help keep the press back. They're going to be climbing over the gate before long."

"Done." The phone was ringing almost constantly. He waited for a lull and called headquarters again. Still no word from Maggie. He arranged for more workers to come out and called the Bel Air Patrol number posted by the phone. He hung up, and again the phone rang.

"Just take this damned thing off the hook for a while."

"Have you had a chance to check the TV coverage?"

"What? No. Not recently. Listen, I have to get back to the hospital. Take care of her, okay? It was rough on her."

"Are they really going to get married?" Christie's eyes were glowing.

Ramsey remembered the way the two of them had looked when he walked in on them in the hospital room. "Any day now, I'd say."

Theodora was sitting on the front steps, staring at

the sidewalk. She didn't look up when Carter pulled in the driveway. Something in the line of her posture told him what had happened.

He pulled to a stop and bolted from the car. He ran to her and took her arms and pulled her to her feet. There were tear tracks down her cheeks.

He started to let her go and push past her, but she clung to him. "She's dead, Daddy. She just let go all of a sudden like life wasn't worth clinging to any longer. One minute she was here, and the next minute I was all alone in that room."

"Theodora . . ."

She was crying now. "Oh, Daddy, why weren't you here?"

"I'm here now, baby," Nolan Carter said. "I'm here for good."

"How are you feeling?" Amanda Blake asked her son.

"I'm all right," he said stiffly.

"If you're expecting a lecture from me, you might as well relax. Things have gone too far now. At least your Grandfather Lewis wasn't alive to see you make a fool of yourself on live television." But she was smiling as she said it, a poignant smile, but still a smile.

"You're not angry?" Devon asked with some confusion.

"I think you're crazy to throw away the kind of political future that you had, but no, I'm not angry." She patted his hand. "That was a brave thing you did, Devon."

"I didn't have any choice."

"I think you did, and that's what makes me proud of you. You saved her life, Devon. You must love her very much."

"I do."

As she watched the play of emotions across her son's handsome face, Amanda wondered what it would have been like if her husband had felt that strongly about her. She had pushed him into a career he hadn't wanted, and in the end that career had been more important to him than either his wife or his son. To have had Robert's love—instead of being the wife of a congressman—wouldn't that have been enough?

But of course it wouldn't have, she reminded herself. Not while her father was still alive.

Devon's face was turned to the window. Ramsey hesitated, wondering whether he should wake him or not, and then Devon turned to face him.

Ramsey pulled a chair close to the bed. "How are you doing?"

"I was just lying here thinking how ironic life is. All those years my mother tried to force me to go into politics, and I was having none of it. Then I decided, with a push from Andrew, that, by God, that was exactly what I wanted." He looked Ramsey straight in the eye. "I could have had it, couldn't I? The governorship. Probably the presidency."

Ramsey sat down heavily. "It sure looked that way."

"Before the interview."

"Winding is a bastard."

"I won't argue that one with you. What are my chances now?"

Ramsey hesitated, wondering whether he should lie or not. With another candidate he would have at least shaded the truth a more palatable color. But this was Devon. "I haven't been able to get in touch with Maggie since this afternoon."

Devon nodded. "She would be the first one off the sinking ship."

"Are you up to hearing some more news?"

"Might as well."

Ramsey told him what the police had said about the senator and Lucette and her husband.

"I knew those bastards were after her!"

"They would have gotten her if it weren't for you."

"And Carter. Do you know that man is seventy-three years old?"

"He'd sure beef up the Raiders' defensive line."

Devon turned back to the window. "You know, Ramsey. I just can't figure it out. Andrew treated me like a son. Why would he hire killers to go after Savannah?"

"He must have just flipped out. Thought if he could get rid of her, you'd be the candidate of his dreams. Hell, I don't know. The man was obsessed."

"I guess," Devon said slowly, but Ramsey could tell he was still troubled. "How's Savannah doing?"

"She's holding up okay. I have Christie staying there tonight, and some of our people are running interference with the media."

"You think of everything, Ramsey. You know,

there's only one thing I would have given up this political dream for and that's Savannah. This afternoon just convinced me of that even more. We're going to be married as soon as we can get the paperwork taken care of.''

"Great,'' Ramsey said with enthusiasm. As he let himself out of the hospital room, he reflected that he'd never been more happy to see a candidate lose his chance at the political gold ring.

The only problem was that it was going to be the American people who would be the losers in the long run. Not Devon Blake.

Savannah showered and dressed slowly, and then lay down on the bed to try and take a nap. Somehow, everything about this day reminded her of the day Kit died.

The day Mama killed him.

And like that awful day, she could not rid herself of the conviction that it had all been her fault. Even the police said that she had been the target, not Devon. Devon could have been killed just for sitting beside her.

Just like Kit.

The girl who Ramsey had sent to stay with her had whisked away her bloody dress while she was in the shower. Savannah was reminded of when the policewoman had taken away her dress, the dress Mama had torn, not Kit, and entered it as evidence.

Everything in her life seemed to go back to Mama and the things that Mama had chosen for her to do—the modeling and the acting—before she was old enough to make a choice herself. Thanks to Mama, she had lived in one glass house after another since she was three years old.

When Devon went into politics, he too had moved into a glass house. And now, because of the rocks thrown at her, both their houses had been shattered. Permanently.

When Savannah woke from a fitful sleep, she found Christie in the den, glued to the television set. "The news is coming on," she said over her shoulder. "There's a sandwich for you on the kitchen table."

Savannah saw the dress she had been wearing soaking in the kitchen sink. Somehow that lightened her mood. She took the sandwich and a glass of milk and went back into the den.

"They've been running this all day long," Christie said without turning from the screen.

With a start of surprise, Savannah saw that the image on the screen was herself, eyes wide with terror, on the stage of the Gary Winding Show. Devon was beside her. Then, more quickly than she remembered, Devon was throwing his body between Savannah and the gunmen, shielding her from the spray of bullets while he pushed her to the floor of the stage.

Savannah drew a ragged breath as she watched his body shudder with the impact of the assassins' bullets. The bullets meant for her, not him. Guilt raged through her.

"He's a real hero," Christie said proudly. "Oh darn," she said when the phone rang. She turned the volume down and answered it, and then covered the receiver with her hand. "Lucette Edwards. She says she's your business partner. Isn't she the woman in the studio audience who starts screaming?"

Savannah nodded as she took the phone. "Hello, Lucette." On the screen the commentator was speaking, and then the same scene was repeated from a different camera angle.

"Savannah! My God! I can't believe it's you!" Lucette was sobbing into the phone. "I've been trying to get in touch with you for days."

"I suppose I should thank you," Savannah said slowly. "If you hadn't started screaming—"

"I swear to God, Savannah; I didn't have anything to do with those men! They killed Jerry. They murdered him right in front of my eyes. They were trying to kill me, too. I thought they were trying to collect a gambling debt. I never thought—"

"If you needed money, why didn't you come to me, Lucette? You should have known I would help you."

"Five hundred thousand dollars? We'd have crippled Royale if we took that much out."

"Royale never meant as much to me as it did to you." Savannah took a deep breath. She knew what she wanted to say, and what it would do to the other woman. "That's why I want out of it, Lucette."

"It's because I blackmailed Devon Blake, isn't it? I wouldn't have done it if I'd thought there was any chance you two would ever get together. You were wrong for each other. I knew that even if you were

attracted to him, I should discourage anything per-
menent between you two.''

Fury blazed into full flower inside Savannah. All
her life others had made the important decisions for
her.

Mama.

Paul.

Lucette.

And she had let them!

Now Lucette's decision had come close to costing
her Devon's life. That was too high a price to pay.
''Who were you to decide that?'' she said coldly.
''Who gave you the right to play God with my life?''

''Savannah, we've been friends for so long,''
Lucette was sobbing again. ''I know I made a mistake, but you can't just cut me out of your life.''

''I won't do that, Lucette. But I won't go back to
Royale either. That was your dream. Not mine. We'll
divide up the assets, and you can continue with it if
you want. But under your name, not mine.''

''Savannah, please! Don't abandon me!''

''I'm not,'' she said soothingly. How strange it
felt to be the one who was making the choices. The
one who was offering the comfort. ''It will be all
right,'' she said awkwardly. ''You'll see.''

''What about the blackmail? Will I go to prison?''

''I'll talk to Devon,'' she promised. ''I'm sure he
can work something out with the authorities.''

Finally, with a promise to call her tomorrow, she
was able to get Lucette off the phone.

''Get this,'' Christie told her, motioning to the

screen. "The crewman they've interviewed from the Gary Winding Show says that Winding was fit to be tied because no one kept a camera on him. Did you know he wears a bullet-proof vest everywhere he goes?"

Savannah shook her head wearily as the girl turned back to the television, switching it to another channel where the same piece of video tape with Devon lunging in front of her was beginning once more. She couldn't stand to see the bullets hit him again. She stood up swiftly. "I'm going to bed now," she said. "It's been a long day."

Christie murmured something, still intent on the screen, and Savannah went to her bedroom. She felt better than she had in a long time, she thought. Maybe ever. She felt like her life was finally her own. She would be able to share it freely with Devon. Whatever happened, there was only one Savannah Royale Marsdon now. Her nemesis, that other woman with her name that the public knew so well, would never have the upper hand again.

Her only regret was that she had cost Devon any chance he had to be governor of California . . . or President of the United States.

When Ramsey pulled into his driveway, he saw that Maggie Evans's car was already parked there. Every bone in his body ached with fatigue as he pulled himself out of the car and trudged into the house.

When he opened the front door, he could hear the

shower running. A bottle of champagne was chilling in the ice bucket on the bar. He ignored it and opened the refrigerator for a beer. Then he plopped down in front of the television and switched on the news channel. He found himself watching a replay of the shooting.

Maggie walked between him and the screen, wrapped only in a towel. When she leaned over and switched off the television, he could see the firm fullness of her breasts exposed almost to the nipples. "There," she said as she straightened. "Isn't this a better view?"

"Didn't we play this scene earlier today in San Francisco, Maggie?"

"But there you weren't the leading man. Now you are," she said, grinning at him.

"I'm still not a politician, Maggie, so I'm trying to figure out why you're suddenly giving me the treatment you only reserve for those guys. Let's see. The last time you bedded down with me . . . the only time, as a matter of fact . . . you wanted something. Could it be that you want something now, too?"

"You know I do, Ramsey. It's a simple business arrangement that I'm proposing. You give me what I want, and I give you what you want." The towel dropped. "And you know you want it."

"I see what you're offering. What do you want in return?"

"Just a recommendation, that's all. I've been a busy little girl today." She walked over slowly and sensuously, not stopping until she was directly in front of him. "I managed to get myself a job this afternoon."

"My memory must be failing. I was under the impression you *had* a job. Public relations adviser on the Devon Blake campaign." She was so close, he could have reached up and taken her breasts in the palms of his hands like ripe melons.

"There is no Devon Blake campaign," she said harshly. "Not after that fiasco of an interview you talked him into." She reached out and ran her fingers through his hair, and her voice softened again. "I've got a reservation for a spot on Senator Hopkins's campaign staff. All I need is a word from you to your old buddy Smitty over there, and I'm in solid."

"Hopkins is gay, isn't he? You'll have a little difficulty adding him to your collection."

She shrugged as she began to unbutton his shirt. "Stranger things have happened. Besides, I'll be back and forth between here and D.C. all the time." She opened his shirt and rubbed her palms across his chest.

"I'll give Smitty a call," Ramsey told her. "In fact, I'll be glad to."

"I knew you would," she said softly as she knelt in front of him. She paused for a moment, her hands on his belt buckle, dark regret in her eyes. "You know I've always been attracted to you, Ramsey. If it weren't for this thing about politicians . . ." She fumbled with the buckle again.

Ramsey caught her hands in his, preventing her from opening his belt. She looked up, startled.

"No need for the bribe," he told her. "I'll be glad to call Smitty. Because I want you off my campaign."

She rocked back on her heels. "Are you trying to say you're dumping me, you bastard?"

"Does it surprise you that there's one poor slob you can't call to heel, Maggie?" He stood up so fast, she went over backwards, sprawling gracelessly on the carpet at his feet. "Devon runs an honest campaign, and you're the most dishonest little bitch I know. I wouldn't be surprised if you didn't have something to do with Senator Harrison finding out about our PR plans for Savannah. Did you try fucking him, too?"

Something flashed across her face.

"Jesus!" Ramsey said. "You really did it, didn't you? Do you know how disgusting you are? I want you out of my house and off my campaign."

Maggie scrambled to her feet. "You don't have a campaign and you don't have a candidate. You have a former candidate who's engaged to a *National Enquirer* regular. I'll be watching to see what you do with that combo, Ramsey."

She stalked back into the bedroom. Ramsey got another beer and turned the TV back on. They were playing that same film clip again. He watched Devon lunge across Savannah, shielding her with his own body.

The bedroom door opened.

Ramsey didn't look up.

The front door slammed.

Now they were showing the shooting from a different camera angle.

It made tears prick Ramsey's eyes to think that this brave and honest man's political career was ruined, just because he had fallen in love with a woman of whom the public did not approve. A woman who was just as brave and wonderful as he was, Ramsey thought. Given half a chance, he might fall in love with her himself. Maybe he already had.

He switched off the television and went up to bed.

Chapter 29

Savannah woke up slowly, feeling groggy and drained instead of refreshed. She could hear a television blaring somewhere in the house, and she remembered that the girl from campaign headquarters had spent the night. Suddenly everything that had happened yesterday came flooding back, and she had an overwhelming desire to climb back in bed and pull the covers over her head. It was only the thought of Devon lying in his hospital bed that made her get up.

She showered and dressed quickly. The phone rang, but was answered on the first ring. When she went into the kitchen, she found Christie already there fixing coffee.

"Ramsey called. He'll be by in a little while to take you to the hospital." Christie was looking at her with a curious expression that Savannah found difficult to define. If it had been directed at someone else, she would have said it was a mixture of deference and admiration. But there was certainly no reason for this girl to feel that way toward her. "Are you ready for breakfast?"

"Just a piece of toast," Savannah said.

"Oh, no, you have to eat!" Christie cried. "You certainly don't have to worry about your figure. Let me make you some scrambled eggs and bacon. It will only take a few minutes."

"No, really," Savannah protested. "I couldn't face a big breakfast this morning." Not until she had seen Devon and assured herself that he was all right. She felt guilty, though, at the disappointment in the girl's face. When Christie brought her toast, Savannah saw that she had toasted four slices and found a generous selection of jellies in the pantry.

While she ate, the girl busied herself straightening up the kitchen, but Savannah could feel the girl watching her out of the corner of her eye as she moved around the room. It reminded her of that awful time after Kit's death, when everyone seemed to be looking at her, watching her. But instead of the judgmental glances she remembered, this girl's face was filled with . . . adoration?

"Don't you want to eat something, too?" Savannah asked desperately.

"I ate earlier. I've been up since the crack of dawn watching the news and reading the paper." Christie's face was glowing. "Did you know you and Devon are front-page news?"

She spread out the paper on the counter, and Savannah saw that the photograph on the front page of the Los Angeles *Times* was that of Devon lunging in front of her. "Isn't he gorgeous?" Christie said. She wasn't looking at Savannah. She had reached out to touch the photograph with one hand. "He's a real hero."

Savannah's vision swam for a moment, and her stomach flip-flopped as she remembered the way the gun barrels had swung toward them. That had been the last thing she saw before Devon shoved her to safety, shielding her from the bullets with his own flesh. She gripped the table, the blood draining from her face.

"Do you want to read the story?" Christie asked shyly.

"No!" Savannah ignored Christie's startled stare and bolted from the kitchen.

She looked so delicate and vulnerable, Ramsey thought as he escorted Savannah down the corridor to Devon's hospital room. Yet the lady had a surprising core of inner strength he had not been aware of before. She had made her way through the crowd of reporters and cameramen without a pause, and without betraying by word or gesture that she even knew they were within a thousand miles of her. When he commented on that in the elevator, she said, "Experience, unfortunately," with a wry grin.

Just outside the door she paused and said, "Tell me the truth, Ramsey. The campaign's over for Devon, isn't it? I've ruined it for him."

"Devon has exactly what he wants," Ramsey protested. "He told me so himself last night."

But she had already seen the answer on his face and turned away.

He followed her into the room and watched Devon's face light up in a way that made him feel like an intruder by just being there with the two of them.

He said as much and added, "I just wanted to make sure you were resting comfortably, Devon. Is there anything you two want before I take off?"

"Just one thing," Devon said. He was holding both of Savannah's hands in his. "I'd like for us to get married right away. As soon as you can arrange it. Here in the hospital, if we can." He looked up at her and she nodded her agreement.

"I'll get right on it," Ramsey said happily. "I'll give you a call later. We'll have to rearrange your schedule of appearances, but—"

"Let's not kid ourselves, Ramsey. The campaign is over and the three of us know it. Savannah and I want to wind things down as soon as we can. There's no use struggling in such an obviously hopeless cause."

Savannah turned to the window, but not before Ramsey had seen the glint of unshed tears in her eyes.

"Oh, Devon," she cried when Ramsey had closed the door behind him. "I'm so sorry for everything that has happened. I thought I was making the right decision about us, but now I don't know."

"I know." He pulled her close. "I love you, Savannah. There's nothing—not the governorship, not the presidency—that's worth losing you."

She let him enfold her in his arms, but all the time she was wondering if he would continue to feel that way. Especially since they both knew that without her his side, it all would have been possible.

*   *   *

Ramsey paused in astonishment.

He had expected headquarters to be half-deserted and any workers who were there to be moping and depressed.

Instead the air was electric.

"What in the hell's going on?" he asked a passing volunteer.

"It's about time you got here," he was told. "Maggie hasn't shown up yet, and the whole place is falling apart."

"Maggie's not going to be in," Ramsey said. "She's off the campaign."

"But who's going to coordinate things? The phones have been ringing off the wall this morning."

"Why?"

"Why?" The worker looked at him in astonishment. "Everyone wants exclusive interviews with Devon and Savannah Marsdon. *Newsweek, Time, People. TV Guide! Today, Good Morning America Donahue.* Somebody's gotta decide who gets first crack at the royal couple. This is the hottest campaign I've ever worked on."

"What in the hell are you talking about?" Ramsey asked as two more staffers crowded up. "We're dead in the water after that interview yesterday. Devon couldn't get elected as dogcatcher today."

"Where have you been? They've been running that clip from the Winding show over and over since yesterday. Hinckley's shot at Reagan didn't get this much coverage."

"It's the most romantic thing I ever saw," one of the women chimed in. "Like the Duke and Duchess of Windsor."

"American royalty," said someone else. "Better than Kennedy and Camelot."

"A hero," said another. "We've got a genuine honest-to-God hero."

"We've got it made. Our boy's going all the way to the top."

When he finally got back to his office, Ramsey sat down behind his desk and stared at the wall in disbelief. Only when they buzzed him that he had a call from Maggie Evans, did the full reality start to sink in.

"I outsmarted myself this time," Maggie said ruefully. "I wanted to move before the campaign sunk. I should have waited until all the votes were in." She paused. "I don't suppose there's any chance you'll let bygones be bygones and hire me back?" Her voice was promising him things he would have sold his mother for a chance at a week ago.

He thought about Maggie and Senator Harrison. Maybe she had gone to bed with him, maybe she hadn't. He no longer cared. But she had told the old man their plans for Savannah and had almost gotten Savannah and Devon killed. That he was sure of. "Not a chance in hell, Maggie."

"Well," she said, her voice a soft caress, "I am sorry we didn't complete that little transaction last night, Ramsey. I hope you are, too."

When she hung up, Ramsey sat there staring at the phone. He had a candidate and he had a campaign. Hell, he had an express train to Sacramento! And possibly the White House, too. If he'd had any doubts left, Maggie's call had laid them to rest.

He started to dial the hospital, and then slammed down the receiver. This was the kind of news that had to be delivered in person, with a bottle of champagne under each arm.

Besides, he wanted to see the light come back into Savannah's eyes when he told her Devon was going to be the next governor of California.

Everyone loves a winner.

Etiquette might call for a small wedding for Savannah Royale Marsden's second marriage, but the American people were demanding more from Devon and Savannah. The wedding guest list was expanded four times as frantic calls poured in from all over the United States. Ramsey was in charge of winnowing the list down to a manageable size, and the task was driving him crazy. He could have used Maggie's help; it was the kind of job she would have been fantastic at. Besides, she would have been beside herself trying to decide which of the politically powerful guests to go after first.

There was only one "regrets." Savannah's former chauffeur, Nolan Carter, had turned down his invitation. Savannah refused to believe Ramsey when he told her. As soon as she could slip away from the hundred and one pre-wedding details, she called Carter herself.

"I'm sorry, Savannah. I'd like to be there. But I have a prior commitment."

"I understand," she said, although she didn't. And then she couldn't help asking, "It's not something I've done to offend you, is it, Carter? You know how much your friendship has meant to me."

"I'd give anything to be there," he said softly, and she knew from his voice that it was true.

"Then why don't you? You're my family, you know. You're really all the family I've got."

"No, Savannah. You have Devon, and you two are going to be very happy together."

It nearly tore Carter in half to hang up that phone without giving in to Savannah's wishes. He would miss not seeing that little girl get married. But he did it.

He had put off being a father to his daughter all these years. Maybe that was Odessa's fault, maybe it was his own. But it was time to change that. He had made Theodora a promise when Odessa died. From now on, she came first. He owed her that.

He found her sitting on the front steps. He sat down beside her. For the first time he saw that there were streaks of gray in her hair, and he wondered how that little girl who used to ride on his shoulder had gotten to be an old woman while he wasn't watching. "That was Savannah Marsdon," he said unnecessarily. Theodora had answered the phone.

Theodora was nibbling on a thumbnail. "What did he want?"

"She wanted to know why I wasn't coming to the wedding."

"Are you wanting to go?"

"Not as bad as I want to be here with you, Theodora."

"Oh, Daddy! Everybody calls me Teddy. I told you that." But she was crying and hugging him when she said it, and Carter knew he was finally home.

When she slipped the engraved invitation out of the envelope, Lucette's first thought was that someone had made a mistake. Why would Savannah invite her to the wedding? She hadn't talked to Savannah since the day of the shooting, but she had talked to Savannah's lawyer. Savannah was closing Royale. That wasn't what the lawyer had told her; the fiction was that if Lucette could come up with the money, she could buy Savannah out and continue to run a jewelry store at that location. But she couldn't use Savannah's name, and she wouldn't have Savannah's designs to sell, or Savannah's fortune to fall back on when the new store's profits dipped too low to cover the expenses of a Rodeo Drive address.

Customers were still crowding into the store in the same numbers, still vying for Lucette's good will, as though that would get them closer to the elusive Savannah. But Lucette knew with an awful certainty that even if she could find other jewelry designs to carry, and came up with enough cash to meet expenses until then, it would do no good. The store would die as soon as the name "Royale" was removed.

So far, nothing had been leaked to the press about the blackmail, but Lucette knew it was only a matter of time. Then the women who were courting her, taking her to lunch, asking her advice on a thousand and one things, and *begging* her for an invitation to the most important wedding of the year—the women who made her feel important—would cut her dead.

She slipped the invitation back in the envelope. Mistake or not, she had been invited and she was going to the wedding. It wasn't over until it was over.

Armed security guards were watching over the rooms of wedding presents displayed inside Amanda Lewis Blake's home. Six hundred people crowded into the garden, where roses and orchids, camellias and lilies, joined the jungle profusion of palms and jacarandas, philodendron, ivy, fuchsia, and begonias. Lucette wandered down the garden paths, past statues and pools, gawking like a tourist at the famous personages she had only seen before on television and in magazines and not seeing a single person she really knew. When she finally spotted two Beverly Hills matrons, frequent customers of Royale, she started toward them eagerly.

Before she reached them, the two women turned and walked away, not with haste, but with a finality that couldn't help but register on her.

Lucette stood there watching them until they disappeared behind a clipped hedge. Then she turned and hurried back through the garden as fast as the spindly heels she had worn could navigate the path. When she reached the front of the house, she ordered one of the boys who had been hired to park cars to go and bring hers back. It took a few minutes and a twenty-dollar bill before the startled attendant would believe an invited guest actually wanted to *leave* the wedding while so many uninvited guests were still trying to crash.

"It's over," Lucette told him sadly.

Shaking his head, the boy went to get the car for the crazy little monkey of a woman who didn't realize the ceremony hadn't even started yet.

In a pale icy-green summer gown of organdy, carrying one perfect ivory rose, Savannah made her way through the crowd of guests in the sun-dappled garden to where Devon and Ramsey Porter waited with the minister, in front of a row of Italian cypress. Although her future life was only moments away, her mind was on the past.

Yesterday, the police had told her about the file they had found in Senator Harrison's safe at his house in Santa Barbara. The man had spared no expense in trying to track down any information he could about her.

Yet for all the thousands of dollars the senator had spent in his attempt to keep her and Devon apart, the trail ended with Irene. There was a scribbled notation from the private investigator that Royale was not really Irene's last name, but he had not been able to find out what her real name was.

What was the story of her family? Savannah wondered. Who had her father been? What about his parents? Mama's parents? She wondered if any of her grandparents could still be alive . . . or her father. . . .

It was a mystery she would never be able to solve.

Just as she was never again able to hate Mama, after those awful minutes in the hospital room where

Irene lay dying, when she finally understood the terrible thing that had made her mother what she was.

The man who waited for her beside the minister was just that, only a man. He was not the Prince of her dreams, the perfect man who would make everything all right. The girl she had been might be disappointed with Savannah's choice of a husband. But how could that little girl have known that there was something far better than fantasy.

"Who gives this woman to be married?" the minister asked as Savannah reached Devon's side.

Savannah took a deep breath. Two men filled her thoughts in that moment: her father, that mysterious figure who might have stepped forward to answer the minister's question if Irene Royale had not been so secretive about her past—and the Prince, who had been her defense against reality for so many years.

The minister looked at her expectantly.

Firmly, finally, Savannah put the past behind her forever. "I do," she said in a strong clear voice that carried over the crowd. "I give myself in love to Devon Blake." She held out her hand and Devon took it.

A murmur of approval from the wedding guests drowned out the next few words of the ceremony, but Savannah was aware only of Devon standing beside her, of his hand in hers, and the future, beckoning.